BGSU LIBRARY
DISCARD

KI-GOR

THE COMPLETE SERIES VOLUME 2

KI-GOR

THE COMPLETE SERIES VOLUME 2

WRITTEN BY

JOHN PETER DRUMMOND

BOSTON

ALTUS PRESS

2011

© 2011 Altus Press

Printed in the United States of America

First Edition — 2011

Visit AltusPress.com for more books like this.

EDITED AND DESIGNED BY
Matthew Moring

THANKS TO
Rick Ollerman, Rob Preston & Ray Riethmeier

REPRINT HISTORY
"Ki-Gor—and the Paradise That Time Forgot" originally appeared in JUNGLE STORIES *(Fall 1940), "The Empire of Doom" originally appeared in* JUNGLE STORIES *(Winter 1940-41), "Lair of the Beast" originally appeared in* JUNGLE STORIES *(Spring 1941), "Ki-Gor—and the Temple of the Moon-God" originally appeared in* JUNGLE STORIES *(Summer 1941), and "White Savage" originally appeared in* JUNGLE STORIES *(Fall 1941).*

ALL RIGHTS RESERVED

No part of this book may be reproduced or utilized in any form or by any means, electronic or mechanical, without permission in writing from the publisher.

TABLE OF

CONTENTS

STORY VII

KI-GOR— AND THE PARADISE THAT TIME FORGOT

CHAPTER I

THE LITTLE TREE SNAKE wriggled cautiously along the top of the broad bough toward the trunk of the tree. It stopped momentarily and tested the air nervously with its tiny red forked tongue. Its unwavering eyes stared at the unfamiliar bulk resting in the big crotch a few feet away. When the bulk did not move, the snake concluded that nothing was amiss and the sinuous progress continued. A moment later the articulated ring-scales gripped the hairy surface of a ruddy brown shaft that extended from the strange body in the crotch. A pleasurable feeling of warmth was communicated to the little serpent's dull brain, but still no untoward movement warned it of danger. Happily, the little creature slithered across Ki-Gor's forearm, and proceeded down the tree.

On another occasion, Ki-Gor might have smiled a little to himself. He was secretly proud of his ability to keep so still that not even a tiny muscle twitching would betray him to the alertest creatures of the jungle. But at this moment, his attention was riveted on the scene in the little clearing below him.

A few shafts of noon sunlight penetrated the leafy ceiling of the jungle and shimmered on the white helmets and clothes of the three whites down in the clearing, the big man, the little man, and the little woman. A few yards away from them, a narrow-headed black Somali boy was squatting, and beyond him a score of skinny-legged porters stood uneasily by their bundles and stared at the three whites.

Even if Ki-Gor had not understood English perfectly, he would have been aware that an acrimonious dispute was going on. Just the rasping quality in the big man's voice would have told him that.

"I tell you," said the big man, "I've got to have a drink, and furthermore, I'm *going* to have a drink!"

"But, Morton, dear," the woman said, "you promised—"

"I haven't touched a drop for three days," the big man interrupted, "and as a result, my nerves are completely shot. I should never have let you two beguile me into a promise like that. As a medical man, I know perfectly well that it's extremely bad for the nervous system to shut off alcohol so abruptly."

"But, darling," said the woman, almost tearfully. "You've tried that way so often, and it never worked."

"Look here, old man," it was the little man speaking, "my whole reason for bringing you and Sheila out here to Africa was to get you away from temptation. Use your will-power. Concentrate on getting through each day without giving in. Before you know it you'll be able to hold a scalpel once more in a steady hand. You can be the old Morton Brett, the greatest brain surgeon in New York—"

"Yes, yes, yes," the big man whined. "But, as a medical man, I tell you it's dangerous to cut off so sharply."

There was a long silence. Then the little man looked at the woman and shook his head.

"Well, Mort," he said slowly, "I'll give you one drink—but only one—"

"That's all I want," the big man said eagerly, "just one. And then maybe one before we turn in tonight, eh?"

"Just one, I said," and the little man moved toward the group of porters.

KI-GOR SHIFTED his weight gently. The dispute was over and the big man had won. It was too bad, thought Ki-Gor. He didn't like the big man, instinctively, and he didn't like to see the big man win. But there it was. Ki-Gor stretched out a long bronzed leg slowly, preparatory to leaving the scene. He glanced upward and caught the eye of the little Pygmy crouched in the tree above him. Ngeeso could stay and keep an eye on this safari and report later. Ki-Gor was going home now to his mate.

Stealthily, he crept down the tree, keeping the broad trunk between himself and the halted safari. He heard the little man say something to a porter. There was a rustling then, and a long silence. A tin cup clinked then, and the big man muttered a throaty word of thanks. There was a brief gasping cough followed by a long shuddering sigh.

"Aaaah!" the big man exclaimed. "That's more like it! In twenty seconds I'm going to feel like a new man. I think, er—I think, David, that since I haven't had any whiskey now for three whole days—I think I'll have another one."

"I said you could have just one," the little man's voice was stony.

"Yes, and you said we would shoot gorillas!" the big man flared up. "Well, we haven't seen a trace of gorilla since we've been out."

"We will, Mort, we will." The little man was patient. "I admit I got off the track back there somewhere. I turned west too soon. We're going to retrace our steps now for a while and then head north toward the Belgian mountains. I have a hunch we're almost into Angola right now."

Ki-Gor was standing on the ground by now. When he heard the little man's words, he drifted off through the trees. As long as the safari was going away out of Ki-Gor's territory, he had no further interest in it. The voices in the clearing faded out of his ears as he slipped noiselessly through the jungle.

The last thing he heard was the big man bellowing for another drink.

All the way back to the Island in the middle of the rushing river which he and Helene had adopted as their permanent home, Ki-Gor puzzled over the scene he had left. The big man's craving for whiskey was something he couldn't understand. Months before, in Nairobi, where Ki-Gor had first come into contact with civilization, he had tasted whiskey. Almost instantly he had spit it out. How on earth anyone could wish the stuff so badly that he would create a scene before the porters, Ki-Gor could not figure out.

Helene would know, Ki-Gor reflected. She was, after all, born and brought up in civilization. It had not been so many months now—although it seemed much longer—that she had put aside civilization forever and come to live in the jungle as Ki-Gor's wife.

Yes, Ki-Gor told himself, Helene would know the reason for the unpleasant white man's strange desire for whiskey. Something told Ki-Gor, however, to omit any mention of the white woman when he described the safari to Helene. Women are rather funny at times, he had found, and if Helene knew another white woman was near, she might do some unpredictable thing or another. The one thing that Ki-Gor did not want now was to have the secret of his island-home revealed to anybody but the friendly Pygmies who roamed that section of the jungle.

A murmuring rumble grew to a roar as Ki-Gor approached the falls above the Island. It was music to his ears. That falls and the other one downstream were two of the many reasons he had selected that island to settle down. They rendered the river un-navigable, blocking approach to the Island by boat or canoe from both directions. Incidentally, the falls kept that part of the river free from any adventurous crocodiles who might stray up into such rugged country.

SUDDENLY, ABOVE the roar of the falls, there came a crashing sound from the undergrowth near the river. Then pealed out an awesome blaring—the sound of all the trumpets of doom. Ki-Gor's head lifted for a moment, attentively; but at once a smile broke across his weathered face and he stopped in the jungle path. Throwing his head back, he whistled a peculiar two-toned note; waited, then whistled again.

In a few moments the huge form of Marmo, the elephant, pushed through the tangled undergrowth of the forest. The elephant advanced, bobbing his trunk up and down in greeting.

"Behold!" Ki-Gor said in Swahali. "Thou comest in good time, O great gray sluggard. Lower thy trunk, that I may ride upon thy broad neck."

The great trained elephant chuckled and lowered his trunk obediently. Ki-Gor walked up it to the elephant's broad head. Reaching out a long muscular leg, he heeled the elephant gently behind a great flapping ear. Grunting softly, Marmo moved off along the forest path, Ki-Gor resting easily on his neck.

A little later they came out on the river bank overlooking Ki-Gor's Island. Ki-Gor told the elephant to stop, while he examined the scene before him.

It was always a pleasant sight to Ki-Gor, this two-acre oblong of land rising steeply out of the swift currents that washed its banks. It was the safest and the most comfortable location Ki-Gor had ever found for a place that he and Helene could call home. The upstream end of the Island was a tumbled mass of boulders and huge rock slabs strewn in mighty confusion over a series of fissured ledges. During some earlier geological day, a subterranean upheaval had hurled and tossed the ledges into the shape they now appeared, and incidentally had formed a half dozen or so roomy caves. Not all of these caves were proof against the violent rains that descend on that part of Africa, but two of them were weather-tight, and high and snug. These two Ki-Gor and Helene had furnished after a fashion, and here they lived in almost luxurious cosiness.

The lower end of the Island was well-wooded and contained a small grove of the same species of tall tree as the one in which Ki-Gor was standing, now. This was a fortunate circumstance which made possible the remarkable means of ingress to the Island which always gladdened Ki-Gor's heart whenever he used it.

It was a bridge of woven vines and reeds, fifty yards long, that swooped from a treetop on the mainland a hundred feet above the river to a corresponding treetop on the Iisland. It had been constructed by the devoted Pygmies, and it was a masterpiece of primitive engineering. It sagged considerably in the center, and swayed perilously as one walked across it to the Island. But, in point of fact, it was extremely strong and would hold a dozen people at once.

Ki-Gor was about to descend from Marmo's shoulders in order to cross the bridge when behind him, muffled by distance and the jungle growth, there came a faint scream. At the sound of that scream, fear leapt in Ki-Gor's eyes.

"Thou flying mountain," he roared, "take me hence! Carry me through the jungle with the speed of the windstorm! Forward, Marmo!"

For the white hunter's jungle-trained ears had recognized Helene's voice. What she was doing in the depths of the forest, and what danger confronted her he could not even guess. He had ordered her sternly never to leave the safety of their island retreat unless he was with her, but Helene, Ki-Gor knew, was apt to do many unpredictable things and there was nothing he could do about it. Now, he urged Marmo on to greater speed, wondering anxiously what had happened.

The elephant crashed through the jungle, with Ki-Gor stretched out flat on his neck. Ki-Gor gripped his assegai in readiness, and roared encouragement into Marmo's great ears.

Suddenly they came out into a clearing. In an instant, Ki-Gor's eyes caught the salient details of the scene before him, and he cried out once hoarsely, urging Marmo to his greatest speed.

Across the clearing Helene was backing up, slowly and carefully, keeping her eyes steadily on the young lioness that crouched menacingly over the body of a dead gazelle. The lioness' tail was twitching. It was obvious that she was angry and preparing to charge. Helene was crooning in a soothing voice: "Nice girl! Helene doesn't want your lunch. Nice girl...." But just as Ki-Gor entered the clearing, the lioness, with a coughing roar, sprang from her prey and bounded across the grass. Helene turned like a flash and leaped for the lower branch of a tree behind her. Ki-Gor's heart nearly stopped as he saw her hand catch hold of an overhanging bough—then slip unavailingly.

"Speed, O faithful friend!" he roared at Marmo. They dashed across the clearing like a runaway express. Ki-Gor shifted the assegai in his hand. The lioness sprang in a driving leap. Ki-Gor's arm tensed and with a mighty throw the assegai sped through the air.

Even from a stationary position, it is hard enough to hit a running lioness with a spear. For Ki-Gor to score a hit from the back of a charging elephant was indeed a triumph of skill and nerve. The assegai struck the big cat directly behind the left shoulder, with such force as to bowl the lioness completely over. She turned, snapping, at the protruding shaft of the assegai, and then with a grunt she rolled over and lay still.

Ki-Gor, knife in his hand, was off Marmo's back before the great jungle creature could stop. Helene threw herself into his arms, sobbing.

"Oh, Ki-Gor!" she said. "I thought I was so careful! I wanted to come to meet you! And then I ran smack into this lioness who had just killed a gazelle and dragged it in here. I looked her in the eye the way you told me, but she finally got angry and charged."

She was so frightened that Ki-Gor didn't have the heart to scold her. After a while, he called Marmo to him and they both mounted to his broad neck. And so they rode homeward.

"A SAFARI! What is a safari doing over here? Oh, Ki-Gor! You mean a regular safari—white men?"

Ki-Gor nodded. "Two white men."

"But when we settled down here, you said you thought there would never be any white men coming through this way."

Already Helene, once the spoiled, pampered daughter of civilization, was beginning to acquire Ki-Gor's deep-rooted distrust of white men in Africa. Genuine perturbation showed in her face as she watched Ki-Gor and waited for fuller information about the intruders.

They sat beside the small fire under a great overhanging ledge which served as an open-air fireplace. Here in their island sanctuary, they felt far distant from the dangerous jungle outside. Ki-Gor was recounting his experiences of the morning to Helene.

"Don't be afraid," Ki-Gor said, "they lost their way. They are looking for the gorilla country and they came the wrong way. I watched them until I heard them say they were turning back. Anyway, I left Ngeeso to keep his eye on them. If they don't go away soon, Ngeeso will come and tell us."

"I hope they go away soon. What were they like?"

"They were quarreling," Ki-Gor said pithily.

"Quarreling?"

"Yes." Ki-Gor frowned. "Helene, you have drunk whiskey. Why should anyone want whiskey so badly he will quarrel about it?"

"Well—" Helene shrugged, "some people just sort of acquire a taste for it, I suppose. After a while, it gets to be a habit and they just can't seem to do without it, that's all."

"Acquire—a taste," Ki-Gor repeated slowly. "You mean they taste it, and the first time they don't like it? But because they are foolish they taste it again, and three or four times they taste it and still they don't like it. But one day they like it a little better and so they keep on until they *do* like it."

Helene laughed indulgently. "You're not far off, dear."

Ki-Gor's eyes twinkled benevolently at her.

"Everybody is such fools," he pronounced, and picked up her hand and held it.

Helene looked at him with eyes full of love.

"Everybody *is* such fools," she whispered.

Suddenly Ki-Gor jerked his head around and stared back over his shoulder. Helene had heard nothing, but as she followed his gaze, she saw a Pygmy hurrying across the bridge. Ki-Gor stood up with a frown.

IN A few moments, Ngeeso was scurrying out of the underbrush toward them. His round little belly bobbed importantly as he ran, and his wrinkled, monkey-like face was contorted in an expression of satisfied glee.

"Hai! Big Brother!" he squeaked in the peculiar click language of the Pygmies and Bushmen. "Thou leftest too early! Thou hast missed a great scene!"

"Peace, Little One," Ki-Gor commanded. "Take a breath and relate calmly what thou hast seen."

"Hai! Rare it was!" Ngeeso exclaimed happily. "The big one—the buffalo with the voice of a crocodile—went among the porters bellowing and knocking down two of them. The other two came up behind him, the two whites, I mean. And they pleaded with him, and he heeded them not. Instead he pulled a brown bottle from a bundle, and tilted it up to his mouth and drank deeply. And nothing the other two said took any effect. Then the woman—*oohee!* but it was comic!—the woman reached up and tried to take the brown bottle from the buffalo! Never did I see such impudence in a woman—even a white woman. The buffalo drew back his right hand and smote her across the face—"

"What is this you are saying!" Helene cried. She was not so fluent in the click language as Ki-Gor, but she was picking it up rapidly.

"Ngeeso! A white woman? Ki-Gor, you said nothing about a white woman!"

"Aye, a white woman," Ngeeso said with a sardonic twitch of his wrinkled mouth, "A little white jungle mouse of a woman with eyes that pop out of her head with sadness. Well, the buffalo struck her full on the mouth and, of course, knocked her down. *Oohee,* it was a sight!"

Helene was on her feet, eyes snapping.

"Ki-Gor!" Her voice was imperative. "Why didn't you tell me there was a white woman on the safari? Some poor creature is out here in this wilderness with a drunken brute who's mistreating her!"

"There is nothing to be done," Ki-Gor said simply. "It is not our affair."

"Of course it isn't our affair," Helene retorted, "but just the same, it's not right. If a white woman is being mistreated right here on our home grounds I want to know about it. Come on. We're going right back and have a look at that safari. Whoever that poor little thing is, we're not going to let her be beaten—not if I have anything to do with it!"

Ki-Gor sighed. Whenever Helene's lovely red hair grew redder like that and suddenly seemed to bristle off her forehead, he knew that there was not much use trying to oppose her in anything she decided to do. He turned to the Pygmy.

"Proceed, Little One," he said, wearily. "We will go back with thee to the place where thou leftest the safari."

Ngeeso took them by the tree-route until they got quite close to the intruders. Helene swung along from branch to branch with almost as much agility as her preceptor and teacher, Ki-Gor, and when the three descended to the ground, she stole through the undergrowth as silently as Ngeeso himself.

Long before they came in sight of the safari, they heard the agitated voices rising high on the still afternoon air of the jungle.

"Get out of my way, Sheila! Or I'll knock you down again! You're a pair of foolish idiots, the both of you! And don't think for a moment that you fooled me with this bottle of whiskey! I can tell when whiskey has been diluted—"

"Mort! Please!" the little man appealed. "That's a ridiculous idea! Of course it wasn't diluted! Why—with your own eyes, you saw me pull the cork!"

"Well, this time—" the rasping voice was heavy with meaning, "—*this* time, I'll pull the cork myself! Now—out of my way! *Out of my way, damn it!*"

The Bull of Bashan voice rose to a savage yell.

HELENE SANK to her knees between Ki-Gor and Ngeeso and peered out with horrified eyes through the screening leaves of a wild banana bush. She saw a heavy-shouldered, bull-necked man with a mottled red face and a cropped mustache lurching toward the huddled group of porters to her left. Behind him in the center of the clearing stood a little man and a woman in attitudes of despair. Her slender frail body drooped, and her once-beautiful, ravaged face was white with fear. The spectacled little man beside her took two irresolute steps forward and peered nearsightedly after the raging figure of Morton Brett.

A sudden clamor broke out among the black porters, and as Helene shifted her gaze in that direction, she saw them milling and pushing against one another in terror as the berserk white man reeled toward them mouthing imprecations. Five paces away from them, he flung an arm up suddenly, and the whole mob of them flew into a panic. The black mass broke up—as it were, exploded—from the pressure within itself. The yelping porters scrambled off in all directions, back into the undergrowth, back up the trail that led into the clearing, off to one side or another—anywhere, to get out of the way of the maddened purple-faced white man.

One poor creature, finding his way to the rear blocked, tried to dash away past Brett's right hand. In his panicky haste, he tripped on one of the bundles on the ground. Black arms flailed as the porter tried to arrest his fall. But his balance was gone. With a despairing shriek, the black fell heavily against Brett's legs.

This, to Brett's drink-dimmed mind, was a final deliberate insult. He staggered back a step shouting curses and his hand groped for the revolver on his right hip. The miserable porter gave an agonized bleat and tried to scramble away on all fours. Brett's huge hand flipped open the holster.

"No! No! Mort! No!"

It was the little white man. Still shouting, he sprinted across the clearing. He was still three paces from Brett when the drink-crazed man sent a bullet through the porter's brain.

"You fool! You bloody fool!" The little man sobbed and flung himself on Brett's right arm. Brett's reaction was instantaneous. He flicked his right arm twice, and shook the little man off as if he were a beetle. The little man landed sprawling on his back five feet away.

So swiftly had all these events taken place that Helene behind her screen of leaves could hardly believe her eyes. But there was more to come.

The little woman in the middle of the clearing uttered a terrified cry and ran forward.

"Morton! How could you!"

She sank to her knees beside the fallen white man. Then Morton Brett laughed a hideous laugh. The muzzle of the revolver swung around slowly, relentlessly, and pointed down at the two white-clothed figures on the ground.

Helene drew a sharp breath and half-rose behind the concealing bush.

"So, that's the way it is, is it?" Morton Brett roared. And then as the noise of the fleeing porters died away in the distance, and a fearful silence took possession of the scene, he repeated in a leering whisper, "So *that's* the way it is, is it?"

The little man raised up on one elbow.

"Put that gun away, Mort," his voice was clear and unafraid. "You've done enough damage for one day."

"Oh! So you want me to put my gun away, David Gray," Brett sneered. "How nice for you if I did. Then you could draw your own and have the drop on me. And you could kill me and leave my body here for the hyenas while you and my dear devoted little wife went off together and lived happily ever after. Which is just what you have been planning to do ever since we came to Africa."

"I don't know what you're talking about," David Gray said. "And I don't think you do either."

HELENE'S HEART was beating like a trip-hammer as she watched the tense scene before her. A slight movement to one side of the menacing figure of Brett caught her eyes, and her heart pounded. It was the Somali boy on his hands and knees, crouched to spring at the drunken white man.

"I know exactly what I'm doing," Brett retorted, his mouth working. "I've been on to you. Try to cut me off liquor, would you? You know damn well it might have been fatal, and that's exactly what you wanted, isn't it?"

"Mort, that's ridiculous! Sheila and I are the last friends you have left on earth. We've stuck to you long after the rest dropped you. We've stuck to you and tried our best to bring back the old Morton Brett we knew and loved."

Helene clenched her fists in excitement. That's right, David Gray, she whispered to herself, keep stalling—keep his attention away from the Somali boy!

For a fraction of a second, Gray's words seemed to have an effect on Brett. A momentary doubt clouded his bloated face and the gun in his hand wavered. But it was only momentary. The cunning bestial grin returned, and the gun muzzle came up again.

Then the Somali boy sprang.

Whether some sixth sense warned the drunken man or whether he just happened to turn his head at that moment, Helene never knew. But as the Somali boy hit him in a slicing high tackle around the shoulders, Brett somehow swung his right arm free. For the space of two heartbeats, the white man and the black man swayed, locked in tense embrace. Then Brett's right arm thrashed out and in again. The gun muzzle jabbed the Somali under the left armpit. The gun roared. The Somali screamed and went limp.

Red froth bubbled out from the black lips, and the black fingers relaxed their hold and twitched. Brett gave a mighty heave and the faithful Somali collapsed in a heap on the ground.

"That's done it!" Brett roared and once again aimed the revolver at his wife and his friend. "My last friends, are you! So you sic your damn native on me!"

Without taking her eyes off the scene, Helene groped beside her with trembling fingers. Ki-Gor had to intervene! But her hand blindly pawed empty air! She jerked her head. *Ki-Gor was not there!*

"Say your prayers, my last friends!" the big man snarled.

Brett's face was contorted into an inhuman mask. The hand holding the fearful gun shook with demoniacal fury.

Something snapped in Helene's brain. Throwing all caution to the winds, she leaped out from behind her hiding place.

"Drop that gun!"

She stood in full view at the edge of the clearing, her blue eyes blazing. Brett threw her a horrified look and staggered back, the revolver suddenly loose in his fist.

"What's this!" he croaked, his bloodshot eyes bulging.

Helene began to shake all over. Now that she was out here, what was she going to do? She was unarmed. She certainly could not overpower that drunken brute. It would only be a matter of seconds before he recovered from the shock of her appearance.

"Drop that gun, I said!" she repeated, and hoped Brett wouldn't notice the hysterical quaver in her voice. "I've—I've—you're surrounded by—by—"

"By what?" snarled Morton Brett, and Helene's heart sank as she realized that the first shock of surprise was leaving him.

"Who are you, anyway?" Morton Brett's mouth worked and his eyes narrowed. The gun jerked up in his fist, and he took two steps forward.

Helene sucked her breath in. What a fool I was! She told herself bitterly. Ki-Gor, Ki-Gor! Where are you? *Where are you!*

Then she saw him.

HE APPEARED from nowhere a few paces behind Morton Brett, cold fury in his bronzed face. He stepped soundlessly, almost deliberately, and yet so swiftly that he was beside Morton Brett before Helene could catch her breath.

His left hand snaked down, seized Brett's gun-hand by the wrist and flicked the revolver loose in one terrific motion. At the same instant, his right hand crossed over and chopped upward in a fearful uppercut. He hit Morton Brett on the point of the chin with his palm open like a gorilla. There was a sound like the crack of a rifle. Brett's head flew back and his feet left the ground. He seemed to hang in the air for a moment, then he crashed heavily to the earth and lay perfectly still.

Helene's knees felt weak and she had to summon up all her will power to keep from sitting down right where she stood. She had never seen Ki-Gor hit a man harder in her life.

Ki-Gor walked across the clearing toward her, stony-eyed, ignoring the awed little couple who stared at him.

"Never do that again, Helene," he said severely. "Trust Ki-Gor. I would not let him shoot his friends. That is why I left your side."

Helene could not trust herself to speak for a moment. He was right and she knew it. Hereafter, she would always trust Ki-Gor. She was glad now that the little woman, Sheila Brett, came stumbling toward her, sobbing.

"I—I—don't know—what to say. You saved our lives—I don't know how—it just seems like—like a miracle. I know him—he would have killed us—and then you just appeared—"

Helene put her arm around the woman's thin shoulders.

"Well, there now," she comforted. "It's all over. Just relax."

"Is he—is he dead?" Sheila Brett asked fearfully.

"No." David Gray was coming toward them, his face white and drawn. "He's still alive. If he hadn't been so drunk, that blow would have broken his neck. However, he won't recover consciousness very soon."

Ki-Gor's face showed the slightest trace of irritation as he glanced toward the recumbent body of Morton Brett.

"Too bad," he said, and turned back to the man and woman. "Maybe I better kill him—now?"

David Gray looked up at him solemnly.

"A man like that," Ki-Gor said, "is like a mad elephant. He is bad, all bad. He should not be allowed to live."

"No-o," David Gray said slowly. "He's not all bad—only when he's under the influence of whiskey. Then he becomes somebody else. He would have killed us, no question about it, if you hadn't come along when you did. But—when he wakes up, he'll be all right. He will be horrified to think what he nearly did. It may be the one thing that will cure him of ever drinking again."

Ki-Gor shrugged contemptuously and turned away.

"It is impossible," David Gray said, "for us to express our real gratitude. We owe our lives to you, this moment, and we—we haven't the faintest idea who you are—unless—" A light began to dawn behind the little man's spectacles. "—unless you are—Ki-Gor!"

"Yes," said Ki-Gor with a pleased smile. "I am Ki-Gor. How did you know?"

"Well, I've heard about you, of course," Gray said, excitement creeping into his measured tones, "the whole world has heard about you. Then you—" and he turned to Helene, "must be Helene Vaughn, the American heiress, who crashed in a trans-African solo flight."

"Yes," Helene smiled, "and Ki-Gor picked me out of the wreckage and protected me from the man-eaters of the jungle."

"Oh, I remember," Sheila Brett put in, "the papers were full of it when you showed up in Uganda. You started back for America and only got as far as London."

"Yes, I never did go on from there," Helene explained, "Ki-Gor found out that he couldn't get along without Africa, and I—I found out I couldn't get along without Ki-Gor. I flew back and joined him and we were married at Fort Lamy."

"You left your wealthy, cosmopolitan life," Sheila Brett said wonderingly, "to settle down in the jungle with—nothing?"

"I have Ki-Gor," Helene said simply, "and as far as that goes, life in the jungle compares favorably with, say, life in Europe, today. After all, lions don't kill wantonly, and even leopards don't slaughter millions of innocent people at the command of a Super-Leopard."

"AH! YOU'RE so right," David Gray said heartily. "I've been making trips to Africa for fourteen years, and I've found that if you mind your own business and see that you don't infringe on the lives and rights of others—beast or human—you are as safe as you could be anywhere on earth."

Ki-Gor looked at him steadily. He said without expression: "I think it is better to take away all the guns from your friend before he wakes up."

And the jungle man coolly strolled across to the prone figure and stripped the revolver belt off it. Then he picked up the revolver, and walked past the dead Somali boy to where two gun-cases were lying. He returned then to the group, bearing the three weapons and the belt.

"Don't let him have these," he said putting them in David Gray's arms, "for any reason."

"Perhaps you're right," murmured the little man. "Now, let's see. I suppose I'd better start thinking about what to do next. I wonder just how far away those porters have gone."

"By now," said Ki-Gor, "they are miles away. You will never get them back."

"Oh Lord!" Gray groaned. "What in the world am I going to do?"

He threw a helpless glance at the row of abandoned packing-cases and bundles lying beyond the prone figure of Brett.

"The worst of it is," he added, "that I've lost my way. I suppose if I followed this trail back I would eventually come to more familiar country, unless—unless the trail branched and I took a wrong turn."

"Don't worry," Ki-Gor said suddenly. "I'll guide you."

"Would you?" Gray cried eagerly. "That would be terribly good of you! I wouldn't let you do it if I could possibly get out myself. Heaven knows you've done enough for us for one day!"

Ki-Gor shrugged again. Helene shot him a shrewd glance. She knew perfectly well that it was all he could do to conceal his irritation at the recent turn of events.

Two basic urges ruled the conduct of Ki-Gor's life. One of them was the fierce desire to be left alone. He prized his independence and privacy above everything else. The other urge or emotion was disgust, contempt for, and even fear of white men.

He had only the dimmest of memories of the Scottish missionary who was his father and who had been killed by treacherous blacks when Ki-Gor was a tiny boy. The boy had grown to manhood, surviving the rigors of the jungle by sheer native wit, adaptability, and physical endurance. Until Helene had come into his life, he had imagined himself unique in the world.

She had persuaded him to return to his own people so that he could have the benefits and comforts of civilization rather than live the rest of his life as a naked savage in the humid forests of Africa. The experiment had been an unfortunate one. Ki-Gor had found the comforts of civilization hampering and constricting. The standards and conventions of civilized society he had found arbitrary and capricious, if not downright false. And the competitive spirit of white men, their boundless greed, their lust for power, their capacity for any treachery to achieve their ends, he found revolting and far less ideal than the impersonal Law of Tooth and Claw of the jungle. Ki-Gor reflected that a lion, viewing his legitimate prey, an antelope, did not whip himself into a rage because he and the antelope differed in their ideas of God. The lion killed the antelope without rancor and ate her—because he was hungry.

Helene's eyes followed Ki-Gor now, as he walked over and stared down at Morton Brett's bloated face. Poor Ki-Gor! Helene thought. He had found his ideal homesite, the Island, and had established himself and her in the snug dwelling in this remote mountainous region safe from all intrusion, so he thought… only to have these whites come blundering in on him and start killing each other off in a manner only too typical of white men. Not only did he have to save their lives for them, but now he was saddled with the responsibility of leading them back to civilization.

No wonder Ki-Gor looked glum.

THEN HELENE looked at the sad-faced little woman in the beautifully cut white riding breeches and the high laced boots. Poor Sheila Brett! What a life she must be leading with a husband who could drink himself so quickly—and so frequently—into irresponsible and homicidal lunacy. She stood apart now, staring apathetically at the ground. Helene wondered if fundamentally she was really grateful at being saved from death. Ngeeso's phrase came into Helene's mind—"a little jungle-mouse of a woman with eyes that pop out of her head with sadness." Helene was on the point of voicing an impulsive invitation to the poor woman to come to the Island with her, when Ki-Gor and David Gray began to talk.

"When will he wake up?" Ki-Gor said, indicating Brett.

"He ought to pretty soon," was the answer. "If he doesn't, we ought to bring him to if we can. I'll try and empty his stomach of some of that poison, and then I'll give him a sedative and let him sleep a while."

"How soon can he march, then?" Ki-Gor asked gloomily.

"I'm afraid not until tomorrow morning at the earliest," Gray replied apologetically. "His face is badly bruised. It's a wonder to me that his jaw isn't broken. I guess it's true that Providence watches over drunkards and fools."

Ki-Gor's expressionless face did not for a second betray the fact that he did not know what "Providence" meant. Ki-Gor never admitted ignorance unless he felt that there was something to be gained by it.

"Look here," said David Gray, "I feel very badly about all this. I might be able to find the way back into Rhodesia by myself, especially if you could draw me a rough map. I hate to ask you to leave your home just to guide us goodness-knows how many miles."

"This is not my home," Ki-Gor said quickly with a warning glare at Helene.

"Oh!" Gray seemed surprised. "I thought it was."

Ki-Gor shook his head, still looking ferociously at his wife. Then he turned to Gray with the blandest of expressions.

"No, we are just here for a little while, and then we will go back North. Anyway, I won't have to guide you far. I know a short-cut over the mountains that will bring us to a trail that goes to a place called Muyanga."

"Oh! Muyanga!" Gray exclaimed. "I know Muyanga. If you can get us to Muyanga, I'll know how to go on from there. How long will it take over this short-cut?"

"Three days, maybe, even going slow," Ki-Gor answered with a significant glance at Sheila Brett.

"That's splendid," said Gray, "much better than I could have ever hoped for." He regarded ruefully the bundles abandoned by the fleeing porters. "It seems a shame to have to leave all that behind—there's some fine camping equipment there among other things. But I guess the only thing to do is to pick out a few items and make up a couple of small packs."

The little man knelt down beside an opened box.

"This is something we're going to get along without," he said grimly, and one by one he took out bottles of whiskey and carefully smashed them on a rock beside him. When he came to the last one, he held it a moment and looked at it.

"I think perhaps we'd better save one and hide it away in my pack. After all, Africa is full of poisonous snakes and it might not be a bad idea to have a stimulant along."

He stood up still holding the bottle and started toward the haversack lying in the middle of the clearing. Then he paused momentarily and looked down at Brett. The big man moved slightly.

"He's coming to, at last," Gray observed, "its about time."

He walked on to the haversack and stowed the bottle of whiskey away in it. Then he picked up a canteen and returned to Brett.

The big man's eyes were half open, now, and he was rolling his head feebly and groaning.

"Help me get him up, will you, Ki-Gor?" Gray appealed.

Helene turned her head away as Ki-Gor dragged the stupefied creature to his feet and propelled him toward the bushes. A moment later there was a sound of dreadful retching. Then came silence.

A LITTLE later Ki-Gor and Gray joined the two women in the clearing.

"Mort doesn't know the score yet," Gray informed them, "but we helped him get rid of a lot of that stuff in his stomach. I think after he's slept a couple of hours he'll be better. In the meantime, Ki-Gor, I suppose we'd better think about looking for some place to spend the night."

The jungle man shot another warning glance at Helene, and she knew he meant her to keep silent about the Island. Very coolly, he answered Gray.

"We don't have to look anywhere. Right here is a good place for your camp. It is high and dry, and there is good water not far from here that I will show you."

"Ye-es," said Gray dubiously with a grimace, "but those corpses aren't very pleasant—"

"Don't worry about them," Ki-Gor cut in. He looked up into a tall tree and raised his voice.

"Ngeeso!" he called, "thou nimble squirrel, come down here! There is naught for you to fear and I have urgent business for thee."

David Gray's face lighted up with interest as he heard Ki-Gor speaking the Pygmy language. And when a moment later, Ngeeso stood shyly at the edge of the clearing listening to Ki-Gor, Gray cocked an attentive ear.

"Behold those two unhappy creatures from whom life has fled," Ki-Gor said to the Pygmy, pointing at the bodies of the porter and the Somali. "They must be removed far from here. Therefore, Ngeeso, collect thy kinsmen with the utmost haste and dispose of them. Within the month I shall reward ye all by killing a wild elephant."

"My kinsmen are at hand, Big Brother," Ngeeso squeaked, "and straightway, we will do thy bidding. Without a reward, we would perform this task, but—" the Pygmy licked his long upper lip comically, *"oohee!* It is long since we gorged ourselves on elephant-meat!"

He disappeared into the undergrowth uttering shrill commands to unseen relatives. In a short time, a horde of potbellied little men and women swarmed out of the forest and scurried about the macabre task of removing the dead from the clearing.

David Gray looked at Ki-Gor wonderingly.

"The language you used just now," he said, "sounds remarkably like the language of the Bushmen down in the Kalahari. I have studied their speech, and yet I could not understand what you said."

"There are some words alike," Ki-Gor nodded, "but not many. But as you say, there are many sounds common to the two languages. Perhaps, at some time in the distant past, they were one people—the Pygmy and the Bushmen, and they split apart to live in different places and in the course of time, their languages grew apart."

"Ah!" said Gray, a fascinated expression stealing over his scholar's face. "That is precisely the theory that is held by one school of African anthropologists. It is a theory which has always interested me."

HELENE LAUGHED as she intercepted the questioning glance from Ki-Gor.

"I assure you, Mr. Gray," she interposed, "that Ki-Gor is not an anthropologist in the accepted sense. He has eyes that see and ears that hear, and he can always put two and two together."

"But that's marvelous!" Gray cried enthusiastically. "As I've said, languages, races, and customs of Africa, are of tremendous interest to me, and I count myself very fortunate to be able to talk to you, Ki-Gor, and get the benefit of your observations. They should be worth twice as much as the mere theories thought up by European and American scholars far removed from the actual scene."

Ki-Gor could scarcely conceal his bewilderment at this outburst, but he had felt from the beginning that there was a quality of honesty and integrity in this little man, Gray, which was rare among white men, or at least the white men that Ki-Gor had encountered. He, therefore, listened attentively as Gray went on:

"As a matter of fact, one of my deepest interests is this very possibility of some relationship or common ancestry between the Pygmy and the Bushmen. Both races are under-sized, yellow in color, and have thin lips in comparison with the Negroes around them. Both races have a very primitive culture, and both use a language of clicks. We're pretty sure both races were in Africa before the Bantu Negroes came along and drove them into the forests and the deserts. But—the question that is still unanswered is—where did the Pygmies and the Bushmen come from?"

If Ki-Gor was still overwhelmed by Gray's scientific zeal he showed it no longer. He merely grinned, and then suddenly reached out and seized an unwary Pygmy scurrying by.

"Tell me, Little Brother," Ki-Gor demanded, "where didst thy father's father's father come from?"

"I know not, Big Brother," the little creature replied, "but my mother's mother's mother was hatched from a crocodile's egg on the bank of a great river."

Ki-Gor translated this to Gray, and the little man with the glasses grew even more excited.

"The same kind of folk-lore as the Bushmen," he cried. "One of them once told me that his mother's mother's mother was hatched out from an ostrich's egg on the sunny side of a sand dune. You notice that both peoples apparently trace their ancestry through the female line. Matriarchy is, of course, much older than patriarchy in the growth of human society."

This was getting far too complicated for Ki-Gor to follow and he was secretly very relieved that Ngeeso stepped up to him at that moment and asked if there were any further commands to be carried out. Ki-Gor suggested that the Pygmies collect some firewood for the camping place, and Helene put in another suggestion that they break out the tents and try and put them up. Helene realized that Ki-Gor was getting a little uncomfortable under the learned questions that David Gray was putting to him, and she was glad of an opportunity to break up the conversation.

FOR THE next hour there was a great running about of Pygmies as they worked with the best of will and in a shrill uproar to put up the tents. But the Pygmies had never seen a tent before and were in consequence less than efficient in the task. Even Gray's supervision could not balance their ignorance, and when the tents were finally set up and pegged down, they presented a laughably lopsided appearance.

However, the tents would do to sleep in for one night if there were no heavy rainstorms, and the activity of getting them up had a beneficial effect on Sheila Brett. The shock of the dreadful scene with her husband wore off to some extent, and she was able to laugh a little with Helene and David Gray at the results of the Pygmies' labors.

About an hour after the Pygmies left, and just before sunset, there was a sound of thrashing in the undergrowth, and Morton Brett appeared at the edge of the clearing. He stood for a moment, swaying, one hand to his head. Gone was his high color, and his face, now, was a pasty white.

"Sheila!" he cried hoarsely, "Dave! What happened? What happened to me? I feel awful! I think I'm going to die!"

"I shouldn't be surprised," said Gray, getting up and going toward him.

"But what happened?" Brett insisted. "I feel as if I'd been on a terrible drunk."

"You have," Gray replied.

"But how—" Brett paused. "Oh Lord!" he groaned. "You gave me a drink. I asked you for a drink and you let me have it. You shouldn't have, Dave. You should never have let me have it!"

"There wasn't much we were able to do about it," Gray replied dryly, "that is to say, we weren't able to stop you from having more than one drink, it seemed."

"Oh Lord!" Brett groaned again. "I remember now. I insisted on having another. And then—oh, this is frightful! I remember I tilted the bottle up to my mouth! That's the last thing I remember at all clearly. Dave—did I—did I drink the whole bottle?"

The big man flopped down on his knees and started shaking all over.

"Yes, Mort," Gray said, "you drank the whole bottle—and more, too."

"Tell me, Dave," Brett whimpered, "did I act badly? Oh, this hideous curse that's fastened itself on me! Dave! Sheila! You've got to help me shake it—you've got to."

"You're in no condition to discuss anything now," said Gray. "I want you to drink this cup of hot condensed milk, and then I want you to go into your tent and sleep for a while."

"I couldn't sleep, now!" Brett whined, "I couldn't possibly! My nerves are shot to hell."

"I know that, Mort. I'm going to give you a pill to go along with the milk."

Brett lifted his twitching face and looked around unhappily. He seemed to see Ki-Gor and Helene, now, for the first time.

"Dave! Sheila!" he whispered in a frightened tone. "Who—who are they? Who are these people? They're dressed in leopard-skins—like savages—. *Who are they?*"

"They're friends," Gray said quickly. "They came along just in time to save your life—and ours. Drink that milk, Mort, and take that pill. After you've had a good long sleep, you'll be feeling much better. Then I'll tell you what you did while you were drunk. Come on, now. Here, come into the tent, and take off those clothes. I'll bring the milk along. Quick—do as I say."

Brett lurched to his feet, his swollen face suggestive of a hurt child.

"Dave," he whimpered, "my jaw aches, and my head aches."

"I'll bet it does," said David Gray and followed the big man into the tent.

Ki-Gor seized this opportunity to drag Helene to her feet and to say good-night to Sheila Brett.

"Oh, aren't you going to stay here with us, this evening?" the little woman said, her large brown eyes growing larger.

"We found a very comfortable tree last night," Ki-Gor said coolly. "We will come in the morning for you."

HELENE FOLLOWED him out of the clearing into the undergrowth. A moment later, Ki-Gor boosted her up to a bough she could not have otherwise reached, and then the pair swung homeward by the tree route.

Ngeeso was waiting by the bridge.

"The mad elephant, hath he finally waked?" the Pygmy asked.

"Yes, Little Brother, and feeling very bad because he drank too much mad-water."

"Hah! Serve the beast right!" Ngeeso spat. "By the Sacred Crocodile, I thought for a moment there thou hadst killed him with thy right-hand blow."

"It was something of a glancing blow, Little One, or else I had."

"Thou came in the very nick," Ngeeso declared, wagging his head importantly. "I was afraid for a moment when thy lady stood out in the open unarmed and dared him. If thou hadst not come then, I had a poisoned-tip shaft all notched and ready."

"Ah! it's as well he lived," Ki-Gor sighed, his manner belying his statement. "Go, Little One, and tell thy kinsmen that Ki-Gor thanks them deeply for their assistance this afternoon."

"They are glad and proud to help thee, Ki-Gor," Ngeeso said simply. Then a roguish expression twisted his scarred features. "Already, I can taste that elephant meat. Ki-Gor, when shall we go hunting the elephant?"

"Mercenary little rascal!" Ki-Gor roared and aimed a jesting blow of his right hand which would have killed the Pygmy if it had landed. Ngeeso chuckled with delight and ducked his head five inches, which was precisely the distance by which Ki-Gor's blow missed him.

"However," Ki-Gor said, "if thou wilt send out some young men to scout the plain below, I will be back from my journey in—" he held up a palm outspread, "five days. Then we will hunt any herds these young men may have discovered."

"Journey, Big Brother?" Ngeeso said sharply. "Dost thou indeed journey with these dull-witted whites back there?"

"I don't want them around here," Ki-Gor retorted, "therefore I shall guide them away by the shortest, quickest route possible."

"Ah!" Ngeeso murmured approvingly. "Over the mountain, Big

Brother? And across the Lost River?"

"The shortest route, I said."

"It is good, Big Brother, and thou art wise, as ever. Let me come with thee."

"No, Little One. Thou wilt best help me by staying and watching over my woman so that no harm shall befall her."

"What do you mean, Ki-Gor?"

It was Helene, speaking abruptly and forcefully in English.

"Did I understand you to tell Ngeeso you were leaving me behind?"

"It is best, Helene," Ki-Gor said with more authority than he felt.

"Well, you're not going to do anything of the kind, Ki-Gor!" Helene brushed an insect off her bare arm indignantly. "There isn't the slightest reason why I shouldn't go along with you. It's just a short trip, and there isn't any danger."

"I don't like that big man. I think he is danger," Ki-Gor said, with a frown.

"No, Ki-Gor, you're wrong," Helene said earnestly. "He's dangerous when he's drunk, and only then. I've seen his kind before. Honestly, Ki-Gor, you don't have to worry about him. Tomorrow, you'll see a different man. It's only when the whiskey gets him that he will cause trouble. And you saw David Gray destroy the whiskey."

"He didn't destroy one bottle," Ki-Gor pointed out.

"No, but he hid it. And Brett will never know it's in Gray's pack, because nobody will tell him."

"Well—I don't know," Ki-Gor shrugged moodily. "Maybe there is no danger but for some reason I don't want you to come along."

"Nonsense!" Helene scoffed. "You're just letting your imagination get the best of you. Now, it's all settled. I'm going with you, tomorrow."

Ki-Gor knew when he was beaten, and so did Ngeeso, even though the Pygmy didn't understand a word of English. He slid down the tree-trunk to the branch below and called up.

"Until tomorrow morning, then, Big Brother. If thy woman journeys with thee, why then, Ngeeso journeys with thee also, the better to watch over thy woman."

He ducked around the bole of the tree with a shrill cackle as Ki-Gor flung a piece of bark down.

CHAPTER II

BEFORE SUNUP THE NEXT day, Ki-Gor was stirring around. He spent an unusually long time examining his primitive arsenal of spears, clubs, bows and arrows. Finally he selected his longest, strongest bow and slung it on his back. He had other bows that shot more accurately, or faster, but none that could send arrows as far as this one. Out of his spear rack, he selected a short, heavy and very strong assegai with a broad double-edged blade.

Helene looked at him in amazement when he came in answer to her call for breakfast.

"What on earth are you doing with your war equipment, Ki-Gor?" she demanded. "Anyone would think you were going to trek through a country infested with cannibals."

"I don't know," Ki-Gor said unhappily. "I don't know at all. I seem to smell danger on this trip. Even going three days with these white people, I feel queer about something. I feel as if I should be well armed."

"That's silly, Ki-Gor," Helene said, but in a sympathetic tone. "I think seeing a man drunk for the first time in your life sort of got you down. I don't blame you in a way, because he was awful—I've never seen anybody worse drunk in my life—and I've seen a few. But you shouldn't let it bother you quite so much. You see, he can't get drunk again, and I think you'll find that when he's sober he'll be perfectly all right, really I do."

Ki-Gor shook his head impatiently.

"The little man," he said, "and the woman—they seem all right. Then why do they have anything to do with a mad beast like—like—"

"Brett," Helene supplied. "Well, the answer is probably just what I say—when he's sober he's a perfectly fine man. From what I overheard, he was once apparently a great doctor in America. Those two love the man he is when he is sober. When he is drunk, nobody could love him."

"It sounds unhealthy to me," Ki-Gor said. "And, once more, Helene, I wish you would not come with me—"

"Please, darling!" Helene pouted. "Don't let's go all over that again. It's all settled. I know you're just worried because you're upset from seeing a drunken man."

"Maybe," said Ki-Gor staring into the fire.

A moment later he stood up with sudden decision and went into the main cave. When he returned, his long bow was still slung over his shoulder, but the war-assegai was missing. Evidently, he had thought better of bringing it. However, a little bulge under the leopard-skin trunks at his right hip indicated to Helene that he was carrying iron rations of dried antelope meat.

"Helene," he said, "when we get to their camp, it will be a good idea, I think, if we don't go in openly. We'll listen quietly for a little while and see how that man is behaving."

Helene nodded and stood up. As long as Ki-Gor agreed to let her come with him, she was perfectly willing to follow his orders, even when he might seem to be over-cautious.

Again, Ngeeso was waiting for them at the far end of the bridge. He had probably slept in that very tree all night, although Helene noticed that the quiver on his back was newly filled with tiny arrows. He greeted the couple formally, betraying no surprise in his gnome-like face at Helene's presence. Swiftly, then, the strange trio swung through the trees toward the camp of David Gray and Morton and Sheila Brett.

THE THREE Americans were fully dressed and sitting around a small fire eating breakfast when Ki-Gor noiselessly slipped into a comfortable crotch in a nearby tree.

"He should be along soon, shouldn't he?" Morton Brett was saying. His manner was far different from the day before. He was humble and subdued, even timid. His face was swollen and purple.

"Yes," Gray answered, "I expected him before now. We were a little late getting breakfast."

"Lord!" the big man muttered. "I don't know how I can face him. It's bad enough to have to face you and Sheila after you told me what I did yesterday. Unworthy as I am, you two love me and understand me. But this man, Ki-Gor, must think I'm a pretty strange sort of person."

"He'll understand that you were just in liquor," said Gray.

"Oh *that!*" Brett shuddered. "You have my most solemn word on that. Any time I ever feel a thirst coming on, all I need to do is to think back on how I felt this morning when you told me how close I came to—to— Oh, Dave! Sheila! Can you ever forgive me!"

The big man held his hands out in agonized appeal.

"Mort," said Gray gently, "if that scene yesterday is the means of curing your dipsomania for good and all—then Sheila and I will consider that our moment of horror and agony was not in vain."

Brett buried his face in his hands for a second.

"Bless you, Sheila!" he said brokenly. "Bless you, Dave!"

Up in the tree, Helene nudged Ki-Gor.

"You see?" she whispered triumphantly into his ear. "He's an absolutely different man when he's sober. You can trust him now."

Ki-Gor nodded slowly, but his blue eyes were cold and unconvinced. He unfolded a long leg silently and easily and began to descend the tree.

The three white-clothed people around the breakfast fire jumped nervously at the sound of Ki-Gor's voice saying, "Good morning."

Morton Brett struggled to his feet as Ki-Gor and Helene crossed the clearing toward the tents, little Ngeeso trailing shyly behind. Brett's face was chalk-white, his lips gray as he spoke the first words.

"Ki-Gor and—er, Mrs. Ki-Gor," he stammered, "before anything else is said or done, I must first try and make my peace with you. You saw me yesterday a homicidal maniac in the grip of a frightful curse that has enslaved me for five years. I cannot apologize adequately, or in any way excuse my actions."

Ki-Gor's eyes held the other man's steadily, but a deep flush spread over his weather-beaten face, and he shifted his feet uncomfortably. Helene could see that he was acutely embarrassed by Brett's abject apology. She stepped forward and held out her hand.

"I think we understand, Doctor Brett," she said calmly, "and let us consider the whole incident as forgotten. The most important thing now, I think, is to get you three started back toward civilization."

"We're all ready to go now," David Gray said promptly. "We just have to sling light haversacks over our shoulders, and we can walk right out of here. It seems a shame to leave these tents here to rot, but I guess there's nothing to be done about it. By the way, Ki-Gor, I buried two hunting rifles and a revolver with a quantity of ammunition last night. If you want them we can go and dig them up now."

Ki-Gor shook his head thoughtfully.

"We don't need them," he said, at length. "They are better where they are. One gun is enough. Let me have yours, Gray."

"Mine?" said Gray, startled. "Why—er—"

"Give it to him, David," Morton Brett said, unexpectedly. "I don't blame him at all for wanting to be the only one in the party with a gun."

"Very well," said Gray, unstrapping the cartridge belt around his waist. "We want you to trust us as completely as we trust you, Ki-Gor."

The jungle man took the belt without answering and fastened it about his own waist. Then he looked impassively at the little group.

"We'll go in this order," he said finally. "I will lead the way. Then you behind me, Brett. Then Helene. After her, Sheila. And then Gray."

He said a few rapid words to Ngeeso which Helene understood as a command to the Pygmy to bring up the rear of the party and to keep a sharp eye on the three Americans.

In this manner, the strangely assorted group finally got under way.

FOR ABOUT a mile, Ki-Gor followed the trail which Gray had come down the day before. But when the trail left the thick jungle for a short distance to cross a stretch of high ground, Ki-Gor turned abruptly off at right angles and began a long, gradual climb up a sparsely wooded side of a mountain. While the ground underfoot was not too rough, there was not much protection from the brassy glare of the sun, and the progress of the column up the long persistent upgrade was slow and halting. Morton Brett, in particular, appeared to be making heavy work of propelling his beefy frame up the slope, in spite of Ki-Gor's considerately slow pace. However, the big man did not complain, possibly because he was saving his breath.

A little after midday, there were expressions of satisfaction from the three Americans as Ki-Gor halted the party on the crest of a ridge and sought out the shade of a clump of tall bushes. There were sighs of relief when the jungle man indicated that the way led down hill from there for some distance. But the relief changed to dismay when Ki-Gor went on to say that after they descended to the shallow valley, they would have to climb a still higher mountain.

Nightfall found the party camping well up on the slopes of this higher mountain. Everyone, including even Helene, was too tired to talk very much, and after a light meal all promptly went to sleep.

The climb was resumed early the next morning, with the Bretts and Gray seemingly much refreshed by their long sleep in the cool mountain air. It was not long before Ki-Gor halted again on a crest of ground and pointed out the direction their way was to take that day.

"We go down hill some more," he said, "until we come to the Lost

River. It's too wide and swift for us to cross without a boat, so we will walk along it until we come to the place where the river goes into the mountain and get across it that way."

"The Lost River," said David Gray, thoughtfully. "I've heard about that somewhere. You say it's a large river, but it disappears into the side of a mountain?"

"Into the side of a mountain!" Helene exclaimed. "What happens to it? A big river just can't lose itself entirely, can it?"

"I don't know," Ki-Gor shrugged. "Maybe it comes out the other side. I've only traveled this route once, and that time I didn't stop to—to scout—"

"To explore?" Helene supplied.

"To explore it," Ki-Gor finished with a grateful smile.

"Wait a minute," David Gray said, frowning. "Are there Bushmen along this Lost River?"

"I don't think so," Ki-Gor replied. "Anyway, I didn't see any. It isn't Bushman country. It's pretty heavy jungle along the banks."

"Well, somehow I seem to connect up a Lost River with Bushmen," Gray pondered. "Now, just what was that connection?"

"You'll see it when we come to it," Ki-Gor said. "It really isn't as strange as it sounds. The river cuts down between two mountains. They have very steep sides, those mountains and they form a sort of—sort of—how do you say it, Helene?"

"Do you mean a gorge?" Helene smiled.

"Yes. A gorge," Ki-Gor said. "That's just what it is—a gorge. And sometime, a long time ago, there was an earthquake, probably, and great piles of rock fell down across the river from both mountains. Maybe it blocked up the river for a while, but now the water has found a way down under the rocks."

"Say!" Gray said with a mounting excitement. "It's coming back to me, now! I know why I connect this Lost River with the Bushmen! It's because I heard about it from them!"

"But, Dave"—it was Morton Brett—"I thought all the Bushmen were way south of us down in the Kalahari desert."

"Most of them are," Brett returned, "and that's where I heard the story—down in the Kalahari. I spent three years off and on down there studying the Bushmen. They have a remarkable folk-lore, rich and colorful. And I remember distinctly a story about two mountains who loved each other. These mountains were separated by a river. At first they pleaded with the river to flow somewhere else, but the river impudently refused to do so. Whereupon the mountains, in a rage, shook their sides and rolled masses of rocks down and blocked off the river. And the river swelled its sides and tried to burst the barrier of the rocks but was unable to do it. And eventually, the river grew ashamed and hid its face among the fallen rocks."

"Why, how extraordinary!" Helene exclaimed.

"Well, it's all the more extraordinary," Gray went on, "to find a natural phenomenon that would bear out that story—give it a basis of truth, so far away from the Bushman country. I wonder whether this region might have once been the home of Bushmen. Perhaps they lived around here hundreds of years ago and were driven south when the big Bantu came in."

KI-GOR REGARDED the little American with genuine interest. Then apparently he thought of something.

"There are not many Bantu here now," he said. "Just a few Pygmies."

"It's very strange," Gray mused. "Are you sure there are no Bushmen somewhere along that river?"

"I never saw any," Ki-Gor replied. "Maybe Ngeeso would know. He has been along the Lost River much more than I have."

Gray listened intently as Ki-Gor questioned the little Pygmy, but try as he would to make sense of the click language, he was unable to translate the conversation. Ki-Gor's eyes were gleaming as he turned back to him.

"It's very interesting," the jungle man said. "Ngeeso says there are people along the Lost River. They may be Bushmen, but he wouldn't know because he has never seen Bushmen. But they are not Bantu and they are not Pygmies."

"Then they must be Bushmen!" Gray cried. "Say, I hope we catch sight of some of them when we get to this river!"

Ki-Gor was talking to Ngeeso again.

"I don't think we will," he said a minute later to Gray. "Ngeeso says these people are not found where we will cross the river. They are all on the other side of the great rock barrier, where the river comes out again."

"Where the river comes out again?" Gray cried.

"Yes. He says the river comes out into a long narrow valley with very steep sides. The people are in that valley. Ngeeso says he thinks they are trapped in that valley. The sides are so steep they cannot get out, and other people cannot get in."

"How could they be trapped, Ki-Gor?" said Gray. "Couldn't they just go in and out of the lower end of the valley?"

"Ngeeso says not," Ki-Gor returned. "He says the steep sides of the valley get very narrow at the lower end, and there is just room for the river to go through the gorge."

"Well, that is fascinating!" said Gray. "I wonder just who those people are that live down there. They must be Bushmen. Did Ngeeso tell you what they looked like?"

"He doesn't know how to describe them," Ki-Gor answered, "and anyway, he says he has only seen them from a distance—he up on the edge, and they down at the bottom of this valley. It's called Glaclanda, this valley."

"Glaclanda!" Gray fairly shrieked the word. "That's the name the Bushmen called the Lost River! Great Scott! Ki-Gor! I want to see that valley and the people that are trapped in it!"

Ki-Gor nodded with an approving smile.

"Over there," he pointed to the eastward, "you see that mountain with two peaks? When we get closer, you'll see that it is really two mountains. In between them is the valley of Glaclanda."

FOUR HOURS later, the party stood on the edge of a high bluff and looked down on a rushing mountain river. Its turbulent, tumbling waters swept away to their left. About an eighth of a mile away it broadened out into what seemed at first glance to be a small lake. But as Ngeeso guided the party along the bluff nearer to it, they could see that the lake was in reality a gigantic pot-hole full of fierce whirlpools and eddying boiling currents.

On either side rocky banks rose steeply upwards. But on the downstream end of the pool a titanic mass of piled rock filled in the ancient gorge to the height of something like five or six hundred feet. It was an awe-inspiring sight, that gigantic heap of tumbled rocks, boulders and ledges—millions of tons that at some time in the distant past had slipped or rolled or fallen down into the gorge.

Helene thought of the folk tale of the Kalahari Bushmen far away to the south. Two mountains loved each other and they shook their sides one day and poured down these rocks to punish the offending river which divided them. But it was the river who won out in the end and circumvented the might of the mountains. Somewhere under that massive heap of rock the river had cut a subterranean channel.

After a brief rest, the party began the task of climbing to the top of the great rock barrier. Morton Brett had objected to the idea in the beginning. He had argued that, being without porters and supplies they should waste no time getting to an outpost, and therefore should not attempt to make a side trip to peer into a valley into which they could not descend. But Gray's enthusiasm overruled him finally, the little man pointing out that they had to climb the rocks anyway to cross the river and that therefore they might as well climb a little higher and look down into Glaclanda. The possibility of seeing the inhabitants of the cliff-bound valley even at a distance had aroused all the scientific curiosity in David Gray's make-up.

It was an arduous climb, though not especially hazardous. Much of the face of the barrier was overgrown with lichen, moss, and in some places grass and even small bushes. And even the patches of bare rock were broken up into comparatively small boulders by the force of the original convulsion that had tossed them down there.

Ki-Gor ordered Ngeeso to lead the way, depending on the Pygmy to go by a route which even Sheila Brett could traverse. The jungle man had rearranged the order of precedence and now brought up the rear of the column, just behind the panting, perspiring bulk of Morton Brett. The little argument between the big white man and Gray had revived Ki-Gor's instinctive dislike and distrust of Brett. And, although Brett had eventually given in with good grace, Ki-Gor wanted him where he could watch him every minute. But Brett made no further complaint during the entire forty minutes or so that the party toiled upwards, and when they all arrived at the top, he joined the rest in the exclamations of delight and admiration at the view from the top of the barrier.

"Isn't it beautiful!" Helene gasped as she gazed out of the mile-wide valley that stretched out below to the northwards.

"I should say so!" Sheila Brett exclaimed, joining her. "It's—why, it's sort of like a miniature Grand Canyon, isn't it!"

David Gray stood spell-bound for a minute, then began fumbling at the leather binocular-case at his belt.

Thousands of years before, the two mountains must have stood shoulder to shoulder, only a high grassy vale separating the two peaks. But in the course of the ages, the rushing waters of the river had cut a channel down through the sandstone. Time and the persistent, unrelenting pressure of the swift-flowing water had finally produced this little jewel of a valley, lined on both sides by perpendicular cliffs that shone brilliant red in the slanting rays of the afternoon sun. It was, as Sheila Brett described it, like a miniature Grand Canyon of the Colorado.

Ki-Gor looked downward and saw the river boiling out from the foot of the barrier a thousand feet below on this side. It flowed rapidly, then, only for a short distance before it evidently found level ground. Then it broadened out and traced a beautiful silvery ribbon down the center of the valley. Ki-Gor tilted his head back and squinted, his eyes following the line of the river until it disappeared. It was about five miles away, he judged, that the mountains seemed to come together again. It must be there, he decided, that the valley narrowed again as Ngeeso had said to form a natural flume just wide enough to let the river through.

"WELL, THERE it is," Morton Brett remarked. "I can see how nobody could ever get down into that place. Look at those sheer cliffs. They must be four or five hundred feet straight up and down. What do you see through your glasses, Dave?"

"Nothing very much," Gray replied, dropping the binoculars from his eyes. "Although, I think there's some smoke rising off in the distance near the cliffs to the right. That's the shady side—the west—this time of day, and it's a little hard to tell much at this distance."

"Well, there you are," Brett grunted. "Climb all the way up here and all you see is a little smoke, and you aren't even sure it's that. Let's get along, shall we?"

"As a matter of fact," Gray turned apologetically to Helene and Sheila Brett, "I would dearly love to walk along the top of the cliffs for a couple of miles and see if I can't catch a glimpse of something more down there."

"Oh, for heaven's sake, Dave!" Morton Brett snorted. "We've got to get back to civilization. We haven't got time to sit around while you indulge a fantastic hobby. Ki-Gor, tell him we've got to push on."

Ki-Gor regarded the big man coolly. What an unpleasant man! Ki-Gor thought, and how ungracious he was to his friend, Gray. Ki-Gor had begun to like the little man, and he quickly decided to take Gray's part.

"It's getting late," Ki-Gor remarked, looking up at the sky with elaborate care. "We'll have to camp somewhere, soon. We might as well look for a place near here. Then, in the morning, before we go on, Gray can walk around and look down the cliffs."

Brett expostulated, "We can't afford to take the time out for—"

"I think I can see a good place," Ki-Gor broke in, and moved away abruptly. "Just off this barrier over there, and a little above it. Come on, we'll all go and look at it."

A dark flush crept over Brett's face and his mouth clamped shut under the cropped mustache. Then he made a defeated gesture with his hands and followed the jungle man.

The camp-site was by no means ideal, being a rather small rocky shelf only partly shaded by two low-branched trees. But as there was very little level ground anywhere about there, Ki-Gor made it do. After the light evening meal had been prepared and consumed, the party improvised sleeping places for themselves and presently dropped off to sleep. Ki-Gor took the precaution of moving away and climbing a nearby tree to spend the night. He was taking no chances with Morton Brett, although the latter had seemed to regain his good humor over supper.

Just at dawn the jungle man woke with a start, feeling something close over the big toe of his left foot. Instantly he shook the foot and he heard a squeaky exclamation. He peered down through the blue dusk and saw that Ngeeso was hanging from a limb below him by one hand.

"Thou art nervous, Big Brother," the Pygmy complained, as he drew himself up to safety. "I thought to play a joke on thee and pinch thee by the toe. By the Sacred Crocodile, I was nearly kicked out of the tree into the valley below."

"Cease thy chatter, Little One," Ki-Gor demanded. "I hear someone move there near the ledge."

"Aye, it's of no matter," Ngeeso said. "It is merely the small white man. The Bull Buffalo still sleeps."

Ki-Gor slipped down the tree and came silently beside David Gray who was peering down into the valley of Glaclanda through the binoculars.

The little man was quivering with excitement. He lowered the glasses and looked around him eagerly as if seeking somebody to share his excitement with him. His eyes lighted up as he saw Ki-Gor.

"I CAN see smoke again!" he cried. "Three or four columns of it. And what's more, there seem to be a number of little black dots at the base of the cliffs way down there—little pin-pricks they look from here, but I wouldn't be at all surprised if they were not caves. Think of it, Ki-Gor, caves! The Bushmen live in caves, you know! I think there's no doubt that we've stumbled on to a rare group of Bushmen, Ki-Gor, a group that somehow survived the Bantu invasions, long ago, and stayed on here instead of fleeing south to the desert. Let's walk along the rim of the cliffs, Ki-Gor, and try and get a closer view of them. We might even find some way of getting down there."

Ki-Gor smiled tolerantly at the little man's outburst.

"Yes," he said, "in a little while. We'll have some food first, and then we'll all walk along the cliffs."

The jungle man had no intention of leaving Morton Brett unguarded.

If Helene could have read Ki-Gor's thoughts, she probably would have told him that he was being needlessly wary about the big surgeon. Brett grumbled somewhat, when he was awakened, and during breakfast he expressed impatience with the idea of delaying the journey back to civilization to walk four or five miles along the edge of the valley on the chance of seeing some of the inhabitants of Glaclanda far below. But there was no appearance of treachery or even unfriendliness in Brett's attitude, merely the disagreeable grumpiness of a selfish, spoiled child.

The matter of walking along the edge of the escarpment proved to be not quite so easy as David Gray had thought at first glance. The line of tree-growth came down very close to the rim, leaving only a narrow alley along which to walk. More than that, this narrow avenue was by no means level. There were many stretches where it canted perilously sideways, so that Helene, picking her way carefully, felt as if she were on the roof of a house, uncomfortably close to the eaves.

Like a house roof, the escarpment had a considerable overhang over the sheer cliffs for most of the distance—a fact which did not increase the safety of the party walking along the rim. In spots this overhang had washed away entirely revealing only too clearly the precipitous drop of four or five hundred feet straight down to the valley floor. In places like these, Ki-Gor who was leading the way and testing every foot of the going before trusting his full weight on it, would climb up hill a short distance, toiling through the thick undergrowth of the hillside.

However, the jungle man felt no annoyance or boredom at having to make this tricky and unnecessary side trip. On the contrary, his curiosity had been thoroughly aroused by David Gray's enthusiasm, and he kept a wide-awake and speculative eye on the valley as he led the party slowly along the escarpment.

For such a comparatively restricted and small area, the Valley of Glaclanda offered a remarkable variety of terrain. Many sections, especially at the base of the cliffs on both sides, were well wooded with beautiful tall virgin timber. The banks of the river were fairly open, however, being narrow green meadows dotted here and there with copses of graceful trees. Toward the lower end of the valley, there were stretches of open veldt and the river broadened out and even divided into several channels separated by sandbars.

David Gray remarked excitedly on the plentiful animal life in the valley, the hordes of monkeys in the trees, and the small herds of antelope on the miniature veldt. But as far as any human life was concerned, Gray was disappointed. In spite of the fact that there were two or three thin columns of blue smoke curling out of what were quite evidently cave mouths in the opposite cliffs, there was not a single Bushman to be seen anywhere. By the time the party had gone half way along the escarpment, the little ethnologist expressed his disappointment.

"Ki-Gor," he said, "isn't there any way at all of getting down these cliffs?"

Ki-Gor shook his head with a smile. He had been keeping a sharp lookout for a place where descent might be feasible, but so far he had seen none, and he was inclining to the belief that there were none. A few minutes later, though, Gray, undaunted, halted by the top of a narrow half-chimney that had been worn away by erosion.

"KI-GOR," HE shouted. "Look down here. I think it might be possible to get down this way by very careful stages. There's a slight slope outwards—it isn't quite so straight down—and the rock is a little rougher. I think I can see some footholds."

Ki-Gor came back and stared down for a minute, then a grim smile came on his lips. He pointed.

"Somebody else thought the same thing a long time ago," he said. "See—down there—at the foot of the first tree?"

Gray's face paled as he stared down at what was unmistakably a human skeleton. The little man was silent as he followed Ki-Gor up and around the half chimney through the undergrowth.

But David Gray could not keep blankets on his scientific zeal for long. In a few minutes he was excitedly pointing out a break in the line of cliffs just ahead.

The rim of the escarpment dipped down suddenly at this place to a height of less than three hundred feet above the valley floor. Here, also, the smooth rock wall of the escarpment was divided by a thirty-foot wide vein of much softer rock—rock so soft, in fact, that in the course of the ages it had broken down and worn down to a great sandbank which sloped away to the valley below at a forty-five degree angle.

"Here, Ki-Gor!" the little man cried enthusiastically. "Don't you think something might be done at this spot?"

Ki-Gor did not answer for a moment. He was peering critically down in the treetops of the valley. He could not be sure, but he thought that he had seen something move down there out of the corner of his eye—something flitting from shadow to shadow. He called to Ngeeso to ask him if he had noticed anything like that. Just as he spoke to the Pygmy, Morton Brett came lumbering over to the edge of the sandbank. Ki-Gor's attention was fixed on Ngeeso's reply, or he might perhaps have prevented the incident.

As it was, the jungle man saw it happening and shouted a warning. But he was too late. Morton Brett blundered out too far on the overhang. Without warning the rotted tangle of roots gave way. Ki-Gor's rescuing hand just missed the beefy shoulder, and Morton Brett went plunging down the sandbank.

It all happened so suddenly that the rest of the party did not grasp it until they saw Brett halfway down the bank, arms and legs flying, rolling, sliding, turning grotesque cartwheels. There were a few seconds of awful silence until the plunging body reached the foot of the sandbank and slowly rolled to a stop. Then Sheila Brett gave a low moan as her husband lay very still.

A small avalanche of sand and tiny pebbles shaken loose by Brett's awful plunge slowed and came to rest, half covering his inert form.

"Mort! Mort!" Gray shouted in entreaty. "Answer me! Answer me, Mort!"

Ki-Gor's brown hand restrained the little man, and drew him back from the treacherous overhang. Then Gray gave a shout.

DOWN BELOW, Brett's right arm stirred under the sand. After a breathless pause, his great bulk heaved, and a moment later, he dragged himself to a sitting position, the sand pouring off his white clothes.

"Mort! Are you hurt badly?" Sheila Brett and David Gray shouted together.

There was a faint mumble from below, and then the big man slowly got on one knee, and finally stood up on his feet. He looked around him in a dazed way, then looked up. Then he took a few uncertain steps, lifting his feet high out of the sand, and paused to feel his elbows and knees and ribs. Eventually, he looked up again and spoke.

"I don't know why," he called in a high, querulous voice, "but I seem to be all right. I don't think I've broken anything."

"Oh, thank goodness, Mort!" Gray shouted fervently. "I thought you were a goner for a minute!"

"So did I," Brett returned, "but—I guess there's no harm done. That's going to be quite a climb."

"It's no use, Brett," said Ki-Gor suddenly. "You can't climb it."

"Nonsense," Brett retorted. "Why can't I?"

"The sand," Ki-Gor said, laconically.

"Don't be silly," said Brett contemptuously. "Of course, I can climb back."

Suiting the action to the words, the big man plunged up the slope. The initial impetus of his rush carried him almost ten feet before the sand began to give way under his feet. He managed to get a few more steps upward, and then the shifting sand poured down on him in torrents. He swayed and almost fell over backwards, but regained his balance momentarily. Then more sand moved inexorably down on him, swept him off his feet and rolled him choking and sputtering to the foot of the slope.

Brett gasped, picking himself up. "You—you may be right—at that—"

But Ki-Gor had moved away from the top of the slope and did not answer. He was talking to Ngeeso. After a moment, he unbuckled the gun-belt and held it out to Helene.

"Keep this, Helene," he said. "Ngeeso and I are going to find some vines. Tell Brett to save his strength. He can never get up the sandbank by himself. I'll be back in a little while."

CHAPTER III

OVER AN HOUR LATER, Ki-Gor and the Pygmy returned. Ki-Gor was in a somewhat grim humor. He had had to go far to find the yards and yards of stout vines that he was carrying coiled up, and he was thoroughly out of patience with Morton Brett's clumsiness.

The jungle man and the Pygmy sat down on the top of the sandbank and began to knot the vines together swiftly. In a remarkably short time a rope which looked more than long enough to reach down the sandbank to the bottom was completed. One end was secured around the base of a big tree trunk, and Ki-Gor began to pay out the other end toward Morton Brett.

"Thank goodness!" Brett shouted as he saw the rope end descending. "I've had about enough of this down here. It's spooky. I have a feeling I'm being watched, but I haven't any idea who it could be."

"Have you seen anything?" Ki-Gor asked sharply.

"No," Brett admitted. "Not directly, that is. A couple of times I thought I caught a glimpse of something dodging among those bushes there. But when I looked again, I couldn't see anything. And I didn't feel like walking over and exploring."

"All right. Be ready to take the end of the rope as soon as you can reach it," Ki-Gor commanded, "and then come up hand over hand. Don't waste any time."

Gray and the two women looked anxiously at Ki-Gor, but he said nothing and concentrated on getting the rope to Brett.

"Now!" Ki-Gor said suddenly. "Come up two steps—you should be able to reach it. Hurry!"

But even as he said the last word, Ki-Gor saw that he was too late. A snake-like object flew out from the bushes near Brett and floated through the air toward him.

"Look out, Brett! Duck!" Ki-Gor shouted.

But before the big surgeon realized what was happening, the lasso dropped neatly over his thick shoulders. He gave a startled cry and plucked frantically at the soft pliable lasso-rope. But, at the same moment, the loop tightened and nearly jerked the big man off his feet.

"Never mind the loop!" Ki-Gor shouted. "Get hold of the rope and pull! You can pull the Bushman out!"

But Brett was lunging around like a panicky steer. Just then a second lasso drifted through the air and ringed Brett's neck with deadly precision. A third and a fourth followed immediately, and in less than fifteen seconds, Brett was rolling on the ground, arms pinned to his sides, and completely helpless.

Without hesitation, Ki-Gor shouted a command to Ngeeso and then lowered himself over the edge of the sandbank by the vine-rope. Instantly he sank deep into the sand and began to slide downwards. But he held firmly on to the rope, kept his balance and checked his progress. A glance over his shoulder showed him that Ngeeso was loyally following him down.

Before Ki-Gor was halfway down the sandbank, he saw that Brett was being dragged toward the bushes by his unseen lassoers. Helpless though the big man was, his legs were still free, and he managed to dig his heels into the ground. For a few precious moments, he resisted the pull of the lassoes. It was just long enough.

Ki-Gor hit the bottom of the bank in a shower of dust, sand, and pebbles. He reached Brett's side in three bounds and seized one of the taut lasso ropes. Ngeeso, scurrying nimbly after, notched a poisoned arrow in the little bow.

The jungle man gave a swift, prodigious heave on the lasso rope. There was a high-pitched cry of astonishment from the other end, and out of the bushes tumbled the oddest looking human being Ki-Gor had ever seen.

Instantly, Ki-Gor sprang at the creature to capture him. But the Bushman or whatever he was, was incredibly agile and started scrambling back into the bushes like a frightened pig. Ki-Gor just managed to seize a hairy ankle. He straightened up and hauled the babbling stranger back into the open.

IMMEDIATELY, THE bushes erupted half a dozen more creatures just like the first one. They flung themselves shouting on Ki-Gor, and tugged at his arms, scratching and biting. Ngeeso dashed up alongside chattering fiercely, but lowered his bow as Ki-Gor shouted at him.

"Don't kill! They are unarmed, Little Brother! There is no danger!"

The Pygmy stepped back in astonishment and watched Ki-Gor shake off the strange men like a terrier shaking off water. A moment later, Ki-Gor was in full command of the situation. With each hand he gripped one of the strangers by the nape of the neck. The other five picked themselves up and stood a healthy distance away from the giant white man.

Ki-Gor shouted a command to Ngeeso to strip the lassoes off Morton Brett, and then he turned his attention back to the wild looking creatures twisting and struggling in his hands.

Aside from the fact which Ki-Gor had instantly noted, that these men were unarmed, he had felt a strong instinct that they were not dangerous. A lifetime of continual physical competition to survive had taught Ki-Gor to size up the temper of an adversary in the first moment of contact. And Ki-Gor judged that these curious men were in no sense real fighters in spite of the way they had attacked him.

The two prisoners soon stopped struggling and one of them twisted his head around to look up into Ki-Gor's face. Suddenly, he spoke, in a curious guttural voice. He said just two words, but they were in a click language, and they sounded remarkably like the first two words Ki-Gor had shouted to Ngeeso.

"Don't kill!"

Ki-Gor regarded the wild man with surprise, and finally answered in Pygmy.

"No, Brother, I will not kill. And you will not kill?"

The wild man followed the words anxiously, but did not seem to understand them too well. Ki-Gor repeated them very slowly, then, and a dawning light came over the savage face.

"Yes! Yes!" he clicked. "I not kill—you not kill!"

Ki-Gor gently released both of his prisoners, and a chorus of excited jabbering broke out from all seven of the wild men. One or two of them came forward and touched Ki-Gor gingerly on the hand and shoulder. He turned quickly as he heard his name being shouted behind him.

It was David Gray toiling down the sandbank by the vine-rope. The little man hit the bottom with a rush, and ran toward Ki-Gor fairly quivering with excitement.

"Ki-Gor! Ki-Gor! Are you talking to them? Can you understand them? Man, this is the most fantastic discovery in the history of Africa—or the whole world for that matter. What do these men call themselves?"

"I don't know," Ki-Gor responded slowly, a little puzzled by the little man's excitement. "Their language is something like the Pygmies, but they are not Pygmies—"

"And they're not Bushmen, either," Gray broke in. "Look at them, Ki-Gor! They're Pre-historic Men! They're like no Africans that anybody has ever seen!"

Ki-Gor regarded the strangers with a prickle of interest, even though he still could not quite understand why Gray was so excited. He spoke to them again in slow precise Pygmy words.

"Who are you, Brothers?" he asked. "By what name is your tribe called?"

"Tribe?" they answered blankly. "What is a tribe? We are the Men."

"The Men!" Gray fairly screamed the syllable. "Did they say 'the Men,' Ki-Gor? It sounded like the Bushman word for 'Men!'"

"Yes," Ki-Gor said, "but wait a minute, I'll ask them more."

"The Men!" Gray exulted. "That is what all primitive races call themselves!"

"Listen carefully, Brothers," Ki-Gor addressed the savages. "What other name are you called by? What do your enemies call you?"

"Enemies?" The savages were stumped. "We have no enemies. They were killed long ago."

GRAY WAS understanding more than half of the conversation and the effect of it was to tie him in knots. Ki-Gor hushed him and questioned the savages further.

"Very well, Brothers, you are the 'Men.' Now, do each of you have names?"

"Oh, yes," answered one of the savages, the tallest. "I am Dlook Danala—he is Chaak Danala—next to him is Tseep Danala—"

"Ah!" Ki-Gor interrupted. "But you are all Danala?"

"Oh yes," the savage answered, as if that should be self-evident.

Ki-Gor turned to Gray.

"They are the Danala," he said, and Gray's reaction was a reverent sigh.

"The Danala!" he whispered. "Amazing! Ki-Gor, for heaven's sake I must see more of these people! See if you can't get them to take us along to their caves."

Ki-Gor grinned and then told the savages that he and his party were hungry. He used, of course, the Pygmy word which is merely the sound of smacking lips that little children the world over use before they learn to speak any language. The savages promptly came back with an invitation to follow them.

During the course of this conversation, Helene and Sheila Brett had come down the vine rope and were standing in fascinated silence at the foot of the sandbank. It was Morton Brett, freed of his lassoes, and feeling very irritable who broke in now on Ki-Gor.

"Well, Ki-Gor, we've given Dave his look at these Bushmen. Let's get out of here, now, shall we?"

Instantly Gray was up in arms. He insisted that they all go with the wild men and look at their caves and observe something of their living habits. Again, Brett acted like a spoiled child and only agreed to go along when Ki-Gor intervened firmly in the argument in favor of Gray. Eventually, the travelers followed the Danala off through the undergrowth toward the center of the valley.

As a matter of fact, Ki-Gor himself was quite curious about these strange men. He had never seen anything like them before. They were fairly tall, almost six feet, and well-formed, with large heads and rather handsome faces. Their large luminous eyes counteracted to some extent the slightly bestial effect of their protuberant bushy eyebrows, and long undershot jaws. They were quite heavily bearded, and their erect bodies were entirely covered with coarse golden brown hairs. They wore not a stitch of clothing of any kind.

To Ki-Gor, accustomed to the hairless bodies of the Bantu, the Danala were probably a stranger sight than they were to David Gray, who had imagined similar physical types in the course of his studies in anthropology.

"Except that they're lighter colored," Gray murmured to Helene as they walked behind the savages, "they're extraordinarily close to the pictures and sculptures that scientists have reconstructed from remains of Pre-historic Man. Not the ape-like Neanderthal Man, but the higher type of Aurignacian Period in southern France and Northern Spain. Cro-Magnon Man who left those remarkable drawings in the caves at Altamira. Helene, I can hardly believe it! How do you suppose this group ever survived?"

"I'm sure I don't know," Helene answered. "Although I suppose the fact that it's almost impossible to get in and out of this valley had something to do with it. They couldn't get out, and their enemies couldn't get in."

"Yes, of course, that must be it," Gray replied, lost in speculation. Suddenly, he pounded a fist into the palm of the other hand.

"By Jove!" he exclaimed. "Danala! Curious how that sound 'Dan,' the Dan-root, keeps cropping up in legendary history. One of the twelve tribes of Israel was called 'Dan.' Homer and Virgil called the Argive Greeks who besieged Troy, 'Danai.'"

"Why, so they did!" Helene said. "I remember my high school Latin. The old priest who stood beside the Trojan Horse and said, 'Timeo Danaos dona ferentes'—I fear the Greeks bearing gifts."

"Certainly," Gray exclaimed, "and far up in Ancient Ireland, their legendary history tells of many invaders. Actually, the last group but one was called 'Tuatha Dé Danann,' the Dan-root again. To this day, one of the tribes up in Abyssinia is called the 'Danakils.' Oh, Helene, this is so tremendous that I can hardly believe it! The Danala! I can't wait to see their caves. If there are drawings in those caves, then I'll be practically certain that we've stumbled on a remnant of Old Stone Age Men."

THE CAVES, when the party reached them an hour later, fulfilled David Gray's wildest hopes. They were beautifully decorated with handsome line drawings in black, white, red, and yellow. They were mostly of animals, only a few caves containing representations of humans. But all the drawings were in perfect proportion and accurate in every detail. Furthermore, they were not the stiff, flat pictures that are associated with the ancient Egyptians—they had plenty of motion and vigor.

The artistic bent of the Danala was not confined to pictorial representations on the cave walls. The women—whose hairy bodies were far less attractive than the men—wore elaborate necklaces and anklets of a dull yellow metal, and there were also in evidence well-made little statuettes of the same metal as well as well-turned round containers for water.

David Gray was everywhere, looking, examining, questioning the strange people with Ki-Gor's help.

The Danala showed themselves to be a thoroughly friendly people with a loose tribal organization of a hundred or so monogamous families. Their dwelling habits were individualistic, but their hunting and eating customs were completely communistic. The women, rather than the men, seemed to have the dominating influence. But men and women together were extremely peaceful and even courteous.

Apparently, there were no predatory animals in the Vale of Glacanda. It was possible that they had been destroyed centuries before and no others had come to take their place. But there was plenty of small game, and medium-sized antelope which the Danala hunted with lassoes and the small wolfish dogs which were their only domesticated animals.

They also used metal-tipped spears in their hunting, and cut up their prey with dull knives made of soft yellow metal. This circumstance puzzled Gray at first, knowing as he did that the men of the Old Stone Age had never learned to smelt metal. He guessed at the answer later, but the answer was accompanied by a discovery which was to have fearful consequences.

As regards physical appearance, the Danala ran remarkably true to form and resembled one another closely. There were a few exceptions to this rule—some individuals who were much less shaggy than the rest and who had darker skins, smaller heads, and thicker lips. Notably, the man who seemed to be the sort of chief of the Danala, named Kleeklee, and his wife, Ulip, were quite Negroid in appearance.

Evidently, Gray mused, in the course of the ages, other people had fallen down the landslide and survived to transmit their Bantu characteristics to future generations. It must have been these late comers too, he reflected, who introduced the art of smelting metal into Glaclanda.

IF DAVID Gray and his companions were curious about the Danala, it was nothing to the tremendous round-eyed curiosity which those innocent savages felt toward their visitors. The news of their arrival evidently spread through the valley like wildfire. They came from every direction to gape at the white clothes of the three Americans, at Ki-Gor's great size, at Helene's smooth-skinned beauty, and at Ngeeso's diminutiveness. However, their courtesy through everything was unfailing, and the Chief, Kleeklee, had three freshly killed antelope brought to the broad open space in front of the cave mouths. This place was evidently the community eating place of the Danala, for there was a good-sized fire burning in it, being constantly replenished. Kleeklee cut ragged steaks from the antelopes with his dull knife, and toasted them over the flames on green sticks. After an all too brief period of cooking, he handed the steaks with immense gravity to the visitors. They were charred black on the outside, and undercooked and tough on the inside. However, everyone politely and manfully chewed on the meat without comment—everyone, that is, except Morton Brett, who was inclined to complain rather than eat. As for Ki-Gor, he would just as soon have eaten the steaks raw, the cooking of food being a custom he had only recently acquired from Helene.

His strong jaws enabled Ki-Gor now to finish his meal before the rest, and he rose to his feet to thank Kleeklee and to congratulate the Danala hunters who had brought in the antelopes. Privately, he marveled that the Danala were able to kill anything with such poor weapons. He examined the metal tip of one of the hunter's spears. It was a clumsy affair very inexpertly fastened to the wooden shaft. The point was quite dull and bent over to one side, indicating that the metal was really too soft to be used for such a purpose. The Danala hunter, however, was proud of the weapon and handed it to Ki-Gor with a triumphant air. Ki-Gor hefted it, and found it very badly balanced, the metal tip being extraordinarily heavy for its size.

It was at this moment that Morton Brett decided that this yellow metal that the Danala used for their knives, spear tips, statuettes, and ornaments, was—gold.

Ki-Gor heard the big man whispering excitedly to David Gray, and he turned to watch them. A moment later, they got to their feet and came over to him. Brett's eyes were glittering, while Gray wore a thoughtful, almost troubled expression.

"Look, Dave," Brett said impatiently, and seized the tip of the spear that Ki-Gor was holding. "Look here. I don't know anything about gold but this stuff can't be anything else. See how heavy it is, and how soft. See? I can easily make a deep scratch in it with this nail file."

A wave of anger swept over Ki-Gor at the big man's rudeness, and it was with difficulty that he restrained himself from thrusting him through with the spear.

"You may be right," Gray said uneasily, "but even if you are, Mort, I don't know just what—"

"Why, good heavens, man!" Brett shouted. "Don't you realize there's a fortune lying around here! Just this spearhead alone is probably worth four or five hundred dollars—just this one spear-head! And the women's ornaments and those little statuettes—there's any amount of pure soft gold already smelted up. Now, it must have come from somewhere in this valley. What we've got to do is to find out where these Danala are getting it."

"I wish you wouldn't," Gray said, shaking his head, "I wish—"

"You wish I wouldn't what?" Brett demanded.

"Well, I mean—" Gray threw out his hands helplessly— "we've made a discovery here that's so much more valuable than mere gold—"

"Have you gone soft in the head!" the big man shouted. "Here we find a bunch of ape-men sitting on top of a goldmine, and all you're interested in is their language and marriage customs. Well, if you're not interested in grabbing off a stupendous fortune, I am."

The big man turned to Ki-Gor with a snort.

"Ki-Gor," he said, "see if you can find out where these monkeys get their gold, will you?"

The jungle man stared at him coldly and then spoke to Gray.

"Do you want to know?" he asked deliberately.

"Er—well, yes," Gray said, flushing. "It—it would be interesting to know."

THE GOLD was in the lower end of the valley, along the sandy banks of the river and out in the sandbars.

"Placer gold!" Morton Brett said in an awed whisper. "Millions and millions of dollars' worth! It's perfectly fantastic! Dave! Sheila!" He whirled around and faced the silent quartette of whites, and his voice rose to a yell. "Think of it! We're rich! All five of us! Rich as Croesus! For heaven's sake, what are we standing here for? Let's get going—fast! Let's go back to civilization as quick as we can. We'll file a claim to this place and come back and mine it. And, while we're about it, we'd better take along some of those statuettes in our pack."

David Gray's face was a study. Helene's eyes were cold. Ki-Gor looked embarrassed. Of the four, Sheila Brett was the only one who seemed at all interested.

"Well, what's the matter with you!" Brett shouted in exasperation. "What are you all standing there for? Don't you realize what I'm telling you? There's so much gold here that even split up five ways it'll make us rich beyond our wildest dreams. Ki-Gor, think of it! You can have anything you want! Anything!"

"I don't understand what you mean," Ki-Gor growled. "I have everything I want."

"Oh, good Lord!" Brett groaned. "Tell him, Helene! Tell him what it means to be rich. You were brought up in wealthy surroundings."

"Exactly," said Helene sharply. "And since I've lived in Africa with Ki-Gor, I've found out that riches don't matter in the least. I've found out I'm much better off without riches. As Ki-Gor says, we already have everything we want."

"Well spoken," said David Gray coming to life. "There's your answer,

Mort! We are not going to take a thing out of this valley, and when we get back to civilization we're not going to say a word about the gold. We have made a discovery—probably the greatest discovery in the history of anthropology. We have found a group of humans who are without any doubt directly descended from the men of the Old Stone Age in Europe, and who furthermore are living in the same state of culture as their ancestors did fifteen or twenty thousand years ago."

"Don't talk rot, Dave—"

"And you, Mort," Gray went on, "would disregard that tremendous contribution to science just to satisfy your own personal greed. Well, we're not going to let you. Now, I think we'd better get on back to the caves before it gets dark. Ki-Gor, did you say that Kleeklee had offered us a cave to sleep in tonight?"

The jungle man nodded without taking his eyes off Morton Brett. More than ever, now, he disliked the big man, and he determined to keep a strict guard on him.

Morton Brett was not a man to give up easily. All the way back to the caves, he argued long and persistently for the idea of seizing the Danala gold. But Gray and Helene were adamant, and Ki-Gor kept out of the argument. He kept out of it, that is, until the party got all the way back to the community gathering place of the Danala in front of the caves. By this time, Brett was almost raving, and Ki-Gor decided to put a stop to his bellowing.

"Look here," the jungle man said quietly, and took Brett's arm. "You stop talking for a while, or I'll hit you."

Brett's face grew apoplectic. But one look into Ki-Gor's eyes convinced him that the white giant of the jungle meant business. Brett subsided into stony silence.

The ever friendly Danala provided more food for the visitors, and their hospitality seemed to have a beneficial effect on Morton Brett. Rather than complaining about the toughness of the meat, he seemed to grow more affable. He remembered that there was a small supply of coffee crystals in his pack, and volunteered to go and get some. Returning with the tin, he even offered to prepare the coffee.

Ki-Gor felt that the big man was not quite sincere in his new and sudden affability, but he drank the coffee, making a mental note to stay on his guard all night. Not long after the meal, however, he began to feel unaccountably drowsy. He muttered an excuse and withdrew from the campfire. Several hundred feet away, he found a good-sized tree and curled up in its lower branches to take a short nap.

WHEN HE opened his eyes again, it was broad daylight and Ngeeso was whispering agitatedly and tugging at his shoulder.

"Wake up! Wake up, Big Brother! Thou hast slept like the dead! Wake up and hear my news! There is bad trouble brewing!"

Ki-Gor tried to shake the sleep out of his eyes. He felt strangely groggy. Once before he had drunk drugged coffee. He wondered if that was what had happened to him now. Ngeeso chattered on.

"I have looked in ten times ten trees to find thee, Big Brother. Thy woman and the little man and the little woman are prisoners. Whilst thou slept like a river-pig, the bull buffalo crept away in the middle of the night and took with him a number of those yellow metal idols. The Danala are in an ugly mood—they like not thieves and thieving."

Before the Pygmy had half finished his tale, Ki-Gor was climbing stiffly down the tree.

"What is thy plan, Big Brother?" Ngeeso inquired, following him down.

"I have none as yet, Little One. I must see my woman first and find out how it is with her. Then I will talk to the Danala. They are a kindly, generous people."

"Their kindness has turned to anger," Ngeeso said. "In thy place, I would be careful."

"Where my woman is concerned, there is no other consideration," Ki-Gor said grimly. "Thou, Little One, keep to the trees and stay out of sight until I need thee."

The Danala, the entire tribe, were squatting in a silent circle around Helene, David Gray, and Sheila Brett. Gray was trying to talk to Kleeklee, the Danala chieftain, as Ki-Gor came across the open ground. One of the tribesmen looked around and gave a shout as he saw Ki-Gor, and immediately a score of the cavemen ran toward him.

Ki-Gor walked through them as if he had not seen them and the expression on his face warned them not to touch him.

"Thank heaven you're here!" Gray said eagerly as Ki-Gor strode through the silent crowd of Danala. "We're in a nasty spot—thanks to Morton Brett."

"There was something in that coffee," Ki-Gor said without the slightest expression.

"Yes, he must have dropped in some of those sleeping pills of his. We were all drugged."

"Where is he?" Ki-Gor asked quietly.

"I haven't the faintest idea," Gray confessed. "When Sheila woke up, he was gone. His pack was gone and so was mine. He took five little gold statuettes that were on the ledge by the cave mouth. He left behind an empty bottle of whiskey."

Ki-Gor digested this information for a moment and then turned to the chief of the Danala.

"Our companion has disgraced us, Kleeklee," he said solemnly.

"He has stolen," Kleeklee said.

"Let us go out together and find him and bring him back," Ki-Gor said.

"Go where, Ki-Gor?" Kleeklee said bitterly. "He is not in the valley."

"How do you know?"

"We have been to the foot of the sandbank where you all came down by the rope."

"Yes?" said Ki-Gor.

"And the rope has been pulled up."

Ki-Gor's face was a mask. That rope was the only possible means of getting out of the Vale of Glaclanda. Kleeklee spoke again.

"We Danala do not steal. We can hardly remember the time when anything has been stolen."

"Yes?" said Ki-Gor with a shrewd glance.

"If you and your companion had not come to Glaclanda, our little statues that we made with our own hands would not have been stolen."

Kleeklee paused and looked straight into Ki-Gor's eyes.

"We look on all of you as responsible for this stealing—"

Not a muscle in Ki-Gor's face moved.

"And," Kleeklee finished with great dignity, "we Danala punish stealing—by death."

CHAPTER IV

IT WAS ALL MORTON Brett could do to haul himself up over the overhang at the top of the sandbank. His arms ached from dragging his great bulk up across the sliding, sifting sand, and he was sadly out of breath. He was also very, very drunk.

After he attained the top, he sat panting for several minutes and leaned back to ease the weight of the two packs off his shoulders. Lord! but they were heavy! Who would have thought that those little gold figures would weigh so much?

His mouth worked triumphantly. The heavier the better! Why those five blocks of gold alone were worth probably three thousand dollars apiece. Fifteen thousand dollars on his back! And heaven knows how many millions of dollars more where that came from! Whew! He wiped the sweat dramatically off his forehead.

And that fool of a David Gray and the rest of them! Try to stop him from making a fortune, would they? He chuckled evilly. They didn't know Morton Brett!

An idea suddenly occurred to him. He reached down between his legs and felt for the vine rope. His fingers curled around it and he stood up. Swaying precariously in the pitch darkness, he pulled and hauled until he felt the end of the rope in his hands. He dropped it then with an exclamation of triumph.

Now!

Which way to go?

Ki-Gor had been heading south-eastwards, until they had digressed to look at Glaclanda. But the river that flowed through Glaclanda—Lost River—flowed northwest. There were certainly less mountains in that direction. Why not follow the river? It's bound to come out somewhere, Brett thought. It was probably the best way, anyway, Ki-Gor or not. He was nothing but a savage, Brett told himself, a big brute of a savage, for all his blond hair and blue eyes. What a surprise he and the rest of them were going to get when they woke up out of their drugged sleep to find Morton Brett gone!

For a moment, he had a drunken notion to stay where he was until morning—until they came running to the foot of the sandbank and begged and pleaded with him to let down the rope for them. Oh! that would be rich, he gloated. He would lean over the bank and jeer at them.

But after a while, he decided against it. Time was awasting, and he should be on his way. Slowly he began to pick his way along the rim of the escarpment—north-westwards.

It seemed to Morton Brett that he had gone miles before he heard the cascading roar which told him that he had passed the Vale of Glaclanda. The roar came from the rapids of the Lost River as it boiled through the narrow rock flume at that end of the valley. The sound made Brett feel even more triumphant. Any rapids that sounded like that certainly would be sure death to anyone trying to swim down them. No, he decided, his companions were locked up in that valley for as long as he felt like keeping them there.

The ground sloped down now steeply, and after a short time, Brett found himself on comparatively level ground. By the same token the trees and undergrowth were much thicker. He stumbled in the direction which he thought the river was, and was soon rewarded by the sound of gurgling water.

As he lurched along beside the river, he began to get acutely conscious of the passage of time, of his aching legs, of the blackness of the jungle. He also began to feel very hungry. Morton Brett was beginning to sober up.

He debated with himself whether to stop a while and look for something to eat in one of the packs. But his courage was oozing fast as the liquor wore off. The jungle suddenly grew very menacing. Maybe he wasn't so clever after all, Brett thought, going off by himself like that. He had no idea where he was going. The impenetrable blackness around him might be swarming with fearful dangers. Why, at this very minute a lion might be stalking him!

He stopped suddenly, his skin crawling as far away a leopard roared a fiendish contralto challenge. Cold panic settled over Morton Brett.

There was a heart-stopping crash, then, as a heavy body blundered through the undergrowth somewhere in front of him. He gave a despairing yelp, turned to his right, and scrambled blindly up the slope away from the river.

AFTER WHAT seemed like agonized hours, he emerged from the trees and fell down panting at the crest of a grassy knoll. He looked around and shivered. He hardly knew whether it was better to be out in the open or to be enveloped in the velvety blackness of the jungle.

Suddenly Morton Brett's heart leaped. A thrill of hope went through him. His hunted eyes had caught sight of a flickering light far away and below him.

He sprang to his feet with a yell. Cupping his hands to his mouth, he shouted again and again.

Black figures crossed and re-crossed in front of the light. There could be no doubt—it was a campfire!

In a moment, another smaller light appeared and moved slowly up the hill. There was an answering shout. In English!

Brett's knees felt weak under him. He tried to run down hill toward the approaching light, but his legs buckled. He sank to the ground sobbing and almost fainting from relief.

The moving light bobbed up the hill toward him and stopped about twenty feet away. It was an electric torch, and Brett felt that its owner was scrutinizing him.

"I don't know who you are," Brett croaked, "but thank Heaven you were near. I'm lost."

The answer came in a cold high nasal voice.

"Well, 'oo the bleddy 'ell are yer?"

"Doctor Morton Brett of New York." Brett's voice shook. He didn't quite like the tone of the man behind the electric torch.

"Doctor Morton Brett of New York, eh? Well, wot the bleeding 'ell are you doin' wanderin' 'round this Gawd-forsayken bush?"

"I'm lost, I tell you," Brett replied with asperity. He didn't like that man's tone at all. "Who are you?"

"Wot d'you care 'oo we are? Now, I'll just thank you to stand up, very quiet like. There! That's more like it! Crod! Look at the size of 'im, Ben!"

"You—you sound like an Australian," Brett offered querulously.

"Yus, I have been towld that," came the voice. "Sound like a bleddy kookaburra, I been towld. I see you're wearin' a gun. In that cayse, just put yer 'ands up, Bully Boy—way up. Naow then, Ben, go tayke it off 'im."

"Here! What's this all about?" Brett demanded, but his hands stayed up in the air.

"Two bleddy packs, too!" the mocking voice went on, ignoring Brett. "Let's 'ave a look at 'em, Ben. Ayn't this a pretty mystery! A bleddy New York medico running around the bush in the dark with two bleddy packs! W'y, Ben, it fair shimozzles me!"

Morton Brett stood rooted to the spot. His mouth and throat suddenly became too dry to speak. The first signs of approaching dawn stole over the landscape as the man called Ben dumped the two packs on the ground and opened them one by one. The Australian stood motionless holding the flashlight in an unwavering hand. A third man squatted down beside Ben, and gave a low whistle as one of the Danala statuettes rolled out of a pack.

Brett felt sick with horror and frustration. He wanted to cover his eyes with his thick arms and shut out the terrible reality of the scene.

The cold nasal voice snarled promptly.

"Keep those 'ands up! That's better, Bully Boy. Naow then, suppose you tell us w'ot that little idol is."

Brett could not have spoken to save his life.

"It's mayde of gowld, ain't it, Bully Boy? Awl right, yer down't 'ave to answer. I know it's gowld—I can tell with 'arf an eye. But look 'ere, Bully Boy, 'ere's one question you'll answer, or I'll blow yer bleddy 'ead off yer shoulders. *W'ere did yer get this 'ere little idol mayde of gowld?*"

Morton Brett shivered and gulped. Dully, he thought of the Vale of Glaclanda, serene in its centuries-old seclusion, and how it was to be visited by strangers twice within twenty-four hours.

CHAPTER V

KLEEKLEE BEGAN HIS SPEECH of accusation at sunrise in front of the assembled Danala. A half hour later he was just beginning to swing into form. Ki-Gor stood opposite him ten feet away, his head bent to one side in an attitude of patient listening. Fifteen yards behind him, Helene, Sheila Brett, and Gray sat very still on the ground. Ki-Gor's position enabled him to see the slow, idle motions Helene was making with her hands. Her movements meant nothing to the innocent Danala whose only weapons were spears, knives, and lassoes. They had been unable to understand the use of Ki-Gor's great bow which lay on the ground beside Helene. And the bundle of long hardwood arrows they had regarded as small ineffectual spears.

As Kleeklee went on and on, outlining to his tribesmen the guilt of the four white visitors, Ki-Gor noted with satisfaction that Helene was following his instructions. She was planting his arrows one by one point downward in the ground so that they formed four short rows. Her manner was that of a person with no especial purpose, and the Danala, not knowing the use of the bow and the arrows, had no idea that she was planting the arrows so that if the worst came to the worst they would be ready for Ki-Gor to do the fastest shooting of his life.

Long after Helene's task was completed, Kleeklee was still talking. His oratory, Ki-Gor recognized, was restrained but eloquent. Unlike the hysterical Bantu, who under similar circumstances would be shouting and leaping high into the air, the Danala remained quiet. What they were witnessing was a legal form which only the oldest among them had ever seen before.

Finally, Kleeklee finished, and in accordance with the fair-minded custom of the Danala, invited Ki-Gor to speak up in his defense.

"I have this to say, O My Brothers," Ki-Gor began. "First, that my companions and I are fully as angry as you are because your community works of art have been stolen. We hate thieves just as much as you do. We four, whom you are accusing, did not steal those little statues. The man who climbed up the sandbank stole them and took them away. It would be the part of justice not to accuse us of the crime which we did not commit, but rather to release us so that we may pursue the thief and bring him back to your justice."

He paused and looked over his audience. He could tell that his words were making not the slightest impression on the Danala. "Pursue the thief where?" he knew they were thinking—these people who had never gone outside their little valley for uncounted centuries. They knew nothing of an outside world. One of five strangers had stolen. He was gone. Therefore, the remaining strangers should be punished. And the punishment was death.

Ki-Gor sighed. It was a tight situation. Not counting the women and small children, there were more than a hundred men and boys squatting in front of him, all armed with gold-tipped spears. If he were alone, it might be barely possible for him to cut his way through and win to safety. But with Helene, and the ineffectual little couple, Sheila Brett and Gray, such a maneuver was foredoomed to failure.

It was time, Ki-Gor realized, for the demonstration of the bow and arrows.

"I have this other thing to say, O My Brothers," he declared, and turned and strolled negligently toward Helene. "You cannot punish us for a crime which we did not commit. You cannot punish us because I will not let you."

With these words he reached Helene's side and took the bow which she held up to him. With an easy motion he plucked an arrow from the ground and notched it in the bowstring. Then he turned swiftly on the Danala.

"With this Magic Stick," he roared, "I can kill swiftly and silently from a distance! Nobody make a move, or you are dead! It would be unwise to doubt me! Look, I will show you! That dog—coming out of the cave—you all see him—" the dog was about fifty feet from Ki-Gor, "—he is alive now—but—"

The bowstring twanged.

"Now, he is dead!" Ki-Gor grated.

The Danala gasped. The arrow sped almost faster than their eyes could follow it. The dog gave a choked gurgle and leaped into the air. It hit the earth in a heap, twitched a few times, then lay still. A small trickle of blood oozed out from around the arrow which transfixed its chest.

KI-GOR'S EYES flashed truculently at the gaping Danala.

"Let him prepare to die," he snarled, "who tries to lay a finger on any of us!"

With his left hand he motioned behind his back to his companions to stand up. Would his bluff work?

He never had a chance to find out.

The Danala were getting to their feet, appalled and outraged, and perhaps frightened. Kleeklee turned to face them. Suddenly a startled cry broke from his lips. He pointed over the heads of the crowd to the edge of the woods behind them.

"The thief!" cried Kleeklee. "He has come back! And three other strangers are with him!"

The Danala whirled in their tracks with an indignant yell and promptly charged toward the four newcomers—the frightened, sagging Morton Brett, and his three unsavory looking captors.

For a moment, Ki-Gor stood undecided. Then he saw the three men with Brett throw themselves to the ground and quickly open fire with rifles on the unsuspecting savages. He and the two women and Gray were directly in the line of fire. The nearest shelter was the caves and Ki-Gor hurriedly herded his companions to the nearest one as rifle bullets whined uncomfortably close.

Even before they reached the cave mouth, however, the Danala were in full flight, scattering in all directions. The noise and the deadly effect of the rifle fire was too much for them, coming on top of Ki-Gor's demonstration of the bow and arrow.

Ki-Gor stood by the cave entrance and stepping over the bodies of more than a half dozen fallen Danala. Morton Brett was in the lead, mouth slack and eyes bulging with fright. Behind him came a thin-lipped, lantern-jawed man, smaller than average and dressed in dirty, ragged khaki. Of the two others, one was swarthy and wore a black eye-patch on one side of a beaked nose. The other was a coffee-colored man, broad-shouldered and wearing only dirty shorts.

Ki-Gor's eyebrows gathered. He smelled danger—worse danger even than the Danala threatened. The thin-lipped man behind Brett leveled the rifle toward Ki-Gor's stomach and looked coldly at him.

"This the party you was speakin' of?" he demanded of Brett. "The w'ite savvidge?"

"Ye-es," Morton Brett quavered. "Ki-Gor."

"Ki-Gor, eh?" said the Australian. "Well, naow, Ki-Gor, suppose you just chuck that there bow 'n' arrer on the graond. Come on, make it snappy, or 's'trewth, I'll plug yer!"

Ki-Gor dropped the bow gently and bent a venomous look at the sweating Brett.

"I couldn't help it, Ki-Gor!" Brett whined. "They captured me and found the gold, and made me bring them back here!"

"Naow then," said the Australian briskly, "w'ere's the rest of yer? Eh? W'ere are they?"

As he spoke, David Gray appeared at the mouth of the cave.

"Mort!" he cried. "What—"

He stopped in alarm and stared at the villainous looking trio around Brett.

"Come aout 'ere, Sonny," said the leader. "Let's 'ave a look at yer. W'eres yer gun?"

Gray pointed at Morton Brett.

"He took the only gun we had. I see you have it yourself, now."

The Australian chuckled. "Bit of luck, eh mates? Only one gun and we've got it."

"What do you want?" said Gray sternly.

"Oo, us?" The Australian chuckled. "W'y we're interested in wild flaowers, ayn't we, mates? Thought we'd 'ave a bit of a look-around daown 'ere, and pick up some new spessimins."

THE OTHER two roared with laughter at their leader's wit, but suddenly stopped as Helene and Sheila Brett appeared beside Gray. A low whistle of admiration broke out from the Australian.

"'Ere's a bit of luck," he observed, "a pair of proper good lookin' females to w'ile away the time with after we get sick of pickin' up solid gowld."

Helene's eyes flashed.

"Well, Doctor Brett!" she snapped. "I should think you'd done about enough damage for one day, without getting mixed up with a gang of jail-birds! Who are they?"

"Strike me dead!" exclaimed the Australian. "These 'ere gals are 'igh clahss, yer know wot I mean?" He leered at Helene for a moment then spoke again. "You ayn't far wrong on the jayl-bird angle, Miss. I'm Wallaroo Jones, *at* your service. This 'ere is One-Eye Mendoza, and that there is Black Ben. We *did* 'ave a bit of trouble back on the West Coast, but I dare say they won't 'ave 'eard abaout it on the *East* Coast w'en we arrive there with our packs full of little gowld idols."

David Gray took a step forward determinedly.

"Ki-Gor," he said, "we can't permit this—this robbery of the Danala. If these men get outside with gold statues and ornaments, it will start a stampede here, and that will mean the end of Glaclanda. We can't permit it, I tell you!"

A bitter smile came over Ki-Gor's face. How unpredictable, unbelievable white men, the men of his own race, were! The ones with generous, decent instincts were invariably weak, irresolute, and foolish like David Gray. While the strong ones had no decent instincts at all, and were twice as pitiless and cruel as the fiercest Masai or Zulu.

The slit-eyed man with the nasal voice who called himself Wallaroo Jones proceeded now to demonstrate his ruthlessness. He interrupted Gray's futile protests with a series of brisk commands which his henchmen carried out briskly. As a result of these commands, Ki-Gor, Helene, Morton Brett and Gray sat in a row out in the open, ten yards or so from the cliffs. Wallaroo Jones sat in the mouth of a cave, his gun across his knees. The muzzle of the gun was less than twelve inches away from the shrinking body of Sheila Brett.

"The first one of you out there maykes a move," the Australian drawled, "and this 'ere lovely little thing beside me gets it."

Having thus effectively hamstrung his captives, Wallaroo Jones ordered his two companions to go through the caves and systematically strip them of all gold ornaments.

David Gray raged and threatened until Wallaroo shut him up with a contemptuous wave of his rifle. But Ki-Gor was silent throughout. He realized perfectly clearly how hopeless any resistance was under the circumstances, and he was not in the habit of wasting his energy in futile vituperation. So he merely sat quietly and pondered the situation, trying to think out a solution.

He knew that as long as the Australian kept his gun trained on Sheila Brett's frail helpless person, there was nothing to be done.

Helene would never forgive him, if by any action of his, the white woman was killed. Therefore, he must simply wait until something happened to alter that situation.

It was fully an hour before the possibility of any action opened up. During that hour, the Australian's two henchmen moved leisurely in and out of the caves with armfuls of gold ornaments and piled them up in a great heap to one side of the four captives. As the pile grew larger and larger, Ki-Gor began to get an inkling of Wallaroo Jones's plan. There was far too much weight of gold for the three desperadoes to carry away by themselves. Undoubtedly, Wallaroo intended to impress his five captives into beasts of burden to bear away the load of treasure.

Ki-Gor stole a glance at Helene beside him. She was looking at him in mute appeal. He turned away quickly. Helene expected him to do something. But just what he could under the circumstances, Ki-Gor did not know.

He bent a glance toward the woods three hundred yards away where the Danala had fled. He thought he detected some barely perceptible movement over there. Could the Danala be planning to attack?

KI-GOR LOOKED up at the sky, and then down again, and inspected the palm of his right hand with elaborate casualness. If the Danala were going to attack, he must not call the Australian's attention to them prematurely. The poor cave-men could not possibly succeed in coming to grips with the desperadoes—they had to come too far across the open. The three rifles would mow them down again as they did before.

But a sudden charge by the Danala might divert Wallaroo Jones's attention for just long enough for Ki-Gor to take some action that would not endanger Sheila Brett's life.

The jungle man leaned back casually from his hips, placing his hands behind him to support himself. His hands were thus hidden from Wallaroo Jones's vision. And to Ki-Gor's great joy, the fingers of his right hand closed over a good sized stone half buried in the hard-packed earth of the Danala meeting grounds.

The fingers began to scratch the dirt around the stone. At the same time, Ki-Gor turned his head slightly to one side and down, and drooped his eyelids sleepily. From this position, he could see a small stretch of the woods. And he could see that that there was definitely some activity among the Danala.

He was not surprised when, only a short time later, they attacked.

They broke from the line of woods with a sharp yell, and came running out into the open in a shallow crescent. Wallaroo Jones was not caught napping. He shouted to his henchmen to join him. But while his eyes flicked away toward the Danala momentarily, he did not allow his attention to be drawn off the captives in front of him.

A thrill of dismay went through Ki-Gor. The Danala were attacking but they were not diverting the Australian's mind. Worse yet, the gimlet-eyed little man coolly got to his feet without once taking the muzzle of his gun off Sheila Brett.

That fool of a woman! Ki-Gor fumed. Why didn't she grab the gun barrel and point it in the air? Helene would have under like circumstance. It would be risky, but the situation called for desperate measures. There was the Australian pointing the gun at her but watching not her but the four people in front of him.

Then Ki-Gor stiffened. Evidently that same thought had occurred to Wallaroo Jones. He looked down at Sheila.

Ki-Gor's right hand came around in a swift arc. The stone left it and hurtled toward Jones's head. It was a snap shot and not accurate. The stone struck the desperado a glancing blow over one ear, doing no damage. It did, however, make Jones jerk the gun up as he pulled the trigger, and the bullet went over Sheila Brett's head.

As Ki-Gor flung the stone, he threw his weight forward and upward, following his balancing right hand. With one continuous motion he shot to his feet and sprang forward. It was a matter of four long steps to Wallaroo Jones—to knock the rifle down or twist it out of his hands.

Ki-Gor moved with unbelievable swiftness. But Wallaroo Jones was quick, too. He swung around with a strangled curse, as Ki-Gor leaped toward him. Ki-Gor left his feet in a flying tackle. But just then something seemed to explode in his head and he did not remember anything more for a long time.

CHAPTER VI

ONCE MORE KI-GOR RETURNED to consciousness with Ngeeso whispering in his ear.

"Open thine eyes, O Big Brother!" the Pygmy was whispering agitatedly. "For pity's sake, open thine eyes! Behold it is thy friend and servant, little Ngeeso, who begs thee! I see thy chest rise and fall, therefore, I know thou art not dead! But open thine eyes that I may know that thou art not seriously hurt!"

Ki-Gor groaned and stirred uneasily. His head felt the size of a boulder. He tried to lift it and multiple sickening pains went shooting through it. With difficulty he opened his eyes and saw Ngeeso's lugubrious little face close to his. The little woolly beard on the end of the Pygmy's pointed chin wabbled with grief.

Ki-Gor essayed a twisted smile.

"Grieve not, Little One," he croaked in a voice he hardly recognized as his own. "A herd of wild Zebra hath galloped across my head. Otherwise, I am not hurt."

Slowly, he raised himself up on one elbow. His head felt as if it would roll off his shoulders. He put a hand to his forehead, and the hand came away sticky.

"Ai! but thou are a fearsome sight," Ngeeso whispered excitedly, "with thy face covered with blood! Yet I could dance and sing at the sight of thee, for thou art alive! Ki-Gor lives and will smite his enemies!"

"Patience, Little One," Ki-Gor grunted, easing himself to a sitting position. "Tell me how things stand. First, how long have I slept?"

"Not long," the Pygmy answered promptly. "The shadow of the trees hath moved this far."

By the distance Ngeeso indicated, Ki-Gor judged that he had been unconscious nearly half an hour.

"I was too far distant," the Pygmy went on, "to see accurately what happened to thee. I saw thee spring, and I heard two shots fired. Thou layest still then, and the three bad white men fired at the Danala, till the Danala fled away again. Quickly, then, the three bad white men forced thy woman and the other three whites to carry the Danala gold. I followed them a distance and saw that they went toward the sandbank, and then I hastened back to thy side."

Ki-Gor struggled to his feet and stood a moment swaying. Gently he touched the side of his head tracing the angry welt ploughed by the bullet. Then he flexed his shoulder muscles determinedly and spat.

"Wah!" he exclaimed. "We must hurry, Little One, if we are to catch those hyenas before they climb the sandbank!"

He paused only long enough to pick up his bow and collect his arrows. Then he set off at a swift lope, running with bent knees to avoid jarring his head as much as possible. Beside him, legs twinkling, Ngeeso ran—like a little gray mouse.

"They went by the long way," the Pygmy shouted, "through the fields, to avoid the lassoes of the Danala."

"Then we may yet cut them off," Ki-Gor replied.

"Aye, if the Danala do not again try to take us prisoner," said Ngeeso. "They may hold thee responsible for these."

The Pygmy waved at the Danala corpses still lying in the open where they were felled by the bullets of Wallaroo Jones and his crew. Ki-Gor knew there was something in what Ngeeso said. Nevertheless, he headed straight for the woods and the directest route to the sandbank.

But he kept Ngeeso's warning in the back of his mind and as he came toward a suspicious looking thicket halfway through the woods trail, he slowed down and stopped.

"Come, you foolish Danala!" he addressed the thicket chidingly. "Save your lassoes for those who are your enemies! Have you not learned by now that Ki-Gor is your friend? If Kleeklee is there, let him step out in the open and talk as man to man."

There was a moment's silence. Then a figure came out from the bushes and stood in the path. But it was not Kleeklee. It was his wife, Ulip, and her face was distorted with grief and rage.

"You talk of friendship!" she shrilled. "How can you be a friend? You are one of many strange people who came to our valley yesterday and today. We treated you with respect and hospitality as if you were, in fact, Danala like ourselves. But you turned out to be thieves and killers. Why should we call you friend?"

"BECAUSE I am your friend," Ki-Gor said patiently. "Those who stole from you and killed your brothers are as strange to me as they are to you. They are as much my enemies as they are yours. Remember, Ulip, that I have not killed any Danala."

"That may be so," Ulip said glowering, but there was a note of doubt in her voice.

"Where is Kleeklee?" Ki-Gor asked. "I must speak to him."

"Kleeklee is gone!" the cave-woman said savagely. "They took him! Your friends or enemies or whoever they are!"

"Took him?" Ki-Gor exclaimed. "Then, come! All of you! Come with me, follow me as your leader and we will save Kleeklee!"

"How can you save him?" Ulip asked bitterly. "They forced him to go up the rope up the sandbank. Kleeklee is gone from Glaclanda—gone who knows where? And who can follow him?"

"*We* can follow him!" Ki-Gor cried. "Come on! There is no time to be lost!"

Evidently, Ki-Gor's words were at last having some effect on the Danala. They began to push out from the thicket, clutching their poor ineffectual spears, and gazing at him with mournful eyes.

"Remember, O Danala Brothers!" he cried. "Ki-Gor is your friend! Follow me—up the sandbank and out of Glaclanda—but follow me, and we will save Kleeklee and punish the evil strangers!"

With that Ki-Gor sprang forward on the trail, Ngeeso close to his side, and the Danala fell in behind him silently.

He had forgotten his aching head now, forgotten everything but how to get Helene out of the hands of the desperate white men who had kidnaped her along with the rest of the party. He turned a dozen different plans over in his mind but settled on none of them. After all, the first thing to be done was to pursue Wallaroo Jones until he caught up with him. Then there would be time to plan. One thing would be helpful and that was that the Danala padding along behind him now were skillful woodsmen, and should be able to travel fast and quietly. And they must be brave, too, to set out to face death a third time at the hands of those murderous men with rifles.

From Ulip's words, Ki-Gor gathered that Wallaroo Jones and his men had already scaled the sandbank. He doubted whether the desperadoes would stay long at the top of the bank for purposes of beating off pursuit. But he decided to take no chances, and as he neared the foot of the sandbank, he slowed up and approached it very cautiously, staying well hidden.

There was a rude shock awaiting him.

To be sure, there was no one in sight anywhere along the rim of the escarpment. There was no one to contest the climbing of the sandbank. It was the sight of the vine rope which made Ki-Gor curse.

It had been cut at the top, and lay in a tangled heap at the foot of the slide.

Ngeeso took in the situation with a grunt of dismay. He trotted out, examined the rope, looked up the sandbank and then returned to Ki-Gor.

"*Ayee,* Big Brother!" he exclaimed. "How do you now propose to get out of this prison?"

Ki-Gor right then had not the faintest idea how he was going to climb out of Glacanda. He knew perfectly well that it was impossible to get up the sandbank without a rope which was well secured at the top. He walked over to the rope, lifted one end of it and thought a moment. It would be impossible to try and throw the rope—it was stiff and heavy, and besides, even Ki-Gor could not throw a rope three hundred feet straight up in the air, like a lasso.

Lasso! That gave Ki-Gor an idea.

Quickly, he commandeered a score or so of the light flexible lassoes of the Danala, and he and Ngeeso set to work knotting them together. Presently, he thought he had a light rope long enough to reach to the top of the sandbank.

He coiled it carefully on the ground by his feet, and then tied one end securely around the base of one of his long arrows. Then he notched the arrow and aimed it at the crest of the sandbank. While the Danala looked on in awed silence, he bent the great bow.

BUT EVEN as Ki-Gor released the string, he knew he had failed. The arrow went up, up—one hundred—two hundred feet and more. But it fell short of the rim, weighed down as it was by the rope that spiralled under it. Ngeeso scratched his head and squinted apprehensively up at Ki-Gor.

"Hast thou failed indeed, Big Brother?" he said. "No one else could bend a bow deeper than thee, and yet the arrow fell short."

Ki-Gor stared around him desperately for a moment. Then he slapped a thigh with a vexed exclamation.

"Stupid, stupid Ki-Gor," he told himself, "not to think of that before!"

Quickly, he pulled the rope down off the sandbank, coiling it as he drew it in, until he held the arrow in his hand. Then he looped the coil of rope and the bow around his neck, selected the tallest tree in the vicinity and went surging up into its branches. The tree was nearly a hundred and fifty feet tall, and Ki-Gor climbed nearly up to its swaying, feathery top.

From this precarious perch, he took aim again. His target was the thick tree trunk on top of the sandbank around which he had originally fastened the vine rope when he descended the sandbank. Back, back he pulled the bowstring.

It was now or never.

Ping!

The arrow sped up and out, straight as a homing bee. This time it hit home with a thud and quivered in the tree trunk. The soft lasso-rope feathered out behind and snaked to the ground. Ki-Gor slipped down the tree with a triumphant smile on his weathered face.

Ngeeso regarded him thoughtfully as he hit the ground.

"Will it hold, Big Brother?" he asked doubtfully, his quick mind having grasped Ki-Gor's plan.

"I ask you to try it, Little One," Ki-Gor answered simply.

"Very well," the Pygmy shrugged. He stooped, picked up one end of the heavy vine rope and walked to the foot of the sand slide. There he picked up the end of the length of lasso rope which dangled from above. Gently, the little man started up over the sifting sand.

For the space of four heart-beats Ki-Gor watched. Then he drew his breath, gratefully. The tiny, light body of the Pygmy worked steadily upwards, one hand clinging to the lasso rope, the other hand drawing up the heavy vine rope.

In a remarkably short time, Ngeeso leaned over the rim of the sandbank with a shout of triumph.

"It is made fast!"

Promptly, Ki-Gor made a running dash up the sand slide. Twenty feet up he began to slide back. He clutched at the newly secured vine rope—and it held. Shouting to the Danala to follow him, he hauled himself upward.

Ten minutes later, he was pushing through the underbrush up the mountain side with Ngeeso beside him, and twenty Danala hunters at his back.

Ki-Gor could never understand why Wallaroo Jones chose to cut his way straight up the mountain, instead of taking the easier route along the escarpment toward the great Barrier at the upper end of Glaclanda. Perhaps the desperadoes were afraid their captives would be tempted to throw their precious loads of stolen gold over the brink to the valley below. At any rate, this circumstance greatly facilitated Ki-Gor's pursuit. The fleeing jail-birds and their prisoners could not hope to make the fast time through the bush that Ki-Gor and his allies, all trained woods travelers, could make. Furthermore, the party of whites left a broad unmistakable trail behind them.

As Ki-Gor toiled up the mountain side, he tried to evolve the best possible plan of action. Against desperate men armed with rifles, obviously the plan most likely to succeed was ambuscade if that were possible. The spears of the Danala were effective only at very short range. But how could an ambuscade be set up?

He had first to catch up with the criminals and their prisoners without their knowledge. Then he had to guess their probable route, and send his Danala allies out in a swift silent maneuver to reach a point ahead of this probable line of march and set themselves for the surprise attack. It would be a doubtful undertaking, with many chances against it succeeding.

BUT WHEN he caught up with the fleeing party, Ki-Gor saw at once that he would have to change his plans. From the vantage point of a tree, whence he had climbed when he came within earshot, he could see them plainly, less than four hundred yards away, crossing a bare rocky shoulder of the mountain. And as Ki-Gor watched, Wallaroo Jones called a halt, and the entire party sat down in the middle of the rock slope.

From the standpoint of the desperadoes, the position was well chosen. There was no cover of any kind for yards around them. Nothing could approach them unseen. Ki-Gor pondered the situation with a trace of dismay. What was he going to do now?

Wallaroo Jones might decide to go in any of three directions—to the right along the hillside, to the left along the hillside, or straight up toward the not-so-far distant crest of the mountain. Ki-Gor could see that the little Australian was himself undecided.

Sheila Brett was still being used as a hostage for the good behavior of the other prisoners. She alone was unburdened with a pack full of Danala gold. But she was made to walk in front of Wallaroo Jones, just a few inches ahead of his menacing rifle muzzle. And now, as Ki-Gor watched, the Australian waved her to her feet. With drooping shoulders she trudged in front of him for a dozen paces and then stopped at his command. At a safe distance from the other prisoners, Wallaroo looked around warily, seemingly trying to make up his mind which direction to go.

Ki-Gor moved gently down his tree a few feet, to make sure that he would not be seen by Wallaroo's sharp eyes. He bit his lower lip discontentedly. Which way was Wallaroo Jones going to go?

The jungle man hissed to Ngeeso, and the Pygmy obediently scrambled up the tree to him.

"I think he will go straight up and over the summit of the mountain," the Pygmy said in answer to Ki-Gor's question. "It is steep that way, but it is not far. And on the other side, there is a long gentle slope downward."

"That will be bad for us," Ki-Gor observed, "it will take us so long to catch up with them."

"I think that is what he will do," the Pygmy persisted, "if he knows the country."

"Let us hope he does not know the country, Little One," Ki-Gor murmured. "Go thou down back to the ground and tell the Danala to be ready to leap forward as soon as I give the signal."

The Pygmy faded down the tree silently, and Ki-Gor fixed his attention on the group out on the ledges above him. Suddenly he stiffened.

Wallaroo Jones was ordering Helene and Morton Brett to come toward him. They reluctantly did so and took their places on either side of Sheila Brett. Then came Kleeklee and David Gray side by side, and behind them, the other two desperadoes. The party then started to march—but not to right or left or up the hill.

They were coming straight down the mountain again!

Ki-Gor wasted no time wondering why Wallaroo Jones had decided to retrace his steps and back-trail down the hill. He fairly flung himself down the tree from branch to branch. There was no time to be lost in setting the Danala into an ambuscade. Wallaroo Jones's decision was the sheerest good luck as far as Ki-Gor was concerned, and it might well offset some of the strokes of ill-fortune that had fallen on Ki-Gor during the past two days.

The Danala understood the principle of ambush perfectly and quickly lined the trail by which Ki-Gor was sure Wallaroo Jones would come. Thick undergrowth screened them perfectly, and Ki-Gor swung himself up into the lower branches of a tree, slightly uphill from the Danala. He notched an arrow in his great bow and waited.

The positions were taken not a minute too soon. The Danala lay waiting for Ki-Gor's whistle signal to swoop out from undercover and attack the desperadoes before they could use their rifles. And especially before the leader, Wallaroo, could fire into Sheila Brett's frail back.

IN A moment, the bushes crackled with the weight of trampling feet, and the Australian's high-pitched nasal snarl hung on the air.

"W'y the bleeding 'ell didn't yer tell us about that trail goin' nor'west?" he complained. "We'd a been miles away by naow. Awl of you better get this strayght—I down't want none of yer tricks from naow on, see?"

There was a sob which must have come from Sheila Brett, and then the party came into Ki-Gor's line of vision. He looked downhill swiftly to make sure the Danala were still hidden, then slowly began to draw his bow.

Then Wallaroo Jones did something that Ki-Gor could not possibly have predicted.

He commanded Sheila Brett, and her husband and Helene who were flanking her, to turn to the right—slightly off the route by which they had climbed the mountain.

Ki-Gor's muscles tightened as he realized that this new direction would ruin the ambush. The party would stumble over half the hidden Danala. There was nothing to be done, except give the signal to attack beforehand.

The attack would be successful—but at the cost of Sheila Brett's life.

There would be a few seconds before the Danala could reach the Australian—a few seconds in which he could pull the trigger of his rifle and send a bullet through Morton Brett's wife.

Automatically, Ki-Gor aimed his arrow. There was a chance in ten thousand of saving Sheila Brett.

Down came the party—captives and captors. They would pass nearly under the branch on which Ki-Gor was crouching. A spreading branch and another tall bush screened him from their eyes if they happened to look upward. But that same branch and that same bush might interfere with the flight of the arrow that Ki-Gor was going to attempt to put through Wallaroo Jones's right wrist.

Step by step, the three captives came and close at their heels the little Australian, rifle watchfully leveled. Ki-Gor cursed silently. It was a hideously difficult shot. A twig might so easily deflect the arrow from its target and send it at Sheila—or Helene.

But again, it was now or never.

Ki-Gor in a split-second calculated when the Australian would pass by a tiny opening in the foliage. Then with a prayer on his lips, he released the arrow.

Without pausing, Ki-Gor whistled shrilly and leaped out of the tree. There was a panicky yelp and Ki-Gor's heart stood still. That was the Australian's voice—but there was no shot fired.

Two seconds later, Ki-Gor burst out of the bushes in front of Morton Brett, and bedlam broke loose all along the trail.

The Australian was staggering back, his right wrist transfixed by Ki-Gor's arrow, and dangling loose. But he still held the rifle in his left hand and he was yelling wild curses. Quickly the little cutthroat cradled the wooden gunstock against his hip.

"Helene!" Ki-Gor shouted agonizedly. "Down! Down!"

Wallaroo Jones's left hand slid back down the barrel to the trigger guard. Ki-Gor made a despairing lunge forward to try and knock the gun barrel down. But Morton Brett was in the way, right between his fear-paralyzed little wife and Ki-Gor.

A white shaft of relief flashed across the jungle man's brain as he saw Helene falling away to one side. Then came the gun shot.

Ki-Gor heard Sheila Brett's agonized scream as he threw himself off his feet at Wallaroo Jones. His fingers closed on the Australian's scrawny throat. He wrenched upward and down and felt, rather than heard, the desperado's neck snap.

Sheila Brett was still screaming when he looked over his shoulder at her. But to his astonishment, she was apparently unhurt. She was kneeling beside the crumpled figure of Morton Brett.

Ki-Gor threw a quick glance at Helene. She was also unhurt, crouched on her knees to one side and staring round-eyed at the two Bretts. Then the action farther up the hillside took away Ki-Gor's attention.

The other two desperadoes had each managed to fire their rifles twice. One shot had hit David Gray, how badly Ki-Gor had no way of knowing yet. Another shot had killed a charging Danala hunter. But that was the sum total of damage that One-Eye Mendoza and Black Ben could do before they were swarmed under by the hairy cave-men.

The gold-tipped spears dipped again and again, and came up dripping crimson. The long-suffering Danala were taking their vengeance.

IT WAS all over in a remarkably brief time. Ki-Gor had to whistle repeatedly to bring the maddened Danala back to their senses. But finally they gathered around him, laughing hysterically with bared teeth. In their midst was the rescued Kleeklee, half dazed by the sudden turn of events.

It was Helene tugging at Ki-Gor's arm who informed him that Morton Brett was dead.

"He threw himself between Sheila and the gun-muzzle," Helene said, "and just a fraction of second later, the rifle went off. I think the bullet went in under his left shoulder-blade."

It was some time before some semblance of order was restored. David Gray had been hit but not seriously. The bullet had gone through the fleshy part of his upper arm, missing bone and artery. One Danala had been killed, and Morton Brett had been killed. The sudden onset of Ki-Gor and his allies had not given the desperadoes time to do any more damage before they were annihilated.

Helene leaned over Sheila Brett who was still sobbing beside the body of her husband.

"Come, my dear," Helene said gently, offering her hand. "Try to control yourself."

"He—he saved my life!" the little woman sobbed. "He took the bullet that was intended for me!"

"Yes," Helene agreed quietly. "He died heroically."

Sheila Brett suddenly stopped crying and stared at her husband's still body. David Gray, one shirt sleeve soaked with blood, came and stood beside Helene. The little woman kneeling on the ground looked up at him.

"David," she faltered, "he died heroically."

Gray nodded soberly. "Yes, Sheila," he murmured, "for one fleeting moment, he was the old Morton that we knew and loved for so long. Perhaps, it was best, after all, that this thing happened. He had changed so the last few years—and I think he knew it, and hated himself for it."

"And now he's dead," Sheila Brett said blankly.

"I think he died happy, Sheila," said Gray. "He saw an opportunity to save your life and to redeem his own character at the same time."

Ki-Gor took Kleeklee aside and talked to him earnestly. A few minutes later the jungle man and the Chief of the Danala returned to the group. Ki-Gor touched Gray's shoulder lightly.

"We must bind up that wound," he said, "and then decide what you are going to do. Kleeklee understands now that we are his friends. He wants to know what he can do for us. He is willing to have us take as many of these gold figures as we can carry and go away with them. Or he is willing to have us come back to Glaclanda with him and stay there as long as we want to."

Appreciation glowed in David Gray's eyes. "What did you tell him, Ki-Gor?"

"I told him I could not answer for you. As for Helene and myself, I said we did not want the gold, and that we would probably continue our journey."

"And I don't want the gold, either," Gray declared. "In fact, it would be my dearest wish that every one of these little statuettes be returned to the Valley. The outside world must never learn about the gold down there, or a great scientific discovery will be lost to civilization, to say nothing of the destruction of a generous and happy group of human beings."

"Good," Ki-Gor approved. "I will tell Kleeklee."

"As a matter of fact," David Gray said with a hesitant, pleading glance toward Sheila Brett, "I—I would like to go back to Glacanda and spend some time studying the Danala. That is, if—if Sheila would come with me."

The little woman got to her feet and held her hand out to Gray.

"I will come with you, David," she said simply. "I think that is what Morton would want me to do."

"That is good," said Ki-Gor. "Helene and I will not come with you, but if you will tell me how long you want to stay in Glaclanda, we will come back for you, and guide you to an outpost."

"That's most generous, Ki-Gor," Gray said fervently. "Under the circumstances, I couldn't ask for a better arrangement."

THAT EVENING, Ki-Gor, Helene, and Ngeeso camped on the barrier at the upper end of Glaclanda. Morton Brett had been buried where he died on the mountain side. Then his wife and Gray had gone down the sandbank with the Danala, and Ki-Gor had cut the vine rope. Sheila and David Gray were prisoners in Glaclanda until Ki-Gor came to bring them out again, but at the same time the precious secrets of the valley were preserved from other marauding intruders like Wallaroo Jones.

As the soft African dusk gathered, Ngeeso chewed a strip of dried meat reflectively and stared out over the Vale of Glaclanda. Ki-Gor, watching him, nudged Helene with a grin.

"What art thou thinking about so intensely, Little Brother?" said Ki-Gor. "The strange hairy cave-dwellers down there? Or perhaps the unaccountable ways of the white men?"

"Who, me?" said Ngeeso. "Certainly not! I am thinking of that marvelous feast I am going to have soon, when Ki-Gor kills an elephant."

STORY VIII

THE EMPIRE OF DOOM

CHAPTER I

IT HAD COME AT last—the day for which Ki-Gor had so carefully prepared, the day when his beautiful, secluded domain would be invaded by strangers.

Ki-Gor had wandered the length and breadth of Central Africa before he had come upon the verdant intervale which he had decided was to be the permanent home of himself and his beloved wife, Helene. Some ten thousand acres were set like a jewel amongst high mountains on two sides, a vast impenetrable swamp to the north, and an inhospitable desert to the southeast. For ages, apparently, the region had been overlooked by Bantu-speaking hunters or settlers, and it was populated only by a small group of Pygmies who roamed the forests and veldts in security and lived well off the abundant game. Ki-Gor, who had always befriended Pygmies wherever he had found them, was hailed by this little tribe as a Big Brother and protector.

But the price of safety in this earthly paradise was eternal vigilance. Ki-Gor and his shy little friends kept a constant watch on the boundaries of the region lest uninvited strangers should intrude their unwelcome presences into the rich intervale. The likeliest route for invaders was the narrow pass through the rugged mountain chain to the east.

It was at the outer end of that pass that Ki-Gor stood now, his blue eyes fixed keenly on several columns of smoke far away rising straight up from the distant jungle. It was early morning. The second morning that Ki-Gor had seen those smokes. The day before they were considerably farther away.

There was no doubt about it—there were strangers heading for the pass, and there were a lot of them. The smokes began to thin out as he watched them. Evidently, the strangers were breaking up camp.

From the distance of the smokes, Ki-Gor judged that the invading party was unlikely to get to the entrance of the pass before late afternoon. That gave him plenty of time to prepare for their arrival. But just the same he had better be going about it.

The jungle man brushed the mane of tawny hair off his forehead, then turned and swung his long, bronzed legs up the pass.

KI-GOR HAD spent a great deal of thought and energy preparing against this day. He had contrived a number of devices by which he hoped to be able to hold the pass single-handed, or with only Helene to help him, against any number of invaders. The Pygmies could be useful, with their tiny arrows tipped with deadly poison, but they went

their own way, and were sometimes far away across the intervale. This was the case now. Ki-Gor had not seen them for three days. It was up to him to defend the pass with only Helene to help him.

The contrivances which he needed to set up his defenses, he kept in a small hut he had built in the lower branches of a great baobab tree. This tree stood not far from the head of the pass, the inner end of it, and Ki-Gor headed for it now. He had left Helene there about an hour before while he came down and explored the outer end of the pass.

But when he arrived back at the foot of the tree, Helene did not answer his call. Ki-Gor muttered impatiently. Helene had learned the ways of the jungle astonishingly quickly, and was well able to handle herself in most contingencies. But she was still helpless against the great beasts of the jungle. Ki-Gor had told her to stay in the tree until he returned because he had crossed the spoor of a gorilla near there, the evening before. What the big man-apes were doing in this country he did not know, but he did not like it. The gorillas were dangerous.

Ki-Gor stood beside the tree and hallooed in all directions without hearing any answer. Finally, he picked her trail and began to follow it.

He felt no great alarm for Helene's safety, but rather an impatience with her for disobeying him. Especially, at a time like this when he should be getting right to work on the defense of the pass.

But Ki-Gor's impatience suddenly changed to alarm when, after ten minutes of trailing Helene, he saw that something else was following his mate. Alongside Helene's tracks ran the unmistakable spoor of a gorilla.

The jungle man sprang forward, running swiftly but silently along the twin trails. It was another ten minutes before he came to their end, and he stepped out from a clump of bushes with a horrified glance at the scene before him.

A hundred feet away out in the open, the great gorilla danced on bowed legs, hairy arms beating his chest menacingly. Twenty feet beyond, crouched precariously on the lower limb of a baobab tree, was Helene.

She was holding a six-foot assegai in both hands, poised like a lance straight at the gorilla. A wave of pride swept over Ki-Gor at Helene's courage. As an offensive weapon the assegai was nearly useless against the gorilla. But it served for the moment to confuse the great ape, frighten it a little, and keep it temporarily at a safe distance.

Ki-Gor glided noiselessly to one side, cursing the mischance which had caused him to come out armed only with his hunting knife. He was afraid that if he shouted the gorilla would spring forward over the assegai and crush Helene in mid-spring.

Cautiously, the bronzed jungle man crept away from the bushes, the hunting knife held ready. So silently, so stealthily, was his progress, that not even Helene noticed him.

At that moment, a resounding cry echoed through the jungle. Helene looked up and her face blanched as she saw another man-ape swinging through the trees. The gorilla on the ground roared once, then waddled forward. Helene gave a little cry, but grasped the assegai firmly. The gorilla reached the bottom of the baobab tree and stared up with baleful eyes. He reached up one tremendous arm to start climbing.

At that moment, Ki-Gor leaped from behind Helene to a position on the baobab limb beside her. He crouched a moment, knife poised, then with a threatening roar dropped to the jungle floor beside the gorilla.

It was not his first fight with the man-apes. Ki-Gor had a veritable contempt for the vicious creatures, in spite of their great strength. He circled the gorilla warily, watching for an opening. It came when the great man-ape screamed and sprang forward with open arms. Ki-Gor lanced in like the hunting leopard, weaving under the powerful arms that sought to crush him. The knife flickered too fast for Helene's eyes to follow it. Twice it sank home in the broad breast of the gorilla before Ki-Gor stepped back. The man-ape coughed horribly, and the murderous red glare left his eyes. He took one step toward Ki-Gor, then crashed like a falling tree to the earth.

Instantly, Ki-Gor turned and snarled at the other gorilla, which stood prudently at some distance, growling and snapping. "See what I have done to your hunting mate!" he roared in the jungle language. "Go—before a similar fate overtakes you. Behold, Ki-Gor speaks!"

With a scream of frustration, the other gorilla turned and made off through the jungle, crying and beating its breast. Ki-Gor's great strength and hunting ability were well known in the jungle.

Helene slipped down from the tree, laid the assegai to one side and then very carefully sat down. She smiled composedly at her mate as he reached her side, but her face was paper-white, and her hands were trembling.

"Good girl," said Ki-Gor admiringly. "How did you happen to have an assegai with you?"

"Oh," she said, tossing her head in an attempt to be jaunty—an attempt that nearly failed—"I remembered your telling me once that an assegai, or even a long pole or a sapling, would hold off a leopard or—even a gorilla—for a little while. So I brought this along, just in case—"

"Good girl," Ki-Gor said again, and stared at the dead gorilla for a moment. "We can use this beast."

"You mean—" Helene began.

"The smokes were nearer," Ki-Gor said briefly. "They are coming here. We must prepare for them right away."

He bent over and hoisted the great carcass onto his mighty shoulders. Helene stood up a little shakily, and they went off toward the baobab tree at the head of the pass. Between his relief at Helene's narrow escape and his concern with the problem of defending the intervale, Ki-Gor completely forgot to scold his mate for disobeying his orders. Helene prudently avoided the subject herself.

WHEN THEY arrived at the baobab tree, they climbed up into the hut. Ki-Gor reached into a pile of assorted objects and drew out two large flat carved pieces of hardwood to which were attached leather thongs. These curious objects he proceeded to fasten to the soles of his feet. Then he leaned back and regarded them with a roar of laughter, in which Helene joined.

They were, in effect, enormous wooden sandals, three or four times the actual size of Ki-Gor's feet. They were circular in shape, and carved on the under side to represent a giant catspaw with four claws. When Ki-Gor walked across soft ground with these sandals, the track they would leave would convince a stranger that some monstrous lion had been in the vicinity.

The other objects in the tree hut included a number of sturdy cross-bows mounted on thick stakes, a basket of cross-bow ammunition—short, thick bolts or quarrels—two big gourds which Helene had carved into leering faces like Hallowe'en jack o'lanterns, a quantity of strong but very fine twine, and a big Ubangi war drum.

These objects, together with the carcass of the gorilla, Ki-Gor carried down the pass, taking care to leave plenty of the terrifying cat tracks where they could easily be seen.

The pass was, for most of its length, a deep gully or donga. It was wide enough at the bottom for eight men to march abreast, and on each side a bank rose steeply for fifty or sixty feet. Except for a few scattered patches of bush and trees, the greater part of the donga was dry and open. However, Ki-Gor's plans were laid to take advantage of the several patches of foliage.

Down near the outer entrance to the donga, a lone tree drooped over the broad trail, its lower branches a full twenty feet above the surface of the ground. By ingenious use of several lengths of the strong twine, Ki-Gor hoisted the body of the gorilla into the lower branches. Then he climbed the tree and fixed the brute in such a way that it hung downward over the trail.

WHEN THE operation was complete, Ki-Gor grunted with satisfaction and paddled off up the donga on his huge sandals. He stopped at the next patch of bush and began driving the cross-bow stakes into the ground on each side and a little above the path. When he had finished there were six cross-bows concealed on each side of the pass and aimed at right angles to it. Ki-Gor carefully drew back the bowstring on each of the twelve weapons, and attached a length of twine to each delicate trigger release. He carried each piece of twine down to the middle of the path and there knotted it to the string from the opposite cross-bow. He made no attempt to conceal the six lengths of twine, but merely left them temptingly lying on the surface dust of the path. Finally then, Ki-Gor loaded each cross-bow with a heavy iron bolt.

Still higher up the pass was another clump of bushes. Amongst them was a single young tree which was rooted in the steep bank and which grew out almost horizontally across the path. Now, Ki-Gor performed his most ambitious operation. He fastened a thirty-foot length of rawhide to the outermost branches of the young tree and then slowly and carefully bent the tip of the tree all the way around to the bank again. He fastened the other end of the rawhide cable to a huge boulder, and secured it by driving a stake in front of it. In that way, the tree was bent in a semicircular arc. When Ki-Gor released the stake in front of the boulder, the tree would spring back to its normal position like a giant whip, carrying the boulder with it.

By now it was mid-afternoon, but Ki-Gor still had two more things to do. One was to set the Ubangi war drum up on the bank of the pass but out of sight from below. Then he attached one end of a well-rosined cord to the taut drum head by means of a wad of tree-gum. He turned to Helene by his side.

"You remember how I told you to work this?" he asked.

"Yes," Helene answered promptly. "I take this little bow, make sure there is plenty of rosin on it, and then draw it back and forth across the cord."

"Good," Ki-Gor said approvingly. "Try it once."

Helene took the free end of the cord that was attached to the drum head and held it taut with her left hand. With her right hand she poised a small two-foot bow at right angles to the cord.

"Shall I?" she said. "Aren't those people, whoever they are, close enough to hear?"

"So much the better," Ki-Gor observed. "Yes, go ahead."

Helene looked down again at the improvised one-string bass viol, then drew the bow sharply across the rosined cord. Instantly, a hideous shattering roar went up as the Ubangi war drum picked up the vibrations of the cord, magnified them many times, and sent them crashing forth on the still air. It had something of the quality of a lion's challenging roar, that ear-splitting din, except that it was much louder than the roar of any lion yet seen in Africa.

"Whew!" Helene exclaimed. "That's some noise!"

"Yes," Ki-Gor agreed with a ferocious smile. "It sounds just like a great big ju-ju lion."

There remained one thing to do and Ki-Gor did it. He lighted the thick homemade candles that were fixed inside each of the big jack o' lantern gourds. They would burn now for several hours. Then he and Helene took up positions in some bushes at the top of the bank above the donga. From here they commanded a view of the entire pass, and of a stretch of open veldt beyond.

At last, they were ready for the invasion.

CHAPTER II

THE SUN WAS DIPPING low toward the mountains behind them, when they first caught sight of the intruders. Far away on the veldt, some black specks appeared, moving very slowly. In a few minutes, some other specks came up and joined the first ones. They all converged for a moment like ants on a drop of spilled treacle. Then they separated and fanned out over the veldt.

Presently, a narrow black stream took shape behind these forerunners and began to flow straight toward the foot of the pass. Longer and longer grew the black ribbon, until Helene began to feel a flutter of panic in her breast.

"Heavens!" she murmured. "I had no idea there would be *that* many. And they're still coming! How many do you estimate, Ki-Gor?"

"It's a big party," Ki-Gor replied, eyes narrowed at the approaching menace. "There are more than a thousand."

"Gracious!" Helene said, shivering. "If that many really want to come up the pass, do you suppose we can stop them?"

"I hope," said Ki-Gor slowly, "that they won't really want to come up the pass—after they have met one or two of our surprises."

Helene hoped fervently that her mate was right, but as the black column came nearer and nearer, she began to have grave misgivings.

It seemed to her that the safari was a small army, and not so small at that. The two dozen or so men in the lead were naked trackers, armed only with light spears. But the main body were heavily armed warriors, carrying great bullhide shields, broad-bladed assegais, and ten-foot knobkerries. All of them wore light-colored kilts of some kind, and many of them wore tall feather headdresses.

"What kind of men are they?" Helene asked.

"I don't know," Ki-Gor answered. "They look something like the warriors I saw once when I was in southeast Africa—Swazis and Zulus. Tall, big-chested men like these. But we are a long way from Swaziland here, and I don't know what manner of men these could be. Their weapons are like the Zulus', too," he added.

There was less than an hour of daylight left when the trackers preceding the main body came toiling up the pass. They did not see the suspended carcass of the gorilla until they were almost under the tree. Then one of them apparently caught sight of the huge prints.

He gave a shrill shriek and leaped backward, looking wildly around. His mates promptly turned and fled down the pass. Left alone for the moment, the tracker crouched on one knee in abject terror. His head twisted this way and that, as if by an uncontrollable impulse.

Then, he evidently caught sight of the suspended gorilla. He jerked himself to his feet with a hideous scream and went shooting down the pass after his fellows.

By this time, the head of the main column was just reaching the foot of the pass. They met the fleeing trackers and halted their flight.

At the same time, the forward progress of the column stopped. The rear ranks, however, pressed on, and the column bulged out to either side, forming, as it were, a black lake ever widening, fed by the black stream coming across the veldt.

Evidently, an excited conference was taking place between the panic-stricken trackers and the advance guard of the warriors. Far away as they were, Ki-Gor and Helene could hear the shrill uproar.

Helene looked questioningly at Ki-Gor.

"It looks pretty encouraging for us, doesn't it?" she ventured. "I mean, it looks as if those tracks and the gorilla have scared them off, doesn't it?"

"They might have," Ki-Gor admitted with a smile, "but I'm not sure yet. Those warriors look like brave men. It all depends on whether they think the tracks were made by a real lion or not. If they think it is a real lion—but just one that's bigger than they ever saw—they may come on up. When I made those tracks I hoped that no one would believe a real lion could make them. I hoped everyone would think that a ju-ju lion had made them. We'll see."

Helene was momentarily sobered by those words, but the next few moments renewed her optimism. The conference at the foot of the pass mounted higher and shriller. And, significantly, none of the milling, shouting blacks seemed inclined to venture up the pass.

"Oh, I think we've done it!" Helene gurgled, clapping her hands. "Look, they're all too scared to do anything but yell at each other."

But even as Helene spoke there came a change in the tone of the uproar from below. From shrill, excited terror, it deepened into a challenging, defiant roar.

THE MILLING, shifting sea of heads began to converge toward the center where an irregular patch of white and a cluster of tossing banners indicated the presence of a high leader or chief of some kind. The noise stilled momentarily, then broke out afresh. Again it hushed, and a single high, clear voice could be heard by itself. Then the din rose up in mighty applause.

The triumphant smile on Ki-Gor's face changed to narrow-eyed concern.

"The chief is making a speech," he said. "I think we are in for it, after all."

The actions of the warriors ten minutes later showed only too clearly the accuracy of Ki-Gor's judgment. The black lake began to surge forward noisily toward the entrance of the pass. A solid phalanx, at least eight men abreast, began to advance up the donga. A wall of the six-foot shields was raised protectively, and knobkerries and assegais were brandished defiantly, but for all that, the phalanx moved with extreme slowness and caution.

Ki-Gor grunted impatiently.

"There's just enough daylight left," he muttered, "for them to try and come up the pass. If they had arrived just a little later, they wouldn't have dared."

Gradually, the column pushed up the pass until it came within fifteen feet of the tree where Ki-Gor had hung the gorilla. There it paused with shrill outcries. Evidently, the advance guard was looking at those giant lion-prints in the dust very thoroughly.

Helene began to take heart a little. She tried to imagine what was going through the minds of those warriors, down there. They were perhaps brave men. But the evidence in front of them pointed to the fact that a prodigious lion had killed a gorilla as though it were an ant, and then had reached fifteen feet up in the air and impaled the carcass in the boughs of a tree. What a monstrous lion that must be!

But again Helene's hopes were doomed to disappointment. The column moved forward again. Reluctantly, perhaps, but it moved forward. Onward it came, cries of encouragement going back and forth among the close-packed ranks, right under the swinging body of the gorilla and over the fearful lion-tracks.

Helene's skin prickled with alarm as the savage phalanx came inexorably up the donga. What would happen when they saw the six strings lying across the path? The strings which, pulled ever so gently, would set off a dozen cross-bows at short range? Helene had never quite understood the scheme of the cross-bows, and now with danger coming nearer and nearer, she doubted their effectiveness even more. Right now, for instance, the column was marching securely behind their shields. The shower of cross-bow bolts would rattle harmlessly off the tough bull-hides.

The front line had reached the strings now and halted with shrill cries. There was a long pause while the strings were investigated—at a safe distance. No one ventured to touch them.

"Ki-Gor," Helene whispered, "maybe they won't dare cross the strings!"

"No," Ki-Gor answered gloomily, "that won't stop them. I'm afraid they've decided that it is just a big lion—not a ju-ju lion."

Again Ki-Gor was right. The column slowly advanced. The front line carefully stepped across the first string, evidently at great pains not to touch it. The renewed outcry was apparently to warn the rear ranks to do the same thing.

Helene began to feel something akin to panic in her breast. What was Ki-Gor going to do? The first two surprises had not stopped these invaders one whit. Would the others?

Ki-Gor's face was reassuringly calm as he turned toward her.

"I'm going down to the boulder," he said. "When you hear me whistle, make the ju-ju lion roar."

With that, he slipped over the edge of the bank and crept downward through the bushes that grew down to the floor of the pass. Helene shivered at being left alone. It was getting quite dark now, too dark to be able to distinguish the faces of the front line of the advancing phalanx, although they were getting quite close. Beside her, concealed in the bushes, and with their leering faces turned toward her and away from the pass, the two jack o' lantern gourds flickered wickedly at her.

Helene's left hand tightened on the rosined cord and pulled it taut. Her right hand swung the bow around ready to saw it back and forth across the cord. Ki-Gor must be nearly down to the tethered boulder now. Her ears strained for the signaling whistle.

THE BLACK phalanx was coming frightfully close. Helene's hands shook with agitation. Could anything go wrong? she asked herself. To unleash the boulder, Ki-Gor had to go awfully close to the trail. Suppose he were seen crouching in the bush. A sick wave of fear went over her, as she pictured those massed warriors surging forward and plunging their assegais into her mate.

Helene's agony of apprehension mounted with every step the phalanx advanced. Why, the front rank was almost abreast of her now! The sweat broke out on her brow. *Where was Ki-Gor!*

Suddenly, above the babble of the advancing warriors, there came a welcome sound. A shrill, sweet whistle!

Helene hauled the cord taut, and drew the bow vigorously across it. Instantly, there came that shocking sound, that earsplitting, paralyzing roar. Again and again, Helene drew the bow across the rosined cord, and a mighty ju-ju lion bellowed its war cry out over the pass.

Down beside the path. Ki-Gor waited for the first roar. When it sounded, he gripped the restraining stake with both hands and gave a titanic heave. Out came the stake from the ground. There was nothing now to prevent the young tree—bent almost double—from springing back to its normal shape.

Rather slowly at first, because of the weight of the boulder tied at the other end of thirty feet of rawhide, the tree began to straighten out across the path. But in a fraction of a second, the motion was taken up by the boulder.

The young tree snapped straight. The rawhide with the boulder on the far end acted like a gigantic whip. Five feet above the hard-packed earth of the path—shoulder high on the advancing phalanx—the fearful whip snapped.

It mowed down the first two ranks of warriors before it broke under the terrific pressure. But the boulder was in midair, traveling at the speed of a cannonball. Crushing bullhide shield and woolly skull indiscriminately, it plowed a frightful furrow of death and destruction down the congested mountain pass.

Over and above the sudden leaping death, however, came the crashing, numbing roar. It could only be a ju-ju, a fearsome, vengeful ju-ju, unleashing supernatural powers of destruction on a presumptuous, overbold band of warriors.

As peal after peal thundered from Helene's sound-effect, the close, orderly ranks of the phalanx melted into a screaming, frenzied mass of terrified black men. The rear ranks broke and fled down the pass, immediately, and relieved some of the pressure up ahead. But for a while they fought each other in hopeless panic, as each man clawed and struggled to get away from there.

Before the last roar of the ju-ju lion died away, the survivors of the column were in full flight. Shields and weapons were flung aside in terror, as the warriors plunged down the pass. Forgotten was the warning to step across those mysterious pieces of string farther down the path. Flashing black feet tripped over them in heedless flight.

Thus the miserable warriors were beset by another unseen terror. Twelve cross-bows discharged their deadly bolts waist-high into the serried mass out on the path. Without their shields, the warriors were cut down as if by a scythe. Some of the terrible bolts went clear through the first soft body and found a second victim.

At the foot of the pass, the leader and his bodyguard, who had prudently stayed behind, made an attempt to stem the headlong rout of the column. They met with little success. The warriors poured out of the pass in a black torrent, insane with terror, and swept the chief and his entourage far out onto the veldt.

There, as darkness closed down entirely, a few of the warriors stayed their flight and gathered, moaning, about their leader. But it was only a brief halt.

One of them screamed suddenly and pointed back toward the pass. A hysterical babbling arose as the sorely tried blacks gazed at a frightful apparition.

Two monsters, or a twin-headed monster—who knew which?—was glaring down at them from the bank at the end of the pass. Yellow flame shot out from the baleful eyes and from the frightful grinning mouths.

It was too much. This time, the chief himself led the flight.

CHAPTER III

AS THE LAST FAINT cries of the fleeing invaders died away in the distance, Ki-Gor blew out the candles in the huge gourd jack o' lanterns, and drew a satisfied sigh. A death-like stillness hung over the evening, punctuated only by an occasional groan from one of the dying warriors in the pass.

"Never again will this happen," Ki-Gor observed to a trembling Helene beside him. "The news of tonight will go all over Africa, and it will not lose in the telling. From one ju-ju lion, the story will grow to a thousand ju-ju lions guarding this place. Not even the Masai would dare to set foot near here."

"Thank goodness," said Helene with a shuddering sigh, "I don't think I could go through such an ordeal again."

"Well, you won't have to," Ki-Gor said, and Helene knew he was smiling, even though she couldn't see his face. "From now on our home will be safe. No intruders will ever dare to bother us. We can live in peace and security with no one near us except the Little People and they are our friends."

"Oh, I hope you're right," said Helene fervently. "Speaking of the Pygmies, I wonder where they all went. I sort of expected them to come and join us after that first roar I produced."

"Yes, I did, too," Ki-Gor replied. "I can't think where they might have gone. Maybe we'd better go back to the Island right now and see if they are there."

"Through the dark?" said Helene, suddenly feeling a little chilly. "I thought probably we'd sleep in the baobab tree, and go on back by daylight."

"Why, Helene!" said Ki-Gor in a tone of jesting reproof. "It's only the Bantu who are afraid to travel at night. Surely, by this time, you know that the jungle is safer at night than the veldt, and our way back is all through jungle."

"Who's afraid?" said Helene boldly. "Not me. Not as long as I have you with me, Ki-Gor."

Ki-Gor mused for a moment on how quickly she had learned the ways of the jungle in those months that had elapsed since the plane she had been piloting on a trans-African solo flight had come down in the middle of the steaming equatorial forest. Whenever Ki-Gor thought of that time, he blessed the fates that had set her down in his bailiwick. He had taken her under his protection, saving her from fearful death in the leering shadows of the jungle.

And then the pampered daughter of civilization, the wealthy American society girl, had learned to love the silent white giant, Ki-Gor, who had hunted alone in the humid Congo since early boyhood. She gave up the world to settle down in Africa with him as his wife. Now, brown, healthy, and strong, she was a fit mate for him.

He chuckled deep in his throat and took her hand in his, and they started back through the jungle to their home on the Island.

IF THE intervale with its teaming game and its healthful, high mountain air was an ideal region to settle down in, the Island provided the ideal home. The Island was situated almost in the exact center of the intervale, in the rushing stream that rose in the mountains to the southeast and flowed northward to the great swamp. Above the Island there was a considerable falls, and below it there was an even larger one. The swift water which swept past either side of the Island made it dangerous to swim, but it abounded in succulent fish and it harbored no crocodiles.

The upstream end of the Island was high and rocky. Dozens of upthrust boulders and ledges had formed a series of natural caves which Ki-Gor and Helene had shortly turned into a fine set of apartments. Lower down on the long, narrow Island, there was sufficient grass to graze a goat, and at the lower extremity there was a grove of tall trees.

When Ki-Gor had selected the Island as a permanent home, he was immediately faced with a problem of transporting himself and Helene back and forth across the swift water of the river. It was a test of strength even for Ki-Gor to swim the river and was therefore out of the question for Helene.

The Pygmies, led by old monkey-faced Ngeeso, promptly solved the problem, by constructing a bridge of vines high above the turbulent stream. From the top of a tall tree on the mainland, they swung tough vine cables over to the top of a correspondingly tall tree on the Island. In a remarkably short time they wove supporting vines together, and completed a masterpiece of primitive architecture.

The bridge sagged frighteningly in the middle, but it was amazingly strong, and could easily support upward of a dozen full-grown persons.

As Ki-Gor and Helene came downstream now past the upper falls on their way to the bridge, the jungle man halted abruptly. Helene, three paces behind him in the almost total darkness, ran into him with a little squeal.

"Oh! you scared me!" she gasped. "What's the matter? Why did you stop?"

"Something just came into my mind," Ki-Gor replied. "This is a good place to leave you alone for a minute. If you should be frightened by anything, you can just step off the bank and duck under the waterfall. Nothing would ever follow you under there."

"Well, what are you thinking of doing?" Helene asked. "Why must you leave me alone?"

"I'll only be gone a little while," Ki-Gor explained. "The Pygmy village is just a little distance off to the right. I'm just going to step over there for a minute and find out where Ngeeso has been. I don't understand why we haven't seen them today. Unless—" Ki-Gor paused significantly—"unless we have had some invaders from another direction."

"Oh, we couldn't have!" Helene exclaimed. "Not two sets in the same day."

"I don't think so, myself," Ki-Gor admitted, "but I'd just like to make sure. It's possible that that *impi,* that body of warriors that we met back on the pass, was just half the force. Another section of the same party might have tried to come in the other way."

"But, Ki-Gor, that's desert over there," Helene protested. "Why would anybody come across that desert?"

"I'm not really worried about it," Ki-Gor said, "but I just want to make sure. Stay here, now, and I will be back very soon."

He disappeared into the impenetrable blackness of the jungle night, and Helene settled down to an uncomfortable period of waiting for him and listening to all the multitudinous disquieting sounds of the tropical forest about her.

Ki-Gor had hardly left her aside before she began to regret that she had let him go. Why did she, now that she came to think of it? She could just as easily have gone along with him. Or better still, she could have gone along by herself to the Bridge-Tree, climbed up and crossed the bridge and been safe on the Island. She could have kindled a fire in front of the main cave and waited there in safety and relaxation for Ki-Gor.

The more she thought about it, the more irritated Helene was with herself.

SHE EDGED toward the waterfall and its comforting roar. Down in her heart, she knew that there was really very little to be afraid of—that Ki-Gor would not have left her alone if there had been. At the same time, she was still new enough to the African jungle to be terrified now and then, even though needlessly. And she was mightily tempted to go on downstream and home by herself. The only thing that prevented her from doing it was the knowledge that Ki-Gor would be alarmed if he came back and found her missing.

So Helene stayed put.

Ki-Gor was not long away. She heard an unseen body crash through the undergrowth off to the right of her, and suddenly went into a mild panic. But almost at the same instant, Ki-Gor's voice floated cheerily through the humid air, and a moment later he was holding her hand.

"Well," she said, "what did Ngeeso say?"

"He wasn't there," Ki-Gor replied. "Nobody was. In fact, they've moved the village."

"Moved the village!" Helene exclaimed. "Why, they only just set it up there a little while ago."

"Yes, but you know Pygmies," Ki-Gor said. "If they happen to feel like it, they'll just pick up and move any time."

"I know that," Helene said, "but, even so, I think it's sort of queer."

"Well, we won't worry about it now," said Ki-Gor. "Let's go home and get some sleep. Tomorrow we can go looking for the Pygmies."

Ki-Gor's tone was reassuring, but Helene wondered shrewdly whether he was hiding something—hiding a private worry of some kind. She knew him well enough to know that he had an extraordinary sixth sense about impending danger. They were never exact premonitions, just vague hunches. At times when, as he put it, "he smelled danger," Ki-Gor would be restless and uncommunicative.

"Ki-Gor," Helene said, as they approached the Bridge-Tree, "do you smell danger?"

"Um—yes, a little," Ki-Gor admitted. "I don't know whether it's danger or not. I just have a feeling something is going to happen. I don't know what."

When they reached the Bridge-Tree Ki-Gor paused and carefully sniffed the base of the trunk all around. His acute sense of smell was able to distinguish the slightest deviation from the normal. While he could not, perhaps, identify individual persons by the slight scent they left behind on hands or feet, he could certainly identify groups. The Pygmies, for instance, smelled quite differently from other races.

"Everything seems all right," he said at last. "There is only Pygmy smell on the tree. Go on up the tree. But wait for me at the top, and I'll go across the bridge first. In case someone or something unfriendly should be waiting on the other side."

Helene pulled herself deftly into the lower branches of the great tree feeling ashamed of herself for picking up some of Ki-Gor's uneasiness. Good heavens, she told herself, if his acute senses could not mark any tangible reason for being uneasy—why, there could not be much real danger around. At any rate, she was thoroughly glad to be back home.

She reached the top of the tree and automatically stepped toward the bridge, forgetting Ki-Gor's warning. But his hand suddenly clamped on her ankle like a vise.

"Wait, wait," Ki-Gor said steadily. "I want to go first."

"All right," Helene answered, "I just forgot for the moment."

Once again, Ki-Gor sniffed the trunk of the tree, and again he found nothing to alarm him. He drew himself up beside Helene.

"Don't come over until I call you," he said and stepped on the bridge.

Without warning, the bridge gave way under his feet.

FOR A long, sickening moment, Ki-Gor felt as if he were standing in mid-air. One hundred and twenty feet below was the river. Time seemed to stand still. When would he start falling? Ki-Gor wondered. It seemed to him that it was an age before he could command his arms to reach out for an unseen bough of the tree.

The tips of his fingers grazed some leaves. Then Ki-Gor knew he was falling. Then some twigs whipped his wrist. Frantically, his hands clawed.

He felt himself gripping a slender branch—heard the branch crack. But instinctively he twisted his body, flung himself forward toward the trunk of the tree. His other hand closed over a larger branch. Instinctively, again, he knew this branch was not strong enough to hold his plunging weight.

He loosened his grip and grappled blindly with his other hand. It fastened on a branch as thick as his wrist. He clung onto it for dear life.

He was still hanging there by one hand, swaying dizzily in the pitch-blackness, when he heard the vine bridge hit the water with a great splash. It seemed hours since he set foot on that bridge.

There was an appalled, incredulous quaver from Helene just above him. Then, suddenly, as realization dawned on her, she shrieked:

"Ki-Gor!"

All the raw agony and primitive horror of the human race poured out onto the night air in that scream.

"Ki-Gor! *Ki-Gor!*" And Helene started to scramble down the tree, numb with horror.

"Don't worry, Helene. I'm all right."

Helene collapsed against the tree-trunk, shuddering.

"Where—where are you?" she quavered.

"Just—below," Ki-Gor grunted. "Stay—there. I'm coming up."

He was inching his way, hand over hand, along the slender branch that was his only deliverance from disaster. It was none too sturdy a lifeline, and he worked his way along it with the greatest caution.

After what seemed an eternity, he reached the tree-trunk, and dug his toes firmly into the mass of vines that entwined it.

He was safe now.

He paused the merest second, then carefully climbed up beside Helene.

"Oh, Ki-Gor!" She buried her face in his shoulder and clutched him convulsively. "What—what happened? The bridge—broke?"

"It was cut," Ki-Gor said bitterly.

"Cut?" Helene said, unbelievingly. "But who would cut it?"

"I don't know. It was cut very skillfully. So that it would barely hold its own weight. As soon as an added weight was placed on it, it gave way."

"But why, Ki-Gor, why? And who could have—?"

"I can't understand it, Helene. Unless my sense of smell has gone wrong, there has been nobody up here but a Pygmy. And I think it was Ngeeso."

"But Ngeeso—" Helene said aghast. "Ngeeso wouldn't do that to you!"

"I don't think he would," said Ki-Gor. "Ngeeso is our friend."

"Then what—?"

"I don't know," said Ki-Gor. "But we must get out of this tree. Follow me down closely. We will go over to that low-branching tree that hangs out over the river. There is nothing more to be done now until daylight. We may as well get some sleep."

As Helene curled up in Ki-Gor's arms in the other tree, she squeezed his arm.

"Ki-Gor, I'm so frightened."

"Never be frightened. Not when Ki-Gor is beside you," the jungle man said, serenely.

Helene felt better, and in a little while she was lulled to sleep by the swirling waters of the river below.

CHAPTER IV

IT WAS EARLY DAWN when Helene opened her eyes again. She started to make some sleepy remark, when a warning pressure of Ki-Gor's hand shut her off. She looked up at him, startled, and then followed the direction of his eyes.

Standing on the river bank, a little bit downstream from them, was a tiny, disconsolate figure.

It was Ngeeso.

He was staring horror-stricken at the wreckage of the vine bridge. Then a dreadful falsetto lament issued from his weazened mouth, and he began to beat his breast mechanically.

"Ai me! What has happened? What fearful calamity has caught Ngeeso unaware? Did my Big Brother come back before I could warn him? O Woe! O Misery!"

Noiselessly, Ki-Gor slid to the ground. Ten feet away from Ngeeso, he spoke, in the Pygmy tongue.

"Greetings, Little Brother."

"E-e-e-eekh!"

The Pygmy squeaked and leaped straight up in the air. He spun around, and landed facing Ki-Gor. He ran forward and threw himself at the jungle man's feet.

"Thanks to the Sacred Crocodile!" the Pygmy gasped. "Thou art safe, Big Brother! For a dreadful moment, I had thought thee dead—drowned in the rushing waters."

"Then thou knewest about the bridge?" Ki-Gor asked.

"Knew about it? Most certainly," the Pygmy returned. "Who but I would know. A clever trap—"

"Who cut the bridge?" Ki-Gor interrupted.

"Who cut it?" said Ngeeso. "Why, I cut it!"

"Thou!" Ki-Gor thundered.

"Wait! Wait! Big Brother," Ngeeso pleaded. "I did it to protect the Island. I never dreamed thou wouldst return last night and attempt to cross in the dark. Never!"

"Go on," said Ki-Gor grimly.

"Nay, I laid the trap, thinking to return here by daylight and catch thee before thou couldst—"

Ngeeso broke off, looked at the ruined bridge and shuddered.

"Ai me!" he lamented. "Miserable Ngeeso who unwittingly nearly contrived the death of his Big Brother!"

The Pygmy clapped a palm dramatically against his forehead. Ki-Gor grinned. He knew it would serve no purpose to scold Ngeeso—the little man was already punishing himself.

"By a miracle," Ngeeso went on, slapping his forehead, "Ki-Gor was saved. A miracle! I cut the vines just so—it would be hard to notice them. I don't know how thou didst not fall to thy death, Big Brother."

"By the very skin of my fingers," Ki-Gor retorted. "But, tell me, why didst thou cut the bridge? For whom wert thou laying the trap?"

"Invaders."

"Invaders?" said Ki-Gor sharply. "This becomes serious. Last evening, Helene and I repelled a whole *impi* of tall men at the Northeast Pass."

"Aye, we heard the ju-ju lion roar even where we were, by the pass from the desert."

"From the desert they came, these invaders of yours?"

"Aye, and thou tellst of tall men. These who came here were black giraffes! Never have these old eyes beheld such monstrous men!"

"You say they came here—to this spot?"

"To this very spot," said Ngeeso stoutly. "There were ten of them, and a leader who was not so tall but much broader than they. We were caught unawares. The first thing we knew, there was a crashing in the bush by the river like a herd of elephants. We took to the trees, and by the time we came here, there were these invaders. The leader stood right here and called your name across to the Island. When there was no answer, he started for the Bridge-Tree. Then I shot a poisoned arrow in his path. He stopped and shouted up at me, though I was well hidden and he could not see me. I made no answer, and he moved toward the Bridge-Tree again. I shot a second arrow, this one a little closer. He kept shouting at me and making signs with his hands indicating friendship. He spoke your name again, too."

BY THIS time, Ki-Gor was openly chuckling. Ngeeso looked at him sharply and went on.

"But he was no friend of mine," he said, "and Ki-Gor has no friends except Ngeeso and the Little People."

"That is not quite true, Little Brother," Ki-Gor said now. "Here in my home, thou and thy people are my only friends. But when I travel far away, up north to the land of the giants who drink blood—why, then I have another friend."

"What's this?" said Helene, who had just descended the tree and come up beside Ki-Gor.

"Our invaders," Ki-Gor informed her, "were ten Masai. They were with George."

"George!" Helene exclaimed. "How wonderful! Where are they?"

Ki-Gor put the question to the crestfallen Pygmy.

"They are near the desert gate where we herded them," Ngeeso replied. "Were we wrong to do so, Big Brother?"

"Nay, there is no damage done," Ki-Gor replied. "But I must go immediately and make amends to my friend from the north for your rude hospitality to him."

"I will lead thee," said the Pygmy eagerly, "and whilst thou visit with him, I will gather my people, and we will come back and build thee another bridge, bigger and stronger than the old one."

It was a bewildered and reproachful party of Masai that Ki-Gor and Helene hailed shortly before midday. The immensely tall, slender warriors were evidently at the end of their patience. Their leader, a giant, bull-necked figure, hurried toward Ki-Gor and Helene.

This was George Spelvin, the American Negro from Cincinnati. Ex-Pullman porter and ship's cook, he had jumped ship at Mombasa and "kep' on walkin'" until he had reached the country of the gigantic Masai who had made him welcome amongst them. He was a full inch taller than Ki-Gor and at least fifty pounds heavier. On several occasions in the past, he had proved himself a strong ally and devoted friend of Ki-Gor and his mate.

Helene and the jungle man greeted him warmly.

"We're so glad to see you, George," Helene said.

"No more'n I am to lay eyes on you-all," the giant Negro rumbled. "Man alive, them li'l cullud midgets"—indicating the Pygmies half-hidden in the trees—"has made us feel pow'ful uncomfortable. We got a feelin' they goin' make a pin-cushion out of us any minute with them poison arruhs."

"Don't worry any more, George," Ki-Gor smiled. "They thought you were an enemy. They know better now."

"Well, that's good news," George breathed. "Say h'lo to the boys. They's two-three of 'em you'll re'connize."

And Ki-Gor did recognize several of the grinning Masai warriors. They had fought by his side in the desperate war against the Wanderobo cannibals.

"Greetings, Tall Trees!" Ki-Gor chanted, as he walked toward them.

"Greetings and long life," the Masai chanted in return, and rattled their huge spears against their shields to signify their respect and approval.

"Well, tell us, George," Helene said, "what are you doing so far away from home?"

"Ma'am, just look me ovuh," said George, with a prodigious grin. "I bin promoted. I bin made a Ambassador."

"An ambassador!" Helene cried. "Tell us about it."

"Yes, ma'am," said George. "Ambassador-Extryo'dinary an' Ministuh Peniplo-ten-shary fum the Masai to His Majesty, King Dingazi of the Kara-mzili!"

"My gracious! what a mouthful!" said Helene.

"Yas'm," chuckled the Negro. "Ol' George, he gettin' up in the world. Well, I tell yuh—it's a long story."

STRIPPED DOWN to its bare essentials, the story that George had to tell was an old one in Africa. Years before, a considerable tribe of fighting Zulu stock had trekked northwestwards into the southern Congo. Their leader was a wily ambitious chief called Dingazi. The local tribes soon fell under the domination of the bigger, fiercer, and more intelligent newcomers.

Dingazi was a shrewd conqueror. He did not unduly oppress his new subjects, and at the same time, he did not allow the martial spirit of his own people to die down. Every year the triumphant Kara-mzili bit off new chunks of surrounding territory. Their weapons, their military organization, and their tactics were far superior to the usual run of jungle warriors. Before long, Dingazi took the title of "King," to which he had earned the right. The rhythm of conquest was maintained, and in the course of time, Dingazi had made himself absolute ruler of an enormous territory, with a population of over four million, and a trained, standing army of more than thirty thousand magnificent warriors.

But now Dingazi was getting old and his conquering ambition was slowing up. He looked back on a full life and saw that it was good, and that there was no real necessity for continuing the seemingly interminable wars that had marked his great career. So one day, Dingazi hit on a device which would, without his resorting to war, maintain his prestige and increase his domains. He placed Mpotwe, his nephew and designated heir, at the head of the nations and tribes that bordered on Dingazi's domains. The most attractive part of this roving commission was the considerable military escort assigned to Mpotwe, who was young and strong, and as ambitious and crafty as his uncle had been at the same age. In recognition of his exalted office of Special Ambassador, Mpotwe was given well over a thousand seasoned warriors.

"That's a good sized Legation Guard," Helene observed.

"You said somepin', Miz Helene," George agreed. "Well, here's how the thing wuk out. Mpotwe traveled 'round, visitin' all these neighbors. An' each new tribe he drapped in on, he'd jest kinda *suggest*—he wouldn't *tell* 'em—jest *suggest* that they'd be bettuh off if they was ruled ovuh by Dingazi. He'd tell 'em Dingazi is a great king, and the Kara-mzili is pow'ful good fightuhs and why don' they think ovuh his proposition."

"Nice Ambassador," Helene commented ironically.

"Well, some o' these boys," George went on, "that Mpotwe talks to thataway, they pretty tough customers, themselves, an' they tell Mpotwe they ain't figgerin' to make no changes, right now. But some of them othuh neighbors, they ain't quite so big and tough. When Mpotwe says, 'Why'n't y'all come ovuh on my side?'—why they takes a look at them thousand warriors behind Mpotwe. And they very liable to answer back and say, 'Mr. Mpotwe, looks lak you got holt of a right good idea.' An' Mpotwe has done got hisself a conquest, without strikin' a blow."

"I remember a country that was once called Austria," Helene murmured.

"Whazzat, Miz Helene?"

"Nothing, George. Go ahead. What has this all got to do with your embassy to King Dingazi?"

"I'm comin' to that, Miz Helene. You see this Mpotwe an' his ahmy come a-wanderin' up into the Masai country."

"WAS THERE a fight?" Ki-Gor asked bluntly.

"Oh, no!" George laughed. "Nuthin' lak that. Mpotwe took hisself a little look 'round, an' decided they wasn't no percentage fightin' the Masai. An' when he kinda hinted 'round about us jinin' up with the Kara-mzili, why we jest laughed at him. An' at that they was only th'ee-fo' hundred Masai went out to meet him. But he knew fightin' men when he see 'em, so he was real polite an' we all exchanged presents, an' he said why don't the Masai come an' call on *him,* sometime, an' then he went away."

"So, now you're returning the call, is that it?" said Helene.... "But you've only got ten men with you."

George chuckled. "Well, Miz Helene, we-all talked it ovuh an' we decided I'd only take 'long ten of the boys. It's jest a li'l way of tellin' the Kara-mzili we ain't afraid of them nor nobody else. When they-all go out on a ambassador job, they got to take a thousand men to be safe. But the Masai—well, *ten* men ought to be plenty. I went down an' picked out the ten tallest boys outa the unmarried fellas, the *Morani.* Look at 'em, they ain't a one of them that's less'n seven foot tall."

George turned his head and looked pridefully at his "boys." They were, Helene thought, the most magnificent physical specimens she had ever seen, their long tight robes accentuating their whipstock slenderness.

"Even so, though," said Helene with a frown, "aren't you a little anxious about walking in amongst thirty thousand warriors with just that little handful?"

"We might be a takin' a li'l chance," George admitted, "but you know, Miz Helene, even in Africuh, they got what you call 'diplomatic immunity.' A Ambassador got a right to come in an' see you an' go way again safely—even if he bringin' you bad news."

"That's true," Ki-Gor said. "I don't know Dingazi, but any king as big as he is would not break that Law. You are perfectly safe, George."

"Tha's kinda the way, I figguh, Ki-Gor."

"Where is his country?" Ki-Gor asked.

"Up yonduh to the no'th-west," George informed him. "I come a li'l outa my way, jest so's I could stop in say h'lo to you-all. It's been a long time since I seen you, so I just took this yere opportunity."

"Well, we're glad you did," said Helene warmly, "and now that you're here, I hope you'll spend a few days with us before you go on to Dingazi's country."

"Miz Helene," George rumbled, flashing a smile, "sounds great. I'm goin' to accept that invite."

"Good," said Helene, heartily. "Shall we go back to the Island?"

"If them li'l Pygmies'll let us move," said George.

But the Pygmies had quietly disappeared while George had been relating the story of the Kara-mzili. George scratched his head sheepishly and Ki-Gor chuckled when they discovered that fact.

"The boys ain't really afraid of nobody they kin *see,*" George pointed out. "But when them li'l fellas hide behind a green apple an' shower down with poison arruhs, why even the Masai is goin' to go slow."

"You don't need to worry about them any more," Ki-Gor laughed, "now that they know you are friends of Ki-Gor."

WHEN THE party reached the bank of the river opposite the Island, they found the Pygmies already hard at work preparing to construct a new bridge to replace the one that Ngeeso had destroyed. The leader of the Little People was thoroughly chagrined over his mistake in taking the Masai for enemies, and he was determined to make up for it by putting up a new and finer bridge in the shortest possible time.

While the work of construction was going on, Ki-Gor made a temporary camp upstream a few hundred yards to be out of earshot of the chattering, swarming Pygmies. And during the course of the next few days, George filled in some details in his account of the Kara-mzili—especially details concerning Mpotwe, the Heir-Apparent.

"He's a mean lookin' boy, that Mpotwe," George declared, "an' I wouldn' trust him as fur's I could heave an elephant. But I guess as long's Dingazi's still goin', the ol' man'll keep a grip on him. Fum what I heah, th' ol' man is quite a fella. Say, by the way, lemme show y'all the presents I'm takin' to him."

"Oh, yes!" Helene exclaimed. "I'd love to see them."

"Well, you know, it's a kind of a tricky business," George grinned as he reached for his knapsack. "Pickin' some gifts for a big chief who is used to gettin' a couple hundred cows or a couple dozen female slaves brought to him. Anyways, I sent down to Nairobi for somepin' I don' think Dingazi has ever seen before."

He drew from the knapsack a flat package which unfolded proved to be a long raincoat with hood attached. It was made of bright red transparent material—a common enough sight on the college campuses of America, but a miraculous article to a savage emperor in the South Congo. Next, George produced a large alarm clock, and finally, a small hand-mirror.

"Oh, I think those are very smart presents," Helene said, "and I bet they'll make a tremendous hit."

"Do you honest, Miz Helene?" said George. "Well, I'm right glad. I wanted to take somepin' that was easy to carry, but the same time was goin' to please th' ol' boy."

As George returned the articles to his knapsack, Helene caught sight of something she had not seen since she left civilization.

"Is that a pair of boots in that knapsack, George?" she demanded.

"Sure," George replied, bringing out a pair of laced knee-boots. "My feet's pretty tough, but I carry these 'round jest in case I got to walk th'ough some tall, dry grass, or across some hot rocks."

He turned them over showing the metal plates fixed to the soles at the toe and heel.

"Tap plates," he explained. "One time, I used to do a little tap-dancin'. Not awful good—I mean, I couldn't never do them triple-taps clean lak Bill Robinson—but I wukked out a coupla routines. Nowadays I put these on an' have masse'f a li'l fun—kinda remind me of the days downtown in Cincinnati."

HELENE LAUGHED and turned to Ki-Gor to explain tap-dancing to him. But Ki-Gor was lost in thought, and she hesitated. Suddenly, he lifted his head.

"The Uruculi feathers," he said.

"The what!" said Helene, in astonishment.

"The headdress," said Ki-Gor patiently, "made of Uruculi feathers. You remember, the Pygmies gave it to me. They are beautiful feathers, and the bird, the Uruculi, is very seldom seen any more—anywhere."

"Yes, I know," said Helene, wonderingly, "but what has the feather headdress—"

"I will never wear it," Ki-Gor went on, "but it is fit for a great king. We will take it as our present to Dingazi."

"Our present!" Helene exclaimed. "You mean—"

"We are going with George to see the King of the Kara-mzili."

Long ago, Helene had learned to expect the unpredictable from Ki-Gor. But this calm statement was a complete surprise. As a matter of cold fact, she herself had felt her curiosity strongly aroused by George's story of the Kara-mzili, and had felt a definite urge to go with the giant American Negro on his mission from the Masai. But, it had never occurred to her to bring up the idea, because she had assumed that Ki-Gor would be extremely unwilling to leave their home in the intervale.

"Do you really mean that, Ki-Gor?" she cried delightedly.

"Yes," he answered with a slow grin. "That is, if you would like to go?"

"Oh, I'd love to!" she declared.

"Good," said Ki-Gor. "Tomorrow, the Little People will have the new bridge finished, and we can go over to the Island and pick up what we need to take with us."

"Well, tha's good news, Ki-Gor," rumbled George. "I sho' would enjoy havin' you folks come with me. I woulda said so, but I nevuh thought you'd tear yusse'f away f'um heah."

"Good then," Ki-Gor smiled. "Tomorrow, we'll look for Marmo, and make our preparations—and go."

"Marmo!" exclaimed George. "You mean, the big elephant? Man, tha's wonderful! That'll be ridin' in state up to ol' Dingazi!"

THE SUN had not been up two hours the next morning before a great clamor from the Pygmies indicated that the finishing touches had been applied to the new bridge. As Ki-Gor, Helene, and George walked downstream, they could see the Little People running back and forth in childish delight on the new span.

It was, as Ngeeso promised, a bigger and better bridge than the old one. Big George was lost in admiration for the work of the primitive Pygmies.

Helene was glad to get back to her home, so much so, that she felt a curious reluctance to be leaving it again so soon. The goat bleated a welcome as they went toward the caves. And the little mongoose, called Whiskey, who kept the Island free from snakes, came chattering up to Helene in evident delight. George looked horrified as the rat-like little animal jumped on to Helene's outstretched hand and scampered up her arm to her shoulder. There it crouched, red eyes gleaming, and grizzled fur standing up in untidy patches.

"My, he's a ugly little fella, ain't he?" George commented.

"He is not," Helene retorted, "he's beautiful!" She stroked the mongoose. "Very beautiful, and very brave. You ought to see him tackle a snake—they don't come too big for him."

"Well, I guess I jest take yo' word for it, Miz Helene," George said, looking dubiously at the mongoose. "But he don't look lak no kind of a pet I'd want hangin' round *my* neck."

To George's further discomfort, it turned out that Ki-Gor intended to take the mongoose along on the journey. Ki-Gor, in fact, made unusually elaborate preparations for the trip. Besides two assegais, he took his powerful warbow and a quiver full of hardwood arrows. He also packed the two wide-sleeved, ankle length robes he had once made for Helene and himself out of lionskin. Their original purpose had been to provide warm body-covers for mountain journeys, but Ki-Gor realized that they would serve very usefully as ceremonial robes in which to greet His Majesty Dingazi. As a last-minute idea, Ki-Gor also added a duplicate of the rosined cord and small rosined bow that had produced the ju-ju lion roar when affixed to the head of the war drum by the wad of tree-gum.

Eventually, the preparations were complete. Marmo, the giant elephant, was summoned by Ki-Gor's shrill whistle. Helene, Ki-Gor, and George settled themselves on his mountainous back, Helene clutching a light bark cylinder which contained the precious Uruculi feathers. The Pygmies lined the trees with excited farewells, and Marmo moved majestically away, followed by the Masai in single file.

CHAPTER V

FIVE DAYS OF CONSTANT traveling through wild country largely uninhabited—desert, jungle, marsh, and veldt—brought the little company to the first frontier outpost of the Kara-mzili. It was a good-sized village located beside a ford across a considerable river. The round huts of the village were shaded by well-spaced trees, and behind them the black jungle loomed up ominously. But to approach the village, Ki-Gor and his little party had to cross a treeless veldt in full view of the ford.

Long before Ki-Gor halted the elephant at the ford, there could be observed signs of great activity in the village, and a company of at least a hundred warriors splashed through the shallow water of the river and drew up to meet the newcomers. As Marmo pushed forward toward these frontier guards, Helene noticed that in dress and weapons, they closely resembled the warriors who had attempted to invade the intervale.

"Them boys," George remarked, "is liable to act awful officious, if we let 'em. Th' only way to handle 'em, is act like we don't even know they are theah. Keep a-goin', Ki-Gor, ontil you get right up close to 'em."

The massed Kara-mzili warriors swayed restlessly as the huge elephant and the ten escorting Masai moved straight toward them. Excited cries of warning rose from among them, and eventually one broad-shouldered spearman—evidently the leader—rushed forward with a high-pitched yell. But it was a very short rush, and when the people on the elephant and the gigantic Masai paid no attention to him, the leader danced backwards to the safety of his own spearmen.

Twenty-five feet away from the howling, gesticulating Kara-mzili, Marmo stopped on a murmured command from Ki-Gor. George stood up on the elephant's back and stared insolently over the heads of the frontier guard. Then his Bull of Bashan voice rolled out, topping the clamor of the indignant Kara-mzili.

"Make way!" George roared. "Make way for the illustrious and sacred embassy to the great Dingazi, King of the Kara-mzili!"

The tumult of the frontier guards suddenly stilled, and an astonished silence fell over them. Then the leader found his voice again.

"An embassy?" he inquired, and then gained courage. "What embassy? Who dares to come unannounced and in such small force to claim audience with the Most High, the Emperor of the World?"

"Who dares?" George retorted. "Who dares to bar the way to an embassy of two kings and a queen riding a sacred ju-ju elephant, and escorted by ten royal princes of the Blood-drinking, All-conquering Masai, Scourge of the North!"

There was a hasty, concerted backward movement by the Kara-mzili accompanied by apprehensive glances at Marmo. From a safe distance, the leader spoke again, but with far less conviction than before.

"No one may come into the lands of the Kara-mzili without the express permission of the Most High Dingazi, Emperor of the World."

"Send fleet messengers, therefore," George commanded, "and inform Dingazi that Tembu George of the Ngombi-Masai is pleased to return the visit of Mpotwe, and comes bringing presents and words of good will. With Tembu George is Ki-Gor, White Lord of the jungle, together with his reigning queen. Send these messengers promptly, and we will follow along at a leisurely pace as befits our high station."

The leader of the frontier guards was visibly impressed by George's ringing words, but his bureaucratic soul would not permit him to give in without a further show of authority.

"It is against all precedent," he said uncertainly. "You will have to give up your arms and be tied with ropes. Then we will take you to Dingazi and he will decide your fate."

"Miserable worm!" George thundered. "By your ignorance you have sealed your own fate! We will stand for no such nonsense! Rather will we immediately turn our backs on you and go back the way we came. And when your master, Dingazi, hears of the intolerable offense you have given to friendly ambassadors, he will cut your foolish tongue out and stake you to an anthill!"

George folded his enormous forearms across his chest, and for the first time he deigned to look at the man whom he addressed. It was a ferocious, beetling look. The captain of the frontier guards was wild with shame and confusion.

"No! No!" he shouted. "Don't let them go! Attack them! Capture them!"

ON THE instant, Ki-Gor rose up beside George, and a three-foot arrow was notched in the great war bow in his hands.

"Attack them!" the captain screamed. "You heard my orders!"

But his followers were none too eager to carry out his orders. Although they outnumbered the Masai ten to one, they did not like the look of those giants from the North. They were apprehensive, too, about the ju-ju elephant. None of the Kara-mzili had ever seen a tamed elephant before.

At a brief command from George, the huge Masai sauntered forward a few insolent steps, their great spears held negligently in the crook of their elbows. They tilted their long narrow heads back proudly and stared over their pointed chins at the wavering Kara-mzili.

Helene held her breath for a long moment.

In the meantime, Ki-Gor's brain had been working fast. He realized that the captain of the frontier guards had worked himself into a situation from which there was no honorable retreat. The jungle man's knowledge of the savage mentality told him that the captain was probably trying frantically to think of some way of reversing himself without losing face. Ki-Gor decided to furnish the captain a way out.

A murmured word to Marmo, and the elephant swung his trunk upward and backward. Ki-Gor leaned forward and allowed the groping tip of the trunk to graze his ear. The crowd of warriors suddenly hushed. It was evident to them that the ju-ju elephant had just whispered something into the ear of the extraordinary white man.

Then Ki-Gor spoke out loud in the same Bantu dialect that the Kara-mzili used.

"Aye, Marmo," he declaimed. "I am of the same opinion. That poor captain is temporarily bewitched."

The Kara-mzili sucked their breath in. The captain went gray and began to tremble.

"Otherwise," Ki-Gor continued, "he would never invite upon himself the fearful punishment which will certainly be his when Dingazi hears of his boorish treatment of our embassy."

The Kara-mzili began to back away fearfully. But the captain stood rooted to the ground, the sweat pouring off his glistening face.

"Happily, Marmo," said Ki-Gor, nodding his head wisely, "thy supernatural gift hath divined that this poor fellow is only temporarily bewitched. And if thou wilt but step forward five paces, reach out thy trunk, and harmlessly touch the man on the shoulder, he will be freed of his horrid enchantment. He will be once more a normal man, and he will order his men to let us pass without further ado."

A breathless silence hung over the scene. The captain's eyes bulged with fascinated horror as the elephant slowly moved toward him. The long, wrinkled trunk reached out and brushed his shoulder. Then Marmo lifted the trunk high in what might have been a ritualistic gesture, and trumpeted once, very discreetly.

An audible sigh went over the Kara-mzili. The captain looked around him in amazement. He was convinced he had just been freed from an enchantment.

"*Hai!* Brainless fools!" he shouted at his men. "For what reason do you stand thus in attitudes of war? Are you so blind as to contest the path with these royal visitors to our land? Make way instantly for the illustrious and sacred embassy to our lord, Dingazi, Emperor of the World!"

The frontier guards were only too glad to obey the new orders. But the captain hounded them to move faster.

"Make way, I say!" he shouted, and pointed to several of the warriors. "And you—and you—and you—be off immediately—run with the wings of the wind to Dutawayo, the kraal of our king. Tell them there that Tembu George of the Ngombi-Masai is coming, that Ki-Gor, White Lord of the jungle—and his queen, also—are coming, and ten Royal Princes of the Masai—all are coming with presents and words of good will for Dingazi, Emperor of the World. Quickly! Go, ignorant louts! Would you keep this illustrious embassy waiting for one tiniest fraction of a moment?"

Ki-Gor's face was a haughty mask as Marmo moved slowly through the wide opening made by the frontier guards. The chiseled ebony profiles of the Masai were models of insolence, too, as the colossal warriors stalked along on either side of the elephant.

But on Marmo's back, the two Americans, Helene and George, buried their faces in their hands, and their shoulders shook with barely concealed laughter.

CHAPTER VI

FROM THE FRONTIER POST to Dutawayo, Dingazi's capital, it was another five days' journey. The countryside was peaceful, and relatively thickly settled. The way led past many cultivated fields and through small villages. Now and then herds of domestic cattle could be seen along the way. These the Masai appraised critically—being themselves herdsmen—and found not so beautiful as the big-horned, small-hooved cattle of the North.

Evidently the messengers which the captain of the frontier guards had despatched to Dutawayo arrived in good time, and with tall tales. Because, on the morning of the fifth day, a large and resplendent welcoming party made its appearance.

The leader, dressed in ceremonial peacock-feather headgear, stood at a safe distance, announced that he was a son of Dingazi, and bade the visitors welcome with flowery phrases. This young man, while he was obviously impressed with Marmo and the towering Masai escort, seemed a trace disappointed with the numerical weakness of the embassy. Ki-Gor smiled to himself, knowing the African tendency toward exaggeration. However, George pointed out loftily that in this particular case, it was not quantity that counted, but quality. With a sweeping gesture, he declared that only an embassy such as this—limited to members of kingly blood—could do honor to the great Dingazi.

The son of Dingazi saw George's point and presently gave the order to proceed toward Dutawayo.

"George," said Helene, keeping her voice low and speaking English, "there's something I don't understand here. If Dingazi has a son, why is it that his nephew, Mpotwe, is the Heir-Apparent? I should think his son would be."

"Well, heah's how I figger it, Miz Helene," George replied. "This yere Dingazi has prob'ly got him a whole raft of sons, because he prob'ly got a whole raft of wives. He would have a hard time pickin' out th' oldest son. That mean he jest goin' to have to say 'Eenie meenie' and catch one of 'em by the toe. Well, it maybe turn out, he like this yere nephew, Mpotwe, just about as good as any of his sons. Maybe Mpotwe is a whole lot sma'tuh than any of the sons. So he jest pick Mpotwe and say, 'Boy, you' the one,' an' sho nuff he is!"

Before many days had gone by, Helene was to find out that George had appraised the situation very accurately.

It was a noisy, but on the whole, friendly escort that accompanied the visitors toward Dutawayo. But Helene noticed that they all kept a safe distance during the journey. Putting herself in the place of the Kara-mzili, she could not blame them much. Probably very few of them had ever seen white persons before, and if they had, they would have been dressed far differently from Ki-Gor and Helene. George, himself, was as big if not bigger than the burliest of the Kara-mzili warriors, and in addition, he wore a European-style white shirt and shorts. Then, too, the unbelievably tall Masai must have seemed like beings from another planet. And finally, the tame elephant was something outside their experience, and they must have readily accepted the idea that Marmo was a powerful ju-ju.

All in all, Helene did not blame the Kara-mzili for keeping their distance from this strange embassy. It was just as well, Helene thought to herself. These Kara-mzili were no whimpering, cowering forest blacks of the Guinea Coast. They were alert, strapping warriors, who held their heads proudly high in the manner of the Zulus. And if they took it into their heads to be unfriendly, they could easily wipe out the little party. To be sure, both George and Ki-Gor had said that even savage jungle monarchs recognized the principle of diplomatic immunity. But just the same, it was good insurance to have the Kara-mzili stand in superstitious awe of them.

For the first time since she started on this journey, it suddenly occurred to Helene that there were thirteen members of the party. Ki-Gor, George, herself, and ten Masai. She shivered a little.

THEY ARRIVED at Dutawayo just before sundown, and this time it was the turn of the visitors to be astonished. They had expected to see a collection of straggling mud huts, such as they had noticed on the way in—a larger group, perhaps, but more or less the same sort of village.

But Dutawayo was a city.

None of the visitors had ever seen a native African town as big as that. Ki-Gor quickly estimated that there must have been at least five thousand well-made thatched-roof dwellings in Dutawayo. They covered a gentle slope that rose from the banks of a placid river to a low knoll. There, a considerable group of these houses were perched, surrounded by a palisade, and dominated by one house much larger than the rest.

"I guess tha's Dingazi's kraal up theah, all right," George murmured to Ki-Gor. "He got him quite a layout, ain't he?"

Ki-Gor nodded. "Well made houses," he remarked.

"Yeah," George agreed. "Look to me like Bechuana style. Them small peeled logs standin' upright for walls. An' the way the roof is raised off'n the walls. Tha's how you get a real cool house, thataway."

The populace of Dutawayo turned out in force to greet the visitors. They streamed in from all sides to stare at the elephant and the white couple and seven-foot Masai and to express their amazement and wonderment in shrill shouts. Young and old, big and little, men, women and children—all tumbled over each other to see the extraordinary visitors.

The human members of the embassy somehow kept their composure in the face of the appalling crowd. But Marmo did not like it at all. There was altogether too much noise and disorder to suit the old elephant. Ki-Gor realized this and did his best to keep soothing Marmo by reassuring pats on the head, and encouraging words.

But half way through the town of Dutawayo, Marmo decided that he had had enough. He lifted his trunk high, and trumpeted three times, loudly and imperatively. The crowd suddenly stopped shouting, and those in front of the elephant began to press backward energetically. Again Marmo trumpeted, and then he suddenly flared his great ears. The Kara-mzili knew what that meant in a wild elephant, and they assumed that it meant the same thing in a ju-ju elephant. It might even mean something a lot worse. A near-stampede ensued among the people of Dutawayo. But Marmo was not through yet.

As the panicky Kara-mzili melted away on all sides, Marmo started to bolt.

Ki-Gor did the only thing there was to be done under the circumstances. It was risky, but it had to be done. He slipped the quiver of arrows off his shoulder, thrust it and the war bow at Helene, and stood up. Balancing on his toes he went straight out on to Marmo's broad flat forehead.

By this time, the great elephant was beginning to gather speed. But without hesitation, Ki-Gor gathered his leg muscles and sprang in a prodigious leap straight forward into the air ahead of the elephant.

He hit the ground running just two feet ahead of Marmo's lashing trunk. By a miracle he kept his feet and shot forward, keeping squarely in the path of the speeding elephant.

But as he ran he raised both arms high in the air and repeatedly shouted the command to stop.

Gradually, Marmo slackened his pace. Ki-Gor sensed that the elephant's temper was subsiding. At the psychological moment, he whirled and faced the great creature. He still held his arms up, the gesture which was a command to halt, and skipped lightly backward.

In a moment, Marmo slowed down to a dead stop.

Ki-Gor walked up and patted the corrugated trunk.

"I don't blame you, old friend," he said, in Swahili, which was the language Marmo understood. It is a huge crowd and a fearfully noisy one. But they mean no harm, so curb your impatience, and carry us safe to our destination."

For answer, Marmo benevolently curled his trunk around Ki-Gor's middle, lifted him up over his head, and deftly placed him on top of his broad neck.

An awed murmur went over the terrified Kara-mzili. Surely, they were watching powerful ju-ju at work.

WITH THE crowd much quieter and withdrawn to a healthy distance, Marmo covered the remaining distance to Dingazi's kraal without further incident. But just at the wide entrance gate into the high stockade, the elephant did a curious thing. He halted without a command from Ki-Gor and then slowly began to lower himself to his knees.

"Hey! Ki-Gor!" said George, in an alarmed whisper. "Whut-all's goin' on?"

"Pay no attention," said Ki-Gor quickly. "We will all dismount here, just as if I had ordered Marmo to stop. He doesn't want to go inside the kraal."

George nodded his understanding and slid to the ground. Ki-Gor followed and helped Helene down. Promptly, the great elephant rose to his feet and waved the tip of his trunk over Ki-Gor's head as if in apology. To the watching Kara-mzili, the gesture seemed like a benediction. Ki-Gor stepped up beside one of the long tusks.

"I understand, O Faithful Friend," he murmured in Swahili. "Go now, but not too far away. I may yet have need of thee, and I will trust thee to come when thou hearest my urgent whistle."

Marmo swung his huge head away, then tilted it upward, curled his trunk and trumpeted fiercely. Then he shuffled away back down toward the river, and the townspeople of Dutawayo scattered briskly out of his path.

Ki-Gor beckoned to the son of Dingazi. "I have sent the ju-ju elephant away on my business," he declared loudly and distinctly. "Let no one follow him lest he turn himself into a horde of locusts and come back to plague you all."

Dingazi's son nodded importantly and yelled a warning at the crowd. Then he came forward and gestured to the visitors to Dutawayo to follow him through the gate into Dingazi's kraal.

There were several hundred people in the kraal, mostly women and children, but they were pressed back against the houses that lined the inside of the great circular stockade. There was an awed silence as the little embassy strolled across the open space.

Directly opposite the gate of the kraal stood the house which by reason of its great size was obviously Dingazi's. But half way across the enclosure, the son of Dingazi veered off to the right and led his guests to a house that was almost a quarter of the distance of the kraal's inner circumference from Dingazi's mansion. The women and children in front of it broke away and retreated in both directions.

"This is your house," said the son of Dingazi to George. "This and the ones on each side of it for the royal princes"—indicating the haughty Masai—"There will be servants for you and I hope you will be comfortable until such time as Dingazi signifies his desire to receive you."

"It is good," said George evenly. "We will await Dingazi's pleasure. We will not need servants."

"No?" said Dingazi's son.

"No," said George meaningfully, "not for the short time we expect to stay."

"Your wishes will be respected," said the son of Dingazi and walked away.

George sent a swift glance at Ki-Gor, and Ki-Gor nodded slowly. They both followed Helene into the house.

"Dingazi don't have to see us ontil he get good'n ready," said George, "an' he won't, either. He's a great king an' we got to be real p'lite to him. But I jest thought I'd let that young fella know that we is pretty big shots, ourselves—an' that we don't have to wait aroun' too long, if we don't want to."

"You were right," Ki-Gor agreed. "There is one thing I don't like. You said Mpotwe is next in rank to Dingazi. Then why hasn't Mpotwe come to greet us, instead of that young man?"

"I don' lak that, either," said George. "An' I don' know 'zactly whut we kin do 'bout it. I guess we—"

"Wait a minute," Helene whispered. "There's a lady to see us. And I really mean a lady."

STANDING IN the doorway was a young Kara-mzili woman. She was the most beautiful Negro Helene had ever seen anywhere. She was tall and nobly proportioned, and she carried herself with an instinctive dignity, a majesty that was thrilling. Her skin was the color and texture of milk-chocolate and showed glowing highlights on her sculptured cheek bones and the clean line of her jaw. As she looked in through the doorway, her generous mouth opened in a warm smile showing white even teeth.

"I am Shaliba," she said, in a throaty, pleasant voice. "My father, Dingazi, sent me to make sure you were comfortable. He would have sent Mpotwe, but Mpotwe has not returned from his mission yet. In the meantime, I will do my best to take his place."

Helene was not familiar enough with the Kara-mzili dialect to understand all of that speech, so she turned inquiringly to George. But the expression on the giant Negro's face made her pause. George was smiling a child-like smile of pleased wonderment. His eyes were wide open, and fixed on the beautiful face of Dingazi's daughter.

Suddenly, he seemed to come out of his daze. He walked forward and held out his hand.

"Shaliba," said George, "your father does us great honor to send you to us. Come inside and sit with us, and tell us about the customs of your people. And tell us what we should know before we have our audience with your father."

"I don't know what there is to tell," Shaliba smiled, "but I will be glad to come in and talk to you."

Shaliba stayed for about a half an hour, and both Helene and Ki-Gor were agreeably impressed with her. She seemed to be as sincere and gracious as she was beautiful. She answered questions frankly, and just as frankly asked some questions. She was obviously quite puzzled about Ki-Gor and Helene, and evidently could not quite make up her mind about George. But she kept her curiosity well within the bounds of good manners. When she left, she warned the trio that it might be some days before they were received by Dingazi. In the first place, the old king would not see them before Mpotwe returned, and in the second place, Dingazi was in poor health. In fact, he had been under the care of the chief witch-doctor, Mbama, for some time now.

George saw Shaliba to the door, and when he came back, his face was thoughtful.

"Say," he said, after a minute, "whut did you folks think of Shaliba?"

"Why, I liked her very much, didn't you?" Helene answered, while Ki-Gor nodded in agreement.

"I sho' did," George said, staring at the dirt floor. "I thought she was a swell gal."

"Why, George!" said Helene mischievously. "I do believe you fell for Shaliba a little bit."

A slow guilty smile stole over George's broad face.

"Well, y'know, Miz Helene," he replied, "I shouldn't wonduh but whut maybe I did—a li'l' bit."

Helene felt quite startled. In all the time she had known George, he had been a stout friend and ally, quick witted in trouble and terrible in battle, and somehow she had never conceived the possibility of his falling in love. Ki-Gor interrupted her thoughts.

"I wonder," he said, "how long we will have to wait for Dingazi. I hope it isn't long. I don't like staying here inside the kraal. I don't like spending the night in this house."

He looked about him moodily, and then spoke again.

"If I can help it, I am not going to sleep here at night."

"Well, I don' know, Ki-Gor," said George, troubled. "I don' know jest whut to do 'bout that."

"Here's what we'd better do tonight," said Ki-Gor decisively. "We will stay here, but I will not sleep. I will go in that little room back there now and sleep a while. Then tonight I will be fresh and I can stay awake while you two sleep."

"Jest whutevuh you say," said George. "I don't think anybody heah goin' to want to ha'm us, but it's always a good idea to keep our eyes open, I guess. I'll have two Masai boys mount guard every night, as long as we stay."

"Good," Ki-Gor approved. "I'm going to sleep now."

He picked up the cloth bag at his feet, and there was a faint chatter from the mongoose inside as the little creature momentarily waked up. Ki-Gor clucked reassuringly at it and carrying the bag with him, lifted the hanging curtain that separated the main room of the big hut from the smaller sleeping room. He glanced around the little space—at the deerskin pallets on the floor, and then up above to the foot-wide gap between the top of the side wall and the thatched ceiling. Ki-Gor didn't like it. He felt dangerously shut in. But he lay down on one of the pallets, and the mongoose chirped sleepily in his bag. In a moment, both master and mongoose were fast asleep.

BACK IN the main room, George sat lost in thought for a moment, then got up and went to the doorway. He intended to call one of the Masai boys over to give him directions about posting a guard that night. But his eye lighted on a strange object that was coming across the kraal in his direction.

At first glance, it seemed to be a large bundle of feathers that moved along by fits and starts under its own power in some mysterious way. It scurried along the ground for some distance in one direction, then veered abruptly and headed off in another direction. Then it would stop for a minute, seemingly inanimate, only to go into sudden motion again.

George stared at the weird object fascinatedly, and with growing interest as he perceived its indirect weaving course was bringing it closer and closer to the spot where he was standing. In a short time, the extraordinary bundle of feathers was close enough for George to see exactly what it was.

A pair of thin, wrinkled wrists supporting claw-like hands parted the feathers and a hideous, leering yellow face blinked up at George. The old man—or old woman, George could not be sure which—rose up disclosing bent, twig-like shins, and a cracked, falsetto voice made itself heard.

"That elephant was no ju-ju!"

George stared at the fantastic creature for a moment without answering. He had seen witch-doctors before, but never quite such a weird one as this.

"It was no ju-ju, I say!" the cracked voice shrilled.

George grinned. "I hope he can't hear you," he said, "or he is liable to throw such a spell on you that you could not open your mouth to speak or eat for the rest of your life."

The witch-doctor squeaked in terror and spun around and peered across the kraal. An extra knot of feathers stuck out ludicrously from behind like a rooster's tail. After a long moment, the witch-doctor twisted his wrinkled face around and glared at George over his shoulder.

"Where are the others?" the falsetto voice demanded.

"Who asks?" said George coolly.

"Who asks!" the little creature shrieked. "Why Mbama himself! Mbama—whose ju-ju protects the Emperor of the World!"

"Ah," said George, while he made up his mind just how to treat the grotesque little bundle of feathers. Shaliba had said Mbama was the chief witch-doctor of the Kara-mzili, in which case he would wield a powerful influence with the tribe, and with Dingazi. At the same time, George was determined not to show the slightest sign of fear as long as he was in the land of the Kara-mzili. To do so might prove to be very dangerous.

"Ah," George said again. "So you are Mbama. I should have known. Peace and long life to you, Mbama. I am Tembu George."

THE WITCH-DOCTOR glared suspiciously.

"Why did you come here?" he said at length.

"To see Dingazi."

"What do you want of Dingazi?"

"Nothing," said George patiently.

"You come on your knees," Mbama declared, "imploring favors of the Emperor of the World."

George laughed. "The learned witch-doctor, Mbama, surely knows that the Masai ask favors of no one," he said.

"Humph," the witch-doctor grunted. "Who are the Masai!"

"Mpotwe can tell you," George said quickly. "Mpotwe came to the Masai with friendly words, and bearing gifts. The Masai are returning his favors."

Mbama brooded a moment, then said, "I have only your word."

George took up the challenge, and his tone was dangerous.

"You are being rude, Mbama, and furthermore, you are being unwise. Learn this here and now. The Masai fear no one on earth. They are unconquerable enemies—and powerful friends."

Mbama shrieked with rage. He suddenly hopped away six feet. Lying coiled in the dust where he had been standing was a tiny snake.

George acted swiftly. The snake might be venomous, but he took a chance that it was not. He swooped forward and down, seized the snake by the tail, and snapped it like a whip. The creature hung down from his hand limp, like a piece of string. George flung it contemptuously at the astonished witch-doctor. Then he turned his back and walked into the house.

Helene was standing beside the doorway, round-eyed.

"I saw that," she whispered. "It was a crazy thing to do."

"I didn't take much of a chance," George shrugged. "That li'l' man is crazy, but he ain't crazy nuf to carry round any poisonous snake in them feathuhs."

"Yes, but do you think it was wise to get on the bad side of a witch-doctor like that?"

"Miz Helene," George said, "anything we'd do, we'd get on the bad side of that fella. I know these yere witch-doctors. They're bad cleah through. They only got a little bag of tricks to impress the homefolks, an' when some strangeh come along, they all skeered the strangeh goin' to show up the bag of tricks. Then the witch-doctor goin' to lose his job. So, right away, they goin' to be against strangehs. Only way to do is show 'em you jest as tough as they are."

"Oh dear," Helene said quietly. "I had a little hunch this trip was going to be dangerous."

"Please don't worry, Miz Helene. We won't have no trouble soon's we get to see Dingazi. It's kinda unfortunate that we got heah befo' Mpotwe, but it'll all come out okay. Don't you worry."

"Yes, but aren't you afraid that horrible little man will try and do us some harm?"

"Oh, we goin' to have to keep our eyes open, Miz Helene, but we will. We'll do just that little thing."

CHAPTER VII

JUST BEFORE SUNDOWN THAT day, Mpotwe returned.

His arrival was presaged by a multi-throated roar from far down the hill of Dutawayo by the river bank. The roar grew louder as the townspeople escorted the conquering hero up to Dingazi's kraal. Ki-Gor, Helene, and George stood outside the door of their house, and the Masai gathered around them, squatting impassively beside their huge spears.

The excitement within the kraal soon equaled the clamor outside. Hundreds of royal relatives and slaves poured out of the circle of houses and raced to the kraal gate. From every hand, great war drums commenced an incessant, frightening throbbing, that mounted in a gradual crescendo as Mpotwe's procession came up the hill.

Finally the crowd around the kraal gate surged back and parted with hysterical screams, and the drums pounded frenziedly in a maddening, ear-shattering rhythm. The crowd streamed backward across the center of the kraal toward Dingazi's house.

Helene, clutching Ki-Gor's arm convulsively, peered out at the flitting, dancing figures, caught just a quick glimpse of a broad, squat, black figure in a towering white feather headdress. Behind him marched rank on rank of spears. It was too dark, and the crowd too dense to see much of the procession. But one thing was only too clear, and that was that an enormous throng was pouring into Dingazi's kraal.

The kraal was relatively big, but there were limits to its capacity. As more and more frenzied Kara-mzili swarmed in, they inevitably pressed the others back toward the circle of houses. In a short while, the outer fringe of the mob was coming dangerously close to Ki-Gor and Helene and their friends. It began to get too much for Helene's nerves. She tugged at Ki-Gor's arm and said:

"I don't like this. They're getting much too close for comfort."

George looked at her with a wry smile and said, "Yeh, it kinda look like they goin' to be jest about sittin' in our laps in a few minutes."

"Well, don't you think we ought to all go back into the house?" Helene said anxiously.

Ki-Gor shook his head emphatically.

"No. We are guests of the Kara-mzili, and they must treat us like guests."

"I think you're right, Ki-Gor, at that," George said. "I think we-all will stay right out yere."

He shouted a command to the Masai, and the ten warriors rose to their feet and ranged themselves on either side of the trio. The three-foot blades on their spears dipped forward and down, until the spear-hafts were horizontal.

Helene looked nervously from Ki-Gor to George and back again. To her way of thinking, the situation had not been improved. The hysterical mob was still backing closer and closer toward them. If they kept on coming, someone was going to get hurt. She shuddered as she thought of the possibility of that mass of excited blacks turning on them. Masai or no Masai, they would be wiped out in a minute.

"There he goes," said George suddenly.

"Who?" Helene asked.

"Mpotwe," George replied. "Into Dingazi's house."

As if by a signal, the drums suddenly stopped and the crowd hushed. The sudden silence was almost as appalling as the noise had been before. The air was thick with expectancy. Helene felt oppressed and strangely fearful. But neither her mate nor George seemed to fear any unpleasantness.

Presently a speculative buzz began to creep over the mass of Kara-mzili. As the moments went by, it grew louder. Finally, there came a flicker of a torch, and George said, "He's come out again. He's goin' to tell 'em all somethin'."

Mpotwe made a brief announcement, after which there was a joyous yell from the crowd. The drums began to thump again, and the massed Kara-mzili began to surge back and forth.

"Don't worry," Ki-Gor shouted in Helene's ear. "He said there was going to be a feast right away down by the river. See, the crowd is moving toward the gate of the kraal."

IN A very short while, the throng of blacks ebbed away from their high-water mark so close to the spears of the Masai, and went shouting and jostling down to the other end of the kraal. Helene drew a sigh of relief.

It was nearly night now, and fires began to twinkle from the doorways of the houses in the circle, and here and there torches danced. One of them came close now, borne by a young slave girl.

"Tembu George," she said. "I am sent by Shaliba. If you will come with me, I will take you to the house of Mpotwe."

"What is that?" said George. "Is Shaliba at Mpotwe's house?"

"Yes," the slave replied. "She told him you had come, and he wished to see you right away."

"Hmm," George murmured. "All right. Wait for us while we make ready." He switched to English as he turned to Ki-Gor. "Well, this's a little bettuh. Maybe Mpotwe c'n get us to see Dingazi soonuh—maybe tonight. Then we c'n be on our way in a couple days."

"You think we'll see Dingazi tonight?" Ki-Gor asked.

"We'll soon find out," George said, "when we see Mpotwe."

"Then we'll put on our lionskin robes," Ki-Gor said to Helene, "in case we go directly to the river with Mpotwe."

"Good idea," said George. "I think I'll put on my boots. Make me look kinda official."

Ten minutes later, the trio followed the slave girl into Mpotwe's house accompanied by one of the Masai warriors, the rest being left outside. The main room of the house was swarming with an excited, jabbering crowd of people. They immediately stopped talking and fell back to either side as George's huge figure loomed in the room.

Sitting on an elevated dais across the room was Mpotwe, a sleek, overfed young man with restless, glittering eyes. His glistening coal-black skin contrasted with the soft brown of Shaliba who sat on one side of him, and the wrinkled yellow of Mbama, the witch-doctor, on the other side.

The young prince stood up with a shout of greeting to George and Ki-Gor, and a curious look directed at Helene. Three slave girls came with mugs of native beer and offered them to the visitors.

"We did not expect to arrive at Dutawayo before you did," George said.

"I understand," Mpotwe said. "I was longer coming back than I expected. We journeyed far to the south on our return."

"I hope your trip was successful," George offered politely.

"Oh yes," Mpotwe said, grandly, "very successful. Everywhere we went, we met tribes who begged to be allowed to come under Dingazi's rule."

There was a boastful quality about the young man that aroused Ki-Gor's instinctive dislike. He stole a look at a group of warriors standing at one side, and a great suspicion began to creep into his mind. They were dressed in dark blue kilts, and wore blue feather headdresses exactly like the men who had tried to invade the intervale ten days before!

At the same time, Helene was watching Shaliba. Dingazi's daughter was very quiet, and Helene suspected that the beautiful girl was unhappy about something.

"We might still have got back before you came," Mpotwe was saying, "except that we were attacked by a powerful ju-ju on the way. But we beat him off with great heroism, and continued on our way. You will hear the whole story later," the prince concluded with a satisfied smile, "when I describe the exploit in full at the feast."

"Then we are to see Dingazi tonight?" George asked.

"Yes," nodded Mpotwe. "The king is in very poor health, but he has consented to appear at a great feast to celebrate my triumphal return. You, my friends, will be a part of the exercises."

Ki-Gor did not like the sound of that at all. He decided to keep a close watch on this paunchy young man. Then Mpotwe was addressing him.

"Tell me, Ki-Gor," he said, with a sleepy smile, "where is your kingdom? Does it lie to the north, east, south, or west?"

"Oh-oh!" George murmured under his breath, "make it good, Ki-

Gor."

"My kingdom, O Mpotwe," Ki-Gor replied, "is a strange kingdom. It is where I am. It moves with me. It is to the north, east, south and west."

MPOTWE FROWNED at this strange answer. Then he said:

"I don't understand. Later, perhaps, you can explain it to me. However, I have something very private to speak to you and Tembu George about. That is why I asked you to come here at this time. Will you step into the other room with me? Meanwhile, your queen will be entertained by Shaliba who some day is going to be my queen."

Ki-Gor glanced at George. The big Negro was staring at Shaliba. Then he looked at Mpotwe again and nodded.

"We will hear what you have to say," George said, and he and Ki-Gor followed the prince out of the crowded room.

"I will be perfectly frank with you," Mpotwe began, when the three were alone. "As you know, Dingazi is ill. I hope and pray he will recover with the aid of Mbama's ju-ju. But if he does not, then I will be King of the Kara-mzili. As King of Kara-mzili, I wish to be on the friendliest terms with such great people as the Masai and—" he threw a puzzled glance at Ki-Gor— "and Ki-Gor. There is no reason why we should not be allies. Together we should be very strong."

The prince paused to watch the effect of his words on Ki-Gor and George. The white face and the black one were impassive, and Mpotwe went on:

"My uncle, the great Dingazi, has announced that I shall succeed him when he dies, and that I shall marry his favorite daughter, Shaliba. This will happen soon. My uncle is failing rapidly. It would make his last days happy if I announced publicly tonight, that I had been acknowledged the King of the Masai."

George studied the prince in silence. Ki-Gor began to wish he had not left Helene in the other room, with the single Masai warrior to guard her.

"It will not be true, of course," Mpotwe went on rapidly, "and when I am King I will not hold you to it. We will be allies."

"You mean," said George slowly, "that you want me to take part in a lie? You want me to say that the presents I am bringing to Dingazi are not presents—but tribute?"

"Exactly," Mpotwe breathed, "that would be a most friendly gesture on your part. You can see what great prestige that would bring me, can't you?"

"Yes," George admitted, "I can see that."

"And when I become King, I will repay you handsomely for that friendly gesture."

George looked at Ki-Gor. The jungle man's face was expressionless.

"Well," said George, turning back to Mpotwe, "there are some difficulties in the way of your plan. I will have to think it over."

"There is no time to think it over," said Mpotwe, "can't you give me your answer now?"

"I'm afraid I can't," George said. "That is, I can't say now that I will do exactly what you want me to. I will think it over. But I can say this much: I will act in the friendliest manner possible toward you—and Shaliba."

"I see," said Mpotwe thoughtfully. "I suppose I will have to be satisfied with that. Anyway, think it over well. And remember, you will lose nothing by being friendly to the next King of the Karamzili."

The three returned to the main room of the house. Ki-Gor breathed easier as he saw Helene sitting beside Shaliba, chatting happily. However, the witch-doctor, Mbama, was nowhere to be seen.

In the distance, drums began to throb, and a buzz of excitement went over the room.

"It is time to go down to the river," Mpotwe proclaimed, and his warriors shouted gleefully. The prince called one of them to him and appointed him to guide the embassy from the Masai to the ceremonial grounds. The guide lighted a torch and a moment later led the way out of Mpotwe's house.

"Well," said Ki-Gor, in English, "that young man is as treacherous as he looks. What do you think of that proposal, George?"

"What proposal?" Helene wanted to know. Ki-Gor told her briefly.

"I don't like the sound of that," Helene remarked, "and there's something I want to tell you. Shaliba is supposed to marry him—"

"Yeah, we was told that," George said, gloomily.

"Well, she doesn't want to," Helene declared.

"No?" said George eagerly.

"SHE DIDN'T say so in so many words," Helene admitted, "but I could tell. She loathes the man. And here's something else. The king is in bad health, and from something Shaliba let drop, I think *she* thinks the witch-doctor isn't doing much to cure him."

"I wouldn't put *nuthin'* past that witch-doctor," George said.

"In fact," Helene went on, "he might even be poisoning the king, or something."

"My lord!" George exclaimed. "That don't put us in a very good position. What do you think, Ki-Gor?"

"I don't like it," Ki-Gor said. "The prince wants to be king as soon as he can, and he's got the witch-doctor on his side. We don't know yet how that Kara-mzili feel about it all, but I would guess that they still love the old king."

"I think tha's prob'ly correct," George affirmed.

"I wouldn't trust the prince," said Ki-Gor, "and so I would not do what he asks. Instead of ambassadors, free to come and go, we would be prisoners."

"Yeah," George said, "I guess we bettuh jest go along our original way. We'll be unduh the p'tection of the king, then, an' maybe we c'n get it ovuh to him whut his young nephew is drivin' at."

At this point in the conversation, the party came abreast of their guest house. George told the guide to stop while he went inside to get the presents for Dingazi.

The guide stood beside the doorway and held the torch low so that its light would be shed inside the house, and at the same time not set fire to the thatched roof. George started across the threshold, when he was halted by an exclamation from Ki-Gor.

"Wait!" the jungle man commanded and went down on his knees. He inspected the dust in front of the door by the flickering light of the torch. Then he stood up, grim-faced. Without a word, he took the torch away from the guide with his left hand, gripped his assegai half way down the haft, and stepped into the house.

A muffled chatter came from one corner from the bag containing the mongoose. Ki-Gor advanced two steps holding the torch low. Then he stopped dead with a quiet snarl.

A dark, rope-like object was stretched out on the middle of the floor. Ki-Gor reached out and touched it with the tip of his assegai. The object did not move.

It was a dead cobra.

Ki-Gor's mind worked swiftly. The mongoose was still in its bag. The mongoose had not killed the cobra. The cobra had been killed elsewhere, and then had been dragged along the ground to the guesthouse and left there.

The reason was only too obvious. The dead cobra's mate would follow the carefully laid trail and wreak a terrible vengeance on any humans it found nearby. That particular trait of cobras is well known.

George stared over Ki-Gor's shoulder and swore softly.

"So that's whut the witch-doctor was doin' when he lef' the prince's house so quiet. Only, he nevuh thought we'd be back so soon. He didn' think we-all 'ud come back ontil late tonight, and by that time the cobra's mate would be settin' heah, waitin' fer us."

"Yes," Ki-Gor breathed. "Well, we will just leave it there and go on. We simply won't come back tonight after the indaba down by the river. Quickly, pick up all our things and let's get out of here before the other cobra comes along."

"Yeah, leave it to me, Ki-Gor, and you get right outa heah. I got high boots on, so I'm safe. They cain't strike higher'n a man's knee, you know."

"We're all right, now," Ki-Gor said. "The other cobra hasn't come yet, or the mongoose would be making more noise."

Deftly, Ki-Gor swept the wriggling bag into a wide sleeve of his lion-skin robe, and then held the torch down for George to pick up the remaining objects. Then, quickly, the two men got out of the house.

Ki-Gor handed the torch back to the guide without a word, and the little party got under way again.

CHAPTER VIII

WHEN DINGAZI BUILT HIS capital city of Dutawayo, years before, he had set aside a broad area along the river below the town as a tribal meeting-place, and a parade-ground for his well-trained army. He had had a crude, wooden grandstand built right on the river's edge, facing away from the sluggish water and overlooking the open field. In the center of the grandstand was a magnificent throne of carved wood which Dingazi, of course, reserved for himself. On either side and below the throne, there was room on the grandstand to accommodate some three hundred people—his picked bodyguard, his household slaves, and his fifty-odd wives.

On the ground in front of the grandstand were two huge pits which served as fireplaces during public feasts. And between the two fire pits was a small platform raised ten feet off the ground. This platform had wooden steps running up one side, and was used as a sort of rostrum or speaker's platform for the benefit of anyone who wished to make a public address to the Kara-mzili or to Dingazi, himself.

Open ground stretched away in front of the grandstand and on both sides for yards and yards, and afforded room for thousands of Dingazi's subjects to gather and watch his public spectacles and hear him or his underlings speak.

The great field was already half-filled with excited, chattering Kara-mzili as Ki-Gor's little party followed the guide toward the grandstand. A hundred little fires flickered all over the flat expanse and illuminated the crescent-shaped rim of dark trees that bordered it. By far the greatest light was thrown from the two huge fires that flamed up from the pits in front of the grandstand.

As yet the grandstand was empty. But soon after the guide halted Ki-Gor beside the little rostrum, a great roar went up from the mass of blacks out on the field. A group of powerful blacks climbed up behind a battery of enormous war-drums ranged along the bottom of the grandstand, and began whaling away with padded drumsticks. The din was unbelievable.

In a little while, a procession could be seen winding along the river's edge from Dutawayo. In the lead was a band of strapping warriors, dressed in yellow-and-black striped kilts. They marched four abreast in slow rhythm, shaking their assegais above their heads and shouting fiercely. Directly behind them swayed an open litter, borne aloft on the shoulders of four huge, naked blacks. On the litter a man reclined—a vast, thick-shouldered, pot-bellied man, naked to the waist.

It was Dingazi.

The Kara-mzili yelled ecstatically as the royal procession slowly made its way to the foot of the grandstand. Alongside the litter walked Mpotwe, eyes gleaming, and Shaliba. Immediately behind the litter came more striped kilted bodyguards, and after them streamed a column of women—Dingazi's wives and slaves.

The litter was set down gently in front of the grandstand—not fifty feet away from Helene's fascinated eyes—and the old king slowly and with apparent difficulty got off and stood swaying on his thick legs.

He was a monumental man, prodigiously tall and broad. He was not so fat as he was massive. And while his movements were deliberate he still gave the impression of tremendous vigor, and his great, grizzled head was carried proudly high.

The war-drums banged and the Kara-mzili cheered as Dingazi slowly climbed up to his throne. After he was seated, Mpotwe and Shaliba took seats at his feet. The bodyguard ranged themselves on all sides of him, and the rest of the grandstand was quickly occupied by a swarming, shrilling crowd of wives and slaves.

The throbbing of the drums mounted higher and fiercer until a sudden quick wave of the old man's hand cut off the sound like a knife. Another quick sign and a subdued but gleeful hubbub went over the crowd as they jostled back and away from the grandstand to leave a large open space far out beyond the speaker's rostrum. Dingazi's second gesture was evidently a sign that the festivities should commence. The old man leaned his head wearily to one side, and Mpotwe came down from the grandstand and started for the rostrum.

He paused on his way beside George.

"WHAT IS your answer?" he murmured. "Shall I announce it?"

"I tell you," George said, with his most charming smile, "why don't you let me announce it? It might have more effect in one way—it would make you seem so modest."

Mpotwe's eyes glittered with excitement, and he nodded his head vigorously.

"Good, good!" he said. "Excellent idea! You won't regret this night, I promise you!"

As the fat young prince went on and mounted the steps to the platform, George murmured in Ki-Gor's ear:

"I *hope* we don't regret this night. But, I'm afraid young Mpotwe is goin' to get a surprise, when he heahs jest whut I announce."

Then Mpotwe began to speak in a high, clear voice.

"O Lord of the Kara-mzili! O Protector of the Race! O Mighty Hunter! O Peerless Warrior, terrible in battle! O Emperor of the World! Ruler of the Universe! Listen to the words of your unworthy servant!"

Mpotwe paused dramatically, and Dingazi closed his eyes and nodded wearily.

"I have just returned," said Mpotwe, "from a great mission—which had for its purpose the spreading of the glorious name of Dingazi. And here is the tale I have to tell of that expedition."

Dingazi's nephew had a gift of oratory, and he held the thousands of Kara-mzili spellbound as he told of the rivers crossed, the mountains climbed, the deserts skirted, the jungles penetrated, the miles traveled by his expedition. He announced the names of tribe after tribe who, he said, came and begged to be annexed to the kingdom of Dingazi.

During this phase of his oration, he hesitated momentarily and glanced down at George. As George smiled ironically, he did not add the name of the Masai to that number.

The most thrilling story of all, however, was reserved until the end of his long speech. And during this story, Ki-Gor's face relaxed a little, and he even allowed a crooked smile to show.

On the way home, Mpotwe said, the party ran into a misfortune which, had it happened to any but the mighty Kara-mzili, would have resulted in the annihilation of the party.

They were attacked, Mpotwe said in awesome tones, by *ten thousand ju-ju lions!*

A low moan of horror went over the crowd as Mpotwe said these words. Involuntarily, the Kara-mzili huddled closer to their fires as Mpotwe described the onslaught of these fearful creatures.

"One minute," he said, "we were starting peacefully up a little donga toward a notch in a mountain range. The next minute they attacked—without warning!"

He paused dramatically.

"Each lion," he declared, "was bigger than an elephant—with wings twice as big as eagles—and *two heads,* spitting flame and destruction! And there were *ten thousand* of these monsters!"

The Kara-mzili shivered deliciously.

"But the worst of all," Mpotwe said in sinking tones, "was the frightful roaring they made. Worse than ten times ten thousand thunder storms. It was indescribable."

Mpotwe paused again.

"They caught us unawares—being ju-ju," he picked up again. "And before we could organize our defense, two dozen of our brave fellows were struck down. The miracle of it was that any of us lived to tell the tale at all. Here we were caught in a donga, beset on all sides by these terrifying creatures."

Mpotwe shook his head and paused. Then he looked around with a fierce light in his eyes.

"What saved us?" he demanded. "I'll tell you! Kara-mzili bravery! Kara-mzili discipline! Kara-mzili might! A handful of us beat off the most formidable supernatural attack ever known in the history of the world. We slaughtered them by the hundreds. I, myself, slew eleven of the loathsome beasts with my own hand, and we drove them off. We lost thirty-two brave men that dreadful day, but we left the field victors!"

A yell of admiration went up on all sides. Mpotwe smiled and waved a hand. The war-drums spoke up, and from the far side of the crowd came a column of blue-kilted warriors, four abreast. They were the veterans of Mpotwe's expedition. They marched straight for the speaker's rostrum, keeping fine order.

AT THE rear of the column came a large disorderly band of stragglers, weeping and shaking their hands over their heads. When the warriors had all marched in and lined up in front of the grandstand, Mpotwe waved the stragglers forward and lifted his hand for silence.

"The prisoners, O Dingazi!" he shouted. "Four from each of the new subject tribes! Three out of each four to be slaves! The fourth—for the crocodiles!"

Ki-Gor grunted and glared up at Mpotwe, as the field rang with wild yells. Dingazi waved a sleepy hand, and warriors leaped among the prisoners and dragged screaming, struggling victims down past the grandstand toward the river's edge.

Helene suddenly felt sick all over when she realized what was happening. One by one, twenty-two miserable humans were thrown off the river bank into the black, crocodile-infested water.

Ki-Gor and George stared distastefully at the fearful spectacle. The Masai looked on contemptuously. Primitive savages though the Masai were, they found nothing to approve in such needless cruelty.

But the Kara-mzili went into hysterical raptures. A solid wall of sound beat against the eardrums of the shocked embassy. George placed his mouth next to Ki-Gor's ear and shouted to be heard over the din.

"I got you-all right into the middle of a mess of bad actors," said George, "an' I'll nevuh fo'give musself."

"I'm not afraid," Ki-Gor replied.

"Well, Lawd help us if they evuh turn on us," said George. "I guess we jest got to trust ol' Dingazi, an' keep on the good side of him."

It seemed as if the sadistic appetite of the Kara-mzili would never be satisfied. But eventually, Dingazi himself stopped it by getting to his feet and waving an arm peremptorily. The crowd immediately quieted down. Up on the rostrum, Mpotwe raised both arms petitioningly.

"Are you ready for the war dance, O Dingazi?" he cried.

"Not now," the king replied in a harsh, strong voice. "First—the ambassadors."

"But—" Mpotwe stammered uneasily.

"The ambassadors!" Dingazi roared.

Mpotwe descended from the platform and beckoned to George. As the giant Negro strode up to him, the prince said:

"Explain immediately that you are not ambassadors, but royal prisoners."

Mpotwe's crafty eyes were suddenly anxious. George did not reply, but merely smiled inscrutably as he climbed the steps to the platform. His boots clicked arrogantly on the rough planks. He waited a moment for the crowd to become completely still, then his rich bass voice rose on the air.

"O Lord of the Kara-mzili! Mighty Hunter! Peerless Warrior! Emperor of the World! Ruler of the Universe! My first words to you shall be spoken by the rare and precious gifts I have brought you. My royal retainers will bring them to you now—with your permission."

Dingazi, still standing on his feet, nodded approval. George uttered a command, and three of the Masai started for the grandstand. Mpotwe's blue kilts were massed across their path, and made no effort to clear a way. The Masai trio, however, ignored their presence and marched unswervingly at them.

Dingazi's eyes gleamed with admiration, and just as the leading Masai would have crashed into the motionless Kara-mzili warriors, the old king rasped a command. Hastily, Mpotwe's warriors fell away on both sides, and the three Masai stalked insolently onward through the path they cleared.

The crowd watched with bated breath as the three mounted to Dingazi's throne.

"The first gift, O Dingazi," George announced. "A magic robe. Wear it during the heaviest rainstorm and not a drop of water will touch your skin!"

A gasp of admiration went up from all sides. Dingazi promptly put on the raincoat and looked around with a pleased grin.

"The second gift," said George. "The magic tick-tock box. It measures the movement of the sun. And when the sun is directly overhead—it will ring a bell."

Dingazi stared incredulously at the alarm-clock.

"ONLY A king may touch it with safety," George went on. "Anyone else will sicken and die. Tomorrow, when the sun is directly overhead, you will hear its bell."

Dingazi set the clock aside gingerly.

"The last gift, O King, is your second self. You have seen your second self before, often. But he always hides in the river. I have brought him away from the river and imprisoned him in that frame. Now, you may see him any time you wish by picking up that frame and gazing at it."

Dingazi looked into the mirror quickly, and an expression of rapturous joy stole over his features. George decided to strike while the iron was hot.

"These precious gifts, O Dingazi, I have brought you as tokens of esteem and friendship from the Blood-drinkers of the North, the Embattled Giants, the Invincible, All-Conquering Masai!"

It was not the speech of a prisoner, or a subject. It was the speech of an ambassador.

George shot a glance down at Mpotwe. The prince's fat face was twisted with rage, and he turned and ran toward the grandstand.

"The war dance, O Dingazi!" Mpotwe cried. "The war dance, in honor of the ambassadors!"

Dingazi, absorbed in his own reflection in the mirror, nodded absently. Instantly, the war drums went savagely into action. A shrill concerted yell went up, and Mpotwe's blue kilts streamed away from their post below the grandstand, out past the rostrum to the open space beyond.

Mpotwe went with them, shrieking incoherently, and in a moment his warriors had formed into ten ranks behind him, a hundred men wide. Then, as the drums throbbed their intricate rhythms, the warriors of Mpotwe performed intricate steps and movements in unison.

They danced backward four steps, then rushed forward ten steps, and leaped high in the air. Then they repeated the routine. Each rush brought them closer to the rostrum, and the group of Masai around Ki-Gor and Helene.

George knew perfectly well what Mpotwe's intentions were. The dance was intended to work up the blood-lust of his warriors, to the point where they would keep on rushing forward, fall on the embassy and slaughter them before Dingazi could interfere. In fact, Dingazi would be powerless to interfere, because the entire tribe would become infected with the lust to kill.

Something had to be done.

George cupped his hands toward the grandstand and shouted at Dingazi at the top of his voice. The king heard that Bull of Bashan voice topping the din, and looked up angrily.

George threw up his arms in a dramatic gesture and—began to dance himself!

There were cries of astonishment from the crowd, and the noise of the drums died away. In a moment, the entire tribe of Kara-mzili, from the monarch down, stood in blank amazement and dead silence as George Spelvin of Cincinnati embarked on an American vaudeville tap-dance routine.

CHAPTER IX

IN ALL THAT VAST crowd, only Helene had ever seen that kind of dancing before, and she alone guessed at George's intentions.

The floor of the platform was rough, and there was no music to accompany him, but George did a pretty fair imitation of Bill Robinson. His taps were blurred, and he could only remember a few simple steps, but he tripped around the creaking platform and chuckled gaily. The astounded savages listened eagerly to merry rhythms that clicked off his tap-plates.

No entertainer ever worked harder. The one thing George counted on was the rhythm—the common heritage of all Africans. And he was not wrong.

The first of the Kara-mzili to succumb was Dingazi, himself.

"Hai!" shouted the monarch, with a delighted grin, and his subjects followed suit. Then George knew that he had won. He had broken the spell of the war dance, and substituted a new and gentler spell.

Mpotwe was foiled. Dingazi waved imperiously, when George finished and climbed down the steps. The entire party was beckoned up to sit beside the king.

MPOTWE GLARED malevolently at George as he went past. The witch-doctor, Mbama, was standing beside the prince.

The embassy had just reached the battery of war drums at the foot of the grandstand on their way to the throne, when Mpotwe ran forward, shouting:

"Dingazi! Dingazi! There are two ambassadors! But you have heard only one! What about the white one? Will he not address you? Has he no gift?"

Ki-Gor's face broke into an impatient frown. It was a lapse of judgment on his part and he knew it—not making his speech to Dingazi at once. He thrust the cylinder containing the Uruculi feathers into Helene's hands.

"You give it to him. I will run back to the platform and make my speech."

Hurriedly, Ki-Gor pushed through the crowd of Kara-mzili warriors that swarmed between him and the rostrum. He was vexed at himself for not keeping a cooler head. He had to keep his left arm crooked, because the mongoose was still nestled in the wide sleeve. He had forgotten to dispose of the little animal.

A moment later, Ki-Gor was very glad he had not given up the mongoose. Because Mpotwe, foiled once, played his trump card.

Before Ki-Gor could reach the rostrum, the witch-doctor had scurried up the steps carrying a covered, round basket. As he reached the top step, his shrill falsetto cut the air.

"Mbama speaks! Mbama warns! Beware! Beware!"

Instantly Ki-Gor realized that his haste had put him in a serious predicament. He had not the slightest doubt that the witch-doctor was going to denounce him. And here he was—separated from Helene and George and the Masai by hundreds of Mpotwe's own warriors. He must get to the platform!

"Beware of the white witch!" Mbama was screaming. "He has cast a hideous spell on Dingazi—"

That was all Mbama had time to say. The witch-doctor saw Ki-Gor flashing toward the rostrum. With a shriek, he dropped the basket on the platform, and dashed down the steps. He made it to the ground just in time to elude Ki-Gor's clutching fingers. Then a horde of warriors swept down on Ki-Gor, and there was nowhere to go but—up the steps.

The jungle man whisked upward. He knew perfectly well what he was going to find on the platform, and his eyes very shortly verified his judgment.

The lid had fallen off the basket, and a huge cobra reared up, hooded and swaying, from it.

Ki-Gor's right hand plunged into his left sleeve and shook out the mongoose. The little gray animal landed lightly on its feet and crouched for a moment on the platform, red eyes blinking.

The cobra and the mongoose saw each other at the same instant, and simultaneously, the age-old enemies went into action. The mongoose flew straight at the hooded serpent. The cobra struck furiously. But the mongoose whipped aside and the venomous fangs missed their mark by a hair. The cobra's head hit the platform with a thud, and before it could recover itself, the mongoose was upon it. The little creature sprang lightning-fast on the back of the hood. Its ferocious teeth fastened on the snake's neck at the base of its narrow skull.

There was a brief thrashing around, as the cobra whipped its coils around the mongoose. But in a minute it was all over. The sharp teeth quickly gnawed through the snake's spinal column, and the coils relaxed.

Ki-Gor bent over, picked up the cobra by the tail, and held it up.

A superstitious moan went up from the crowd. It was broken by a shriek from Mbama. The witch-doctor was tumbling up the grandstand toward the throne.

"He's a witch! A witch!" the witch-doctor screamed. "Kill him! Throw him to the crocodiles, before he kills Dingazi!"

A confused mumbling rose on all sides, and Ki-Gor's heart sank. The worst had come.

WHEN A witch-doctor denounced a victim, no one—not even Dingazi, in this instance—could save him. Ki-Gor's first concern was for the safety of Helene and George. For the moment, they were in Dingazi's favor.

"Ki-Gor!"

It was George's voice topping the confused murmur of the crowd.

"Hold on, Ki-Gor! We're comin' to get you!"

"No, George, no!" Ki-Gor shouted excitedly. "Stay where you are—behind the war drums!"

A desperate plan was forming in Ki-Gor's mind.

"Stay there, George," he repeated. "If you come out, you haven't got a chance. If you stay behind the drums, you can hold off an attack for a little while."

"But we can't let 'em throw you to the crocodiles!" George shouted.

"You can't stop them," Ki-Gor shouted back. "Trust me to get out of it somehow. I'll come back—Helene, get the lion-roar ready—"

Mpotwe's warriors were clambering up onto the platform now. Ki-Gor whirled and shouted at them:

"Stand back! I am a witch! I will go to the crocodile pool by myself. You may follow me and watch me. But do not touch me! Whoever dares to touch me, I will instantly change him into a jungle-mouse!"

The warriors hesitated. Ki-Gor strode across the platform straight at them. They quailed under his stern gaze and started to back down the steps.

Ki-Gor followed them down. When he reached the ground, he walked unmolested a few steps toward the grandstand. A tiny hope began to flicker in his breast. If he could frighten the warriors enough to keep them from touching him, he might be able to go straight back to his party, unharmed.

The hope was short-lived, however.

Mpotwe came pushing his way through the massed warriors.

"Up spears!" he barked.

The ring of Kara-mzili around Ki-Gor lifted their spears up and poised them over their shoulders, ready to throw. Ki-Gor bowed his head. Resistance would be futile.

He lifted his head and looked over the plumes of the encircling warriors toward the grandstand. In the general excitement, the fires had been left untended, and it was hard to see much in the dim light. At the foot of the grandstand, he could make out the white robes of the Masai, towering above the drums. Above them, the striped kilts of Dingazi's bodyguard clustered around the throne. Ki-Gor could not see the witch-doctor, but he could hear his incessant yelping—inciting the Kara-mzili to kill. From the crowd, there came a steadily increasing roar.

Ki-Gor threw back his head and yelled.

"Helene! I'm coming back!"

Then he turned and started toward the river.

A howl of triumph went up from the warriors and was taken up all over the field. The savage call for blood followed Ki-Gor all the way to the river's edge, ringing hideously in his ears.

But hope was not dead in Ki-Gor's heart. In all the furious din about him, he could not hear the thump of the drums! Had the Masai ousted the drummers and dug in behind the protecting rampart of the huge tom-toms?

It was pitch dark by the edge of the river. As Ki-Gor and the frenzied warriors drew nearer to it, the light shed by a single torch carried by one of the Kara-mzili could do little to dispel the gloom. The torchbearer was pushed up behind Ki-Gor, and then the jungle man could see the wavering flame reflected on the slick, oily surface of the river. Huge, ghastly shadows danced beyond as the torch sputtered and smoked. A faint odor of corruption hung on the air. Ki-Gor's nose crinkled in disgust, and he searched the dimly lighted surface of the river with his eyes. He could see no crocodiles, but he knew they were there, lurking in the greasy, black depths.

Mpotwe's warriors, by now, had reached the peak of their frenzy. Yelling insanely, they closed in behind Ki-Gor, stabbing at him with their spears.

HE TURNED and faced them, blue eyes flashing and teeth bared. Slowly he retreated three steps, until he stood on the very brink of the low bank.

His hands crept up to the low collar of the lionskin robe. Then, like a flash, he shucked off the robe.

Before the raving Kara-mzili knew what was happening, Ki-Gor had flung the robe straight into the faces of the nearest warriors. With a savage snarl, the jungle man leaped at the torchbearer, snatched the burning brand out of his hand, and flung it out into the river.

And before the infuriated blacks could recover their balance, Ki-Gor seized the miserable torchbearer by both wrists, and swung him off his feet. At the same moment, the torch hit the water with a hiss and immediately went out, plunging the whole scene into darkness.

The first row of Kara-mzili screamed with rage and stabbed out blindly. But Ki-Gor swung the body of the squealing torchbearer in a wide arc, knocking down spears and spearmen alike. At the end of the arc, Ki-Gor released his hold, and the torchbearer went spinning out over the river.

He landed with a prodigious splash in an upstream direction. At the same moment, Ki-Gor hit the water in a long, shallow dive—in a downstream direction. His arms were flailing and his legs thrashing as he touched the water and an unspoken prayer bubbled at his lips.

Then, over the howling bedlam back on the bank, he heard a hideous shriek cut the black night. Ki-Gor took hope. At least the crocodiles had discovered the torchbearer first. There was a chance, now, that they would all move upstream in the direction of the kill.

Ki-Gor pumped arms and legs harder than ever. In this desperate situation, every second he lived increased his chances of pulling out with a whole skin. He had to put a certain distance between himself and the enraged Kara-mzili, before he dared go ashore. At the same time, as far as he knew, a scaly monster might that very minute be pursuing him through that fearful black water. Ki-Gor redoubled his pace.

A hundred thoughts went boiling through his brain as he churned through the water. Would he escape being overhauled by a crocodile? If he got ashore safely, could he find Marmo? Could George and the ten Masai protect Helen until he got back? Had he gone far enough downstream yet to risk turning shoreward?

The sprint was finally beginning to tell on his arms, and legs, and lungs. He shot both arms forward, held his legs still, and coasted for a moment. The maniacal shouts of the Kara-mzili sounded clear and still very close. He wondered if they were following him along the bank.

ROLLING GENTLY over on his back, he was surprised to see how far he had actually traveled. A second torchbearer had evidently joined the group of warriors on the bank. They were, Ki-Gor judged, a good two hundred yards away. The surface of the water served as a sounding board, making their howls sound deceptively close.

Ki-Gor peered around him to try and orient himself. It was literally pitch black. He could see nothing except the distant torch and its dancing reflection in the ripples he had stirred in the oily water. Above him there were no stars; evidently the sky was heavily overcast. He rolled back onto his stomach again and began to swim quietly.

A sudden thrill went shooting up his spine.

A faint musical ripple had sounded right beside him. A crocodile? Ki-Gor held his breath.

Again there was the sound. This time it was in front of him. It sounded almost like a large drop of water. There it was again! Right behind him!

Ki-Gor's cupped hands dug the water. His legs galvanized into action. He shot forward. Ki-Gor put everything he had into this second sprint, teeth clenched, waiting for the moment when he would feel huge jaws clamp over his beating legs.

After a few seconds, he decided to swing to his right and head directly for the bank. But just as he began to turn, his hand plunging down at the end of a stroke, scraped on something rough below him.

He stifled a yell and bulled forward through the water, eyes shut. Again his hand scraped—both of them—and then his knees. For a paralyzing moment, Ki-Gor did not realize that he was aground in the darkness. Then his heart leaped as he recognized finally that he was not scraping a crocodile's back, but a rock.

He rose swiftly and found that he was in water less than knee deep. The ripples sounded again, but now Ki-Gor knew they were caused by raindrops.

He cocked an ear and heard them falling on leaves in front of him. He had blundered ashore in the darkness.

Now! If it was possible, he had to locate, somewhere in this sooty blackness, an elephant named Marmo. He put two fingers in his mouth and blasted a shrill whistle.

Head bent, he stood in silence in the increasing rain, waiting for an answering trumpet-call. From upstream came the confused roar of the Kara-mzili. Ki-Gor's heart tightened as he thought of Helene.

Marmo! Where are you?

Again he whistled. The rain came down harder, drowning out the insane baying of the blacks.

Ki-Gor listened a long moment and sighed. There was no answer from Marmo.

The jungle man stepped out of the water, hands extended, and pushed his way blindly through the thick brush along the bank.

CHAPTER X

AS SOON AS KI-GOR thrust the container of Uruculi feathers into her hands and started back toward the rostrum, Helene knew he had made a mistake. But before she could summon her voice, a wave of Kara-mzili warriors had closed in between her and his retreating back. He was separated from her and George and the Masai now, and it was a tactical error. No matter how strong he was or how fierce the Masai, they could never cut their way to each other through such overwhelming masses of Bantu.

George saw it, too, but like Helene he saw it too late.

"My Lawd, Miz Helene, he shouldna done that. Mpotwe goin' to catch him sure!"

"Oh, George, I know!" said Helene agitatedly. "What'll we do?"

"Nothin' we *kin* do," said George tightly. "If we tried to go get him, we'd jest all of us get killed."

Helene fought down a mounting panic within herself.

"Oh, George!" she said. "He'll find a way out. He's got to! He always has, before. He's got to this time! We must have faith in him, George! Because—because he's *Ki-Gor!*"

The events that followed alternately justified Helene's faith, and then dashed it to earth. When the witch-doctor screamed his curse from the grandstand, and George had been ready to order the suicidal sortie to the rostrum, she was proud that Ki-Gor commanded him not to. She did not know how Ki-Gor was going to escape, but she somehow had faith.

A little later, her faith in Ki-Gor's invincibility was sorely strained. When he shouted to her that he would come back and then walked toward the crocodile-pool at the points of the Kara-mzili spears, she sank down behind a great war drum and rocked back and forth with closed eyes and clenched fists.

Then came the fiendish yells of Mpotwe's men. It could mean only one thing. But Helene refused to believe the evidence of her ears.

"No! George, no!" She scrambled to her feet, face contorted. "I have faith! He's escaped—somehow!"

The expression of stunned horror on George's face indicated that his faith was not quite so strong as Helene's. Mechanically, he turned to the impassive, gigantic Masai.

"They will probably attack us now," he announced to them. "You will fight like Masai, I know. But none of you must leave the shelter of the drums. Stay together and we may come out of this."

Helene's eyes fell on the little bow at her feet and she remembered with a start that she had a part to play. With trembling fingers, she unfastened the rosined cord that was tied around her middle. She held out the end with the big wad of tree-gum.

"George," she said, and her voice was once again strong, "will you press this gum as hard as you can on the head of this drum?"

"Why, whut you got theah, Miz Helene?"

"You'll see. Quickly, George—and I guess you'd better tip the drum over on its side, so that I can hold the cord straight out from it."

Wonderingly, the great Negro did as Helene asked. But there was no time for more questions. A great uproar had broken out in the grandstand above.

Dingazi, Lord of the Kara-mzili and Emperor of the World, was suddenly asserting himself.

Peering up through the gloomy light shed by the dying fires, George could barely make out the grotesque figure of the witch-doctor cowering backwards from the throne.

"It makes no difference that he was a witch!" Dingazi roared at his medicine-man. "He was an ambassador to my Court and his life was my affair! You broke the Law by inciting the warriors to kill him! How dare you come now and propose that I kill these others! How dare you!"

"Dingazi! Dingazi!" Mbama wailed. "You know not what you say! To talk to Mbama thus—you are bewitched!"

"If I am bewitched," Dingazi retorted, "it is because your ju-ju is not strong enough to protect me. But I am beginning to think, Mbama, that I am not bewitched so much as—*betrayed!*"

FOR A moment, the witch-doctor seemed too shocked to answer, but could only retreat farther and farther from the throne.

"Let it be understood," Dingazi thundered, "that these people down here are under my protection!"

George gripped Helene's shoulder.

"Amen!" he muttered. "Maybe we-all got a chance to pull out of this, at that!"

"How's that?" Helene whispered. "What were they saying?"

George translated for her. But in the middle of it, Mbama's hideous cackle broke in. The witch-doctor had crept down the grandstand past the ranks of the king's bodyguard.

"So be it!" shrilled the witch-doctor. "So be it, O Dingazi! But remember! Mbama's ju-ju is all-powerful!"

With that, the fantastic little man scrambled away out onto the field.

George raised his voice toward the throne. "All thanks, O Dingazi," he said, "for your protection!"

"You have it!" snapped the old king. "It is the Law. But all is not well among the Kara-mzili. I have just been learning some things from my daughter, Shaliba, things about my witch-doctor and my nephew which I can hardly believe. Shaliba has told me, too, that you refused to plot with Mpotwe. You have thus doubly earned my protection."

Just then, a great triumphant yell went up from the river bank beyond the end of the grandstand. The thousands of Kara-mzili out on the field fell silent, as Mpotwe and his men came marching back from the crocodile pool, chanting exultantly.

"The witch is dead! The white witch is dead! He has gone to feed the crocodiles! The witch is dead!"

Helene tried to shake off the cold horror that was stealing over her. George went murmuring among the Masai.

"No! No!" Helene whispered to herself. "I won't believe it!"

A drop of rain fell on her clenched fist.

The only sounds on the field now came from the chanting column of men. Through the dim half-light shed by the dying fires, they could be seen marching out in front of the grandstand. Suddenly the chanting ceased and Mpotwe's high, clear voice rose out of the gloom.

"O great Dingazi! Look with pride on your servants! We have delivered you from the white witch who impudently cast a spell over you! No longer can he harm you! We threw him into the river and lo! even while his body was in midair, a great crocodile came halfway out of the water and received him in his jaws!"

There was an ominous silence from the throne. Mpotwe took a breath and went on.

"These others who were with the witch, O Dingazi, do not let them fool you! They are traveling under false colors, telling you they come as ambassadors from the Masai! That is a gross lie! They are no ambassadors—they are prisoners! The Masai recognized me as their king, and appointed these miserable felons to come direct, bearing tribute! They are entitled to no safe-conduct whatsoever! They are forsworn criminals! To the crocodiles with them, O Dingazi!"

A murmur went over the assembled Kara-mzili as their insatiable blood-lust began to rise again. George gripped his huge Masai spear. He knew now that it was inevitable that his little band would be attacked. And he saw little chance of standing off the Kara-mzili hordes for very long. His only consolation was that Helene could not understand Mpotwe when he described the fate of Ki-Gor. Perhaps it was just as well all around, the giant Negro reflected, that they be attacked and killed. He could not see how Ki-Gor could possibly be still alive. And Ki-Gor was his dearest friend.

The muttering of the Kara-mzili swelled and then suddenly cut off, as the voice of their king thundered at them from the throne.

"Silence! This is Dingazi speaking to you. Know then, that my nephew, Mpotwe, whom I selected to be my heir, has broken the Law! He has killed an ambassador who was entitled to my guarantee of safety. He has lied to me about Tembu George and the Masai, attempting to make me break the Law, too. That I will not! Tembu George spoke as an emissary of a free and powerful people on friendly terms with us. His life, and the lives of those with him, are sacred! Whoever does them harm shall feel the consequences of my might."

"Dingazi! Dingazi!" It was Mpotwe. "What words are these—"

"As for you, Mpotwe!" Dingazi roared. "You are no longer my heir! You are a forsworn criminal yourself, and you have until dawn to get away from Dutawayo!"

"BEWITCHED! BEWITCHED!" screamed Mbama. "Close your ears, O People, and avert your faces! Our Lord Dingazi is grievously enchanted! There is a fearful ju-ju still at large! It can only be these fearful Masai—"

"Soldiers!" Dingazi broke in. "Seize that pestilential priest! I hereby command all my soldiers except my bodyguards to surround and take the false witch-doctor, Mbama!"

"Heed him not! Heed him not!" shrieked Mbama. "He knows not what he is saying! He is not responsible! Soldiers! Follow your rightful commander—Mpotwe!"

The close-packed masses on the field murmured in bewilderment as the king and the chief witch-doctor fought each other for supreme authority. It was a puzzling, frightening situation. They feared and loved Dingazi—they feared and hated Mbama.

Mpotwe suddenly seized the initiative.

"Follow me!" he shouted to his own men. "We must save our king from the Masai demons! Fall on them! Kill! Kill!"

"This is rebellion!" Dingazi shouted. "Guards! Down beside the Masai and protect their flanks—"

The rest of his commands were drowned out by the war cry of Mpotwe's *impi* charging between the two smoldering fire-pits.

"Stay behind the drums, O Masai!" George shouted. "And make every spear-thrust count!"

Mpotwe's men came rushing forward with all the bravery and ferocity that has characterized the Zulus since the ancient glory of King Chaka. They threw themselves recklessly against the rampart of war drums, hacking and stabbing with their short assegais.

But these men of Mpotwe were used to quick, cheap victories, against foes who dreaded the name of Kara-mzili. This handful of Masai could not possibly stand up to them, they thought. One headlong charge and it would all be over.

There were only ten Masai, and a gigantic American Negro. But this handful was not afraid of the name of Kara-mzili. They were not afraid of anything.

As the first rank of yelling Kara-mzili reached the line of war drums, the long Masai spears licked out. The prodigious three-foot blades cut Mpotwe's men down like butter. The second rank pressed on. Their short, stabbing assegais could not reach past the fearful Masai spears.

In thirty seconds, the Masai cut down twice their number.

The survivors recoiled momentarily. The onset was slowed down.

"Hai!" cried the Masai gleefully. This was their idea of true sport. They were never quite so happy as when they were engaged in bloody combat.

George ran alertly to the left flank of the line of drums. As he feared, a dozen or more of Mpotwe's men were rushing around to take the defenders in the rear.

He struck down the first man, and saw the rest pause. Then a group of light-colored kilts swarmed up beside him. Dingazi's bodyguards had remained loyal!

They poured down off the grandstand to each end of the line of drums and drove Mpotwe's men back in disorder.

Kara-mzili was fighting Kara-mzili!

The rain, which had been coming down intermittently for some time, now began to pour down in earnest. The untended fires all over the field hissed and sputtered and sent up ghostly columns of steam.

"By golly, Miz Helene!" George cried delightedly. "We beat 'em off! We truly did!"

But George's triumph was premature. A wall of enraged warriors erupted from the darkness. Five and six at a time they leaped up on the drums.

Again the deadly Masai spears did murderous work. The men of

Mpotwe sobbed with rage, as all along the line, their assegais were outreached.

"Blood-Drinkers of the North!" shouted George. "Make your spears drink blood!"

The Masai responded with a cascade of delighted shouts and hurled the attackers back for the second time.

"Well done! Splendid, Masai!" George roared.

But even as he spoke, Mpotwe's *impi* hurled themselves at the drums once again. Rage at their humiliation lent strength to the attackers. They poured and swarmed over the drums in such numbers, that a few inevitably got past the thin line of defenders.

BUT AGAIN Dingazi's bodyguards came to the rescue. A scant dozen cut in from the flanks and cut down those attackers who had broken through, before they could do any damage.

This was the most determined assault of the battle. Mpotwe's blue-kilts came on and on, to be cut down by the untiring spears of the Masai. Eventually, it was more than flesh and blood could endure. The Masai, protected up to their chests by the war drums, had the added advantage of longer spears.

With shrieks of agony and terror, Mpotwe's men broke backward from the holocaust at the drums and turned to get away from those terrible spears.

A joyous yell went up from the Masai warriors.

"They run! The miserable dogs are running! After them! Don't let them escape!"

"No! No!" George shouted. "Don't run after them! Stay behind the drums!"

But the Masai were already vaulting up on to the tops of the drums. The battle-madness was on them, and they could not resist. George clutched at one lean ankle going over the rampart.

"Nay! Let me go, Tembu George!" the warrior cried. "We've got them on the run!"

He wrenched himself free and jumped off to the other side with a joyous whoop.

"Oh, my Lawd, Miz Helene!" George groaned. "Them fools! We were winnin'! We were safe! But, now they'll jest get out theah in the dahk, an' be killed off! Miz Helene, I guess this is the end."

Helene, crouched beside her drum, the rosined cord held ready in one hand and the little bow in the other, drew a deep shuddering breath.

"I'm ready, George," she said, in a dead voice. "Up till now I clung to the hope that—that Ki-Gor would come back. But now—I'm afraid, George—I'm afraid he's not coming back. Ki-Gor is dead, and I'm ready to die, too."

At that moment, there came a sound above the din of battle. Helene and George both jumped and stared. Then came the sound, again!

It was an elephant trumpeting.

"Marmo!" they both cried together.

The noise of the battle hushed.

"Is—is—Ki-Gor—with him?"

Helene whispered the question, hardly daring to hope.

Suddenly a low moan of horror swept over the great field. At the same instant, Helene saw the torch blazing high in the air. It was in Ki-Gor's hand and he was standing on Marmo's back.

"The witch!" cried the Kara-mzili. "Risen from the dead! Ju-ju—ju-ju—most deadly!"

Helene's brain clicked, and she went into action. Her left hand drew the rosined cord taut. Her right hand poised the little bow across it at right angles. Then she drew the bow hard across the cord.

A frightful, ear-shattering roar filled the air, rasping and resonant.

"The ju-ju lions!" Ki-Gor shouted at the top of his voice. "Flee, Kara-mzili! Flee before you are slaughtered by the ten thousand ju-ju lions!"

Again Helene drew the bow, and again the hideous, mangling roar sounded.

The Kara-mzili broke into complete and utter panic.

The men of Mpotwe's *impi* had heard that roar before. At that time, it had been the signal for sudden, swift and mysterious death. They bolted now.

The rest of the Kara-mzili, having heard Mpotwe's dramatic and exaggerated account of the ju-ju lions, caught the infection of panic instantly. Almost all the fires had been put out by the rain. They could see nothing. But that terrifying, insufferable noise rang in their ears from all directions.

And in the center of the field, the ju-ju elephant stalked toward the grandstand, with the ghost of the witch brandishing a torch.

It was too much.

Dreadful gurgling shrieks bubbled from thousands of lips, and inside of ten minutes the field was empty.

THE ONLY people left were Mpotwe's dead and wounded around the rampart of drums, two slightly wounded Masai behind the drums, and eight more Masai out on the field. They were unhurt but badly scared, and were stretched out on the ground under their shields.

And up on the grandstand, Dingazi, Lord of the Kara-mzili, sat on his throne. He was twitching with fright, but he had stayed to await whatever fate had in store for him. His sole companion was his favorite daughter, Shaliba.

As Marmo maneuvered himself alongside the drums, Ki-Gor slid down his side to the top of one of them. Helene stumbled toward him, incoherently blubbering. Ki-Gor leaped lightly down beside her and folded her into his arms.

"O-o-oh, Ki-Gor!" Helene wailed. "I was so afraid that this time you—you weren't coming back!"

"Ah, Helene," said Ki-Gor, and patted her awkwardly on the shoulder. Ki-Gor loved Helene, but this was a scene, and Ki-Gor hated scenes. "I promised you," he said, "I promised you I would come back."

"Jest as simple as all that," George Spelvin murmured. Then out loud he said, "Well, man, I'm always goin' to b'lieve you after this. Anybody who gets throwed into a rivuh o' crocodiles an' then climbs right out again—I'll b'lieve c'n do most anything!"

Ki-Gor released Helene with a smile and held his hand out to George.

"Good friend," he said, "you kept Helene safe."

"Almost didn't," George replied, gripping his friend's hand. "If you hadn't come along—"

"I was late," Ki-Gor said quickly. "I meant to get back much sooner, but it took me a long time to find Marmo."

"Well, Ki-Gor," said George, "you didn't come a minute too soon, but, still an' all, you wasn't late. Or, we wouldn' none of us be standin' heah, now."

Just then there came a timid, querulous shout from up in the grandstand.

"Lawdy, whoozat!" George exclaimed, whirling. His nerves, if the truth were told, were a little edgy as a result of the evening's events. He held up Ki-Gor's torch and peered upward toward the throne.

"Who is it?" he demanded in Kara-mzili.

"Dingazi," was the reply. "Have the ju-ju lions gone?"

"Yes, O King," said George. "We have sent them away."

"A-ah!" breathed the Lord of the Kara-mzili. "That was mighty ju-ju! I never thought to live through such an exhibition."

Then the realization seemed to dawn on the old man that he had lived through it, and was safe now. He spoke again and his voice began to assume royal authority,

"How am I ever going to get out of this rain? I'm too old and fat to climb the hill on my feet, and all my cowardly subjects have run away. All but one, that is," the monarch added graciously.

"All but one?" George asked.

"Shaliba stayed with me," Dingazi said with great satisfaction.

"Oh! Shaliba!" George said eagerly. "We owe her a great deal."

"Yes," Dingazi grunted. "She told me the truth about my traitorous nephew, Mpotwe, and that poisoning schemer, the Chief Witch-Doctor. I'll have his heart's blood."

Ki-Gor said, "If you will come down here, O Dingazi, I will take you up the hill to your kraal on the back of the elephant."

"What's that?" said Dingazi, uncertainly. "The elephant? The ju-ju elephant?"

"He obeys me," said Ki-Gor reassuringly. "You will be quite safe."

There was a pause. Then Dingazi said, "Very well then, I will come down. But you must all come to my kraal, and spend this wet night in my house. Tomorrow, I intend to make gifts to you in return."

CHAPTER XI

IT WAS AN AWED, shaken group of Kara-mzili who gathered the next morning in the king's kraal in answer to the summoning drums. They considered it miraculous that any of them were alive after the terrible visitation of the night before. And when their king appeared in front of his house with the White Witch, it was all they could do to keep themselves from bolting all over again. Then the Masai appeared with their giant leader, and again moans of fear could not be restrained. Several of the tall warriors bore wounds, and their white robes were bloodstained. But they were all there—all ten. What incredible fighters! the Kara-mzili marveled, to hold off an entire *impi!*

Dingazi held informal court in front of his house. He seemed in much better health than he had been for months. And when he announced publicly that Mpotwe and Mbama were expelled from the nation and could be killed by anyone finding them, the Kara-mzili nodded wisely. There were those among them who had long suspected what was going on. No one had said anything, because no one could be sure who would come out on top.

Ki-Gor made a presentation of the Uruculi feather headdress—rescued at the last minute from the shambles behind the war drums-and Dingazi was entranced. He commanded slaves to bring out bales of beautiful buckskin garments and presented them to Ki-Gor and Helene.

Then Dingazi announced to his people that he had selected Tembu George to be his heir, but that Tembu George had declined the honor. But at all events, Dingazi said, when he died, the Kara-mzili must send a delegation to the Masai and offer Tembu George the crown.

"And if you will not stay here as my heir," Dingazi said, turning to George, "I will, nevertheless, so consider you, wherever you are, as long as I live. To bind the bargain—" the old man jerked his head around to the door of his house. "Shaliba!" he cried. "All of you! Come out!"

Shaliba came proudly through the doorway followed by ten other young women, all more or less her age, and all very nearly as beautiful.

"Tembu George," said Dingazi, "I have eleven daughters of marriageable age. I give them to you. They are your wives."

"My—my wives!" gasped George Spelvin of Cincinnati.

"Every one of them is of royal blood on her mother's side," said Dingazi complacently.

"But eleven!" George exclaimed. "Shaliba would—"

"By the tima you are my age," Dingazi broke in, "you will have eleven times eleven wives."

"But, hear me, O Dingazi," George protested. "It is the custom among the Masai to have only one wife."

"Only *one* wife!" Dingazi cried in astonishment. "Well—well, your customs do not concern me. I give you my daughters. Do with them as you wish."

"You—?"

"Take them with you!" Dingazi shouted testily. "If not as wives, then slaves. But they are yours, do you understand, yours."

George paused, staring at Dingazi's eleven comely daughters. Then he strode toward them. He stopped beside Shaliba and took her hand and looked into her eyes. She returned his look. George turned toward his battered warriors.

"O Morani!" he cried. "O wifeless ones! Seek your wives. You are now Morani no longer. You are married men!"

STORY IX

LAIR OF THE BEAST

CHAPTER I

THE SPREADING BRANCHES AND the cool shadows of the grove offered glorious relief to the hot, dusty couple—the huge bronzed man with the thatch of tawny hair, and the beautiful red-haired girl who was his mate. For days now, Ki-Gor and Helene had been traveling along narrow trails in the grassy uplands of East Africa. Immensely tall grass it was, towering up sometimes twelve feet on both sides of the trail. The sun beat down mercilessly on the bare backs of the jungle couple as they wound along the stifling canyon which was the trail.

But by mid-afternoon they had come to this extensive grove of welcome trees and the welcome shade which they provided.

"We'll stay here a while," Ki-Gor said with an appreciative glance around him. "There should be water and probably some game. We're really very lucky to come here."

"M'm!" Helene murmured. "I'm thirsty, and I'm hungry. I think this place is wonderful!"

Ki-Gor grinned amiably at her. "I'll look for something to eat—"

"You look for something to eat," Helene interrupted. "I'll find the water-hole."

"Save some water for me," Ki-Gor admonished jokingly, and standing up, unslung the great war bow from his shoulder. He flipped a three-foot hardwood arrow from his quiver and moved silently through the trees.

For one who, unlike Ki-Gor, was not born to the jungle, Helene had absorbed a good store of jungle lore. And now when she strolled through the grove, she quite naturally looked for the denser vegetation which might indicate the presence of a water-hole nearby. She was not long in finding a little hollow near the center of the grove, where

M. LINCOLN LEE

enormous tree trunks encased in layers of vines stood in gloomy shadow, and where huge dark green leaves grew in clumps straight off the humid ground. A vague passageway through the undergrowth indicated a possible animal trail.

Helene hummed happily. This water-hole was not hard to find. She hummed, too, because it was very still in there in those brooding shadows. She wished for a moment that Ki-Gor was with her, so that they could talk out loud and break up that primordial stillness. She attempted to drive the wish from her mind as being unworthy, and even walked a little faster and more boldly through the damp dark green leaves. Suddenly she stopped short and an ugly little thrill coursed through her.

At the foot of a huge gnarled tree trunk just in front of her, a human skull grinned up at her.

AT ONCE, all desire to locate a water-hole left Helene. It was not that she was not brave. But the presence of that skull indicated that there was danger lurking near. Once upon a time a living, breathing human being had met death in that gloomy glade. Another human might die from the same cause.

Helene stood very still for a long moment and scanned every inch of the leafy scene about her. Then she stepped back cautiously and turned around. There was just the faintest rustle in the leaves ahead of her. And before she could take a step, the leaves parted, a huge tawny gray head appeared, and a lion was glaring at her not six feet away.

Helene fought down an insane impulse to dash away, madly—blindly. She knew that a lion will chase anything that flees from it, chase it automatically, as a kitten will chase a wind-borne leaf. She knew that she must decide on the nearest place of safety and move toward it slowly and gently so that she would not provoke the lion into attacking her. She tried to tell herself that she was really not necessarily in great danger, even though she was at such close quarters with this lion. She reminded herself that the king of beasts minds his own business in general and does not trouble humans unless they annoy him.

Keeping her eye on the great grizzled head, she moved one foot back slowly. The lion continued to glare unwinkingly, balefully. Helene moved her other foot back gently. A broad leaf brushed against her bare shoulder and she just suppressed a startled scream.

She got a fresh grip on her nerves and took another step backward. There was no reaction from the lion, except that the pupils of its eyes dilated.

Helene began to breathe a little easier. She had put three more feet between herself and the great beast. If she could retreat just a few feet farther unmolested, she would be safe. She would be on a line with the huge tree trunk that towered over the skull. A quick leap behind it, and she could scramble up the vines out of the lion's reach before he could touch her.

But just as she was reaching her foot back for another stealthy backward step, a call rang through the glade.

"Helene!"

Sudden alarm shot through Helene's brain. Where was Ki-Gor? Would he walk unsuspectingly through the thick undergrowth into danger?

"Helene!" he called again, this time nearer. "Helene! Where are you?"

Frantically, Helene tried to decide what to do. If she answered, the sound of her voice might provoke the lion into attacking her.

It was the lion who decided Helene's course. Its upper lip suddenly crinkled and laid bare yellow fangs. The head went up abruptly and the great jaws bit at the air. A soft, snarling cough rattled from the shaggy throat.

Helene screamed at the top of her lungs and wheeled about. The lion gave a full-throated roar and sprang. But Helene was running for her life. There was no time to dodge behind the great tree. She must run, run—away from the tawny death at her heels.

But even as she ran, she knew that she could not escape. The bushes crashed behind her, and she knew the great cat would reach her in two bounds. Hopelessly, desperately she dodged to one side of the rail, flinging her body through an opening in the bushes.

At the same instant, one foot tripped over something, and she fell forward headlong. As she hit the ground, a huge tawny form sailed through the air over her prostrate body. And just as the lion hit the ground beyond her, a wild yell rang out. Ki-Gor burst out of the bushes beside Helene and flung himself straight at the lion. The beast was scrambling around to face Helene when the jungle man landed astride the grizzled mane. The great knife blade flashed and shot down with terrific force. Ki-Gor's mighty shoulder muscles followed through, and the steel bit deep into the beast's side.

THE LION gave a choking roar and doubled up convulsively. Ki-Gor sprang away from the kicking, tearing hind claws, and stood watchfully as the huge animal, two inches of steel in its heart, gasped and gagged and died.

Helene stood up trembling. It was good to be alive. At the same time she wanted to show Ki-Gor that she could face death without flinching.

"It's an old lion, isn't it?" she remarked.

"Yes," said Ki-Gor gravely. "The worst kind to meet. This one was a man-eater. I think it stalked you."

He glanced into the shadows beyond the lion's body and gave a startled whistle.

"I wonder," he said, "whether this lion killed those people."

Helene followed Ki-Gor's eyes. Cold chills ran up her spine at what she saw.

There were three skeletons sprawled grotesquely under an evil-looking shrub. Only two of the skeletons had skulls. And lying like a dead snake among the whitening bones was a long, rusty chain.

"Oh, Ki-Gor!" Helene said suddenly. "I don't like this place! I don't like this lovely grove a bit!"

"Neither do I," said Ki-Gor. "There is the smell of death around. I think we'll go on until we find another grove."

They did not speak again until they had been on the dusty trail for nearly half an hour. Then Helene said, "Ki-Gor, did you see the chain around those bones?"

"Yes. Those three were chained together when they were alive. They were slaves."

"Why, are there slave runners around here?" Helene asked.

"I didn't think they came as far south as this," Ki-Gor replied, "but evidently they do."

"Oh, I don't like the sound of that," Helene commented with a little shiver.

"Don't worry," Ki-Gor reassured her. "Slave runners or slave hunters would never bother us. We'd be too much trouble to capture. They usually go among the weak forest blacks who put up a very weak resistance."

Soon after that, the trail wound around the base of a series of craggy ledges. Ki-Gor climbed up several feet to look over the top of the tall grass. When Helene started to follow him, he stopped her, remarking that the ledge was liable to be the home of baboons.

"They're almost as bad as lions," he told her. "They're big and fierce and they travel in packs."

"Well," said Helene, "I don't like this country. I'll be glad when we get back to our home on the Island."

"We will in a few days," Ki-Gor smiled, coming down off the rocks. "Meanwhile, there's another grove not far from here. Perhaps it will be pleasanter than the last one."

The trail curved wide of the second grove, and Ki-Gor halted at the curve.

"We'll have to push through this grass," he said. "Follow close behind me. I don't think we'll meet anything except maybe a snake. But it's just as well to be alert."

"Wait a minute," Helene said, looking up the trail. "What's that black thing over there beside the path?"

Ki-Gor walked up the trail. He picked up the object and looked at it curiously.

"More evidence of slave running," he said. "This looks like an anklet of some kind—"

"Oh, but it's handsome," Helene said, holding her hand out. "Let me see it. Why, it's beautiful—hammered iron. And listen!"

She shook the anklet vigorously and it produced a resonant chiming, quite clear and quite loud. Helene laughed delightedly and jingled the iron fetter again. Far away somewhere, an animal set up a high-pitched yelping.

"Why, this can't be for slaves," Helene said. "It's too musical. Couldn't it be a regular dancer's anklet, Ki-Gor?"

"I don't think so," Ki-Gor said, shaking his head. "It's too heavy. It would be pretty hard to dance with anything as heavy as that riveted on your leg."

"It certainly is a mystery," Helene declared, looking at her find. "It isn't so terribly heavy—I think I'll take it along. I love the sound it makes."

SHE JINGLED it again, and smiled up at Ki-Gor. But he had turned away from her and cocked his head in an attitude of listening.

"What is it?" she said. Then she heard the animal yelping in the distance.

"Can you hear it?" Ki-Gor gestured in the direction of the sound.

"Yes. A wild dog?"

"No," said Ki-Gor, "it's a baboon."

A little chill chased itself clown Helene's spine.

"A baboon!" she murmured. "Maybe it's just as well you didn't stay up on that ledge any longer."

"There only seems to be one of them," Ki-Gor said. "As long as there's only one, there's nothing to worry about."

"I thought you said they always traveled in packs."

"They do, usually," Ki-Gor said. "That's what interests me about hearing a single one calling. Well—let's get along to our grove of trees."

He stepped into the tall grass beside the trail and parted it with his left hand. His right hand dropped to his waist and unsheathed his great hunting knife. Helene followed in his tracks, the slave anklet jingling merrily in her hand.

It was a slow and tedious business, pushing through that jungle of grass. The stalks were as thick as young bamboo trunks and grew even closer together. Ki-Gor had gone some forty feet, swinging his mighty right arm like a club against the tough dry stalks of giant grass, when behind him, suddenly, he heard a crash and a jingle. Looking around, he saw Helene flat on her face on the fallen grass-stalks.

"Don't mind me," she called in an exasperated tone, "I've just got myself a little tangled up here. Go right ahead. I'll be with you in a second."

Ki-Gor smothered a smile and turned back to his task of hacking a path through the dry, crackling wilderness. The slave anklet jingled again and the fallen grass rustled as Helene untangled her foot and stood up.

"Are you all right?" Ki-Gor called, without turning around.

"Ye-es—but—" Helene's voice had taken on a peculiar note.

"Yes but what?" said Ki-Gor.

"I—I think something's following us, Ki-Gor."

The jungle man felt a fearful sense of danger sweep over him. He swung around swiftly. At the same time, Helene screamed.

Her back was to Ki-Gor and she was staring at something that was coming along the broken trail they had made through the grass. Ki-Gor saw what it was over her shoulder.

It was a baboon.

As Ki-Gor moved forward, a question flashed through his mind. The baboon was not the giant chacma native to that country—short-haired and almost black in color. It was a hamadryad, almost as big as the chacmas, but with long silver-gray hair and a silver-tipped mane like a lion's. Ordinarily hamadryads were not common south of Abyssinia. Where had this beast come from?

Helene stood paralyzed. The slave anklet fell from her nerveless fingers and hit the ground with a jingling thump. The noise seemed to infuriate the hamadryad. Its pale eyes glittered in the repulsive, scarlet face. The lips under the flared nostrils lifted all along the dog-like muzzle baring huge yellow fangs.

"Drop! Drop down!" Ki-Gor whispered, his muscles tensed.

Helene fell away to one side. At one and the same instant, the baboon sprang—and Ki-Gor sprang.

The monkey's flying form was just lighting on Helene's prostrate figure when Ki-Gor launched a kick at its leonine head. The force of the blow, with all the power of Ki-Gor's mighty leg muscles behind it, knocked the brute three feet in the air, and sent it crashing against the grass-stalks. Ki-Gor flung himself after it.

But the snapping, snarling beast dodged with incredible agility. The leaping gray form just escaped Ki-Gor's clutching fingers. Like a flash, Ki-Gor was up again. The huge monkey hurled itself at him.

Horny black fingers clutched at Ki-Gor's left knee. The jungle man's left hand shot downwards into the beautiful gray mane. But before he could dislodge the baboon's grasp, the brute gave a horrible growl. Yellow fangs slashed Ki-Gor's left thigh, the powerful jaws snapping like a wolf's.

The knife in Ki-Gor's right hand flashed and sank with terrific force into the thick gray fur on the hamadryad's shoulder. The animal screamed in agony, and twisted its maned head around. The slavering jaws clashed on thin air for a moment. Then they gaped open trembling, and a convulsive shudder went over the gray body. The terrible jaws spread wide and bright blood flooded through them.

The horny fingers relaxed on Ki-Gor's knee, and the huge monkey fell slowly backwards. It twitched spasmodically for a moment and then lay still. The blue-red face froze into a ferocious, vindictive grin.

Ki-Gor wrenched the knife out of the creature's back. For a long minute he stood crouched and peered back along the rough trail, while the knife blade dripped red on the gray fur of his conquered foe.

"Are—are you all right, Ki-Gor?" Helene quavered from behind him.

"Yes," Ki-Gor muttered, "but be quiet. There must be more of these baboons."

"Oh, dear Heaven!" Helene said in a strangled voice, and then kept very still.

BUT THERE was no sound in that grassy wilderness, except the droning and humming of insects of an African mid-afternoon. Gradually, Ki-Gor's muscles relaxed. He straightened up and looked around him with a puzzled expression.

"He must have been alone," the jungle man said wonderingly. "That's very curious."

His eyes still sought the grass restlessly, and his ears strained to catch the slightest rustle of an unseen enemy. But still there was no sound.

Finally, Ki-Gor sighed, stepped forward over the dead hamadryad, and turned to face Helene.

"We were very lucky," he said soberly. "Just one of these brutes is a handful. If there had been more—"

"Ki-Gor!" Helene cried. "Your leg! Look at it! You were terribly bitten!"

The jungle man glanced down at his left thigh. Blood was streaming from five jagged, ragged furrows above the knee. And there were four ugly bluish holes.

"It's not bad," Ki-Gor said quietly. "It could have been a lot worse."

"Oh, darling!" Helene cried, scrambling to her feet. "Doesn't it hurt dreadfully?"

"It hurts a little," Ki-Gor admitted, and sucked his breath in suddenly as he stepped forward, throwing his weight on to his left leg.

"Oh, we've got to do something about that." Helene stared at the fearful wound and bit her lip.

"Yes," said Ki-Gor. "It isn't serious. But I'll have to clean it out."

"Clean it out? How do you mean?" said Helene, startled.

"Don't worry about it," Ki-Gor said. "I'll take care of it—I've done it before."

"You mean—cauterize it?" Helene whispered.

"With a hot knife," Ki-Gor said. "Let's go along, now, and get through to the grove where we can build a fire and heat some water. I should attend to this leg pretty soon."

He moved forward a little stiffly and began to attack the wall of grass-stalks. Helene bent over to pick up the slave anklet, then hesitated. Finally, she straightened up, leaving the iron fetter on the ground.

"I'm not going to take that anklet," she said. "It's brought us bad luck."

It was fifteen long minutes before the jungle couple could pound their way through the tangle of dry grass to the grove of trees. By the time the grass thinned out and disappeared under the shade of the spreading branches, Ki-Gor's leg was throbbing violently.

The grove was comparatively cool, and was quite extensive. The trees grew thickly enough to choke off any undergrowth, so that it was quite open ground beneath them. Helene instantly set about collecting dry twigs for a fire, while Ki-Gor searched for a possible spring.

He found it bubbling out from between two great roots at the foot of a tree. A thin trickle of water flowed from it into a shallow depression where it collected in a stagnant, scummy pool. Ki-Gor deftly fashioned a crude container from a broad banana leaf, filled it with water and carried it back to the little fire Helene had laid, ready to be lighted.

From the rawhide pouch at his waist, he took out flint, steel, and tinder. Deftly, he struck a spark, saw it grow into a tiny flame in the tinder, and in a short while the fire was blazing merrily. The banana-leaf water container was suspended from a tripod of green sticks, and Ki-Gor eased himself to a sitting position beside the little blaze.

WHEN THE water came to a boil, Ki-Gor held the knife blade down in it, taking the first step in his fight to prevent septic poisoning from the yellow fangs of the baboon.

Helene watched with harrowed face, as he pressed the sharp tip of the scalded knife blade into one after the other of the wounds on his thigh. When every wound was thoroughly opened, and the blood flowing freely, Helene, under Ki-Gor's instructions, dropped some moss into the boiling water. Then she fished out small wads of it with a green twig, and swabbed the red, gaping flesh.

Ki-Gor leaned back on his hands and let his breath out very carefully as her trembling fingers probed the fearful gashes.

"Oh, darling!" she wailed. "This must hurt you horribly!"

"It—it hurts a little," he admitted, as the sweat poured off his face. "But—it's got to hurt more than this—before I'm—through."

Helene forced herself to watch him as he laid the knife blade in the hot coals of the fire. She felt that she had to be at least as brave as he was. But it was almost too much for her to bear, when he pressed the heated blade into each wound, and a little curl of smoke went up from each wound. She stood up, white-faced and shaken, when he finished his task and went off to get some fresh water, glad to get away from the smell of scorched flesh.

Ki-Gor was on his feet when she came back with the water, but his bronzed face was considerably paler, and he walked very slowly. He held in his hands some healing herbs and some broad leaves. The herbs were dipped into the fresh water as soon as it came to a boil, and then laid gingerly into the wounds. Then the leaves were dipped into the boiling water. They stayed in just long enough to be sterilized, but not long enough to break down the vegetable tissue.

Patiently and carefully, Ki-Gor wrapped the leaves around his thigh to make a crude bandage and secured them with some slender but tough vine tentacles.

Then he stood erect with a white-lipped smile.

"There," said Ki-Gor, "that's taken care of. There shouldn't be any trouble with poisoning now. But—" he regarded the leg ruefully, "I'm going to have to stay off my feet for a little while. Now, before this leg stiffens up completely, I'm going up this tree to that big crotch. Helene, I'm afraid you're going to have to do the hunting for the next few days."

"Darling, I don't mind a bit!" Helene cried. "I just can't—can't—" her voice broke, "bear to see you in such terrible pain!"

She dropped her face in her hands for a moment and her shoulders shook. But Ki-Gor's voice came to her authoritatively.

"Please don't cry, Helene," he said. "Everything is all right, now. It's all over—I'm perfectly all right now."

Helene's head came up. She wiped her eyes briskly, and essayed a smile.

"I know, Ki-Gor, and I'm sorry to act like a cry-baby. I promise to behave."

Ki-Gor gazed at her earnestly for a minute, then patted her hand reassuringly, and turned to the tree trunk behind him. An ordinary man, after suffering the pain and losing the amount of blood that Ki-Gor had, might have flinched at the task of climbing thirty feet or more up a tree, dragging a useless leg. But Ki-Gor was no ordinary man. And while Helene's heart went up into her mouth several times as she watched him, he made the ascent without any great difficulty.

When he finally reached the great crotch in the tree, he was trembling from the exertion and from the torturing pain in his thigh. He eased himself into a fairly comfortable position with his left leg extended along a small bough that jutted horizontally outward from the trunk. Then he called down some advice to Helene, and finally laid his head back and closed his eyes. Ki-Gor had done all he could. From now on, for a few days, it was up to Mother Nature to heal him, and Helene to do what she could about feeding him—and herself.

CHAPTER II

KI-GOR SPENT THREE FEVERISH, uncomfortable days in the tree. His leg pained him ferociously and continuously, and he was constantly fretting about Helene. She, in turn, had her hands full. It devolved upon her to hunt up food of some kind or other. Unfortunately, the only weapons available were Ki-Gor's knife and his great war-bow. This mighty seven-foot shaft was far too stiff for her to use, although she did try throwing the iron-tipped arrows at some small game that came through the grove. She was unable to kill any, however.

She was forced at last to resort to gathering fruit, wild nuts, and birds' eggs. There were plenty of all these, but after three days of this diet, she longed for a change.

By the third day, the pain began to let up a little in Ki-Gor's wounds, although his leg was swollen and stiff. As his leg improved, so did his disposition, and he was less querulous about Helene's activities.

During the morning of that third day, Helene had an idea and promptly set to work on it. Ki-Gor watched her, grinning from his perch in the tree as she whittled down a stout sapling with his knife. She peeled it with great care and shaved it diligently so that it tapered toward both ends from the middle. Then she notched each tip and strung a piece of tough vine between the tips.

When her crude bow was finished, she looked up at Ki-Gor, brandished her handiwork at him, and laughed in triumph.

"Bring it up and let's see it," he commanded.

"I think it will shoot, all right," she answered, climbing up to him.

He looked at the bow curiously. "It hasn't got any shape," he commented.

"Of course not," Helene retorted, "but I haven't got time to steam it into a proper bow shape. But there's plenty of spring in those horns—"

"Give me the knife," Ki-Gor said. "It needs just a little more shaved off each side at the handgrip. Then I think you'll get a pretty good spring out of it."

SWIFTLY, HE shaved away the wood until matters were more to his satisfaction. Then he gave the bow back to Helene.

"Now that you have a bow," he said, "where are you going to hunt?"

"Well," Helene answered, "last evening I saw some little dik-dik go out through the path we made in the long grass when we came into the grove."

"Helene," Ki-Gor said sharply, "you know I don't want you to go out of the grove."

"Now, wait a minute," Helene said patiently. "Two days ago you didn't want me to go out of your sight even if I stayed in the grove. Well, yesterday I spent a couple of hours out of your sight down by the spring. And nothing happened to me. You don't seem to realize, Ki-Gor, that I'm learning how to handle myself in Africa. I'm not the same idle-rich American society girl I was the day my plane cracked up on your front door step in the jungle. I was completely helpless and useless, then. I wouldn't have survived ten minutes if you hadn't been right there to take me under your wing."

"You were so funny," Ki-Gor said with a smile. "You were very angry with me and hated me and tried to run away from me."

"Oh, yes," Helene said. "I was furious! I didn't know what to make of you. Remember how I commanded you to guide me to the nearest outpost? Not knowing, of course, that the nearest outpost was a good eight hundred miles away through the thickest jungle in the world."

"Then one day," Ki-Gor mused, "you decided that you wouldn't try to run away from me any more."

"And I'll never run away from you," Helene said, her eyes a little moist, "for the rest of my life."

Ki-Gor squeezed her hand. "You're quite sure?" he said.

"Listen, Mr. Ki-Gor!" Helene declared in mock indignation. "I may have been a silly social butterfly once, but I was never the kind who would leave her husband. Especially if her husband happened to be the handsomest man in the world."

Ki-Gor blushed appropriately.

"And you're not sorry that you left your old life behind and married me that day in Fort Lamy?"

"Of course not, Ki-Gor. Why, I didn't really start living until Fate threw us together."

Ki-Gor swung her hand happily—the curious child-like gesture that was his expression of supremest happiness. After a minute Helene sat up very straight and disengaged her hand.

"Now, look," she said severely. "I'm going to take my new bow and some of your arrows, and I'm going to the mouth of the path through the grass. And I'm going to look for signs of dik-dik or anything like them. I may even go a few steps out into the grass. But I'll keep very alert and I'll be sure and keep out of trouble. Now you are not to worry about me, and maybe sometime before dark, I'll be back with some lovely fresh meat for dinner. Won't that be wonderful? I know you like meat, Ki-Gor."

"Don't go far into the grass," Ki-Gor said, frowning.

"I won't—and don't you worry," Helene cried, and she slipped down the tree to the ground. "Good-bye!" she called, and with a last wave of her hand she trotted away through the grove out of Ki-Gor's vision.

THE HOURS passed slowly for Ki-Gor after that. Evidently, Helene had no immediate luck stalking her small game, because by mid-afternoon she had not returned. Ki-Gor had to keep reminding himself that she had said she might not be back before sundown. It was hard not to worry. Helene could take care of herself to a certain extent. It was true that she had learned the ways of the jungle remarkably well in the few months she had lived with Ki-Gor.

At the same time, his own very helplessness made Ki-Gor feel that Helene was in terrible danger from something or other every minute that she was out of sight from him. Supposing something did happen to her? he asked himself. He could do nothing about it. The wounds in his thigh were just beginning to heal. In another two days they would knit fast, thanks to his magnificent powers of recuperation. But right now, he was not ready for any but the slightest physical exertion.

He shifted his position carefully. Then he slowly flexed his ailing left leg, and as slowly straightened it out. The action hurt cruelly, and Ki-Gor grunted. It would be a couple of days yet before he could safely climb down the tree.

Ki-Gor leaned back with a sigh. His eyes roved over the little clearing below, and his ears harkened for a sound which might betoken Helene's return. But the only sign of life that was visible from his perch was a small jungle mouse that scampered past the smoldering campfire. And the brooding, vibrant silence of Africa was broken only by the raucous cry of a lonesome parrot. From the angle of the sunbeams that filtered through the leafy canopy of the grove, Ki-Gor judged that the sun was about two hours past its zenith. There was nothing to do but wait for Helene to come back. Ki-Gor closed his eyes and dozed off to sleep.

He woke up with a guilty start. Instantly, he realized that he had slept much longer than he had intended to. The soft light in the grove indicated that it was quite late in the afternoon. Anxiously, Ki-Gor stared down into the clearing. There was no sign of Helene.

An anxious frown gathered on the jungle man's brow. She should have been back by now—whether she had found any game or not. There was a scant two hours of daylight left. Ki-Gor realized that he was probably being a little over-anxious. It was entirely possible that she was crouching within easy distance of his voice somewhere in the grove. She might at that very minute be aiming her crude bow at a small deer or a game fowl.

But over-anxious or not, Ki-Gor decided that she had been gone long enough. He decided that he was going to call out to her, even at the risk of frightening away her quarry. She would be extremely annoyed if it did turn out that way, but that couldn't be helped. Ki-Gor was taking no chances. He called gently:

"Helene."

There was no answer.

"Helene!" This time he raised his voice considerably.

The lone parrot ceased its squawking, and there was no other sound in the grove. A prickle of alarm went over Ki-Gor. If Helene had been in the grove, she surely would have heard him that time and would have answered him. He could only conclude that she had wandered farther out through the tall grass than she should have. He filled his great lungs and shouted again at the top of his voice:

"HELENE!"

Ki-Gor sat for a long time with his head bowed, listening to the exasperating silence around.

Where had Helene gone? Where could she have gone? That last shout of his must have carried for at least half a mile. Of course, it was possible that she had heard him but was too far away to answer.

He called again—three times—each time as loudly as he could, at intervals of three or four minutes. But ten minutes later, there had still been no answering call from Helene. Ki-Gor was forced to accept the sober fact that Helene was somewhere out of hearing. Or else within hearing but for some reason unable to answer or unable to come back.

There was only one thing to be done, and that was to go and find her. Wounded leg or not, Ki-Gor could not stay up in that tree any longer while the daylight ebbed away, and Helene was missing.

HE LEANED over and gazed down the vine-covered trunk of the tree, rapidly calculating the easiest route to the ground. Then he rolled his body carefully to the edge of the crotch until he could release his good leg and swing it downwards. His right foot sought and found an unseen foothold. Then came the business, the slow and painful business, of maneuvering his stiff, sore left leg into a perpendicular position. Finally it was accomplished, and he was ready for the descent.

With one leg dangling uselessly, this presented somewhat of a problem—especially as that same leg must be swung clear of the tree all the way down to keep from scraping his wounds. But the first few feet of the way encouraged Ki-Gor. He realized that he really did not need more than two hands and one foot if he were careful. As a matter of fact, he reflected, he could have climbed down the trunk of that tree using only his hands, if it had been absolutely necessary. Returning confidence swept over him and he began to let himself down faster.

When he was still about fourteen feet from the ground, the accident occurred.

Whether it was from over-confidence and carelessness, or just bad luck, Ki-Gor never knew—but his right foot missed its hold, just as his right hand was groping for a new hold. He swung for a moment by his left hand. And before he could catch himself, the vines under that hand gave way. With a grunt of dismay, the jungle man fell through the air.

Ordinarily a drop of that distance would have meant nothing to Ki-Gor. He would have landed on the balls of his feet like a cat. His knees would have bent to take up the shock of landing and he would have hardly noticed the jolt at all.

But now he could not bend his left leg. He landed heavily on his good leg. The unexpected fall threw him off balance. He teetered for a second, wildly swinging his arms. Then he crashed headlong on the earth.

A hundred burning knives jabbed his tortured left thigh as he hit the ground. The breath hissed through his clenched teeth as he struggled to his feet. He stood swaying for a moment and fought down a wave of nausea. There was no need for him to look down to see what the fall had done to these wounds. His left knee tickled unpleasantly as the blood flowed down over it from the freshly reopened gashes.

Ki-Gor tried to rest his weight on the injured leg. It was no use. The jungle man looked around him with a snort of disgust. Quite obviously, he was not going very far on one leg. He would either have to crawl along the ground or hop like some grotesque bird. Either way was impractical. He could not only not go far, but he would be extremely vulnerable in case he were attacked by anything.

His eyes fell on a stout young sapling growing some fifteen feet away. Six or seven feet from the ground, the young trunk divided into two equal-sized branches at a wide angle. Ki-Gor felt for the great knife at his waist, and knew that he had found a way out of his problem.

He made short work of cutting the sapling down at its base, and trimming off the two branches until they were mere six-inch horns on either side of the crotch. Ki-Gor tucked the crude crutch under his left shoulder and took several swinging steps forward. It would do, but it would be uncomfortable for his armpit. What could he use to pad the crotch?

His hand dropped to his waist, to the rawhide pouch which contained the flint, steel, and tinder. Quickly, the jungle man emptied out the fire-making materials. In a pinch, he could make fire by cruder methods.

It was the work of a moment to stuff the pouch with moss, and tie the crude cushion around the horns of the crutch. Ki-Gor tried the padded staff again. It was much better.

The jungle man squinted at the slanting sunbeams and estimated not much more than an hour of daylight left to find Helene and bring her back to the safety of the grove. He had to work fast.

Quickly, he replaced the great knife in its sheath at his waist, and slung his great war-bow and the quiver of arrows over his right shoulder. Then he swung off through the grove on the crutch, looking for all the world like a tall, tawny gorilla.

THE PROBABILITIES were that Helene had left the grove by the rough passageway they had beaten through the tall grass on the way in. And Ki-Gor's jungle-wise eyes saw that that was indeed so.

He saw where she had first crouched to one side waiting for an unsuspecting dik-dik to come along. Then he saw how she had tired of waiting and had gone on out through the channel in the grass. He frowned and set out along her trail. He had hoped that she had not gone all the way out to the main trail by which they had been traveling southwards four days before. But it looked now very much as though she had.

It was tricky work handling that crutch in the tangle of fallen grass, but Ki-Gor pushed along at a good rate of speed. He took the greatest care, however, not to fall down again. His throbbing left thigh was a constant reminder to be careful. The blood had finally stopped flowing from the reopened wounds, but Ki-Gor knew that he was risking new infection by not stopping to bathe those wounds and put a new dressing on them. But with the daylight fading fast, there wasn't time to spare.

In a short time, he came to the scene of his furious encounter with the strange baboon. The creature's carcass still lay where it had died. Ki-Gor could see where Helene had trampled the grass to one side where she had gone to give the malodorous body a wide berth.

He stopped for a moment as a thought crossed his mind. His eyes searched the torn grass for the iron slave anklet. It was nowhere to be seen. Evidently, Helene had thought better of her impulse to leave the object behind. Ki-Gor looked at the baboon's carcass again and wondered, uneasily, whether Helene might have run into another one like it. With a muttered exclamation, he swung around and made off through the rough trail toward the main pathway.

When he finally came out on to the regular trail, he looked swiftly to right and left. There was no person or thing in sight. Ki-Gor's eyes dropped to the ground to see in which direction Helene's tracks led.

He sucked in his breath quickly at what he saw.

The dust of the trail told a grim story.

Helene's tracks showed that she had stepped out of the grass and turned to her right—toward the bend in the trail where she had previously picked up the slave anklet. But only a few of her tracks showed clearly. They had been obliterated by a multitude of tracks pointing in the other direction. It did not take much study to figure out that these other tracks had been made by a number of bare-footed splay-toed Bantu. It was not immediately evident exactly how many of them there were. Certainly there were at least six or seven, and perhaps there were a great deal more.

Grim-faced, Ki-Gor swung southwards toward the bend in the trail. He stopped at approximately the spot where the unlucky anklet had lain. The foot prints here in the dust had a story to tell that was even more definite and dramatic.

Quite evidently, Helene had strolled around the curve unsuspectingly, and walked right into the arms of the party of unidentified blacks. She had attempted to run away, but they caught up with her in just a few strides and swept her struggling off her feet. Thereafter, Helene's tracks appeared no more in the dust of the trail.

The hackles rose on the back of Ki-Gor's neck as he visualized the scene.

There was no doubt in his mind that Helene had been made prisoner by these strange savages. The questions that remained to be answered were—who were these Bantu, and why had they captured Helene?

Ki-Gor was unfamiliar with that particular part of Africa and with the tribes that inhabited it. A little to the north lay the country of the blood-drinking Masai, the cannibal Wandrobo, and the highly intelligent Bantu Buganda. The foot prints left by Helene's abductors were not long enough or slender enough for the tall, lean Masai. Nor were they short and broad enough for the dwarfish Wandrobo. They were typically Negro footprints, unmistakable evidence of Bantu-speaking blacks. As far as Ki-Gor knew, the Wandrobo were the only cannibals that lived so far east in the Dark Continent. So it was unlikely that Helene was in any immediate danger from her captors—danger of the kind that Ki-Gor hated to think about.

AS HE wheeled around on his crutch, his eyes fell on an object in the tall grass beside the trail. It was the iron slave anklet, apparently flung there during Helene's struggle with her assailants. He looked at the black fetter for a moment, thoughtfully. There, possibly, was the answer to his question.

As he had told Helene, he did not believe that slavers came this far south. But he did not know for sure. So, it was possible that Helene's abductors were local raiders. They were not slave-runners—the absence of boot prints and horses' tracks demonstrated that there had been no Arabs or white men in the party.

However, there was only one way to find out who had carried Helene off, and why, and that was to follow and catch up with them. Ki-Gor sent a last glance at the slave anklet and then started off up the trail to the north.

The sun had long since settled out of sight behind the tall grass bordering the trail, but Ki-Gor estimated that there was almost an hour of daylight left. And although he could not tell whether Helene's captors had passed that way an hour before or four hours before, he was sorely afraid that he could not catch up to them before dark. After dark it would be unwise to continue his pursuit. The trail branched off to right and left frequently, and without light to follow the tracks he would be unable to tell which direction the abductors had taken.

Ki-Gor was able to swing along at a fair rate of speed on his improvised crutch, but every step taxed his lowered vitality. Every now and then he was forced to stop and rest, standing panting on his good right leg. Time and again he cursed the extraordinarily bad fortune that had sent that strange hamadryad baboon so far from its home country to attack Helene and inflict such painful wounds on him. For without those hampering wounds, he would have sped tirelessly along the trail and would surely have caught up with those marauding blacks some time during the next day. As it was now, he could close the distance between them only very slowly. And when he would actually come up with them, Ki-Gor had not the slightest idea.

He swung his way up the trail as long as there was light enough to follow the tracks in the dust. Then he reluctantly gave up the chase for the night and crawled a short distance into the grass, there to sleep fitfully. At the first sullen signs of dawn he was up and on his way, not pausing even to think about food.

Ki-Gor devoted the next three days to his grim pursuit. Only at night did he stop, and once on the second day to send an arrow through a jungle fowl. Even then he did not stop to cook the bird, but plucked it quickly and ate the warm raw flesh as he went along.

The morning of the third day found him following the footprints along a smaller trail that had branched off to the eastward. This trail gradually moved out of the tall grass country uphill into wooded rolling terrain. And as the day wore on, the upgrade grew steeper and consequently slowed Ki-Gor's progress considerably. The single crutch was harder to maneuver going uphill. Ki-Gor's diminished strength was hardly equal to the demands he made upon it. But he stuck doggedly to his task.

He had scarcely dared to think about what Helene was going through all this time. Instead he clung to the conviction that sooner or later he would catch up with the gang who had captured her and wrest her from their profaning hands. And if he had not come within sight of them yet, at least he had followed their spoor unerringly, never once losing it among the twisting and branching trails.

CHAPTER III

IT WAS LATE AFTERNOON of the third day when the trail, now definitely in mountain country, led Ki-Gor to the crest of a ridge. Ki-Gor halted for a moment to catch his breath and saw that the path dipped steeply downward in front of him, apparently leading into a thickly wooded ravine. Even on the crest of the ridge where he was standing, the trees around him were too thick for him to get any view of the surrounding country. However, to the right, the ground sloped upward slightly and was less wooded. Ki-Gor decided to turn aside for a moment on the chance that he could find a point of vantage somewhere up the slope from where he could survey the land.

Less than a hundred yards from the trail, Ki-Gor came out on an outcropping ledge clear of trees, which afforded a splendid view to the east and the north and the south. It was extremely interesting country.

As far as Ki-Gor could see, bare brown mountains spiked upward. They were not high peaks like the massive Rwenzori Range or the great mounds of Kenya. But although they were comparatively low, they were rugged and alpine in character and sprang up in jutting cones separated by narrow valleys. Ki-Gor looked down into the wooded ravine below and felt a sudden shock of discovery.

There, at the edge of the woods, a miniature mountain rose with bare, steep sides. Unlike the other large mountains, it did not have a conical peak, but a flat top—a sort of plateau, some three or four hundred yards in diameter. And on that flat top were human habitations, gleaming white buildings.

It was really one set of rambling buildings with a white wall running completely around the edge of the plateau. Little black dots moved slowly over the plateau, and Ki-Gor did not doubt that they were human beings.

The jungle man wasted no time conjecturing over this curious mountain retreat, but hurried back to the trail. There was not much daylight left, and he wanted to get a good look at the place from a point much closer. Just as he was nearing the trail, he heard voices. He slipped behind a broad tree trunk to watch.

A group of fifteen stalwart, well-armed blacks came up the trail from the ravine. They were in high good humor, and were laughing and chattering. They spoke a Bantu dialect but one which was unfamiliar to Ki-Gor, and he was only able to catch a very few words of their rapid, confused conversation.

But he noticed that every one of them was carrying a brand-new cheap trade knife. They looked at and admired the knives as they went along. Evidently they had only just come into possession of them.

Ki-Gor could not help but suspect that these blacks had been the ones who carried Helene off. The knives which they were admiring could very well be the price they had been paid for her by some slave-runner. The jungle man's upper lip twitched in an involuntary snarl. If he had not been so crippled by his wounds, he would have attacked the blacks and found out the truth. As it was, he could not successfully assail that large a group.

As soon as the fifteen blacks had gone by, Ki-Gor stepped back onto the trail and swung rapidly down into the ravine.

By the time he moved out through the ravine into the thinning shrubbery near the base of the miniature mountain, night was drawing on. The soft, delusive luminance of the brief twilight gave an unreal fairy-like quality to the extraordinary white buildings above. Even to Ki-Gor's keen realistic eyes, the white walls did not seem to be resting on the rocky plateau at all, but seemed rather as if they were mysteriously suspended in mid-air.

Only once before in his life had Ki-Gor seen anything like this beautiful, fantastic fortress that shimmered above him in the twilight. Far away in northwestern Nigeria, where the jungle contends for mastery with the sands of the South Sahara, Ki-Gor had come upon an old ruin of a Moorish castle. The jungle man then had marveled at the strange beauty of that one-time stronghold of desert raiders. Its graceful pointed arches had caught his eye, as well as its solid foundations and the exquisite architectural balance of the whole.

This fortress on the miniature mountain was built along the same lines, except that it was much larger. The enclosing wall formed a rough square. At three corners stood graceful watch towers, and at the fourth corner—just above Ki-Gor—the main buildings reared up proudly.

AS THE jungle man watched, lights appeared, twinkling through the narrow arched windows, and a muffled babble of conversation came faintly to his ears. There were many people up there behind those walls, and Ki-Gor had not the slightest doubt that some of them were slaves.

Ki-Gor had had experience with slave-runners and slave dealers, before. Moors and Mohammedan Sudanese in the Western Sahara, and in East Africa, Arabs and Mohammedan Somalis. They were universally a cruel and completely ruthless lot, buying and selling poor miserable blacks and careless of the suffering and death they caused by the way. And while on occasion Ki-Gor could be as hard and implacable as any Moslem fanatic, he was incapable of deliberate unreasoning cruelty.

A distant jingling intruded on Ki-Gor's reflections, and he thought back immediately to the slave anklet that Helene had found. He listened closely now, and seemed to hear hundreds of those little bells. Ki-Gor's lips drew back in a soft snarl. He wondered whether Helene was that minute among those slaves on the plateau—with a jingling fetter riveted to her ankle.

His eyes scanned the heights and the wall above him. Dim though the light was, he could see no sign of guards anywhere along the wall or even in the watch towers. However, the rapidly fading daylight was tricky, and there might be guards stationed where he could not see them.

Just at that moment, there was a chorus of staccato barking sounds, and around the base of the little mountain there came a troop of gray shadows. Night was descending swiftly now, and Ki-Gor could see the shapes only very indistinctly. But he saw enough to tell that the gray shadows were baboons.

Could it be that these slavers relied on baboons for guards?

Carefully, Ki-Gor withdrew to the forested ravine. He selected a tall tree and drew himself up into it with the utmost care. High in the upper branches, he found a crotch where he could make himself fairly comfortable for the night. At the same time, when daylight came, he could command a view of the slavers' fortress and observe what went on there while he decided on a course of action. There was no question in his mind but that Helene was a prisoner in the place.

With the coming of the dawn, Ki-Gor had a better opportunity to scrutinize the fortress. Two details which had escaped him the evening before were the doors in the white wall, and the long ramp that led down and across the steep side of the hill.

There were two doors, one small one under the main building, and the other, a larger one, set in the wall halfway along toward the watch tower on the next corner. It was from this second door that the man-made ramp extended down the hill. Ki-Gor guessed that the ramp was for the purpose of enabling horsemen to scale the steep hill to the fortress, and his guess was borne out soon after the sun rose.

The first sounds which Ki-Gor heard that morning were a subdued mumbling coming from scores of unseen mouths, and the same jingling of fettered anklets that he had heard the night before. Then a column of smoke poured up apparently from a great fire in the middle of the enclosure. A while later, there were some shouted commands, and an answering murmur from the unseen crowd. At the same time, two figures appeared on the top of the wall, lounging toward the corner watch tower. These men were dressed in the manner of the Fulahs, the strapping Mohammedan Negroes from the Western Sudan. They no more belonged in this East African picture than did the Moorish castle, itself.

A little later, the arched door in the middle of the wall swung open, and one by one four tall blacks rode out on horses. They looked like Somalis and wore the typical Somali white cap on the backs of their long, narrow heads. They each carried a long-barreled gun which they waved in farewell to the Fulahs on the wall. Then their horses picked their way slowly down the ramp to the bottom of the hill. From there they set off at a gallop toward the east.

KI-GOR WATCHED these activities with the keenest interest. The most significant thing he saw, however, was that at the bottom of the hill, the Somalis walked their horses fearlessly through a large troop of baboons gathered there. The baboons had not paid the slightest attention to the horsemen.

There could be only one explanation to that, and that was—the baboons were not wild ones. Ki-Gor had never tried to tame baboons, himself, but he knew that it was quite possible to do so. The farmers in South Africa, he knew, had pet chacmas, as well trained and intelligent as dogs.

These baboons here were not chacmas. They were beautiful, silver-gray hamadryads.

As far as Ki-Gor could tell, there were about sixty of the animals. They were apparently perfectly free to move about as they liked, yet they never left the steep sides of the hill. They climbed about ceaselessly, here and there on the rocky slopes. Sometimes some of them went up to the foot of the wall, looked inquiringly upwards, and then strutted along its base. None of them ever attempted to scale the smooth side of the wall—it was obviously too high above them—at the same time, they seemed to be keeping a watch. Their actions convinced Ki-Gor that they were the real guards of the slavers' fortress.

It was well into the middle of the morning before Ki-Gor climbed down from his perch in the tree top. The three Somalis had ridden back, one of them with the body of an antelope lying across his pommel, and had gone through the pack of hamadryads and up the ramp to the door in the wall. There was a babble of noises as the door closed behind the Somalis. Human voices shouted, horses nickered, and Ki-Gor even heard the baaing of goats. Then the fortress gradually relapsed into silence. Ki-Gor felt safe in going down to the ground.

His first act was to go down to a little stream in the ravine. There he stripped off the leafy bandage around his thigh, and gently washed the wounds out with the cold water. In spite of the fall, and the strenuous pursuit of the band of blacks, the wounds were beginning to heal. In a day or two more, Ki-Gor thought he might be able to throw away his crutch. He debated with himself whether or not he should apply a fresh bandage of leaves, and in the end decided to hunt for certain healing herbs which might be growing along the banks of the little stream.

He proceeded along the bank of the stream, walking on both feet, now, and using the crutch only to ease the weight on his left leg. He had not gone far when he heard something or someone coming toward him through the underbrush.

It sounded like a human being, but if it was, it was a very heavy and very clumsy human being. Only a stranger to Africa could make such a noise walking through undergrowth that was not especially thick. Ki-Gor limped quietly away from the stream to have a look at the person who was making such heavy work of traveling through the jungle.

Ki-Gor was prepared for something pretty strange, but when he finally caught sight of the person plowing through the underbrush, he blinked in astonishment. It was a short, plump man with lemon-colored skin and large, sleepy eyes. He was waddling slowly along hampered by the most curious costume Ki-Gor had ever seen. He wore a long black full-skirted coat, and below it a quantity of flimsy white muslin flapped around his thick legs. On his wavy black hair was a small round black cap.

Noiselessly, Ki-Gor followed this apparition as he made his way to the bank of the little stream. Now and then the stranger bent over and plucked some herbs. They were herbs with whose medicinal properties Ki-Gor was familiar. Whoever the stranger was, he certainly knew his herbs.

What manner of man this was, Ki-Gor could not figure out. He was not a Negro, he was not a Somali or a Sudanese, and he was not an Arab. And if he were some kind of Berber, Ki-Gor had never seen that kind before. And whatever he was, he was not at home in the jungle, so Ki-Gor reasoned that he must have come from the white fortress on the hill.

Ki-Gor smiled grimly. Chance had offered him a fine opportunity to find out something about that fortress. He crept closer to the unsuspecting stranger. The plump man bent over to pick an herb, and when he straightened up, Ki-Gor reached out his crutch and tapped him smartly behind the ear with it. The stranger collapsed gently.

KI-GOR DEFTLY trussed the flabby arms and legs with vines and then stood in front of the stranger and waited for him to recover consciousness. The jungle man had no idea what language the stranger would speak or even understand, but he decided to try English first.

As the large, heavy eyelids fluttered open, Ki-Gor said, "Who are you?"

The stranger's eyes flew open. He gave a squeak of terror, and began to shudder violently.

"Do you understand English?" Ki-Gor demanded severely. "Who are you?"

"Oh, yess!" the man cried. "Most certainly! Most certainly I am understanding English! I am peace-loving Hindu of utmost European education, having been graduated with honors and degree of M.D. from Bombay University. Doctor Hurree Dass, sahib, and your most willing servant!"

Ki-Gor stared at the terrified stranger for a moment in puzzled silence.

"Please, sahib," the man gibbered, "if it be not too impertinent of humble student of medicine to inquire—what is your name and lofty rank. Surely you are famous English sporting duke in fancy hunting costume?"

"I am Ki-Gor," the jungle man said briefly, "and I will ask the questions."

"Oh, yess!" said Doctor Hurree Dass hastily. "No offense, I am sure! Gladly will I answer all questions, although at the moment I am experiencing slight but disagreeable headache."

"Where do you live?" Ki-Gor demanded.

"At the Jebel Musa, sahib," the Hindu replied. "That is the white edifice on the hill nearby. I am retained as medical adviser to Sheikh ibn Daoud who is master of the place."

"Ibn Daoud?" said Ki-Gor sharply. "Oh, yes, the slave trader."

The Hindu looked startled. "You have heard of him, sahib?"

"Certainly," said Ki-Gor, although until that moment he had never heard of Sheikh ibn Daoud.

"Er—please to enunciate your name again," said the Hindu nervously.

"Ki-Gor," said the jungle man. "If you have never heard of me, perhaps ibn Daoud has."

"Ki-Gor," the Hindu repeated doubtfully. "No, I have not the honor of knowing the name. Perhaps, you are not masquerading English duke at all?"

"I am not," said Ki-Gor. "I wish to see ibn Daoud and talk to him."

"Ah," said the Hindu, "I think there are difficulties in way. Access to Jebel Musa not an easy matter."

"You will take me there," said Ki-Gor, drawing his hunting knife.

The Hindu shrieked in terror, as Ki-Gor reached down with the knife. Then he collapsed shuddering as the jungle man merely slashed the vine ropes on the plump arms.

"Oh, dearie me!" Doctor Hurree Dass moaned. "I mistook knifing gesture. Momentarily, I feared your purpose to be mayhem."

"Stand up," Ki-Gor commanded, and the Hindu scrambled to his feet. "You will take me to Jebel Musa."

"Oh, yess," said Hurree Dass. "But not answering for consequences, you know, my dear fellow. Ibn Daoud and his retainers are men of utmost determination, you see."

"So am I," Ki-Gor growled, placing the crutch under his left arm. "Lead the way."

"My dear fellow!" the Hindu exclaimed. "Look at condition of your leg! You have been most grievously bitten! How did it happen?"

"Baboon," said Ki-Gor laconically, then added, "A wild one."

"Dearie me!" said the doctor. "We must pay attention directly, or septicemia will inevitably set in."

"No, the leg is healing," said Ki-Gor. "This happened four days ago."

"Gracious!" said the Hindu, staring. "I perceive that healing process is indeed setting in. Remarkable!"

"Hurry up!" Ki-Gor commanded.

"Hurrying," said the Hindu, and moved clumsily through the underbrush. "Hurrying like anything!"

A few minutes later, Ki-Gor said carelessly, "A white woman was brought to ibn Daoud last night?"

"How did you know?" said Hurree Dass over his shoulder. Then a thought seemed to strike him. "Oh, of course! Most remarkable woman. Dressed in same bizarre costume as yourself. Some relation to you, perhaps?"

"Yes," Ki-Gor responded grimly. "She is my wife."

"Oh, dearie me!" the Hindu said. "Most awkward situation!"

"Awkward for ibn Daoud," Ki-Gor said.

"Ah," breathed Hurree Dass. "Possibly so. By the bye, have no fear of the sacred baboons up here. They are quite tame, I assure you, and have most loving, affectionate dispositions. They are hurting nobody—except escaping slaves."

Ki-Gor grunted disdainfully and followed the waddling figure of the Hindu out of the undergrowth toward Jebel Musa.

CHAPTER IV

THE GREAT HALL OF Jebel Musa was richly furnished with beautiful deep-piled rugs and carpets, delicately carved tables, and fat silk-covered cushions. But the men who sat on those luxurious cushions and stared at Ki-Gor looked out of place—with one exception. The one exception was ibn Daoud himself. He was a huge, grizzled Arab with a keen, predatory face, and his gorgeous robes would have done credit to the Sultan of Morocco.

But the others—there were fourteen of them besides Hurree Dass—were as vicious a looking gang of cutthroats as Ki-Gor had ever seen. There were two Negroid Arabs, probably Zanzibar Arabs with more than a trace of Zulu blood. There were three Fulahs from the Western Sudan. There was a long, lean villain who looked like a Masai, though he wore a Mohammedan cap, and two others like him who might have been renegade Gallas from Abyssinia. And finally, there were six cruel-faced Somalis.

Ki-Gor stood in the middle of the floor before ibn Daoud, and leaned indolently on his crutch. The grizzled Arab stared over his head and spoke in Swahili.

"You say your name is Ki-Gor," said ibn Daoud. "Well, we do not know that name."

"I am surprised," said Ki-Gor haughtily. "It is well enough known in other parts."

"Be it so," the Arab shrugged. "Here, you are a stranger. And we of Jebel Musa do not take kindly to strangers. What is it you wanted?"

"The white woman who was brought here last night," Ki-Gor said simply. "She is my wife."

"There was a white woman brought here last night," ibn Daoud said slowly. "A party of black men brought her and sold her to us."

"Yes," said Ki-Gor pleasantly. "She wandered away from my camp, and they kidnaped her."

"That is nothing to us," said the Arab. "If you do not keep your women at home, but permit them to go abroad unveiled and scandalously unclothed—you must take the consequences."

"You mean," said Ki-Gor, "that you will not give my wife back to me?"

"Of course not," said ibn Daoud with a contemptuous smile. "Are we mad? We have bought and paid for the woman. She is a great prize—we can sell her for a fortune."

"Well then, the affair is perfectly simple," Ki-Gor said. "I will buy her."

"You will buy her!" Ibn Daoud's eyes flew open. "With what?"

"I will give you one hundred tusks for her," Ki-Gor said calmly.

"One hundred tusks!" the Arab shouted. "Where are they?"

"Oh, I will have to go and get them," Ki-Gor said. "It will take me perhaps ten days to fetch them here."

The Arab's eyes grew cunning. "Pooh!" he exclaimed. "A mere hundred tusks for that paragon of beauty and excellence. Why, she—"

"A hundred tusks is a fortune to you, O ibn Daoud!" Ki-Gor thundered. "And furthermore, you must release the woman to me immediately. You have my word that I will return with her price. No one in Africa questions Ki-Gor's word—and lives long afterward."

Ibn Daoud stared at the jungle man in amazement, and an astonished murmur went over the motley crew in the hall.

"Either you are mad or I am," the Arab said finally, with a mystified shake of his head. "You come here dressed like a Bantu savage and prattle of a hundred tusks and make demands as if you were a sultan. I doubt if you could get two tusks. I really do not know why we waste our time talking to you."

"It is unfortunate, O ibn Daoud," Ki-Gor said quietly, "that you are not familiar with the name of Ki-Gor. Let me inform you of something. It would have been far better for you to have handed over my woman in the beginning and won my everlasting gratitude and friendship. You did not do that. However, if you agree to give me my woman now, I will return with one hundred large tusks in ten days' time, and I will hold no grudge against you. But hear this, O Slave Trader! If I go forth from this place today without my woman, I will return with a thousand Masai tribesmen and I will slaughter you and your puny little band in one night!"

IBN DAOUD looked at Ki-Gor in wonderment and some uneasiness.

"Truly," he said, "we are talking to someone who is insane."

"Not so insane," Ki-Gor drawled, "that I cannot notice that your fortress here is severely undermanned. Fifteen men are not enough to defend a place like this. A good-sized caravan would outnumber you heavily, and could conquer you if they were so inclined."

The Arab studied Ki-Gor with shrewd eyes. Then he said, "We make up for our small numbers by the strength and cunning of each member of the band."

Ki-Gor turned his head and cast a disdainful glance of appraisal at the men sitting around him.

"Are they so strong and so cunning?" he said contemptuously. "Who is the strongest and cunningest among them?"

An angry growl went up from ibn Daoud's men, and the renegade Masai sprang to his feet, eyes rolling. He loomed seven inches taller than Ki-Gor.

"Do you know," said ibn Daoud, "do you know of one stronger or cunninger than Malgo, here?"

Ki-Gor snorted derisively.

"Hah!" he exclaimed. "I am but recently wounded, and yet I could handle two such brittle bean poles as that at a time."

The Masai gave a howl of rage and flung himself upon Ki-Gor. A slender blade flickered at the end of the long snake-like black arm. Ki-Gor pivoted swiftly on the crutch. His good right leg braced hard, and his arms shot up into the air. Fingers like steel springs closed over the descending knife hand of the Masai. Ki-Gor jerked downward. The Masai screamed with pain and fell forward, his long, narrow torso doubling up like a jack-knife.

Then Ki-Gor's right fist crossed over like a bolt of lightning. It caught the falling Masai just below the ear on the point of the jaw. The sound of the blow was something between a smack and a crunch. The Masai was flung back six feet. He wavered a moment, his head rolling uncontrollably on his shoulders, and his lower jaw jutting grotesquely to one side. Then he sagged to the floor, blood oozing from his mouth and ears.

"You fool!" ibn Daoud cried. "You have broken his jaw!"

"Broken his jaw?" Ki-Gor replied contemptuously. "I have killed him."

A heavy silence filled the hall. All eyes were on the limp figure on the floor. Ibn Daoud's right hand crept downward toward the long-barreled pistol stuck in the sash around his waist. Then a shrill voice shattered the silence. It was Doctor Hurree Dass.

"Ibn Daoud! No!" the Hindu cried, and ran across the carpet toward the Arab, his plump body shaking like a jelly. He broke out into rapid-fire Arabic, while ibn Daoud listened, frowning. Ki-Gor could not understand Arabic, but he had a sneaking suspicion of what Hurree Dass was talking about.

AT FIRST ibn Daoud shook his head at the Hindu's idea but when Hurree Dass redoubled his arguments, the Arab grew thoughtful. Eventually, he lifted a restraining hand, and the Hindu fell silent.

Then ibn Daoud stepped forward two steps and addressed Ki-Gor in Swahili.

"We will not give you back your woman, nor will we permit you to take her away with a promise to return with a hundred tusks. But we will do this—we will admit you to our band as a regular member. You will share equally with the rest in the profits we make. When your share has accumulated and you have earned the equivalent of a hundred tusks, then you may go away with your woman, unmolested. You have killed one of our strongest fighting men, but we will not hold that against you. The man was a troublemaker and we are better off without him. But we control a rich trade here at Jebel Musa, and we have plenty of rivals who would like to take it away from us. We need a few more guards—as you yourself guessed. Therefore we make you this fair offer."

Ki-Gor stood silently for a moment. On the surface, it was a fair offer. Certainly, this chieftain was not obliged to make it—he could have ordered Ki-Gor's death if he had wished, for the jungle man was at his mercy. Instead he had offered equal participation in a trade that was as rich as it was unholy.

But Ki-Gor was perfectly aware that ibn Daoud would keep his end of the bargain only as long as he realized a benefit from it. The Arab needed Ki-Gor's fighting prowess, and any agreement between them would very likely end just as soon as ibn Daoud found that he no longer needed Ki-Gor.

However, if Ki-Gor accepted the offer, it would give him an opportunity to stay inside the fortress and devise a means of getting Helene and himself out safely. He guessed that his freedom of action would probably be restricted, but that was a problem he would meet when it arose.

Ibn Daoud grew impatient. "What do you say, Ki-Gor?" he demanded.

"I accept," Ki-Gor said calmly, "on one condition."

"We permit no conditions," the Arab said imperiously.

"One condition," said Ki-Gor firmly, "or I do not accept."

"Well, what is the condition?" ibn Daoud said testily.

"That I can see my wife at any and all times."

The Arab's eyes smoldered for a moment, then he appeared to consider. Finally he said, "Why not? After all, she is your wife. And you will be working with us to buy her release. We will allow you the company of your wife."

"Then I accept," Ki-Gor said promptly.

"Very well then," said the Arab. "Henceforth, you are a member of this band with the rights and privileges of that membership. You will accept all orders without question from me, the leader. But be warned, Ki-Gor. We are no fools. We'll be keeping an eye on you. And at the slightest sign of treachery—"

"Ibn Daoud," Ki-Gor broke in coolly, "I am no fool either, and I shall keep an eye on you."

"Wah!" the Arab exploded in astonishment. Then a crooked smile stole over his hawk-like features. "So be it," he shrugged. "You begin your duty immediately. In a short while a caravan is arriving to do some business with us. Your post will be in the slave kraal, inside the main door. You will permit only two men from the caravan to come through that door to pick out slaves. The rest you will keep out. After the caravan has gone, you will be relieved, and then you can see your woman."

Ibn Daoud said a few words of Arabic to Doctor Hurree Dass and then turned back to Ki-Gor.

"Go with Hurree Dass," he said. "He will look over those wounds, and then lead you to your post."

Ki-Gor knew that his wounds were healing well enough so that they needed no further attention, but he followed the plump Hindu out of the room. It was possible that Hurree Dass could give him some more information about ibn Daoud and Jebel Musa.

HURREE DASS' dispensary was a small, neat room with a window looking down onto the slave kraal. Ki-Gor gazed at the scene below with considerable interest, while Hurree Dass inspected his thigh.

"Remarkable!" the Hindu murmured. "You have performed most remarkable self-medication. This is strong evidence that you are well acquainted with beneficial herbs. At earliest opportunity, I must be comparing notes with you. This leg requires only light protective bandage."

"How long have you been at Jebel Musa?" Ki-Gor asked bluntly.

"Three years approximately," the doctor replied. "Before that, I was practicing physician in Hindu colony in Nairobi. But a peculiar circumstance advised somewhat hasty moving away from that place. During removal operations, I chanced to meet ibn Daoud and received invitation to come here."

"I can only see about a hundred slaves out there," Ki-Gor commented. "That isn't many."

"Ah, that is because of our policy," Hurree Dass replied. "Quality is watchword, not quantity, you see? Ibn Daoud believed old-fashioned slavers' methods were too dreadfully wasteful. Average black fellow who is captured for slave material is mighty poor specimen of humanity, don't you know? Under-nourished, weak, and prone to all manner of disease. Sixty to seventy per cent get sick and die before they even reach ultimate consumer. To slave dealers, they are thus dead loss, don't you see? Forgive feeble joke, please."

Ki-Gor hid a smile at the Hindu's florid English. "Go on," he commanded.

"So," Hurree Dass continued, "we institute policy of taking only good material. We keep them here three months, feeding them only finest nourishing food—I am also skilled dietitian, you see? I inoculate them all for several diseases, and when time comes to sell them, they are finest quality slaves—prime blacks. We ask and get ten times ordinary price from slave dealers. They pay it with utmost willingness because they know they run minimum risk of loss during transportation."

"Hm," Ki-Gor murmured, looking out of the window. "I should think they would hate to be sold—the slaves, I mean."

"Oh, don't worry," the Hindu said. "That does not matter to ibn Daoud. Do not get idea that ibn Daoud feeds them well because of tender heart. I assure you, my dear fellow, he is impelled by economic considerations only. Besides, there is a policy of mental as well as physical conditioning we follow regarding slaves."

"What do you mean?"

"We beat them all regularly twice a day," Hurree Dass said. "That is to put them in proper frame of mind for life of servitude."

Ki-Gor's eyes narrowed at the thought, and he turned away. But evidently, Hurree Dass had caught the expression of revulsion on his face.

"And by the bye," said the Hindu, lowering his voice, "if you object to such ideas, I would suggest not expressing such objection. Ibn Daoud is man of utmost determination, you see?"

"I shall say nothing," Ki-Gor shrugged. "I care only about one thing, and that is to get my wife safely away from here. As long as ibn Daoud does not break his agreement and try to sell her, he can do anything he pleases."

"Ah," said Hurree Dass, and fell silent.

Ki-Gor looked sharply at him. The Hindu was staring thoughtfully off into space. Then he seemed to make a decision.

"My dear fellow," he said, "I am going to tell you something which could be grave embarrassment if not danger to me personally, if ibn Daoud knew I told you. However, you are a good sort, don't you know, and besides you know a great deal about herbs and that is a very admirable thing. So I will risk my precious neck and tell you something. You will not repeat it?"

"No," said Ki-Gor, fixing his eyes on the Hindu.

"Well, then—ibn Daoud has not slightest idea of keeping agreement with you. Our best client, Shere Ali, is coming tomorrow or next day. He is certain to offer great price for your wife and—ibn Daoud is certain to sell your wife to Shere Ali."

Hurree Dass got up quickly and went to the door of his dispensary and looked out. Then he came back to Ki-Gor.

"I will just place bandages on that leg, now," he announced in a loud voice, "and then I will show you your post."

CHAPTER V

A FEW MINUTES LATER, Ki-Gor lolled against the wall beside the main door to the slave kraal, and pondered over Hurree Dass' warning. Was it a genuine gesture of friendship from the strange doctor? Or was it a deliberate trap set by ibn Daoud himself?

It was quite possible that the Arab had directed Hurree Dass to deliver that warning so that Ki-Gor would be led into trying to escape from the fortress with Helene. And when Ki-Gor tried to escape, he would be cut down by a watchful ambush.

Ki-Gor mulled the question over in his mind for the next three hours.

The caravan that ibn Daoud was expecting came along, and its members seemed peaceably inclined. But the owner of Jebel Musa took no chances. The watch towers at each corner of the kraal were manned, and one of the Somalis stood on the wall above the main door, when Ki-Gor opened it to admit two men from the caravan. Ibn Daoud and one of the Zanzibar Arabs, armed to the teeth, conducted the two visiting traders among the slaves. Fifteen sleek, strapping blacks were selected and herded back toward the door in the wall. Then a curious thing happened.

One of the Somalis approached with a hammer and a cold chisel and struck off the jingling anklets from the legs of the newly sold slaves. The visiting traders then put their own chains on the blacks and led them out through the door.

This puzzled Ki-Gor. Why were the belled anklets taken off when the slaves were sold? If the slaves were not to wear them when they left Jebel Musa, why should they wear them when they were inside the kraal? Ki-Gor could think of no satisfactory answer to the question.

Then he looked at the wall around the kraal and he saw a possible reason for the bells.

For a prison wall, it was ridiculously low. The top of the wall was scarcely eight feet above the ground on the inside of the kraal. It would be absurdly easy to leap up, grip the top of the wall with one's fingers and draw one's self up and across. On the other side, perhaps the drop was a little greater, but not enough to prevent even an ordinary man from escaping.

It might be, Ki-Gor reflected, that the belled anklets were for the specific purpose of enabling ibn Daoud and his men to hear any attempted escape over that low wall. However, if the escape were made early in the evening before the slaves went to sleep, the guards would not be able to distinguish one anklet from another. It was most peculiar.

When Ki-Gor closed the great door after the visiting traders, ibn Daoud beside him turned away and called to somebody within the castle.

"Luma!" the Arab shouted. "Luma, come out with the account books!"

A moment later, a small Negro girl with a twisted, emaciated left leg, came limping out of the castle, carrying two ledgers.

"Come on, thou misshapen little monkey!" the Arab snarled. "Don't keep me waiting!"

"Coming, Sidi," the little Negress panted, dragging her crippled leg hurriedly across the kraal.

"Don't answer back, you miserable little ingrate!" ibn Daoud thundered, and went toward the limping girl. A terrified moan escaped her lips as she saw the Arab approaching, and she sank to her knees on the ground. Ibn Daoud strode to her side, and cuffed her brutally on the head.

"Wretch!" the Arab shouted. "I have taught thee how to set down figures and add them up. I have taught thee to read the Koran like a hakim. Let this teach thee to be gratefully prompt, and to obey quickly and silently."

He wrenched the ledgers out of the girl's trembling hands and turned away.

"Get up!" he shouted over his shoulder. "And show Ki-Gor the way to the room of the white woman."

KI-GOR'S FACE was blank as he strolled past ibn Daoud toward the crippled Negro girl, but he had to fight down an impulse to cuff the Arab for his treatment of the helpless slave. She scrambled to her feet as he came toward her.

"This way, Sidi," she said in Swahili, and hurried toward the castle, dragging her leg pitifully.

"Gently, gently, little sister," Ki-Gor said. He spoke not in Swahili but in the Bantu dialect of the Buganda.

The girl threw a startled glance at him over her shoulder.

"Gently," Ki-Gor repeated. "There is plenty of time for two lame ones to go their own pace."

The girl stopped and looked incredulously at Ki-Gor as he swung up beside her on his crutch. Ki-Gor felt a wave of pity go out toward the girl. His had probably been the first kind words she had heard in a long time.

"How do they call you?" he asked genially, as they went slowly toward the castle.

"My name is Luma," the girl replied. "I am of the Banda people, who live not far from here."

"And how long have you dwelt at Jebel Musa?" Ki-Gor said with a quick glance behind him to make sure he was out of earshot of ibn Daoud.

"More than two years, Sidi," Luma replied.

"You are enslaved, aren't you?" Ki-Gor asked. "Why do you not wear an anklet of bells like the others?"

"It should be plain enough," the girl said sadly. "With this withered leg I could never run away. But this is indiscreet talk for me, Sidi—are you not a new member of the band?"

"Yes, I have just had that honor conferred on me," Ki-Gor said dryly.

"And yet you speak to me in kind tones," Luma said wonderingly. "It is not customary. I don't understand."

"If I tried to explain that," Ki-Gor said, "then it would be I who was indiscreet."

Luma stood aside at the door into the castle, and as Ki-Gor stepped past her, she looked up at him with a gleam of understanding in her pinched little face.

"Down the hall to your left, Sidi," she said quietly. Then as she limped after him, she whispered, "The white woman—is she related to you?"

"She is my wife," Ki-Gor informed her.

"Ah!" Luma breathed. "It becomes clearer, now. Ah, Sidi, she is beautiful, and she speaks with kind words just as you do. There is her room at the end of the hall—the door is unlocked, I think."

A moment later, Helene was in his arms, laughing and crying at the same time.

"Oh, Ki-Gor!" she cried, "I knew you'd come—sooner or later—but—but—"

"There now," Ki-Gor murmured, patting her awkwardly on the shoulder. "Don't cry, Helene. I'm here, now, and everything will be all right."

"Oh—it's—it's been an eternity!"

"I know," Ki-Gor said soothingly, "but don't worry, now. Because we're together again, and nobody can separate us."

Helene gulped and smiled through her tears. Then sudden concern came into her face.

"But how—how did you get in?" she said.

"I walked in," Ki-Gor replied calmly.

"Well—how are we going to get out? Are you a prisoner?"

"No, not exactly," the jungle man said. "I'm not supposed to be—"

Just then he caught sight of the iron band on Helene's ankle and a wave of rage swept over him.

"So!" he said tightly. "So they put one of those things on you!"

"Yes," she answered sadly, "and they're not so pretty when you have to wear one, I've decided. Oh, I just go sick all over when I think of that anklet on the trail. Why did I pick it up? We've had nothing but bad luck ever since that minute!"

"Well, don't worry," Ki-Gor said grimly, "you won't have to wear that much longer."

HE TOLD her briefly of how he had tracked her abductors, and found Hurree Dass, and of the fight with the renegade Masai, and of ibn Daoud's proposition.

"But," he concluded, "an agreement like that will be broken whenever the Arab feels like it, and I would be a fool to think otherwise. I think we will just walk out of here whenever we see a chance."

"But, how, Ki-Gor?"

"I'm not sure yet," the jungle man said. "They will be watchful, of course. But you are not locked up—you can walk around the castle. The best thing to do may be the simplest and boldest. Just arrange to meet by the outside door right after the evening meal and then—just walk out."

"Yes, but the anklet," Helene said, "they'll hear it."

"They won't notice it, because early in the evening, all the slaves in the kraal will be walking around."

"No, I mean the baboons will hear it. That's what these bells are for."

"What do you mean?" said Ki-Gor.

"Ibn Daoud said that the baboons are trained to attack anybody wearing bells—"

"Oh!" Ki-Gor pursed his lips. So that was it. That was why the wall around the kraal was so low. Anybody trying to escape over the wall would meet certain and terrible death from the baboons. It was a fearful prospect.

But as he digested Helene's information, a tiny doubt began to creep into Ki-Gor's mind. Ibn Daoud, he knew, was a subtle, tricky Arab. It was quite possible that he would spread a story like that among the slaves, and it would be sufficient to frighten them out of any ideas of escaping so long as they wore the belled anklets. Who would be brave enough to test the story and find out whether it was true or false?

At this moment, footsteps sounded outside the door, and then ibn Daoud walked into the room.

"I am sorry to interrupt your meeting with your wife," the Arab said, "but it is necessary to discuss your duties. I'll give your choice of assignments. You can go out now and stand watch for the rest of the day, or you can have the day free and stand watch all night. Which would you rather do?"

Ki-Gor thought quickly. It was hard to tell which would be better suited for a night escape—to be on duty or off. He finally chose the day assignment, so that he would not have to account for his whereabouts during the night. He embraced Helene briefly and followed ibn Daoud out of the room.

His post was the watch tower at the end of the wall in which the main door of the kraal was set. From there, he was able to size up the walls and approaches of Jebel Musa at his leisure.

He had already estimated the height of the wall on the inside of the kraal at a little less than eight feet—easy enough for a man of ordinary agility to scale. On the outside the ground fell away, so that there was a drop of about fifteen feet from the top of the wall. But even this would not be a serious obstacle. Ki-Gor felt that his wounds were sufficiently healed so that he could make the drop if it was necessary without any ill effects.

However, the plan that had been forming in his mind was not concerned with going over the wall. It occurred to him that the best method of escape was the simplest and the boldest, and would succeed because of its very obviousness. Just after the evening meal, for instance, he could arrange to meet Helene as if by accident near the outside door of the castle. There would probably be a guard there, but it would be the work of a moment to dispose of him, and then he and Helene would calmly walk out. Their disappearance would not be discovered immediately, but Ki-Gor needed only a few minutes to gain the wooded ravine. Once there, he felt confident of holding off any pursuit, or eluding it under cover of darkness.

It all depended on whether or not ibn Daoud's fantastic story about the baboons attacking bells was true or not. Ki-Gor had to admit that it could be true. There were plenty of ways by which baboons could be trained to react savagely to bells. But was it true?

ALL DAY, Ki-Gor pondered the question. But when he was relieved just before sunset by one of the Somalis he still had not decided the point in his mind. But, walking along the wall toward the castle, he saw two things that impressed him.

One was the feeding of the baboons. They were clustered around the outside of the doorway to the castle, and Luma herself was tossing handfuls of food out amongst them. For such fierce-looking beasts, those hamadryads behaved as gently as kittens. Luma showed not the slightest fear of them. Ki-Gor remembered that Luma did not wear a belled anklet, but even so the peaceful scene inclined Ki-Gor to doubt the truth of ibn Daoud's carefully circulated story.

The other thing Ki-Gor noticed when he chanced to look back at the watch tower he had just left. The Mohammedan Somali was making ready to say his prescribed evening prayers. The thought struck Ki-Gor that those evening prayers might provide a moment in the castle when the members of the band would be off guard. They were all Mohammedans, even the two Gallas from Abyssinia, therefore they would all say evening prayers. Whether they would say them all together or not, Ki-Gor did not know. There was the time element to be figured, also. If they were as prompt as the Somali in the watch tower, it would still be too light to attempt a break for freedom.

The jungle man went inside the castle and swung down into the main hall. He was still using his crutch, although his leg was almost strong enough to walk without it. Perhaps it would relax the vigilance of the guards.

Ibn Daoud and nine of the band were assembled in the main hall as Ki-Gor went in, and his heart sank. If they said prayers now they would be finished before darkness closed over Jebel Musa. But ibn Daoud came toward him, in his hand two rawhide whips. The Arab held one of the whips out toward Ki-Gor.

"At this time of day," ibn Daoud said with a wolfish smile, "we are accustomed to whipping the slaves. It is very good for them and is incidentally great sport."

Ki-Gor drew his hand away with a frown. "No," he said.

"Why not?" the Arab demanded, the smile dying on his face.

"I don't think I'd like it," Ki-Gor said simply.

The Arab looked at him a long time, then shrugged his shoulders.

"It matters not," ibn Daoud said. "I will not order you to do it. We of the band usually consider the slave whipping a form of relaxation. So please yourself. Go where you please—anywhere except outside the wall. If you attempt to do that, you will be shot from one of the watch towers."

"Thank you for the warning," Ki-Gor said ironically. "I am going to visit my wife—if it is permitted."

"Oh yes," the Arab said carelessly. "We will have some food in this room in about an hour's time. You may eat with us unless you are too proud to do so. Just before the meal, we will gather here for prayers. If you are a True Believer, you are invited to join those, also."

"No, I am no Muslim," Ki-Gor stated. "I will join you when you sit down to eat."

The Arab bent a sour look at Ki-Gor, then turned away, and a moment later he and the other nine men went out into the kraal snapping their whips and laughing.

Swiftly the jungle man went down the narrow corridor to Helene's room. An hour from then, it would be dark. And the slavers of Jebel would be on their knees for their evening devotions to Allah the Great.

Helene stared at him horrified when he told her what he proposed to do.

"But—Ki-Gor! The baboons! I've got a belled anklet on."

A piercing scream came from the kraal, and the sound of terrible blows of a rawhide thong hitting cringing flesh. Again and again came the screams, interspersed with triumphant shouts.

"Oh, those poor slaves!" Helene whispered. "Every evening and every morning this happens! I can't understand such cold cruelty in human beings."

"And I can't," Ki-Gor said, "but listen. I think ibn Daoud's story about the baboons is not true. I think he is just bluffing you and all the other prisoners with it. Those baboons seem much too friendly to attack human beings, with bells or without."

"But you don't know for certain, Ki-Gor, do you?"

"NO, I don't," the jungle man admitted, "but I think the chances are in our favor. And we've got to get away from this place as soon as we can. Ibn Daoud isn't going to keep his promise to me that he won't sell you as a slave—he isn't that kind. We've got to forestall him with a quick, unexpected move. And these prayers tonight will give us five minutes or so to get away under cover of the darkness."

"Oh, Ki-Gor!" Helene murmured. "I'm so afraid! What if the baboons really are trained to bells?"

"If they are," Ki-Gor said, tight-lipped, "then we will be in a serious situation. But every minute we stay here we are in a serious situation, too, so I think we'll have to take the chance."

"All right, Ki-Gor," Helene said, and lifted her eyes bravely to his. "I'll do whatever you say—even—even if I am afraid."

Ki-Gor gripped her hand hard. "You are braver than you think," he said, simply.

"Well," said Helene, drawing a deep breath, "how are we going to meet at the outside door? The only way I can get there is up the corridor and right past the door to the big hall. They'll hear me walking along the corridor with this anklet, and they'll see me as I go past the door. That is, they could see me if one of them happened to look that way."

"Don't worry about them hearing you," Ki-Gor said. "All the house-slaves except Luma wear the anklets, and the men at prayers will simply think you're one of the slaves."

"That's true," said Helene, "but suppose they catch a glimpse of me going toward the outside door."

"They won't," Ki-Gor replied. "It's a fairly narrow door, and just as you go past it, I'll step into the doorway and cover you from them."

"Well—I hope it works," Helene said, with a tremulous smile.

"It's got to work," Ki-Gor said grimly. "Now, I'll leave you here just before they come in from their recreation at the whipping post. You had better leave your door open, and listen. I think you will be able to hear them start their prayers—"

"Yes," Helene interrupted, "I heard them last night."

"Good. Then just come right up the corridor the minute you hear the prayers beginning, go past me without hesitation, and don't stop until you get to the outside door. I think there's a light there, isn't there?"

"I don't know, Ki-Gor."

"There must be. Probably a big oil lamp. Turn it out if you can, or anyway, turn the flame as low as possible. I'll stay in the doorway of the main hall just long enough to make sure they do not suspect anything going on, and then I'll come up the corridor as fast as I can and join you at the front door. All we need then is five minutes."

"All right," said Helene. "I hope I can find out how to turn the light down or out."

"Do your best," Ki-Gor urged. "Or else when we get the door open, the light will shine outside and attract the attention of the men in the watch towers."

"All right," Helene said again, and then said no more for fear Ki-Gor would detect the terrible feeling of impending calamity that was growing within her.

"I think I'd better go back now," Ki-Gor said, "and look innocent while those cut-throats come in from their sport in the kraal. Listen sharply for the prayers."

Helene nodded dumbly and put her arms on Ki-Gor's great shoulders and her head on his broad chest. He patted her silently and she released him and stepped back.

"That's right—smile," Ki-Gor said. "It looks a little risky—what we're going to do—but it'll be all over in a little while, and we'll be out in the open—*free!*"

HE TURNED and walked up the corridor.

He had taken several steps before he realized that he was not using his crutch. His left thigh hardly pained at all. He gripped the crutch with a grin. It might come in handy as a weapon if the baboons proved vicious. Although, by now he was thoroughly convinced that the baboons were absolutely harmless, bells or no bells.

A few minutes later, ibn Daoud led his crew in from the kraal, sweating and panting and very pleased with themselves. From their conversation, Ki-Gor gathered that one or two of the slaves had taken their beatings very hard, a circumstance which had amused ibn Daoud's band a great deal.

Ki-Gor strolled blank faced out of the main hall as the band poured in.

"Wah!" cried ibn Daoud, as he looked at the jungle man. "No sport, no prayers for the Unbeliever! What satisfaction can Unbelievers get out of life anyway!"

The slavers roared with laughter at their leader's sally, but Ki-Gor made no response. At the moment he was planning the quickest way of rounding up some friends when he got out—the Masai, perhaps—and returning with them to wipe out this iniquitous slaver nest. But his expressionless face told nothing of his thoughts, and the slavers pushed noisily past him into the great hall and busied themselves spreading their prayer rugs.

Ki-Gor lolled in the corridor just one side of the entrance to the hall and waited for the prayers to begin. Then an encouraging thing happened. One of the Zanzibar Arabs carried a big screen over and placed it across the doorway. It was a piece of luck. Now there would be no need for Ki-Gor to step into that doorway in order to cover Helene's passing with his body.

Suddenly, Ki-Gor heard a soft step behind him. He whirled around and saw Doctor Hurree Dass coming toward him.

"Good evening, my dear friend," said the Hindu, unctuously. "It is utmost pleasure to find another non-Muslim. You are Christian, I presume? Excellent religion in many ways—if it were only possible for poor fallible human beings to adhere to all its beautiful ethics."

Ki-Gor stood mute with dismay. Hurree Dass had chosen a very awkward moment to stand in the corridor discussing religion. At any second, now, the Muslims would raise their sonorous voices in prayers, and Helene would come jingling down the corridor.

But to Ki-Gor's intense relief, the corpulent Hindu shrugged comically and turned away, smiling at Ki-Gor apologetically.

"More's the pity," said Hurree Dass, "but no time now for me to expound ideas on ethics. My friends inside have done considerable superficial damage to otherwise valuable merchandise in kraal. It devolves on doctor at this point to proceed to kraal and attempt to repair some of said damage. May I have pleasure of your company while performing these tasks? Or perhaps you are otherwise engaged?"

"No, thank you," Ki-Gor muttered, and the Hindu inclined his head philosophically.

"Cannot blame you," he said. "The cruel waste of it sometimes enrages me, don't you know? Well, until dinner time."

Just as he walked away and out another door to the kraal, a voice sounded in the great hall behind Ki-Gor. "Ya Allah! Allahi ul-Akbar!"

The evening prayers had begun.

Soon a faint tinkle could be heard down the corridor, and a moment later, Helene came into view, walking gently to try and minimize the sound of the bells. Ki-Gor realized that was a mistake. The jingling would be heard by the men at prayer, and it must not sound furtive or it might arouse their suspicions. He waved imperiously at Helene to hurry.

She looked appealingly at him with eyes grown enormous, but she obeyed his gesture and came toward him at a normal speed, the bells in the anklet clamoring. Silently, Ki-Gor moved ahead of her down the corridor toward the outside door of the castle.

The prayers grew louder and louder in the great hall, and Ki-Gor breathed a little easier. Evidently, Helene's noisy passing had aroused no suspicion. Now, if they could only reach that outside door without running into any house-slaves—

HE ROUNDED a corner in the corridor, and his heart leaped. There, just in front of him and completely unguarded was the door to the outside. It was of heavy reinforced timbers and was fastened by a simple large iron bolt. On the wall beside it, a big oil lamp was burning.

Ki-Gor had just a moment's misgiving as he stepped forward toward the door.

It was too easy.

For a fraction of a second he hesitated, wondering whether ibn Daoud had planned things like this deliberately.

But the door pulled at him like a magnet. Just get past that door, Ki-Gor told himself, and we are free! We can escape the band of slavers and be done with it. He reached up and blew out the lamp with one great puff.

Then his hand groped for the heavy bolt and seized it. Gently, ever so gently, he pulled it. Mercifully, the bolt did not squeak. Helene touched his back in the darkness, and he felt for her hand.

"Hold on to the crutch," he whispered, "we're nearly out."

Carefully he slid the bolt free, and with a sound like a sigh, the great door swung slightly ajar. Ki-Gor gripped the edge of it to prevent it from swinging any further and possibly making a louder noise.

The droning of the Mohammedan prayers in the distance seemed to add to rather than detract from the ominous silence that hung over the world at that moment. A breath of fresh air swept through the narrow opening of the door, and it smelt gloriously sweet to Ki-Gor. He let the door open just wide enough to allow him to pass through. Then he moved forward gently, his left hand holding one end of the crutch. Helene holding the other end, followed him reluctantly.

Suddenly, he felt her stop.

"Ki-Gor!" Her voice came in a suddenly terrified, suddenly agonized whisper.

"Ki-Gor! No! No! We can't go out! It's death!"

The jungle man stepped back toward her.

"It's death!" Helene repeated. "Those baboons *will* attack bells! I *know* they will! *I know because a hamadryad baboon attacked us four days ago when I was carrying that anklet!*"

AN ICY sheet seemed to drape itself over Ki-Gor's bare back. He stood for a fraction of a second stunned and sickened.

Helene was right. And he had been too stupid to remember the incident. They must get back into the castle quickly and try to light the lamp. They must not leave evidence of their attempted escape.

Just then the silence was shattered by a hideous shriek. It pealed again and again on the still air. Another voice shouted feebly. The voices came from the kraal. But the shrieks were suddenly nearer.

There was a scrambling noise and then a jingling thump as of a heavy body hitting the ground. The shrieks went up again louder. Three shots sounded. There was more jingling.

Then came the hoarse barking of many baboons.

Sick with horror, Ki-Gor pushed Helene back through the doorway. Then he pushed the heavy door shut and slammed the bolt home. At the same instant, he heard the commotion of voices behind him. There was nothing to light the lamp with, and if there had been, there was no time to do it.

He turned around with his back to the door and watched the

flickering light from many torches coming down the corridor toward him.

There was no way for him and Helene to dodge the oncoming slavers, no way in the world. They were trapped. Ki-Gor stood stock-still.

Ibn Daoud was in the lead carrying a torch high above his head. Behind him one of the Gallas held a rifle pointed forward.

"You!"

All the venom in the world was concentrated in that one word that was spat out of ibn Daoud's beard.

Ki-Gor glared alertly at the throng of slavers that filled the corridor in front of him. He saw now that the other Galla and one of the Somalis were pointing their rifles at him.

There was absolutely nothing he could do.

There was a momentary diversion when Hurree Dass' voice speaking Swahili sounded at the back of the group of slavers.

"Nothing to worry about, ibn Daoud," Hurree Dass was saying. "Only one of the slaves who went out of his mind after the beating you gave him. He jumped over the wall and the baboons got him, that's all."

The Hindu's voice trailed off suddenly and there was a heavy silence. Then ibn Daoud said, "That was not all. And there is more to come."

And Ki-Gor knew that ibn Daoud spoke the truth.

Swiftly then, the huge Arab organized the situation. One of the Gallas held the muzzle of his gun a foot from Helene's breast. Ki-Gor needed no explanation of that move. He held up his hands while a squat, bull-necked Fulah came up close to him clutching an iron rod.

Ki-Gor bowed his head then and made no move to dodge the terrific blow the Fulah aimed at him. There was momentary swift searing pain and a blinding flash and Ki-Gor knew nothing more.

CHAPTER VI

WHEN KI-GOR RECOVERED CONSCIOUSNESS, he found himself lying on stony ground. He heard someone groaning and realized that it was himself. His head and neck and shoulders ached fearfully and his stomach felt like a hard knot pressing up under his ribs. He opened his eyes and winced with pain as brilliant sunshine was reflected into them from a white wall. He closed his eyes quickly and thought.

He had seen enough to tell that he was lying on the ground in the slave kraal of Jebel Musa. Suddenly, a familiar voice fell on his ears.

"Ah, my dear fellow! Ready to sit up and take a bit of notice, no doubt?"

Then a cool wet cloth descended on his aching forehead and bathed it gently. Hurree Dass chattered on in his best possible bedside manner.

"Nasty crack, my boy! Remarkable you survived it! To best of my knowledge before last night, only Bengali babu has thick enough skull to resist such devastating blow. Good thing perhaps you wear long hair."

The wet cloth felt grateful on his forehead, and Ki-Gor opened his eyes again. Hurree Dass was bending over him, an expression of utmost concern on his plump face. Behind him, stood a small tense figure. It was Luma.

"Ah!" Hurree Dass exclaimed delightedly. "Eyes open properly and focusing. Let us sit up a moment and take a sip of small infusion from this cup. A gentle herb stimulant, don't you know, brewed from a little plant whose properties you are tremendously familiar with—no doubt."

Slowly Ki-Gor raised himself on one elbow. To aid his balance he drew up one leg slightly and heard a tell-tale jingle. He did not need to look down at his ankle to know that one of the belled anklets had been riveted on while he was unconscious. He drank from the cup that Hurree Dass held to his lips. Then he scrutinized the bland face of the Hindu.

"Ah," Hurree Dass smiled. "Feeling much better already no doubt?"

"Why?" said Ki-Gor abruptly. "Why are you healing me? You are a member of ibn Daoud's gang. You stood to lose with the rest of them when I tried to escape with my wife."

"Most interesting question," the Hindu replied. "Only possible answer is that I am indubitably great rascal, but I am also doctor. And if civilization denies me privilege of practicing within its borders—because of some trifling deviation from straight and narrow—then I am reduced to practicing somewhere else. And I may tell you, by the bye, old man, that this little practice of mine here is quite enormously profitable. You can't imagine how happy I am being one and same time, great rascal and—doctor."

Hurree Dass stood up straight with the empty cup in his chubby hand.

"In short time," he said, "you will be able to take small dose of nourishment, which I dare say you are needing very badly having missed your dinner last night. Meantime, rest quietly—ah, but wait! Here comes ibn Daoud."

A MOMENT later, the big Arab stood glowering down at Ki-Gor.

"So you are still alive, lying, thieving dog of an Unbeliever!" he snarled. "So much the worse for you! Before many days are over, you will wish you had died last night."

Ki-Gor looked up steadily, but made no answer.

"In the end you will die anyway," ibn Daoud went on, maliciously, "only you will die slower. You have transgressed the rules of our band. And for that, the penalty is death by torture, all kinds of torture. But chiefly the whip. Thousands of lashes will eat the very flesh of your bones. Hour after hour you will be beaten until your unclean soul will sicken of the pain and leave your bleeding carcass behind."

Ki-Gor cleared his throat.

"Ibn Daoud," he said in a low voice. "You will never kill me. I am Ki-Gor. And a miserable jackal like you cannot kill Ki-Gor or even hold him imprisoned for long. I will escape, and escape soon. And when I do, ibn Daoud, beware. For I will return with swift vengeance."

Ibn Daoud gave a choking snarl and snatched the long-barreled pistol from his sash. But at the same moment, there came a shout from one of the watch towers. The shout was echoed from the other watch towers, and in a few seconds one of the Somalis hurried out of the castle and came running across the kraal.

Ibn Daoud's contorted features relaxed, and he tucked the pistol back into his sash.

"Insolent dog," he sneered. "You almost provoked me into giving you a quick merciful death. But you are not to be so lucky. Your torture will begin soon. Shere Ali's caravan has been sighted. As soon as he gets here, we will have some sport with you."

Then ibn Daoud hastened away to the castle shouting orders. Hurree Dass hesitated a moment and shook his head.

"Very much afraid you are in for troublous times, old man," he said. "Ibn Daoud, as I have often stated, is man of utmost determination. However, I will at least endeavor to furnish you some species of nourishment, if not by my own hand, then by Luma. Toodle-oo, my dear fellow."

The Hindu waddled sadly away, and Ki-Gor watched him gratefully. However great a rascal Hurree Dass was, he at least had the heart of a human being.

The jungle man now turned his brain on his own predicament. His head ached and he felt sick with pain and hunger. But Ki-Gor had been in situations almost as bad as this before, and had somehow survived. There must be some way out of his present trouble, and Ki-Gor proposed to find that way.

First, he examined the iron fetter on his ankle. A very brief inspection showed him that it was impossible to strike off the anklet without proper tools. There could be no question of smashing it with a heavy stone—his ankle would break before the anklet would.

Next, he examined the bells in the hope he find some way of ripping them out of the iron band. There was none. They were welded right into the fetter itself.

At this point, Ki-Gor's thoughts were interrupted by the arrival of the slave caravan.

The defense points of Jebel Musa were manned, and ibn Daoud waited behind the main door to the kraal to admit the two traders who were allowed within to select their slaves for purchase. Eventually, after a great deal of shouting and haggling, the door swung in and two scar-faced Arabs entered. As ibn Daoud led them around the kraal, they quickly selected twenty blacks. Then one of them caught sight of Ki-Gor lying near one wall.

"HAI!" CRIED the Arab. "A white one, and a strapping fellow to boot! What is the price on him, Sidi?"

"He is not a slave," ibn Daoud answered promptly. "He is some wild man of the jungle unfit for servitude."

"Are you sure?" the visiting Arab snapped.

"Have you ever tried to enslave the Masai?" ibn Daoud retorted. "You know how those tall fellows sicken and die in captivity for no apparent reason, except that their pride is broken."

"Yes," the Arab admitted, "I have found that is so."

"That fellow," ibn Daoud pointed at Ki-Gor, "is a kind of white Masai."

The conversation was in Swahili, which Ki-Gor understood, and the jungle man took ibn Daoud's last statement as a high compliment.

"But there is another white one," ibn Daoud told the slave dealer, "the white woman I sent word to you about."

"Ah, yes," cried the Arab eagerly, "bring her forth. I am sure she cannot be worth one tenth of what you are asking for her."

"A very houri for beauty," ibn Daoud affirmed. "She will fetch you five times over the price you pay me."

Ki-Gor sank his head on his chest. The torture was beginning. Then he raised his head again. For Helene's sake, he must seem confident.

Nevertheless, the next few minutes were a fearful ordeal. Ki-Gor smiled through it all, and shouted encouragement in English to Helene, while the slave trader peered at her teeth, pulled at her red hair, and pinched her arms and legs. Ki-Gor fought down his rage.

"Never mind him, Helene!" he shouted. "He will pay for this!"

Ibn Daoud started toward him once, mouthing oaths, but Hurree Dass intercepted him and spoke earnestly in Arabic. Ki-Gor did not understand the Hindu's words, but he made a shrewd guess that Hurree Dass told ibn Daoud that physical torture then would result in death for the weakened white man.

Eventually, the fearful scene was over. Helene's belled anklet was struck off, and she was led white-faced from the kraal. She looked back tragically just before she was pushed through the great doorway. Ki-Gor raised a clenched fist, to show her his unconquered spirit. He hoped by that gesture to keep her from despairing of ever being rescued.

While the caravan prepared to leave Jebel Musa, Hurree Dass hastened toward Ki-Gor, bearing a cup of liquid.

"Not acting so sprightly, please," he scolded. "I am continually telling ibn Daoud that he cannot torture you more today or you will die like flies. Therefore, if he desires live white man to torture, he must needs wait until tomorrow, thus giving you opportunity to recuperate."

"I am grateful to you, Hurree Dass," Ki-Gor said.

"It is possibly no favor I do," the Hindu said. "However, do not make a liar out of *me,* for pity's sakes. Lie very still to give impression you are as weak as I am claiming you are."

"I will," Ki-Gor agreed.

"Here is cup of beef blood," Hurree Dass said. "Very bad from standpoint of Hindu religion, but very good as regards human constitution."

"I don't understand you," Ki-Gor commented, drinking the blood gratefully. "You are acting as a friend."

"Not at all," Hurree Dass said, firmly. "Merely as physician. If you are thinking of asking me to bring you instruments to take off anklet, do not do so. I am not your friend, only your doctor. However, I strongly regret your inevitable fate. I have recently run into a curious herb which perhaps you could identify."

With that, the Hindu waddled away quickly, and Ki-Gor stared after him.

APPARENTLY, HURREE DASS' prestige as a doctor was enough to keep ibn Daoud from molesting Ki-Gor all that day. And the jungle man lay beside the wall of the kraal deep in thought. Every scheme for escaping he had ever known revolved in his mind. But at last he came to the conclusion that any plan depended on one thing. And that one thing was to get rid of the bells on his ankle. That could not be done without special instruments. And as the hours went by, no solution offered itself.

Luma came twice with food. She squatted on the ground beside Ki-Gor and watched him sad-faced as he ate. On questioning her, he found that her father was the Chief of the Banda, a gentle peace-loving tribe in the vicinity. The Banda lived in constant terror of the slavers of Jebel Musa, and were forced to deliver fifteen young men a year as slave material. Through some perverse impulse of ibn Daoud's Luma was seized one day and brought back. It had amused the Arab to teach the little cripple to read and write Arabic and to do simple arithmetic.

At dusk, she brought him an antelope steak which she had cooked herself for him, and Ki-Gor ate it gratefully. Already the day of rest which Hurree Dass had gotten for him was making him feel stronger. But just as he finished the steak, a burly figure loomed across the kraal. It was ibn Daoud, and behind him came the two Gallas, rifles ready. Heeding Hurree Dass' directions, Ki-Gor pretended to be very weak.

"Rest well, dog of an Unbeliever!" ibn Daoud rasped. "For tomorrow you must be in condition to suffer! Hurree Dass assures me you will be recovered enough by tomorrow to endure hours of pain before death will rescue you."

"Do your worst, O Hyena," Ki-Gor replied in a faint voice, and ibn Daoud chuckled evilly and strode away.

A moment later, Luma appeared out of the shadows.

"Here is a small cake I have baked for you," she said. "I hope it will be to your taste. It is the last thing I can do for you."

"Ah, thank you, little sister," Ki-Gor said in a voice that trembled a little. "I hope it is not the last thing you can do for me. There is still time for me to escape, if I can only figure out a means. And when I escape, Luma, I will return and free you and every other slave at Jebel Musa. Ah, this cake—it is delicious! Still warm."

"Yes," said Luma, in a choked voice. "Be careful, there is a lump of coconut butter on top. It may be melting and running over your fingers."

"I will be careful, little sister—"

A sudden stupendous idea flashed through Ki-Gor's mind like a bolt of lightning. Coconut butter! The jungle man sat in tense, tight silence for ten seconds.

"What is the matter, Ki-Gor?" Luma said, alarmed at his sudden silence.

"Matter?" said Ki-Gor, letting his breath gently. "There is nothing the matter. I have just discovered how to escape from Jebel Musa tonight, and you have helped me discover the way."

"I have?" Luma said, incredulously.

"Yes, but keep your voice low, little sister. Now, will you do something for me? Go back to your kitchen and fetch me a lump of coconut butter as big as your two fists. Hurry, little sister!"

"Yes, yes, I am gone already," Luma panted and limped frantically away across the kraal.

WHEN SHE returned with the lump of coconut butter, Ki-Gor took it from her with murmured thanks. Then he bent his right knee, and reached toward the fetter on his right ankle. Swiftly, he pressed the soft butter into the cross-slits of each of the three bells. In a few moments, the bell cavities were thoroughly clogged with the butter.

"Now!" Ki-Gor muttered, and stood up. He took six steps around the crippled girl, stamping his right foot hard with each step.

Not a sound came from the anklet.

Triumph surged over Ki-Gor. He reached down and took the crippled girl in his arms.

"Tonight, little sister," he whispered, "you have saved Ki-Gor! Tomorrow night, or soon afterwards, Ki-Gor will save you. Go back now into the castle and let yourself be seen by ibn Daoud. At the same moment that he sees you, I will have scaled the wall and will be walking safely past the baboons. Go, now."

Ki-Gor peered through the darkness and waited until Luma's limping steps told him that she had entered the castle. Then swiftly, he turned and went to the wall behind him. His left leg still pained dully, but it felt strong enough.

A silent leap upward, and his fingers gripped the top edge of the wall. The muscles of his wrists and biceps corded as he drew himself slowly up. Making not a sound, he slid across the broad top of the wall, and let his legs dangle over the outside edge. Fingers gripped again, and his body slid over, until he was dangling full length, arms outstretched.

It was a critical drop, with the ground falling away behind him when he landed. But he had jack-knifed in midair and hit the earth on all fours.

There was a considerable thump as his heavy body landed, and one or two pebbles rolled down the slope. Ki-Gor crouched motionless. The men in the watch towers must have heard that thump and those pebbles. They were probably that instant staring down, trying to pierce the black night with their eyes.

But Ki-Gor did not move, and as the seconds went by and no alarm sounded, he began to breathe easier. He looked over his right shoulder and saw no movement. Then he looked over his left shoulder and made out two indistinct shapes coming toward him.

Ki-Gor stood up and went straight toward them, silent as a ghost. One of the shapes whined but Ki-Gor kept straight on. The hamadryads stayed in their tracks as Ki-Gor, nerve-ends prickling, went between them.

The hamadryads were trained to attack bells. And they heard no bells.

There was just enough starlight for Ki-Gor's eyes to locate the ramp that led down the hill from the slavers' stronghold. Half an hour later, he was a mile away from Jebel Musa, traveling rapidly eastward along the route taken by the slave caravans.

Ki-Gor had no war bow, no hunting-knife, he had not even his crutch. He was completely unarmed as he pushed through the African night.

But Ki-Gor was free.

CHAPTER VII

THE CARAVAN ROUTE WAS a well-defined trail, and even in the dark, Ki-Gor had no difficulty following it. He blessed Hurree Dass and Luma for the rest and the food that enabled him now to travel all night in hopes of catching up with Shere Ali's caravan by morning. The slaver had a start of nearly eight hours, but Ki-Gor knew that slave caravans make slow time, and his leg wounds were sufficiently healed so that they hampered him only very little. He favored his left leg slightly, but still managed to keep up an easy ground-covering lope, for hour after hour.

He began to consider just how he was going to wrest Helene away from this third captivity of hers. The caravan would have numerous well-armed guards on the alert for rival caravans or unfriendly tribes. He, Ki-Gor, was alone and completely unarmed. And the minute he showed himself to the slavers Shere Ali would recognize him, having seen him lying in ibn Daoud's kraal the day before.

One thing was certain: Shere Ali would be doubly alert on this trip because he was transporting a slave of such extraordinary value—Helene.

Another disquieting thought came into his mind, and that was ibn Daoud might send out searching parties as soon as he discovered that Ki-Gor had escaped. Whether the Arab would guess the direction in which he had gone, Ki-Gor had no way of telling. But as he thought about that aspect of his position, the outline of a daring plan began to form in his mind.

As the eastern sky grew brighter, and the stars began to dim overhead, Ki-Gor could see something of the country he was traveling through. Evidently, he had passed through the mountain belt that ranged north and south from Jebel Musa. The terrain that the coming dawn now showed him was much less rugged. It was rolling, lightly wooded country with only a few hills here and there.

Just before the sun came up, the brisk morning breeze blowing into Ki-Gor's face brought a message. His sensitive nostrils caught the smell of horses and men. A few faint shouts, too, were borne to his ears. He had caught up with Shere Ali.

Ki-Gor turned off the trail at this point and made for a series of ridges which looked as though they might command the caravan route ahead. He sped through the sprinkling of woods, keeping well covered and made for the tallest of the ridges. There were no trees on this ridge, and Ki-Gor crouched low and climbed up its back side carefully.

In a short while, he was stretched out flat on his stomach peering down the steep front slope.

He had guessed right. The trail wound around the base of the ridge, less than a hundred yards below. And on the far side of the trail was a caravan just about to get under way.

The first thing that Ki-Gor noticed was that Helene was mounted on a horse. Evidently, Shere Ali was taking no chances of overtiring or otherwise injuring his prize package. The other slaves were manacled together on a long chain. There were ten mounted, armed Arabs or Somalis, and a dozen or so naked blacks on foot and armed with spears. For the relatively small number of slaves, it was a strong, heavily armed caravan.

As Ki-Gor watched, the slaves began to move out of the large boma in single file toward the trail, and the horsemen divided into two groups, one on each side of the line of chained blacks. At the head of one group rode a small Arab, whom Ki-Gor placed as Shere Ali. Beside him Helene rode, and as far as Ki-Gor could tell at that distance, she was not bound or chained.

Ki-Gor debated desperately with himself whether to try his rash plan. It might work, but the chances were strongly against it. For one thing, it involved the dubious business of trying to convince Shere Ali of the truth of a very flimsy story. If Shere Ali doubted the story, Ki-Gor could not bring up a shred of evidence to back it up. But the risk had to be taken. Ki-Gor had only his own strength and audacity to depend on.

SLOWLY THE caravan wound out of the boma and on to the trail, and Ki-Gor steeled himself to action, desperate though it seemed. By chance, he glanced off to the westward, back up the trail. His heart gave a leap as he saw a cloud of dust rising in the distance.

For the next two minutes he kept his eyes glued on the dust cloud. It grew rapidly larger. Whoever was raising it was coming down the trail in a hurry.

Less than a mile away, the trail climbed over the top of a little hill and was clearly visible to Ki-Gor's keen eyes. And while he watched, the dust cloud rose up behind that hill. A moment later, a horseman cantered into view over the crest of the hill. Close behind him came another horseman, and another—until Ki-Gor counted eight.

At that distance, he could hardly identify the riders, but he was pretty certain that they came from Jebel Musa. Ki-Gor sprang to his feet and shot down the slope toward the caravan below.

For all their alertness, the Arabs below did not see him until he was twenty yards from them. And only then, because Ki-Gor shouted. There were answering shouts and someone fired a snap shot at him. But Ki-Gor raised his arms high above his head to show that he was unarmed, and plunged straight toward Shere Ali.

"Shere Ali!" he shouted. "Don't shoot! I am a friend! I bring you a warning!"

"What is this?" the scar-faced Arab cried. "Why—by the beard of Mohammed! It's the White Masai from Jebel Musa!"

Instantly five horsemen spurred forward and covered Ki-Gor with their long rifles.

"You are in no danger from me!" Ki-Gor cried. "Your danger, O Shere Ali, comes from your friend ibn Daoud of Jebel Musa!"

"How do you mean—danger?" Shere Ali demanded.

"He sold you the white woman beside you for a large sum of money—"

"A round thousand Maria Theresa thalers," Shere Ali said.

"Well, then be warned!" Ki-Gor spoke as rapidly as he could. "Ibn Daoud means to raid your caravan and take back the white woman!"

"Ibn Daoud!" Shere Ali, exclaimed incredulously. "He would never dare!"

"I heard him plotting it with my own ears last night," Ki-Gor cried. "Then I escaped over the wall and ran all night to warn you!"

"What cock and bull story is this!" the Arab scoffed. "There is not a word of truth in it—"

"Believe it or not, as you please," Ki-Gor broke in, "but protect your rear—and quickly. For the raiders from Jebel Musa will be on you in less than a minute!"

The Arab threw a startled glance up the trail.

"Listen!" Ki-Gor shouted. "You can hear the drumming of their hoofs behind you!"

"Aye, so I can!" one of the Arabs cried. "So can I!" shouted another. Ki-Gor flung his last effort in to build up the manufactured panic.

"Get the slaves off the trail!" he roared. "And divide your forces on each side of the trail ready to meet them with cross-fire. Give me a gun, O Shere Ali, so that I can help you fight them off!"

Before Shere Ali could answer, Ki-Gor deftly wrenched the rifle out of the astonished hands of a Somali guard. At that second, the pursuing horsemen thundered around a bend in the trail, not a hundred feet away.

"Here they are!" Ki-Gor roared, and blazed away at the group of riders coming down the trail. The shot was like a spark in a powder barrel. Shere Ali's bewildered guards raised their guns and fired wildly at the galloping crew up the trail.

The pursuers—and Ki-Gor saw that they were from Jebel Musa all right—reined up in confusion with shouts of dismay. At that moment, Shere Ali decided that he had been tricked.

"No, no!" he shouted at his followers. But it was too late. An infuriated volley of shots came from ibn Daoud's men, and with yells of rage they spread out on both sides of the trail. Shere Ali's men answered the volley with interest and the battle was on.

THE ONLY person in the whole affair who knew exactly what was happening was Ki-Gor. When the raging Shere Ali spurred forward among his men, the jungle man sprang toward Helene. He saw that she was manacled but that the chain between her wrists was very light and was nearly a foot long.

"Ride, Helene!" he told her, keeping his voice low. "Down the trail as hard as you can! I'll catch up somehow."

Obediently, Helene kicked the ribs of her mount and went flying down the trail. There came an agonized cry from Shere Ali. The Arab swung his horse viciously around. But before he could start off in pursuit, Ki-Gor was beside him. Swiftly and efficiently, the jungle man whipped the squalling little Arab out of the saddle and flung him down in the trail.

By now, the scene was one of utter confusion. Shere Ali's men had been given so many contradictory orders they did not know which to obey. Ibn Daoud's men were pouring vengeful volleys at them. The Negro spearmen were scampering about hysterically, and finally the twenty newly-purchased black slaves added the finishing touch to the demoralization of Shere Ali's caravan. All twenty tried to run away in opposite directions, and succeeded only in tangling themselves and everyone else on the spot in their long connecting chain.

But Ki-Gor had the commanding advantage of knowing precisely what he wanted to do. Hardly had he dragged Shere Ali out of his saddle when he sprang up on the back of the plunging little Somali horse. He slapped the frenzied animal on the rump, and then leaned forward and hung on for dear life.

Shere Ali's horse needed no second urging. It shot eastward down the trail like an antelope. Ki-Gor made no effort to control him in any way. The jungle man was busy enough staying on the little horse's back. Besides, Ki-Gor wanted to place as much distance as possible as quickly as possible between himself and inevitable pursuit. He had no idea how soon the mad mêlée behind him would quiet down and untangle itself. But whenever Shere Ali's men and ibn Daoud's men finally discovered that they were fighting each other for nothing, there would be a grim chase speedily organized.

A half a mile down the trail, Ki-Gor's flying Somali overtook Helene's mount, which had slowed down to a walk.

"Ride!" Ki-Gor shouted, and Helene promptly spurred up her horse. But Ki-Gor shot past her on his terrified Somali, and the two horses led a mad race for three miles down the trail.

At last the Somali pony slowed up, foam-flecked and gasping, and Helene reined up beside him. Ki-Gor looked sharply at her. A variety of emotions struggled for recognition on her lovely face. But Ki-Gor was satisfied with one thing, and that was that Helene was not laughing. The jungle man had been slightly apprehensive that she would be laughing—at him. Because Helene rode a horse beautifully. And Ki-Gor had never ridden a horse in his life before.

The spot where they halted was quite thickly wooded, and not far ahead the trail plunged into true jungle. Ki-Gor quickly came to a decision.

"We'll go as far as those trees," he announced, "and when we find one with boughs overhanging, we'll climb up into them without touching the ground."

A few minutes later, the jungle couple stood on a broad bough over the trail and watched the two riderless horses plunging down the trail.

"Now," said Ki-Gor. "The tree route for a few miles and we'll be safe from all pursuit."

Helene understood by Ki-Gor's attitude that the time had not arrived to ask the questions that were burning in her mind so she swung silently through the tree tops after Ki-Gor. Silently—except for the jingling of the slave anklets.

NOT UNTIL three hours later did Ki-Gor swing down toward the ground. A clear stream rippled over stones and Ki-Gor dipped his face in the cooling water and drank sparingly. Helene followed suit. Ki-Gor looked at her now with a shy smile.

"You see?" he said. "We are all right."

"Oh, darling," Helene responded, "I can hardly believe it! Now, tell me all about it. How on earth did you get away without being attacked by the baboons?"

"I found a way to stop the bells from ringing," he said simply.

"You did?" Helene exclaimed. "Then why are they ringing now?"

An expression of consternation crept over Ki-Gor's face. He shook his right foot gently. The anklet gave forth a clear tinkle.

"Oh, I see what happened!" Ki-Gor said slowly. "With the heat of the day, the coconut butter melted!"

"The coconut butter!" Helene cried. "Ki-Gor, what are you talking about?"

So Ki-Gor told her the whole story.

"And now we must go back," he finished. "Without Luma, I could not have escaped. We've got to save her somehow."

"Yes, but how?" said Helene practically.

"The melting of the coconut butter has given me an idea," Ki-Gor said thoughtfully. "First of all, we must find the Banda people. Luma's father is the Chief and he will be glad to help us, I should think."

TWO DAYS later, just before sunset, the frail old Chief of the Banda addressed his little tribe.

"Ki-Gor has come among us," he said, "to help us be rid forever of the terrible tyranny of Jebel Musa. We must help him in everything he asks us to do. If we do, he tells me that tomorrow night Jebel Musa will be empty—its cruel baboons and its crueler men will be gone—and my—" here, the old man's voice broke "—my little daughter will be back in my arms."

The tribe listened in fascinated silence, and the old man went on.

"The first thing Ki-Gor asks us to do is to dig up our dancing bells, the wristlets and anklets and girdles that we used to use in our tribal ceremonies. Dig them up from the ground where you buried them when the great gray baboons came slaughtering in our village. Bring also a great quantity of coconut butter—but keep the coconut butter well away from the fires, so that it will not melt. Ki-Gor will show you what to do with it. And finally, gather a quantity of the large sweet nuts and good ripe bananas. Tomorrow morning, before dawn, the young men will take all these things and their war spears too, and follow Ki-Gor to Jebel Musa. Let no one shirk this duty. It is our opportunity to throw off the hideous grasp of ibn Daoud and his men."

The old man turned to Ki-Gor who was sitting beside him.

"Is there anything you wish to add?" he asked.

"Just a word, if it is permitted," said Ki-Gor rising. "Men of the Banda, remember just one thing. The baboons do not attack men—they attack bells. So, as long as your bells are silent, you need not fear the baboons. In fact, the baboons are tame. Remember that—do not fear the baboons. For the rest, have faith in me. It may be that some of you will not return from this expedition, but I am going to try to lead you in such a way that not one life will be lost."

Ki-Gor sat down and the old Chief exhorted his people to be off doing his bidding.

The Banda village presented a busy picture that evening as quantities of belled anklets and bracelets were exhumed from the ground where they had been buried so long. Some of the bells had corroded so badly that they no longer sounded, and those were thrown aside as useless. But in the end, there were sufficient for Ki-Gor's purposes.

The young men of the village burnished their spears and boasted among themselves about their bravery the next day. But Ki-Gor spent a tedious hour pounding the iron fetters from Helene's ankle and his own.

CHAPTER VIII

THE SUN WAS JUST about to rise when Ki-Gor and thirty shivering Banda youths arrived in the wooded ravine below Jebel Musa. The young tribesmen did not feel quite so brave as they had the night before, but they nevertheless followed the giant white man loyally through the mists of the ravine. Besides their spears, they carried baskets of fruit and nuts, and baskets of bells. The bells were all carefully choked with coconut butter and were fastened in pairs on light strings. The pieces of string were about six inches long and had a bell attached to each end.

Ki-Gor led his little party through the thick woods toward Jebel Musa and did not halt until the foliage had become so thin that it barely covered them from view of possible watchers up at the fortress. The jungle man bade his party stand still while he skirmished around cautiously in the undergrowth. At length he found a considerable patch of quite thick bushes. It was what he was looking for. A low whistle brought the Banda youths to his side and immediately they proceeded to carry out the plan Ki-Gor had so carefully explained to them.

First the youths with the baskets of fruit pushed through to the center of the brush patch. There they dumped their baskets, rolling the fruit and nuts on the ground. When they returned, the ones charged with the bells went into the brush patch. With them went half a dozen youths carrying gourds full of a thick treacly tree sap, a natural tree syrup which the Banda were accustomed to eat with their fried dough cakes.

Then the six-inch length of string which connected each pair of bells was dipped into the gourds of tree syrup, care being taken not to coat the bells with the stuff—just the string. And finally the sticky string was draped over twigs about two feet off the ground, in the same manner that children in more northerly climates drape short lengths of tinsel on Christmas tree branches.

Ki-Gor watched the operation anxiously. It was going a little slower than he had anticipated and the sun was just clearing the horizon. His trap must be laid and sprung before the sun got hot enough to melt the coconut butter in those bells dangling on the bushes.

The hamadryads up on the slopes of Jebel Musa furnished another cause for anxiety, too. Whether they had heard or smelt the busy group down on the fringe of the woods, they began to show curiosity. One or two huge males started slowly down the slope, sniffing the air and barking.

Ki-Gor watched them intently and urged his Banda to hurry with their task. But he grew more and more uneasy as the big gray brutes came on—not very fast, but steadily.

Suddenly, his uneasiness turned into definite alarm as the whole tribe of hamadryads began to move down the slope after their leaders. He turned and crept quickly back toward the busy group of Banda in the brush patch.

To his intense relief, he saw that the job was practically completed. In the center of the patch was a large, tempting mound of fruit and nuts. And scattered all through the bushes of the patch were hundreds of pairs of bells swinging on the close-growing twigs.

"Back! Back quickly, Faithful Ones!" Ki-Gor whispered. "Back to the trees and up them without delay!"

The Banda required no more urging, but scrambled hastily off toward the ravine. Ki-Gor followed more slowly, keeping his eye on the baboon pack.

The hamadryads were by now thoroughly aroused and were trooping noisily down off the slope of Jebel Musa. Ki-Gor smiled with satisfaction as he saw that they were heading straight for the baited trap. A few moments later and they walked right into it.

There was a squeal of joy from the first baboon who discovered the mound of fruit. It was answered by a disorderly rush from his mates. The gray beasts fought their way through the thick underbrush, chattering and barking. And for the next fifteen minutes, the sounds that came from the patch of brush were sounds of solid satisfaction.

THE SUN began to grow hot on the side of Ki-Gor's neck, but now it did not matter. If Ki-Gor's plan was going right, the baboons were collecting quantities of paired bells in the thick silver-tipped fur of their manes. The treacly pieces of string would stick in that fur—Ki-Gor hoped.

He just happened to shift his gaze from the gorging hamadryads to the white fortress on Jebel Musa and caught his breath sharply. Evidently, ibn Daoud and his men had noticed the behavior of the baboons and were puzzled over it. Several men were standing along the near wall staring down toward the ravine. Ki-Gor recognized the huge green-robed figure in the middle of the group. It was ibn Daoud himself. From the violent gesturing that went on, Ki-Gor reasoned that the slavers were arguing about what to do. One of the figures beside ibn Daoud raised his gun as if to shoot toward the ravine. But the gun was lowered again without a shot being fired.

Ki-Gor held his breath. What would the slavers do?

At length the group on the wall walked inside the castle. At the same time, several well-satiated baboons lurched through the brush out on to the bare ground at the foot of Jebel Musa. Ki-Gor concluded that the slavers had seen these baboons returning and had ceased to worry about the whole matter.

Gradually, the rest of the baboon pack left the scattered mound of fruit and reluctantly pushed their way back to join the leaders out in the open. The sun was mounting higher and hotter, and Ki-Gor's ears strained for the sound of a tinkling bell, freed by the melting coconut butter.

But in spite of the increasing heat, there came no sound. The hamadryads wandered slowly up the stony slope. A thrill of dismay went through Ki-Gor. Could the bells have failed to stick in the great gray manes? He stared after the retreating brutes and tried to see whether they carried any of the bells. The distance was too great, although Ki-Gor thought he caught a slight glint of refracted sunlight in the middle of the pack.

Then to add to Ki-Gor's despair, the outside door of the castle opened, and three men came out. One of them was ibn Daoud. They closed the door behind them and marched down the ramp. The ramp sloped down in an easterly direction away from where Ki-Gor was standing, but he surmised that the trio would turn at the foot of the ramp and come around the base of the hill to see what the baboons had been after. Ki-Gor's mind began working rapidly to figure some way of turning this new development to advantage.

Suddenly, there came a hoarse, savage bark from one of the baboons. Ki-Gor turned his head quickly in their direction. He saw one baboon leap backward, and saw two others leap after him. Others began barking now, and before Ki-Gor's eyes the mass of lazy, lethargic hamadryads galvanized into a screaming, snarling mêlée.

Once the little bells got thoroughly heated, the coconut butter melted fast.

The scene that now played itself on the slope of Jebel Musa would have to be seen to be believed. Sixty powerful baboons, trained to attack whoever wore jingling bells, now found themselves surrounded on all sides by a clamoring jingle. And as each one discovered that his neighbor was the source of the noise, he fell on that neighbor with slashing fangs. All over the slope of the hill the fearful suicidal battle spread. Now the baboons separated into couples locked in death struggles. Then the individual combats merged into general battles royal.

It was an awe-inspiring spectacle. The most fearful thing of all was that not one of the gray monsters thought of flight, or even of defense. Ibn Daoud had trained them to attack at the sound of bells, therefore, they attacked each other with all the savage fury of their implacable natures.

Someone has said that civil wars are the worst wars. But here was a civil war in which a tribe was not merely divided into two warring groups, but in which *each individual* attacked the *rest of the tribe* in a bitter fight to the finish.

KI-GOR WATCHED the battle rage up and down the slopes of Jebel Musa. The din was stupendous. The hoarse, frenzied snarls of each fanatical fighting hamadryad fused into one great fantastic blood-curdling roar. For sheer ferocity, Ki-Gor had never heard a sound that equaled it.

In less than three minutes, the smaller and weaker of the baboons were slashed to ribbons and the still, gray forms began to dot the field of the extraordinary battle. But Ki-Gor took his eyes off the baboons now, to watch events farther to the east.

Ibn Daoud and his two followers were halfway down the ramp when the peaceful pack of baboons suddenly flew into their berserk fury. For a few seconds, the slavers stood appalled and stunned and watched the madness spread through the pack. They were standing perhaps fifty yards from the pack at the time.

Then they seemed to think they should try and stop the fight. They ran across the face of the slope toward the frenzied brutes, shouting and waving their arms. But after they had gone twenty yards, they appeared to realize that the situation had gone far beyond anything they could do. At almost the same instant, they decided that they were much too close to the blood-crazed baboons for safety. The three, with ibn Daoud in the lead, started climbing rapidly up the slope toward the door in the wall.

But before they had taken ten steps, an inexorable Fate sent the tide of battle rolling in their direction. And a single baboon, flung out of the main mass as if by centrifugal force, landed up the slope not far behind the three fleeing slavers. The battle-crazed brute sprang at the nearest man. A fearful shriek rang out over the din of battle, and the man went down. Ibn Daoud whirled and fired at the baboon. But the damage had been done. A dozen or more baboons separated from the main group and started up the slope. Perhaps their brute minds recalled dimly that human beings were to be killed at the sound of bells—or perhaps their blood lust would have led them to attack any living thing within sight. But whatever it was, ibn Daoud was doomed.

His agonized shouts brought four men out on the wall above, who fired methodically into the pursuing baboons. But the great gray brutes came too swiftly, and ibn Daoud went down screaming with three of the monsters on his back.

Ki-Gor watched ibn Daoud die without emotion. It was a curious thing that such a monster of cruelty as the Arab should be killed almost incidentally, as it were. His was only one of sixty-three lives lost that morning. Three humans and sixty baboons died furious, frenzied deaths, victims of an implacable system which ibn Daoud had himself originated.

And it was pure chance, as well as poetic justice, that ibn Daoud should have been bitten to death by his own baboons. Ki-Gor had expected to kill the Arab that night when he stormed the fortress under cover of darkness. But Fate had taken a hand, and now Ki-Gor found that he might not have to wait until darkness to make a final disposition of Jebel Musa.

The suicide of the baboon pack was soon accomplished. The entire slope of the hill was strewn with the bloody, contorted bodies of the gray brutes. Here and there single individuals tottering from mortal wounds sought each other out to deliver the coup de grace. And it was not long before these last hardy survivors succumbed and lay still.

Quickly, Ki-Gor decided on immediate action. He had kept an eye on the walls of the fortress and had seen only four men in evidence while the wild scene of carnage was being played below them. It was possible, he reasoned, that yesterday's pursuit party had not yet returned, or that they might have suffered heavy losses in the clash with Shere Ali's caravan. At any rate, Jebel Musa was without a leader, and was seriously undermanned.

Ki-Gor whistled up the Banda. They came down cautiously from their trees and approached him gingerly.

"There is nothing to fear," Ki-Gor called out reassuringly. "The baboons are gone—wiped out. Now, I am going up the hill to the fortress for an indaba. Do all of you come out and sit at the bottom of the hill while I go up."

OBEDIENTLY, THEY ranged themselves as he directed, and Ki-Gor boldly walked out into the open toward the bottom of the ramp. Promptly a shot rang out from the wall and a bullet kicked dust thirty feet beyond him. Ki-Gor raised his hands high in the air.

"I am unarmed!" he shouted. "Hold your fire until we have talked together."

He never slackened his stride, but went steadily to the foot of the ramp, turned there and climbed up it. No more shots were fired, and Ki-Gor saw a fifth figure join the others on the wall—a short round figure in a long black coat. The five men stood mute and motionless on the wall as Ki-Gor approached, arms high in the air.

Not until the jungle man arrived close under the wall did one of the men—and it was Hurree Dass—step forward and speak.

"My dear fellow," the Hindu cried, "what in name of goodness have you done to us!"

"The baboons have gone, Hurree Dass," Ki-Gor said.

"Oh yes, so I am perceiving with utmost astonishment!"

"Your leader is dead," Ki-Gor went on.

"Most indubitably," Hurree Dass agreed.

"I don't know how many of you are left," said Ki-Gor, "but it does not matter. You cannot last long. I will give you a choice of action. You who are left may go away from Jebel Musa immediately, and I will promise you safe-conduct for a distance of twenty-five miles for a period of two days. If you are not twenty-five miles away on the morning of the third day, you will be killed."

"Ah, most generous," Hurree Dass observed, "and what, pray, is alternative?"

"If you choose to stay on," Ki-Gor said, "you will be surprise-attacked during the night. If not tonight, then some other night. In the meantime, your slaves will know that the baboons are gone, and they will slip over the wall fearlessly."

"Well," Hurree Dass sighed. "I am not sure I can persuade my remaining colleagues to accept your first offer."

"Tell them," said Ki-Gor, "that when we surprise-attack, there will be no quarter at all."

"Ah," said Hurree Dass. "Most persuasive argument in favor of immediate evacuation with safe-conduct. Permit me to confer with colleagues."

There followed a long and heated argument now between Hurree Dass and his "colleagues." The four remaining members of the band consisted of the three Fulahs and one Zanzibar Arab, so the conversation was carried on in Arabic. At length, Hurree Dass walked back to the edge of the wall.

"It was hard fight," he called, "but reason prevailed. At first my friends wanted to shoot you on the spot, but I informed them that you were no doubt powerful Muslim jinni with supernatural qualities—otherwise how ever could you have performed such miraculous escapes and subsequent feats? So now they are ready to accept your original offer."

"Good," said Ki-Gor.

But the doctor went on hurriedly.

"Myself, Hurree Dass, if I may be so bold as to suggest it, respectfully beg to be exempted from expulsion edict."

"Why?" said Ki-Gor. "What do you want to do?"

"I wish to accept gracious offer of Luma, daughter of Chief of the Banda. Offer is to be physician to Banda tribe. Not so much money, but great opportunity to practice."

"All right," Ki-Gor grinned. "Let it be that way."

THAT NIGHT the Banda village was the scene of such tribal gaiety as it had not known for years. Not only was Luma restored to the adoring arms of her father, but twelve of the young men of the tribe were rescued from the slave kraal of Jebel Musa.

Helene sat happily beside Ki-Gor watching the ceremonial dances. On the other side of Ki-Gor sat little Luma, eyes shining with happiness. And beside Luma, Doctor Hurree Dass of Bombay sat cross-legged. At one point, the plump Hindu leaned across Luma and shouted to Ki-Gor.

"On such joyous occasion," he shouted, "I hope you and most beautiful wife will reconsider decision to go away tomorrow. Myself would dearly love to have you stay on for extended visit. Consider, my dear fellow, we have not had proper opportunity to compare notes on herbs."

"Well," Ki-Gor considered, "maybe we could stay an extra day or two, but no longer."

"Then tomorrow," Hurree Dass said, "you will give me your opinion of certain small plants I have been unable to classify. For instance, I have in my pocket one such plant."

He reached into the pocket of the black coat and drew out a small wilted plant. He handed it to Ki-Gor.

"Do you, for instance, know something of this herb?" said Hurree Dass very scientifically.

Ki-Gor looked at the little plant curiously, and Helene peered at it over his arm.

"Why," said Helene, suppressing a giggle, "in America we would call that a four-leaf clover."

STORY X

KI-GOR—AND THE TEMPLE OF THE MOON-GOD

CHAPTER I

KI-GOR LOOKED AT YOUNG Prince Datu as if he had not heard him aright.

"A leopard, didst thou say?" Ki-Gor demanded in the Lunanda dialect. "Surely a leopard is hardly big game for a great hunter like thee."

"Ah, but there are leopards and leopards," Prince Datu laughed, "and this is such a leopard as thou hast never seen or heard of, Ki-Gor. It is as big as a lioness, and as crafty as an elephant. Do I speak truth or not, Father?"

Mboko, King of the Lunanda, nodded his head soberly.

"It is indeed so, O Ki-Gor," Mboko affirmed. "Six people from our village has this monster borne off and eaten. And two of our best hunters who went out to destroy him fell victims instead to his supernatural guile. If thou, Ki-Gor, and my son, can seek out and destroy this monster, it will be a blessed deliverance for my Lunanda."

The old king's face was solemn by the flickering light of the cooking-fire. His wife, Queen Goli, sat impassively at his side. Ki-Gor's gaze swept past her to Datu's handsome, expectant face, and finally came to rest on the beloved form of his own beautiful Helene who was sitting silently beside him.

An almost-full moon began to push up over the tree tops, sending a soft, yellow light over the little group around the fire, and revealing the massive stone ruins which crouched all about them in the gloomy Congo jungle.

"What are they talking about, Ki-Gor?" Helene asked. It was her first visit to the Lunanda and he did not speak or understand their dialect. Ki-Gor told her briefly about the man-eating leopard.

"What a terrible thing!" Helene murmured. "Oh, by all means,

Ki-Gor, you must help Datu kill that leopard! These Lunanda are such sweet people and they seem to be such good friends of yours—It's the least you could do."

Ki-Gor smiled down at her. It was characteristic of Helene now that she never for a moment questioned his ability to wage successful war on any creature, man or beast, no matter how dangerous or formidable.

"I think so, too," Ki-Gor nodded his shaggy head. "I will tell them so."

"There's only one condition," Helene warned him, "the usual one. You've got to let me come along."

Ki-Gor frowned.

"Oh, yes," Helene maintained stoutly. "I always have to share your danger with you."

Ki-Gor knew it was useless to argue with her. He shrugged and addressed Prince Datu.

"I will be glad to hunt the leopard with thee, O Datu," he said, "whenever it suits thee."

"Spoken like Ki-Gor!" Datu exclaimed, eyes shining. His face fell when Ki-Gor went on to tell him that Helene insisted on coming along with them. But Ki-Gor reassured him.

"She is as quick and alert as a Pygmy, this Red-Haired One," Ki-Gor said proudly. "She will be no hindrance."

Finally Prince Datu agreed, though there was doubt in his handsome face.

"Very well, then," he said. "Shall we start out at dawn?"

"At the stroke of dawn," Ki-Gor assented.

King Mboko stood up.

"Thou art a good friend of the Lunanda, Ki-Gor," the old king said. "Go, now, to thy lodging and sleep soundly, that thou wilt be fresh and strong for the hunt tomorrow."

Ki-Gor stood up with a smile. But before he could open his mouth to answer the king, a sudden commotion broke out in the main village of the Lunanda, a hundred yards to the eastward.

"The leopard!" Prince Datu exclaimed and jumped to his feet. He seized one end of a long stick whose other end was burning in the fire. Raising the blazing end as a torch, the young prince ran toward the village. Ki-Gor ran silently at his heels.

They found the Lunanda crowding around the still form of a man lying sprawled on the ground before one of the huts. The man was dead, but evidently he had not been killed by a leopard. Another man was screaming and struggling in the grip of several villagers.

A few moments later, King Mboko arrived. Gradually the true story of what happened was told.

IT WAS the dead man's wife who gave the main facts. There had been an altercation of some kind between her husband and the other man. The argument had grown more and more heated until the other man had struck her husband on the head with a stick. The angry blow had landed on her husband's temple and killed him instantly.

"It was unintentional!" the wretched culprit cried. "I never meant to kill him! It was an accident, I swear to it!"

Prince Datu, standing beside Ki-Gor, shook his head and murmured, "It makes no difference. By the ancient Code of Dera Daga, he who kills another, whether intentionally or unintentionally, shall be adjudged of his crime by the King and the Tribe. And his sentence shall be set by the Priestess of the Moon."

The back of Ki-Gor's neck prickled a little and he threw a glance over his shoulder at the great crumbling ruins that brooded under the light of the moon. The ground sloped upward behind him and far up that slope, great square columns and massive monolithic slabs stood in scarred majesty among the trees. At the very crest of the height, a huge mass of stone gleamed dimly white in the moonlight.

Ki-Gor had once stood beneath that mass of stone. It was an enormous truncated pyramid with uneven eroded steps mounting one face to the broad flat top.

That was the Temple of the Moon.

King Mboko quickly called his people together and a long procession started up the hill through the ruins. The Lunanda wasted no time in bringing their criminals to book.

They were, Ki-Gor reflected, the most civilized of all the jungle people he knew. Ki-Gor had often marveled at the Lunanda's intricate code of manners. They were a simple, warm-hearted people in spite of their formality, however, fond of hunting and like sports. When a messenger from Mboko had come some weeks before with an invitation, Ki-Gor, having some time on his hands and anxious to show the Lunanda to Helene, had decided to pay his old friend a visit.

Ki-Gor and Helene stood at the doorway of the house which they had been assigned, and watched the procession winding its way toward the Temple of the Moon. Prince Datu had told them that they could attend the trial if they wanted to, but that it was not obligatory. Ki-Gor had declined with thanks. For one thing, he wanted to get some sleep. For another, he knew that the ceremonies at the Temple would make him distressingly uneasy.

"Are the Lunanda Bantu?" Helene asked. "They're so quiet—so unlike any Bantu I've seen, so far."

"Yes, they are Bantu," Ki-Gor replied, "but their religion and their Law are not. The cult of Moon-worship and the strict Code is something from the Dera Daga alone."

"Then the ancestors of the Lunanda weren't the men who built these ruins in the beginning?" Helene asked.

"The Lunanda say not," Ki-Gor replied. "Their tribal songs all say that the Lunanda originally came from the North somewhere. And that the ruins were just as they are now. Who did build the Temple of the Moon, and who did put up these great stones, they don't know. And they don't know how they came to be Moon-worshippers, or how they took up the Code of Dera Daga."

"It's very interesting," Helene commented, "and it's a little spooky. But I must say that the Lunanda are just about the gentlest and most charming tribe I've ever seen."

"They are," Ki-Gor agreed. "I've known them a long time and I've never seen a tribe that obeyed its laws so faithfully. This thing that happened tonight is very unusual. I'm quite sure it was an accident, and that the poor man didn't intend to kill his neighbor."

"What do you think will happen to him?" Helene asked.

"I'm not sure," Ki-Gor replied. "I never learned the Code of Dera Daga. But," the jungle man concluded, "I'd guess that it may go hard with that man. We'll find out in the morning."

Ki-Gor stretched his mighty bare arms upward, then relaxed with a sigh. He smoothed the long yellow hair back off his bronzed forehead and looked down with a smile at Helene.

"We'll find out in the morning," he repeated. "Now, let us get sleep."

PRINCE DATU'S eyes were bloodshot and his face puffy when he called for Ki-Gor and Helene the next morning. Nevertheless, he smiled cheerily and waved a hand toward the dozen or so Lunanda hunters who stood behind him blinking sleepily in the cold gray light of dawn.

"We are ready, O Ki-Gor!" he proclaimed. "Ready to seek out and destroy the great leopard!"

"We, too, are ready!" Ki-Gor responded. "Hast thou worked out a plan, O Datu?"

"That I have," said Datu, "and here it is. I think the leopard is pretty sure to be at one or another of a series of waterholes not far from here. If we do not actually find him beside a kill, we will certainly pick up his spoor somewhere along the way. We will search for him in a body—bunched together. He would not dare attack fifteen people, but would run away. So then, as soon as we find him or his spoor, we will spread out in a thin line on either side of the spoor—each man about three yards from the next—and work down the spoor until he turns to make a stand."

Ki-Gor nodded. "That seems to me a good plan," he said. "I notice thy men are carrying throwing-sticks."

"Instead of beating the bush and shouting," Datu explained, "I thought we would advance quietly, using the throwing-sticks to make him show himself. He is a very devil for back-trailing, this leopard. That is how he killed our two hunters before. When he discovered them following him, he circled back on his trail and lay in wait beside it. When the hunters came along, he let them go by and then sprang out at their backs. We will avoid such a thing happening to us by spreading out on either side of his spoor. And by advancing quietly, we will not frighten him too much to run away."

"Good," said Ki-Gor and stepped forward. His left arm was bent and in the crook of the elbow, he carried a long shovel-headed Masai spear and his six-foot hunting bow. Slung on a rope over his left shoulder was a quiver full of formidable arrows, three feet long and made of baked hardwood and iron-tipped. On his left hip rested the huge hunting-knife in a leather scabbard sewn on the outside of the leopard-skin breech-clout which was Ki-Gor's sole garment.

Helene stepped daintily beside him in her brief leopard-skin tunic. Except for the hunting-knife at her slender waist, her only weapons were a pair of matched throwing-sticks of Zulu pattern. Prince Datu grinned good-naturedly at her and swung his long assegai down in salute.

"Glad am I, O Wife of Ki-Gor," he said, "that thou carryest no spear. Else, thou mightest step in and cheat us men of the honor of killing the leopard."

Helene acknowledged the extravagant compliment with a smile and a nod—although she had not understood one word of Prince Datu's Lunanda speech. But she had long ago learned to follow Ki-Gor's custom in similar situations. Ki-Gor never betrayed ignorance of another person's language if he could help it. She had been amazed at how much one can understand when spoken to in a foreign tongue—simply by the expression and attitude of the speaker. Also, she had found, it made for generally smoother relations between strangers if the barrier of language were ignored.

In this particular instance, Datu led the hunting-party off in high good humor, though he had slept very little. He had completely forgotten that Helene did not understand Lunanda, and Helene's warm smile had seemed to indicate that she understood his compliment perfectly.

Then Ki-Gor asked a question of him, casually, and Datu's cheeriness vanished.

"By the way," Ki-Gor said, "what happened last night?"

Datu's face fell, and he said in a changed voice, "It was too bad. The man was found guilty of murder."

"Ah," said Ki-Gor.

"There was nothing to be done," Datu went on. "I spoke for the man's life. I am convinced that he killed unintentionally. But under the Code of Dera Daga, a blow struck in anger which causes death is considered an act of murder. So this man was adjudged a murderer—for whom no mercy could be recommended."

"And the penalty?" Ki-Gor murmured.

"The Priestess of the Moon-God sentenced him to the Crocodile Pool."

"H'm," Ki-Gor mused. "There is no escape from the Pool, is there?"

"Not the slightest chance of it," Datu replied. "The walls are ten feet high and are faced with slippery mud."

Ki-Gor walked several paces before he spoke. Then he said, "It is a harsh penalty for an act which carried no intent to kill."

Datu shook his head slowly.

"We be law-abiding men," he answered, "and we obey the Code of Dera Daga."

Ki-Gor understood that the subject was closed.

DATU HAD said that the water holes were not far from the village. Nevertheless, it was nearly two hours before the little safari came within sight of the series of thickly wooded dongas where the water holes were located. These dongas were gulleys running parallel to each other for a mile or so, separated one from another by low wooded ridges. The bottoms of the dongas were quaggy underfoot with good-sized waterholes, mud-rimmed, every fifty yards or so.

Ki-Gor frowned a little as Datu prepared to lead his little party down into the nearest of the dongas. The ground around each water-hole was clear, having been trampled and beaten down by thousands of four-footed animals of all kinds. But in between the water-holes the undergrowth was lush and dense. Only up on the sides of the donga did the vegetation thin out enough so that a man could see twenty feet around him. Along the bottom of the donga, a man could blunder right into a great cat without seeing it.

Nevertheless, Prince Datu was leading the way straight down to the bottom of the gulley.

Ki-Gor moved reluctantly after him. Then he shook his head and stopped.

"O Datu!" he called. "Thou art the leader here, and I will follow thee wherever thou goest. But permit me a word of caution, as an old lion-hunter. It is extremely dangerous to proceed along the bottom of this donga—even for a party as big as this one."

Datu turned around, incredulous astonishment on his young face.

"What sayest thou, O Ki-Gor?" he gasped. "Thou—of all people—afraid of danger? I never would have believed it!"

"I said naught of being afraid," Ki-Gor answered, a little testily. "Nevertheless, prudence is not unbecoming in a wise hunter."

"I never would have believed it," Datu repeated slowly.

"Oh, come, Prince Datu!" Ki-Gor exclaimed. "Call me not a coward! I have hunted a great many cats—aye, and hunted them alone. But I always bore in mind the old Mballa proverb, and that is why I am still alive and hale."

"What proverb is that?" Datu inquired coldly.

"In the Mballa tongue, it goes, '*Semlon hia dangu ko simba, hia nakan ek,*' and it means, 'Put thy spear in the lion's mouth, not thy head.'"

Datu's eyes flashed, and he bit his lip in vexation. "Thou art making fun of me, now!" he accused.

"No, no, my friend!" Ki-Gor said with a friendly chuckle, "I am only telling thee how I would hunt this donga—and I am quite wrong to do it. Thou art the leader. Lead the way and I will follow."

Datu looked a little mollified, but he did not smile. He turned his head and looked down into the donga, then along the clearer sides. Then he faced Ki-Gor again.

"No, Ki-Gor," he said, "*thou* art right, and I am wrong. I accept thy caution with thanks."

The young prince wheeled about without another word and headed along the side of the donga. Ki-Gor felt a warm glow. It took a lot of character to make an admission like that—especially in a headstrong young Bantu prince with twelve of his own men within earshot. Assuredly, Ki-Gor told himself, Datu was made of good stuff.

THE YOUNG prince now proceeded to modify his original tactics admirably. The safari kept on the high ground until it came abreast of the first water-hole. Then it descended to the cleared ground around the pool, and investigated the maze of tracks for leopard-spoor.

They found none at the first water-hole. Whereupon Datu led them back up the slope out of the dense brush and proceeded in the same fashion to the next water-hole.

There were no leopard-tracks near that one, either. Nor were there any at the one beyond. Eventually, the safari worked its way to the far end of the donga without finding any trace of its quarry. They had found leopard tracks, but Datu said they were too small to have been left by the huge beast they were hunting.

"Well," said Datu, as the party gathered around him, "certain it is that our leopard is not in this donga—although this is the one where he was last seen. However, he might just as well be in any of the other ones around here. Let us go over the ridge and try our luck in the next donga to the east. That is—" he paused and looked at Ki-Gor—"unless thou hast a suggestion, my friend?"

Ki-Gor hesitated for a split second before answering. He did have a suggestion. And that was that the party backtrack and investigate one of the waterholes they had already looked at. It was entirely possible, Ki-Gor reasoned, that a beast as cunning as this one was reputed to be might have followed the safari into the donga, keeping skilfully behind them and well-hidden. But, for the present, the jungle man decided not to offer any more suggestions.

"Nay, Datu," he smiled, "I have no more ideas to offer. Lead on."

However, as the party climbed up the slope in ragged line abreast, Ki-Gor managed to lag behind, little by little. He was the last one to reach the bare ledges at the crest of the ridge, and as he did, he paused for a moment and looked back. His quick scrutiny turned up nothing to justify his suspicions. The donga lay below him in beautiful serenity. The slight breeze produced a gentle movement of the trees and tall bushes, and there was no sign of an animal of any kind.

Ki-Gor glanced off in the other direction where the ridges sloped down to an open rolling veldt, dotted here and there by good-sized copses. A scattered herd of gazelle grazed peacefully less than a mile away, and nearer at hand a small troop of baboons pursued an erratic course across the open.

Ki-Gor sighed and started down the slope after the safari.

But after he had gone about ten paces he stopped again. Then he went down on his hands and knees and crawled back to the crest of the ridge. Cautiously, he raised his head behind a sheltering spur of rock and once more peered down into the donga.

He sucked in his breath sharply. It seemed to him that a dark shape had drifted into the brush near the next-to-last water-hole. He squinted a long moment at the spot. But he saw nothing more.

He twisted his head around and looked up into the sky. The sun had mounted high by now and beat down fiercely on his bare back. There was a tiny cloud almost in the path of the sun's rays. Ki-Gor wondered whether he had merely seen the shadow of that cloud.

He looked back again at that water-hole. There was no dark shape there, now. There was nothing but the gentle, rhythmic waving of the bush tops in the breeze.

Ah, but *was* that the breeze moving those bushes!

Ki-Gor stiffened, blue eyes gleaming. The bushes wavered and shivered. Something, some sizable body was moving through them, forcing a passage through the dense growth. And whatever it was, was moving up out of the donga, up the ridge—straight toward Ki-Gor.

In a moment, Ki-Gor saw the dark shape coming on through the thinning vegetation. It was no shadow of a cloud. It was an enormous black leopard.

THE BEAST came rapidly up the slope. It came in short rushes, dragging its belly on the ground. Between rushes, it would stop for a second, motionless, then dart forward again. It could not be doubted that the leopard had seen the safari disappear over the brow of the ridge and was now following it.

Ki-Gor smiled grimly as he slid his bow away from his body and reached back into the quiver for an arrow. He was turning the leopard's own backtrailing tactics back on it. Instead of his blundering on to the leopard, the leopard was going to blunder on to him.

Ki-Gor notched the arrow, and set himself to spring upright with bent bow and let fly the arrow before the leopard had a chance to turn and run. The brute would soon be in range now. Ki-Gor's upper lip lifted off his clenched teeth in a triumphant smile.

Certainly, it was the biggest leopard he had ever seen in his life. And a creature which combined the size of a lion with the ferocity and treacherous cunning of a leopard would be, next to a wild elephant, the most dangerous antagonist in all Africa.

A few seconds more, now, and— Suddenly, Ki-Gor heard his name called. He threw a hasty glance behind him and saw the safari halted a hundred yards below him.

"Ki-Gor! Ki-Gor!" Datu's voice floated up to him. "What art thou doing? Come on!"

Ki-Gor grunted with dismay and gestured frantically with his left arm. But Datu kept on calling, and the Lunanda hunters joined in with gay shouts.

With a muttered imprecation, Ki-Gor whipped his head around to look at the leopard. Just as he did, the beast seemed to hear the shouts. It swerved sharply to its left without relaxing speed and shot off across the face of the slope away from Ki-Gor.

The jungle man leaped to his feet and sent a despairing arrow after the flying form of the leopard. But the beast was bounding away at an incredible speed, and the arrow tell short. Ki-Gor swiftly notched another arrow and aimed it. Then he relaxed his bow-arm and let it fall to his side without shooting. The leopard was out of range.

But curiously enough, the flying creature was not going back into the undergrowth of the donga. Instead it kept on in plain sight out toward the veldt. A quick hope crossed Ki-Gor's mind. He waved his hand and shouted down to the safari.

"The leopard!" he cried. "It's gone out on the veldt! Follow me!"

With that he leaped down off the ledge and set off in hot pursuit. He had not taken a dozen paces when he realized that he had left his Masai spear behind on the ledge. He debated with himself for a split second whether to stop and go back for it. Then he decided against it. He must not lose sight of the leopard.

The great cat was now down on the veldt, still running at top speed. The troop of baboons caught sight of it and galvanized into action, scrambled away in terror. A moment later, the gazelles flung themselves into full flight and stampeded thunderously toward the horizon.

Meanwhile, Ki-Gor was sweeping down the end of the ridge, swiftly but effortlessly. He was not running at top speed. He knew that he could not overtake the leopard in a sprint. All the big cats are capable of tremendous speed for short distances only. But, sooner or later, they must stop to rest. Ki-Gor's prime purpose now was to keep in sight of the leopard. In a prolonged chase, he knew he could overhaul the brute and bring it within effective arrow shot.

Already Ki-Gor saw that the leopard was tiring after its long sprint. It was slowing down to a lazy canter. Suddenly it veered and made straight for a good-sized copse. A moment later it disappeared among the shadows of the trees.

This suited Ki-Gor perfectly. The grove of trees was probably no bigger than half an acre, and it did not offer such good cover as the dongas. It would be simple enough to surround it, after which it would be merely a question of time before the huge leopard would be slain.

Only one thing now could go wrong. The leopard might sneak out of the copse on the far side and run unseen to the next grove before the rest of the safari could come up. Ki-Gor decided that it was up to him to get around to the far side of the copse as fast as possible and prevent anything like that from happening. He glanced over his shoulder and saw Datu and Helene and two hunters just coming over the brow of the ridge. He gave them a hasty wave and then sped out on to the veldt.

This time Ki-Gor sprinted, and it was as well he did. Just as he rounded the grove, he saw a dark form slink back into the shadows. The leopard had almost managed to slip out of the copse.

KI-GOR NOW began to wish that he had gone back for his Masai spear. Lacking that formidable weapon, he would have time to shoot at least one arrow, and possibly two. Acting on the thought, he noticed one arrow, and stuck a second point downward in the ground in front of him. He had now but to wait until the safari came up.

The jungle man wondered whether Datu really thought he had been cowardly because he had offered cautious advice, and whether Datu would consider him cowardly for waiting like this for help, rather than going into the grove after the leopard single-handed. Ki-Gor smiled. He had killed many leopards armed only with his knife, and once he had killed a leopard barehanded, choking the brute to death. But on all those occasions he had had no choice, and on all those occasions he had been badly clawed. No one, Ki-Gor reflected, but an impetuous boy would risk close quarters with a huge black leopard, except in case of direst necessity.

He began to hear shouts from the other side of the grove, and he increased his watchfulness lest the leopard try to make a break on his side. Then there came a nearer shout, and a moment later Datu and Helene came trotting around the copse to his right. They shouted and waved their hands in triumph at him, but Ki-Gor did not answer for a second. For sudden alarm had caught him by the throat.

They were both much too close to the trees.

They were running almost abreast, Datu slightly in the lead and on the inside between Helene and the grove.

But they were scarcely ten feet away from the wall of trees and brush in which the black leopard might that very moment be lurking.

Ki-Gor waved frantically. "Get away from the trees!" he cried in

English.

Helene slowed up reluctantly as if puzzled.

"Thou too, Datu!" Ki-Gor shouted in Lunanda. "Thou art too close to the trees!"

The young prince stopped and stared into the grove. He shook his head and shouted back.

"There is no danger, Ki-Gor! He is deep in the grove, somewhere. We will have to—"

Just then, there was a terrific roar, and Ki-Gor went cold all over. A huge black form came bounding around the corner of the grove *behind Helene and straight toward her!*

"Helene!" Ki-Gor's voice was agonized. "Drop! Drop to the ground!"

She whirled around and saw the Black Death rushing at her. Promptly she flung herself to the ground.

Ki-Gor's bow was bent, and he said a private prayer as he sighted along the arrow. This shot he could not miss. Datu stood paralyzed ten feet away from Helene. Ki-Gor's arrow alone could save his beautiful wife.

The leopard was two bounds away from her when Ki-Gor let go the arrow. At the same instant, Datu came to life. With a wild yell he lunged toward Helene, his spear tilted upward from his hips. The next moment Ki-Gor was never to forget for the rest of his life.

Datu flung himself squarely in the path of the charging beast. His spear-point caught the leopard just under the wide-open jaws, snicked through flesh and hide, and came out between his shoulder blades.

At the same instant, Ki-Gor's arrow hurtled into Datu's back.

KI-GOR HAD seen Datu throw himself into the path of the arrow. He had seen the arrow bury itself deep into the young prince's back. But the few seconds that followed were a blank in Ki-Gor's memory. He did not remember running forward, a tiny growl deep in his throat.

The next thing he remembered was bending over Datu's still form on the ground. Helene picked herself up quite unhurt.

Prince Datu and the leopard were both stone dead.

Sick with horror, Ki-Gor stood up and faced the Lunanda hunters who were just now swarming around the corner of the grove.

"What has happened!" the foremost of them shouted. Then he gave an agonized cry and threw himself on the ground beside the body of Datu. Suddenly, he seemed to see Ki-Gor's arrow sticking up from

Datu's back. He recoiled in horror, one knee still on the ground. The rest of the hunters quickly clustered in a little knot behind him. A low moan went over them, and then a fearful silence hung on the air.

"Did—did none of you see what happened?" Ki-Gor asked quietly.

There was not a word of answer from the little groups of Lunanda.

"Then I will tell you," Ki-Gor went on. "Prince Datu sacrificed his life to save my woman. He charged the leopard and slew him. Unhappily—he stepped between me and the leopard. And I had already shot an arrow. The arrow has gone into Prince Datu's heart, and it—killed him instantly."

Ki-Gor heard his own words as if someone else were speaking. And he was so numb from the shock of what had happened that he hardly noticed that his words were greeted with stony silence by the Lunanda hunters. But an instinct for action prompted him to do something—anything.

"Come," he said, "we will go along, now. We will take Prince Datu back to his father and mother."

He bent over the boy's still form, took hold of the feathered butt of his arrow and gently pulled it out. He stared at the bloody shaft for a second, then deliberately broke it across his knee. Tenderly, then he picked up the inert body of Prince Datu and bore it sorrowfully toward Dera Daga. Helene walked beside him, and the Lunanda hunters fell in behind them silently.

CHAPTER II

DATU'S BODY LAY ON the ground in front of Mboko's house where Ki-Gor had reverently placed it. Mboko and Goli stood on the threshold stunned and incredulous, while Ki-Gor told them what had happened. Helene stood beside him holding his hand, and glancing now and then uneasily at the Lunanda who were massed behind them.

"And thus your son died," Ki-Gor concluded, "valiantly sacrificing himself to save Helene's life. I would give my right arm rather than my arrow should kill him. But he jumped in the way of it after I had released it. There is nothing I can do now—no power on earth can restore your son to you. All I can say, my old and dear friends, is—he was my friend. And my grief approaches yours. And if there is aught I can do to ease your pain, tell me—and it shall be done."

King Mboko lifted sorrowful eyes to Ki-Gor.

"There is naught thou canst do, O Ki-Gor," the king said in a broken voice. "I know well enough that thou wouldst never willingly harm a hair of Datu's head. I would be ungenerous if I did not say that I hold thee in no way accountable for my son's death."

Ki-Gor breathed easier. He had not been unmindful of the hostile silence of the Lunanda villagers behind him. But King Mboko had not finished.

"I speak for myself only," he said, "but I feel sure that the tribe will agree with me, and that when thou art tried tonight, according to the Code of Dera Daga, thou wilt be acquitted of any crime."

An uneasy little fear lurked at the back of Ki-Gor's brain. So he was to be tried for manslaughter, and by these very Lunanda who stood ominously quiet behind him.

"I will not put thee to the shame and discomfort of arrest," Mboko said. "Simply give me thy word that thou nor thy wife will not leave Dera Daga before the trial tonight."

Ki-Gor hesitated. Something told him that he and Helene should go away at once from those mysterious ruins of Dera Daga and those quiet Lunanda who dwelt there and lived in blind obedience to their ancient Code. Ki-Gor's word was his bond. If he gave it, he could not go away. If he refused to give it, it might make a very bad impression on the Lunanda people. It was a hard decision to make.

However, in spite of a strong subconscious warning within himself to evade the trial, Ki-Gor saw no other way out.

"Thou hast my word, O King," he said simply.

DATU WAS buried that afternoon with full pomp and ceremony. Unlike such occasions among other Bantu tribes, there was no demonstration of grief by the Lunanda or their bereaved king and queen. In a way, Ki-Gor wished there had been. The silence of these people moving among the timeless ruins of Dera Daga oppressed him more and more as the afternoon passed and the day drew to a close. More and more Ki-Gor felt that he should take Helene and escape while there was yet time. Yet there was nothing to be done about it now. He had given his word, and he could not go back on it.

Although he tried to hide his apprehensions from Helene, she knew him too well for him to do it successfully. She finally made him tell her what was worrying him. He found it hard to put into words, and finally he had to fall back on his old expression.

"It's just that I smell danger about here," he said. "I feel that we ought to get away as fast as we can."

"Oh, that's nonsense!" Helene scolded. "You've got nothing to fear from the trial. You yourself told me that the Lunanda are the most law-abiding people you know. The trial is just a formality. After all, you didn't murder Datu—it was a complete and unavoidable accident."

"Yes, Helene," the jungle man smiled. "You're quite right. I won't worry any more."

But with the coming of darkness and later, the rising of the full moon, Ki-Gor's apprehensions returned to him in full force. And, finally, when he found himself standing on the flat top of the pyramid, staring down at the sea of uplifted faces, he felt for all the world like a trapped lion.

During the course of his wandering life, Ki-Gor had watched many tribal ceremonies. From Nigeria to Mashonaland, from Benguela to Lake Rudolph, he had seen dancers strutting and leaping to the booming rhythms of giant drums; he had seen witch-doctors shrieking incantations and slaughtering sacrificial victims; he had seen whole tribes whip themselves into maniacal frenzies.

But this one was completely different. There were no torches, no great bonfires hurling great flame toward the sky. There were no dancers, there were no giant drums thumping. The Lunanda huddled in sullen silence around the base of the pyramid, their only illumination the eerie blue-white light of the full moon. And this ceremony, in which Ki-Gor as central figure awaited the verdict of the implacable Code of Dera Daga, exceeded all the others he had ever seen for sheer brooding terror.

He stood at one corner of the flat top of the pyramid beside King Mboko. At the next corner were Helene and Queen Goli. Halfway between them the Priestess of the Moon crouched over a tiny fire of smoldering embers. Ranged behind her were the twelve hunters who had accompanied Prince Datu on his last safari.

After all had taken their places there was an interminable pause before the Priestess finally rose from behind her little fire to begin the trial. She was a tall, thin, incredibly old woman, dressed in a long white skirt of cloth, and a shoulder-cape of long white feathers. No headdress at all covered her short white woolly hair.

She stepped slowly around the little smudge fire and stood at the very edge of the pyramid-top. For an appalling moment she stood motionless. Then long scrawny arms appeared from under the feather cape. She lifted them high in the air over her head and began a chanting invocation in a sad, harsh voice.

"O Moon-God, who sends his beneficent rays downward to destroy the darkness and light the night for his grateful people—listen, we pray thee! Listen to this trial we are about to hold, according to thine ancient and invariable Code! Guide our minds, we beseech thee, along the paths of righteousness, and help us do strictest justice in thy holy name! So be it!"

The Priestess let her arms fall slowly to her sides, and stood with head bowed for a moment. Then she turned and went majestically back to the little fire, and squatted down behind it.

KING MBOKO now stepped forward and quietly addressed the tribe.

"We are gathered here tonight, O Lunanda," he said, in a voice that shook a little, "to consider the unfortunate death of my son, Prince Datu. His death was caused by an arrow discharged by a dear friend of his and mine, Ki-Gor. There were no witnesses to the happening except the Red-Haired One, who is Ki-Gor's wife and who, therefore, cannot testify. So the only account of the accident we have is Ki-Gor's. But Ki-Gor's words, as you all well know, can be believed. According to him, this is what happened."

And the king related the account of Datu's death just as Ki-Gor had told it to him.

"And thus did the tragedy happen," he concluded. "For my part, I can see no possible reason for holding Ki-Gor guilty even of negligence in this matter. The arrow had been released before Datu moved, therefore Ki-Gor had no control over the instrument of death."

Mboko paused amid a dead silence.

"Is there anyone," he said, "who wishes to speak before we go on?"

"Aye, here is one, O King, who wishes to speak."

The voice came from the hunters grouped behind the Priestess. Mboko turned around in surprise. One of the hunters stepped forward.

"It is I, Aku the Hunter," the man said. "I was the first of Datu's own people to kneel by his side after he had been done to death."

"Speak thy mind, Aku," said the king patiently.

"It is a question I would ask, O King," said Aku. "I would ask why this Ki-Gor did not tell of the dispute between him and our young master, Datu."

"Dispute?" Mboko repeated slowly, and a chill breeze blew gently on the base of Ki-Gor's neck.

"Aye, a dispute," Aku insisted. "There are at least twelve of us who remember how the words flew back and forth—even if Ki-Gor and his Red-Haired One do not."

Mboko swung around and looked at Ki-Gor.

"You told me of no such happening," the king said.

"I deemed it not worth the telling," Ki-Gor answered quietly. "Datu and I differed on a point—as good friends will. It was over in a moment and forgotten."

There was a murmur from the crowd below the pyramid, and Mboko instantly stilled it with a gesture. Then he turned back to Aku, the hunter.

"What was thy purpose, Aku, in asking that question?" the king said.

"We are asked to believe Ki-Gor's story," the hunter replied. "And yet Ki-Gor did not tell you that Datu called him a coward. Maybe the dispute was over and forgotten in a minute—and maybe it was not. But our young master died with Ki-Gor's arrow in his back—at a time when no one but his wife was present."

Again the murmur rose from the Lunanda, and again Mboko waved it down. Quickly he turned again to Ki-Gor.

"Can this man be answered, Ki-Gor?" he said.

Ki-Gor thought for a moment and then said, "It is hard to answer a man who speaks from a bitter heart and who talks of what might have happened—as if Ki-Gor were a liar. But there is this to be said. If I planned to kill any man, friend or enemy, it is not likely that I would choose a moment to kill him when he was engaged in saving the life of the woman I love."

"Well and truly spoken," Mboko observed. Then to the hunter, he said, "It is unseemly and unjust of thee to raise suspicions without basis. Because thy mind is clouded with grief, do not accuse someone of murdering Prince Datu—someone who is as full of grief as thou art. Stand back, Aku."

The restless muttering increased in the crowd, and Mboko whirled to face them.

"The words of Aku, the hunter, were unjust and improper," he thundered. "Make up your minds without regard to those words. Before I call for a vote, I must say this—that I cannot see how you can do else than acquit Ki-Gor. And if we could hear the voice of my son now, I am sure he would say the same thing. In a moment, we will vote. According to our Code, you will shout 'Aye' or 'Nay' as I put the questions to you."

THE KING paused and stared down at the massed faces of his people. Ki-Gor, his heart pounding uncomfortably, looked down too at the people who were to decide his fate. Somehow, he was not encouraged.

"Here is the first question," said the king. "Is Ki-Gor accountable in any way for the death of Prince Datu? Answer 'Aye' or 'Nay'."

Ki-Gor held his breath. Then he let it out slowly.

There was not a sound from the Lunanda.

An incredulous smile broke out on Ki-Gor's face, and he took a step toward Mboko. The king raised a warning hand.

"We have not finished yet, Ki-Gor," he said. Then, lifting his voice to the crowd, he said, "I give you the converse of the question, now. Do you acquit Ki-Gor of all responsibility for the death of Prince Datu? Answer 'Aye' or 'Nay'."

There was a stony silence.

Ki-Gor stared in consternation at Mboko. The king's face was grave.

"According to the Code of Dera Daga," he announced, "if the Tribe neither convicts nor acquits, then the Priestess of the Moon shall decide the question by mystic means."

A great sigh went over the Lunanda massed around the base of the Pyramid. Ki-Gor tried to hide the dismay in his heart. He realized now that the Lunanda in their grief demanded a victim, a scapegoat, to punish for the death of their prince. Yet their instinct for impartial justice would not permit them to convict Ki-Gor on the evidence that was presented to them. They had, therefore, begged the issue and passed the decision on to the old Priestess with the hope that she would find Ki-Gor guilty.

Ki-Gor watched her now. She gave no sign that she had heard Mboko's words, but squatted motionless for a long moment gazing into the glowing embers of her little fire. Then she reached out a scrawny hand toward an indistinct object beside her. She lifted it up and held it over the fire. Ki-Gor perceived then that it was a pouch, and that she was pouring a dust out of it on to the fire.

Thick smoke began to roll upwards, and the Priestess got to her feet. She raised her arms and bent her head forward into the smoke. From where he stood, Ki-Gor caught a faint pungent whiff of narcotics.

The Priestess coughed once or twice, and then began to sway. She leaned back out of the smoke momentarily, but then thrust her face back into it again. She repeated this two times more, and finally shuffled backward unsteadily for several feet.

Arms still upraised, she lurched around the fire with a low moan and came to the edge of the pyramid-top. Here she swayed drunkenly, her hands fluttering rhythmically above her head, and her moans grew louder.

Eventually the words of her incantation could be distinguished.

"Come! Come, O Lord of the Moon!" the croaking voice intoned. "From out the clouds—come and render judgment! Speak! Through the ancient mouth of thy priestess—speak!"

KI-GOR WATCHED her with a horrid fascination as she retreated from the edge of the pyramid-top, and slowly circled the smoking fire three times. And as she tottered around, her arms undulated and a ceaseless muttering came from her seamed old face. Suddenly she stopped and her lean figure became rigid.

"A-a-a-ah!" she exclaimed in a voice that was a wail. "The Moon-God speaks! Hear ye all the judgment of the Moon! Datu is dead—killed at high noon by the arrow of Ki-Gor! Witness to the deed there was none save Ki-Gor's other half, his wife! Truth needs a witness!"

There was a pause, and then the wailing voice rose again.

"Ki-Gor can prove his innocence!"

The jungle man's heart bounded.

"Let Ki-Gor find the star that shines as brilliantly at high noon as it does at midnight!"

A shock of dismay went through Ki-Gor.

"After that, let Ki-Gor at high noon look upon the sun and feel its rays cold upon him!"

Cold despair began to settle over Ki-Gor.

"Then let Ki-Gor return to Dera Daga when next the Moon is full. At that time he must satisfy a third condition which will not be revealed until then."

Ki-Gor's mind set to work trying to interpret the Priestess's words.

"When Ki-Gor has successfully performed this threefold task, then shall he be considered completely guiltless of the death of Datu. If he fail—then shall he be adjudged a murderer. While he is gone on his missions, his wife shall be held for his return. If he does not come back by the next full Moon, then she will be punished in his place. And the punishment will be the punishment of a murderer—the Crocodile Pool!"

A low gasp swept the Lunanda as the fateful voice rose to a shriek.

"Thus speaks the Moon-God! So be it!"

And the old Priestess tottered back and collapsed beside the smoking fire.

A gust of rage swept over Ki-Gor. Why should he, Lord of the Jungle, be victimized by the perverse whim of an old crone stupefied with narcotics? He shot a wary glance at the twelve hunters to his right. Then he swiftly measured the distance between himself and Helene. A desperate plan formed in his mind to dash over to her side, sweep her into his arms and run down the steps of the pyramid. The very boldness of such an action might take the Lunanda by surprise, and he might somehow escape into the night with Helene.

But as he looked across the pyramid top at Helene, his back began to crawl. One of the great paving-stones beside her was tilting up. Two white-robed blacks sprang up from underneath it and seized Helene. Ki-Gor gave a hoarse cry and bounded toward her.

But he knew he could not reach her side in time to save her. In a flash, the two white-robed blacks had borne her down into the hole. And just as Ki-Gor made a last despairing leap, the huge paving block banged shut. He knelt and clawed vainly at the smooth stone.

The twelve hunters swarmed after him shouting, and the Lunanda below were thrown into an uproar. Ki-Gor sprang up whirling to face the hunters, teeth bared and eyes blazing. In another second he would have hurled himself at them.

But King Mboko suddenly came in front of him, hand upraised in a compassionate gesture.

"Nay, Ki-Gor!" he cried. "Violence can avail thee nothing, now. Be calm, I pray thee!"

"What have you done to the Red Haired One?" Ki-Gor raged. "Give her back to me before you ask me to be calm!"

"She is safe, I promise thee," Mboko answered, "and she will be unharmed until thou return from thy missions."

"How can I believe you," Ki-Gor shouted, "when you have done a thing like this to me?"

"I have done nothing, Ki-Gor," the king said patiently. "It is the Code—the Code of Dera Daga. Everything that has happened has been done in accordance with its rulings. Come with me calmly to my house and I will explain anything that needs to be explained."

Ki-Gor looked wearily at the ring of hostile faced hunters, then looked down at the great block of stone which had closed over the head of his beloved Helene.

"Very well, Mboko," he said listlessly, "I will come."

CHAPTER III

SOME TWO HOURS LATER, Ki-Gor walked slowly out of Mboko's house. The situation he and Helene were in was now all too clearly in his mind. He must somehow accomplish the seemingly impossible feats of discovering a star that shone visibly at high noon, and of finding a place where the sun's rays at high noon felt cold. And he had twenty-eight days to locate these paradoxes.

In the meantime, Helene would be a closely guarded hostage. Mboko had warned against any attempts to rescue her.

"If thou returnest with an army," the king had said, "and wipe out the Lunanda, it will avail thee nothing. For Helene will be cast into the Crocodile Pool at the first hostile sign from thee. And no amount of dead Lunanda would bring Helene back to life."

As to the self-contradictory phenomena which the Priestess had commanded Ki-Gor to find—Mboko could not say whether they were to be taken literally or figuratively. But if they were figures of speech, the king had no interpretation for them.

For perhaps the first time in his adventurous life, Ki-Gor felt completely trapped and helpless. He walked into the house which he and Helene had occupied, felt his way around in the darkness and picked up his bow and quiver of arrows. Then he stepped outside again into the moonlight, thinking desperately.

There was manifestly no place on earth where a star shines at mid-day. Nor was there a place where at mid-day the sun's rays are cold. And yet, to save Helene, he had to find those places. But how to go about it, he had not the faintest idea.

Suddenly an idea crossed his mind. He thought of one man in Africa who might possibly be able to help him. That man was old Tsempala, the M'Fang witch-doctor.

He had once saved Tsempala's life and earned the old man's everlasting gratitude. For shrewd, clear-eyed thinking Tsempala was far above the run of witch-doctors, and he had, moreover, an amazing fund of obscure knowledge. If anyone could interpret the commands of the Priestess of the Moon, Tsempala could.

Ki-Gor threw a quick glance upwards and saw that the moon had begun to slide downwards toward the west. The Lunanda village lay sleeping. No one moved among the houses, and there was no sound.

Twenty-eight days, Ki-Gor reflected. There was no time to be lost. Silently he walked through the village and into the jungle.

His route was the same one which Datu had taken at the head of the ill-fated safari less than twenty hours before. Ki-Gor considered that he was entering upon a long journey, and he wanted the Masai spear which he had left on the top of the ridge between the dongas.

Ki-Gor covered the distance to the dongas in quick time, but the moon was hanging low in the western sky as he climbed to the crest of the ridge. However, streaks of dawn were appearing in the east and there was sufficient light for him to locate the bare ledge where he had hidden the day before. Indeed he found the very spot where he had lain watching the black leopard, and where he had left the spear when he sprang up to discharge his arrows.

The jungle man stood at that spot now, and looked down thoughtfully.

The Masai spear was not there.

Ki-Gor proceeded to search the whole ledge carefully, although he was pretty sure he would not find the missing weapon. It was possible, he reasoned, that some member of the safari the day before had picked it up. Yet he did not remember seeing any of the hunters carrying it during the Trial Ceremony on the pyramid-top.

He returned to the spot where he had left the spear, and dropped to all fours. He put his head close to the ground and sniffed. His extraordinary sense of smell should enable him to find tracks where none could be seen.

Almost immediately, his sensitive nostrils caught a strong scent of Bantu. So strong it was that Ki-Gor knew it was quite fresh. The Bantu who had been at that spot had been there less than an hour before.

Ki-Gor stood up grim-faced. He wanted that Masai spear but he did not want to spend precious hours hunting down the man who had picked it up. He sent one last regretful look back in the direction of Dera Daga, and then turned his face resolutely northward and set off at a tireless, ground-covering lope.

MILES OF more or less open veldt stretched before him, dotted by small copses and groves. The grass was short and the footing sure, and by the time the sun had climbed high enough in the heavens to have become unbearably hot, Ki-Gor had traveled an astonishing distance from Dera Daga. He began to think about stopping for a rest through the heat of mid-day, when he saw some distance ahead of him a row of tall trees.

That was an indication of a stream or a narrow lake, and Ki-Gor increased his pace toward the trees. A stream it turned out to be, or rather a small river flowing quietly between two rows of graceful sycamores. The river was not large enough to contain crocodiles, yet was sufficiently deep to swim in. Ki-Gor dropped his bow and quiver on the bank and plunged in.

The cool water felt grateful to his parched skin and he swam in a lazy circle, dipping his head under luxuriously. Arrived back at the bank beside his weapons, he stood up waist deep in the water, and gazed downstream. It seemed to him that about a half a mile away, the fringe of sycamores broadened out into a grove. It would be shady and cool down there. Promptly Ki-Gor picked up the bow and quiver, held them high in his right hand, and half-waded, half-swam downstream until he arrived at the grove.

It was indeed cool and shady under those spreading trees. A great bough bent low over the stream, and Ki-Gor hauled himself up on to it without bothering to step ashore. Forty or fifty feet up the tree there was a wide hospitable crotch. Ki-Gor curled himself up in it and speedily went to sleep.

It seemed but a moment later that he woke up, tense and sharp-eyed. What woke him up, he did not know. He drew himself up to a sitting position and peered around him, listening intently. He heard nothing suspicious, nor could he see any danger of any kind. The sun had not yet climbed to the zenith. There were still more than three hours of intense heat left, and Ki-Gor still felt the effects of not having slept at all the night before. He curled up again and went to sleep.

When he woke up again, he saw that there were only about three hours left before sunset. But he felt strong and refreshed and so he did not grudge himself the prolonged rest. He swung himself easily through the trees to the edge of the grove and slid down to the ground.

Remembering that something had awakened him earlier in the day, he spent a few minutes reconnoitering the grass at the border of the grove. In a very short time, he came across a spoor which he quickly identified as human. A lone Bantu had evidently come along the bank of the river from somewhere upstream. He had circled the grove, then entered it, crossed once and then departed across the veldt.

Ki-Gor looked thoughtful. It was possible that this Bantu had picked up his spoor, and followed it. Losing it where Ki-Gor had plunged into the stream, he had tried to pick it up again along the river bank. Finally baffled, the strange Bantu had gone on his way.

Who was that Bantu? Ki-Gor wondered. And had he followed Ki-Gor's trail by pure chance?

The spoor of the strange Bantu angled off northward—the very direction Ki-Gor was going. He decided to follow it, for a time anyway, and see if he could catch up with the man who left it. It would be extremely interesting, Ki-Gor thought, if the unknown Bantu turned out to be a Lunanda.

IN THE short grass of the veldt the spoor was not over-distant, and but for one thing Ki-Gor would have probably not continued to follow it, because it would have slowed him down too much. However, that one thing was that the trail, faint as it was, went straight as an arrow northwards across the veldt in Ki-Gor's own direction. And by the time night fell Ki-Gor was still on the track of the Bantu who had tracked him.

By this time, however, the veldt had begun to give way to more closely wooded country. And as the last of the brief twilight deepened into the gloom of the African night, Ki-Gor saw that his man had entered a well-defined travel-trail that traversed the ever-thickening forest.

Ki-Gor was not afraid of traveling in pitch darkness. But most Bantu are mortally afraid of venturing away from their camp-fires at night. The jungle man plunged up the narrow trail, confident that he would soon catch up with the Bantu whose spoor had led him in this direction.

It was, however, several hours before Ki-Gor caught the faint flicker of a campfire through the trees ahead of him. He slowed down abruptly and glided noiselessly toward the patch of light. Silent as a cat he worked his way to a great tree beside the trail, and peered out from behind its broad trunk.

Less than ten feet away a lone black man squatted beside the little fire. Ki-Gor saw at a glance that the man was not a Lunanda. He had the broad face and thick limbs that characterized the dreamy tribes who inhabited the steaming forests along the Gulf of Guinea. The man had extremely primitive features, flat nose, heavy recessive chin, and excessively thick, curled lips. But for all that, his expression was that of a man of peace.

Blissfully unconscious of Ki-Gor's unwavering eyes on him, the man sighed gustily, reached out a hand and tossed some faggots on the little fire. For a moment, the fire light shone on the inside of the man's wrist and disclosed there a small circular tattoo-mark. Ki-Gor smiled knowingly to himself.

Although he could not see the tattoo-mark distinctly, he knew perfectly well what it was. It was a crude representation of the head of a dog—a wolfish dog with stand-up ears, and pointed muzzle. And that tattoo mark showed that this strange black belonged to the Brethren of the Dog.

OF ALL the numerous secret societies which cut across tribal and geographical lines in Africa, the Brotherhood of the Dog is by far the oldest. No one can go back far enough through the timeless centuries to find the origins of this mighty society. But it is suspected that the Brotherhood existed ages ago in the Prehistoric Dawn, when Europe and Africa were connected by a land-bridge, and the men of Europe as well as the men of Africa lived in gloomy caves with their only domesticated animal—the Dog.

Unlike most of the other societies of the jungle, the Leopard and the various Snake cults, the Brotherhood of the Dog was purely benevolent and had no hidden and hideous practices of torture and bloody sacrifice. Ki-Gor was, in a sense, an honorary member of the Brethren, having once helped them and accepted help from them.

However, Brotherhood of the Dog or not, Ki-Gor was disinclined to walk into any possible trap. He decided to prepare the way before he showed himself to this strange black. To that end, he spoke in a gentle voice, using the M'Pongwe trade dialect of the Guinea Coast.

"Do not turn around, O Little Brother of the Dog," he said softly, "in fact, do not move a muscle. But announce thy name, tell whence thou comest, and whither thou goest."

The black jumped in terror at Ki-Gor's first words, but as the ghostly voice smoothly went on, he subsided trembling. Obediently he did not move. When Ki-Gor finished, the stranger paused. Then he said in a shaky voice, "My name is Lebo, and I am a student returning to my home in the north from a pilgrimage to a wise man. If thou who speaks to me art a man, then show thyself—for I am a man of peace. If thou art a disembodied ju-ju, be warned: I am a student of ju-ju myself, and I will cast a mighty spell against thee!"

Ki-Gor could hardly restrain a chuckle. These last brave words of Lebo the Student were uttered in a tone that carried very little conviction.

"To what wise man hast thou made a pilgrimage?" Ki-Gor said, in the same gentle voice.

"To Tsempala, the medicine-man," Lebo replied.

"To Tsempala!" Ki-Gor exclaimed in astonishment. "Then we are well met!" He stepped out from behind the tree trunk. "I, myself, am journeying to see Tsempala."

Lebo peeped furtively over his shoulder. His eyes were round with awe as they beheld Ki-Gor, yet there was relief in them.

"Ah!" he breathed. "Undoubtedly, thou art he who is called Ki-Gor."

"I am he," Ki-Gor replied, sitting down beside the little fire. "But tell me about my friend—Tsempala. You hast seen him and yet thou art headed north. How is that? Does Tsempala himself no longer dwell in the north?"

"Nay," Lebo replied. "Recently he moved from his own people to a retreat which is but two days' journey from here up the great river."

"The river?"

"It is not far from here," Lebo said. "I came up the trail to make camp a safe distance from any crocodiles. Possibly, I can be of service to thee, Ki-Gor. I am leaving the river here. It bends southward, and my way is the opposite direction. If thou wish, use the canoe which I came down the river in. It is a good light canoe, and I have left it drawn up on the river bank. Thou canst make good time even upstream, because the current is sluggish."

"That is welcome news," Ki-Gor said slowly. "I will use thy canoe most gratefully."

He paused a moment and thought. So this Lebo had come by water. In that case, he could not be the same man who had trekked across the veldt, first behind, then ahead of Ki-Gor.

Who was that man? And where was he now?

A TINY moonbeam fought its way down through the leaves of the forest and lighted Ki-Gor's knee. He was reminded that the night was advancing. He had no time to speculate on the unseen Bantu. His chance meeting with Lebo had been indeed fortunate in that he had not only discovered that Tsempala was much nearer than he had expected, but he had acquired a swift means of transportation to him.

He determined to resume his journey immediately and received minute instructions from Lebo as to how to find Tsempala. Then, in spite of Lebo's warnings that traveling on the river by night would be extremely dangerous because of the crocodiles, he got up and took leave of the student.

"Farewell, and long life, O Ki-Gor!" Lebo cried.

"Long life to thee," Ki-Gor replied, "and may thy ju-ju become all-powerful."

He set off down the trail swiftly toward the river and the canoe. The moonbeams dancing in the trail lighted the way, and showed him the canoe drawn up on the river bank. Deftly, he pushed off from shore, pointed the nose of the canoe upstream, and dug the paddle deep into the oily water of the river. Full in his face shone the almost-round moon.

There were twenty-seven days left in which to perform the feats commanded by the Priestess of the Moon.

TSEMPALA LOOKED grave. Ki-Gor regarded him anxiously. All through Ki-Gor's recital of the events at Dera Daga, old Tsempalas face had grown increasingly serious.

"Tell me, O Wise One," Ki-Gor urged, "what is the interpretation? What is the hidden meaning behind this gibberish about stars that shine at mid-day?"

The old medicine-man shook his head slowly.

"I fear me," he said at length, "that there is no hidden meaning. I have heard before now of the Priestess of Dera Daga and her fearful Errands. Those commands of hers are not figures of speech. The things she sends men to find are real, or she believes they are real. They exist at least in her dope-crazed brain."

Ki-Gor's great shoulders sagged and a stupendous weariness came over him. He had been counting more than he realized on Tsempala's being able to shed some light on his extraordinary missions. He had hoped that there was some trick about the old Priestess's commands that Tsempala could solve.

"Some years back," the old man went on, "a man came to me for help. He was a Lunanda and he had somehow killed his wife. The Priestess had sent him on just such a pair of Errands as she has done to thee. Only in his case, I was able to help."

"What were his missions?" Ki-Gor asked.

"He had to find the Black Rocks Which Burn," Tsempala said.

"Rocks?" said Ki-Gor. "Rocks do not burn."

"You are wrong," the witch-doctor said. "There *are* some rocks that burn. And they are black. If they are placed on a hot bed of embers, they will presently catch fire themselves and give out a great heat—as well as much smoke and a very unpleasant odor."

"Oh, yes, yes!" Ki-Gor exclaimed. "Come to think of it, I have seen them. Helene has an English name for them—it is 'Coal!'"

"Precisely," Tsempala nodded. "Then this poor wretch of a Lunanda also had to find the river which ran backward."

"That runs backward?" Ki-Gor repeated. Then his face lightened. "Oh, that's easy!"

"Surely, it is easy," Tsempala said, "for those like thee and me who have followed a river to its mouth at the sea, and seen the tide wash it back upstream. But those Errands illustrate what I mean about the Priestess of Dera Daga. If she has sent thee to find a star that shines in the middle of the day, she means thee to look for exactly that."

"But where, then—" Ki-Gor cried despairingly— "where in the name of goodness will I find such a thing? And where in all Africa will I ever find a cold sun's rays?"

"That," said Tsempala, "I don't know. It may be that someone would know. Stay with me for a while, and I will make a Sending. I will make several Sendings of various kinds—with the drums and in other ways. I cannot promise any real help, but it will do no harm to ask in various directions. Just by chance, we might hear of some clue to these things thou seekest."

The medicine-man paused and looked inquiringly to Ki-Gor. His wrinkled old face wore a solicitous expression.

Ki-Gor stared at his great hands. Such powerful competent hands they were. They could choke a raging leopard to death, or they could weave fine reeds into a basket so closely that it would hold water. Yet what good were they now?

"How long can I stay?" Ki-Gor said simply. "How long can I afford to stay? Time is flowing like blood from a severed artery."

"I wish, dear friend," Tsempala said sorrowfully, "that I could promise swift aid. Yet I cannot. I can only try. In a few minutes, I will set the drums to talking. And soon, the Brotherhood of the Dog will set to work furiously, asking and looking. If at the end of three days, we have heard of nothing which might possibly be of help—"

The witch-doctor waved an expressive hand.

"Then thou canst do nothing," he finished, "but go forth and trust to thy good fortune."

FOR THREE days thereafter, Tsempala's drums spoke. Distant drums sounded faintly—acknowledging the question. And other drums far out of earshot were relaying the message from Tsempala, and these in turn sent the message ever farther away.

In the meantime, Tsempala employed other means of communication—means which were less easily understood than the booming drums sending their ancient code. The old man spent hours by himself squatting on his heels, arms straight out in front of him resting on his bony knees, his hands dangling limply from the thin wrists. His eyes at this time were lack-lustre and unseeing, and he was perfectly oblivious of everything that went on about him.

Ki-Gor tried to keep himself occupied by fashioning a spear out of a young ironwood sapling. Although he had to be content to tip it with a small iron hunting tip given him by one of Tsempala's students, the wood was heavy and strong, and by the end of the third day, Ki-Gor had a satisfactory weapon.

For three days Tsempala's drums spoke. But at the end of each day, the witch doctor shook his head gloomily in answer to Ki-Gor's questioning glance. There had been answers to Tsempala's broadcast query, but none of them had presented any strong clues for Ki-Gor to go by.

On the evening of the third day, Tsempala laid his gnarled hand on Ki-Gor's knee.

"Great is my sorrow, O Friend," he said. "I have failed thee. I have called on all my resources to try and solve the riddles of the Priestess of Dera Daga. Far and wide have my questions gone, and yet there has been no one who has answered with definite information. Here and there, voices have been raised whispering that they have heard of the cold sun, or the mid-day star, but where they can be found no one really knows. I am afraid thy three day wait has been in vain."

Ki-Gor let his breath out slowly. So it had come to the worst! He had been hoping against hope that Tsempala's wisdom would somehow find the answer to the riddles. Now he had to face the brutal fact that even Tsempala was helpless in the face of the narcotic-inspired commands of the Priestess of the Moon.

And if Tsempala could not find the answer, how could he, Ki-Gor, hope to do better?

"Thanks to thee, O Tsempala," he said quietly. "Thou hast done thy best, and no man could ask more of a friend. But I have only twenty-two days left to perform these miracles, so I had best be on my way."

"Which way do you go?" said the witch-doctor.

"Reason fails to point the direction," Ki-Gor shrugged. "One must fall back on blind chance. I will go straight east—if for no other reason than the sacred moon of the Lunanda rises in the east."

"It is as good a direction as any other," Tsempala observed. "Also, this mighty river at my doorstep comes from that direction, and in a fairly straight line at that. Its current is slow, and thou couldst make good time on it. Among my students there are two Kroo boys from the North. Excellent canoemen they are. They will be glad to lend the strength of their broad shoulders to help thee speed eastward up the river."

"I will accept their aid with thanks," Ki-Gor said. "Although why I choose to breast the current, I do not really know. As thou hast said, one way is as good as another. But, somehow"—he stared off into the darkness—"somehow, I have a feeling that east is best. It is what Helene would call in English a 'hunch.'"

CHAPTER IV

FOR THE PAST SEVERAL hours, the current had been getting increasingly swifter. Already the little dugout containing the three paddlers, one white and two black, had breasted several small rapids. And now, a distant roar told Ki-Gor that somewhere not far ahead there was a mighty waterfall.

He cast a glance toward shore and saw that the progress of the canoe had been slowed down to a walking pace. It was time for him to leave the river and proceed on foot. He had traveled through this country before, and knew that once he crossed a narrow belt of jungle, a vast highland veldt stretched to the eastward—easy country to make fast time through.

However, he was not dissatisfied with his progress thus far. The two Kroo boys had indeed been mighty canoemen. For four days the dugout had never stopped, or even slowed down. Sometimes, the paddles had dipped and flashed in the muddy water, but always there had been two. One of the three would stop now and then to sleep for a short time, or to drop a hook and line overside to catch the fish which had constituted their only food.

This furious, unrelaxing pace had carried Ki-Gor a prodigious distance in those four days. However, it was time now to leave the river, when he could go faster on foot. He directed the Kroo boys to head for the bank at their right.

"Farewell, O Rivermen," he said, as he stepped ashore. "I can never thank you for this. I only hope that one day, if you should need help of any kind, that Ki-Gor will be nearby to provide that help."

The Kroo boys grinned toothily and wagged their heads in deprecation. They stood still beside the canoe until Ki-Gor disappeared into the jungle.

It was shortly after noon, and the sun was still high in the sky, flaming fiercely. Ki-Gor found it advisable to stick to the shade of the jungle trails as long as possible, waiting until the evening before he took to the open veldt.

This circumstance had rather an important bearing on Ki-Gor's fortunes. For if he had left the jungle sooner, he would not have passed through the small Gwembi village which was ruled by King Makaka.

The first intimation Ki-Gor had that there were any humans near was when he heard a series of agonized shrieks off in the distance. It sounded as if a woman were being horribly tortured.

Ordinarily, Ki-Gor was prone to mind his own business. He viewed dispassionately the jungle spectacle of one beast or human killing another beast or human—it was the Law of Tooth and Claw, the survival of the fittest. But something in the quality of those persistent screams stirred something in him. Thus would Helene scream, he reflected, in the Crocodile Pool, unless he was able to do something to prevent it in the next eighteen days.

He began to run in the direction of the shrieks.

In a short while, he came upon a gruesome spectacle.

A small tribe was gathered in the clearing in the middle of their village. They were ringed around a gibbet-like structure, gazing with sadistic pleasure at a pitiable object in the center.

A young human—a boy of about thirteen—was suspended by one ankle on a rope that hung down from the gibbet. His head was some five feet from the ground. And on the ground, right under his head, was a good-sized pile of twigs and faggots.

While the miserable boy twisted and screamed, a fat, grotesque black danced slowly around him, brandishing a flaming torch. With every other step, the fat man swept the torch downward as if to ignite the bonfire under the boy's head.

Ki-Gor was used to death. Death left him unmoved. But useless, wanton cruelty was another thing. He gripped his spear and moved forward with sudden decision.

He charged across the clearing at a dead run toward the ring of blacks. Without slackening pace, he smacked into the rear rank, knocking several spindly blacks spinning, and hurtled through. The others in his path flung themselves aside with frightened yelps, and when the fat man with the torch turned around, Ki-Gor was standing in the middle of the ring six feet away from him.

THE CRIES of the blacks died away into a shocked silence as Ki-Gor leveled his spear-point at the fat man's pendulous belly.

"What contemptible cruelty is this?" Ki-Gor spat out. "What tribe is this which has nothing better to do than to torture its children?"

The fat man stared at Ki-Gor for a moment, pop-eyed. Then a gurgling, wrathful sound rolled up from his fat neck and out between his thick lips.

"Who calls the Gwembi people to account! Who so arrogantly questions the mighty King Makaka, Ruler of Gwembi, Master of the World!"

"I see no king before me," Ki-Gor snarled. "I see only a petty chieftain, a fat hog of a man whose lips slobber with pleasure at the sound of a harmless child's agony!"

The Gwembi moaned aghast, and the fat man stepped back a pace, his jowls quivering with incredulous rage.

"Know ye all!" Ki-Gor shouted. "Know ye that I am Ki-Gor, White Lord of the Jungle! I am displeased with this spectacle, and I intend to make swift end to it! I am going to cut this child down.... Let no man try to interfere with me!"

King Makaka suddenly found his voice again.

"Death!" he shrieked. "Death to this insolent braggart! Kill! Kill him! Kill—"

Ki-Gor moved forward so swiftly, the Gwembi hardly saw him move. His spear point stopped a half inch away from Makaka's belly.

"Let a hand be lifted," he warned, "and I will puncture your chief like a fish-bladder!"

Makaka jerked his trembling bulk backward in a terrified spasm, and he half turned, as if to flee. The next instant, Ki-Gor's brown arm had whipped around the fat neck, and a moment later Makaka, Ruler of the Gwembi and Master of the World, lay squalling outstretched on the ground. Ki-Gor stepped up on the heaving mound of flesh, and whipped out his hunting knife. The knife flashed against the rope that suspended the young boy by the ankle, and severed it. Ki-Gor's other arm went around the youth's slim body and eased it gently to the ground.

The boy picked himself up and stood looking around dizzily. Ki-Gor stepped beside him and took one hand in his. Meanwhile, the Gwembi were milling around in a shrill uproar. Their chief rolled on the ground, alternately commanding them to kill Ki-Gor, and then imploring them not to, lest the jungle man make swift reprisals on his own fat person. Truth to tell, the Gwembi were a puny breed, and none of them had the slightest desire to come within arm's length of the formidable-looking white man.

So when Ki-Gor waved his spear menacingly and started to walk away from the gibbet holding the hand of the youth he had just rescued, the Gwembi in his path broke and ran in all directions. Ki-Gor stalked slowly out of the village with the boy, while Makaka, still lying on the ground, hurled imprecations after him.

As soon as he had left the village and re-entered the jungle, Ki-Gor began to regret the impulse which had led him to save the life of the boy who now stumbled along at his side. He realized that, having taken on the obligation of the youth's life, he had to take him with him to some place where he would be safe from the Gwembi.

Ki-Gor tried to reconstruct a map of the region in his mind's eye so as to recall the location of the nearest friendly tribe. Soon, he remembered that there was a considerable colony of river-blacks who dwelt only a few miles above the falls on the river which he had ascended with the Kroo boys. Once with those river-blacks, this youth shivering at his side would never have to fear the Gwembi, and Ki-Gor felt sure the boy would be treated well. Those river-blacks had once been loyal allies of Ki-Gor's.

The jungle man decided to take the boy with him for two or three miles along the trail they were on, until it came out of the forest onto the veldt. He would then direct the boy to cut over northward, which would eventually land him on the river bank. From there the boy should have no difficulty locating Ki-Gor's friendly tribe.

NEITHER KI-GOR nor the youth had said a word to each other since they left the village of the Gwembi. Ki-Gor looked down at him curiously. He was a slim, slight boy, undernourished-looking as all forest blacks are. Yet he did not look like a Gwembi. His head was narrower, and his features finer than the Gwembi type, and his expression was sharper, more alert. Ki-Gor wondered vaguely what the boy's history was, and in particular, what had led Makaka, the Chief of the Gwembi, to stage such a cruel punishment.

The boy evidently felt Ki-Gor's eyes on him, for he suddenly cocked his head to one side and looked up.

"Thou art quite a man," the boy said in Swahili.

Ki-Gor looked away and frowned.

"Quite a man," the boy repeated. "Art thou truly a white man? Thou hast a look of it around the eyes, but I never before saw such clothes on a white man, and I have seen many of them. And thy name—Ki-Gor, is it? I never heard of a white bwana with such a name."

"Just a minute, O child!" Ki-Gor snapped. "People do not use 'thee' and 'thou' to me unless they are my friends. Keep a respectful tongue in your head for your elders."

"But thou art manifestly my friend," the boy chirped impudently, "or else thou wouldst never have saved my life."

"Think again," Ki-Gor growled. "I am not your friend, and I truly do not know why I bothered to save your life."

"Ah!" the youth said brightly. "That was spoken like a white bwana. Perhaps, after all, thou art really a white bwana. Although that name—"

The boy broke off and shook his head. Ki-Gor felt suddenly furiously angry at the boy. He had not expected any expression of gratitude from him. The Bantu are curiously lacking in expressions of gratitude. But he had not expected such cavalier treatment from an emaciated black boy who could hardly be fourteen years old.

"Quite a man," the boy said again. "And thou really camest in the nick. Although, it would have been better if thou hadst arrived somewhat earlier, before those brutes strung me up like a springbok."

By this time, Ki-Gor was aghast. Such a complete young egoist he had never in his life come up against.

"However," the boy went on judicially, "thou camest in time, and that is all that matters. Thou wilt not regret it, Ki-Gor. Ekka is a good friend to have."

By now, Ki-Gor was beginning to recover from his rage and his astonishment, and was able to see the funny side of the situation.

"Are you," he asked gravely, "Ekka?"

"Certainly," the boy answered, with a surprised look.

"Ekka," Ki-Gor repeated, as if to himself. "It does not sound like a Gwembi name."

"Certainly not!" Ekka cried. "Of course it is not a Gwembi name! Do I look like a jungle fool of a Gwembi?"

"What are you then?" Ki-Gor asked. "Of what tribe?"

The boy thought for a moment, and said, "I don't know. I have been everywhere, but where I came from originally I don't know. I may be a Kikuyu, or a Kavirondo, or I may be something entirely different. I have wandered all my life. I have been to Mombasa, to Dar-es-salaam. I have been in Mozambique, in Nairobi. I have been through Entebbe and Niangara. I have been everywhere."

In spite of himself, Ki-Gor felt a curiosity about this loud-mouthed, impudent stripling. It was highly improbable that Ekka had ever been in all the places that he named. But it was highly remarkable that a thirteen-year-old Congo boy would even have heard of such places as Mombasa and Mozambique, seaports on the Indian Ocean.

"HM," KI-GOR mused. "You traveled with your father and mother?"

"I traveled alone," Ekka declared. "I have no father and mother. I don't think I ever had a father or mother."

"That is very distressing," Ki-Gor observed.

"Not at all," Ekka retorted. "It is far better to be unburdened with ignorant parents. No man wants a pair of interfering busybodies telling him what to do and what not to do, and when to do it, and 'now you have to go to bed, Ekka!' and 'you are smoking too many cheroots, Ekka'—no man wants that sort of thing."

"No, I can see that," Ki-Gor said, smothering a smile. "It is much nicer when you are on your own."

"Manifestly," Ekka said, with a lordly inclination of his head. "That reminds me, give me a cheroot, wilt thou, Ki-Gor?"

"I'm sorry," Ki-Gor said, "but I have none to give you."

"No cheroots!" Ekka cried. "Why, all white bwanas carry cheroots! What do you mean you have none?"

"I have no cheroots," Ki-Gor repeated patiently.

"By the gods!" Ekka said bitterly. "I don't believe you are a white bwana after all!"

"I never said I was," Ki-Gor replied, blue eyes twinkling. "If you must know, I am really a great white ape."

"An ape!" Ekka exclaimed with a startled glance.

"You don't believe me?"

Ki-Gor suddenly sprang straight up in the air, seized a low-hanging bow with his left hand, and swung his body up in a twisting arc. A moment later, he stood on the bow and looked down at the astonished black youth with a chuckle.

"By the gods!" Ekka cried. "That takes some doing! I believe thou hast some ape in thee, at that!"

Then he darted backward in a panic as Ki-Gor leaped down to the ground. The boy's foot slipped and he fell ignominiously into the undergrowth beside the trail. Instantly, he let out a terrified howl.

"Hush, hush!" Ki-Gor admonished. "Don't you know better than to proclaim your presence to the jungle like that? Get up. We must keep moving. I am in a hurry."

Ekka picked himself up gingerly, shot an awed glance at Ki-Gor, and trotted clumsily by his side. Ki-Gor began to wonder if Ekka's stories about himself might not be true. The boy was not at all at home in the jungle. It was quite possible that he was town-bred.

"That was truly remarkable," Ekka said. "I saw some Persian acrobats in Dar-es-salaam once, but none of them was half so clever as thee. Ai! not so fast, thou great ape!" he shouted breathlessly. "I can't keep up!"

"You had better keep up," Ki-Gor said. "I have no time to lose."

"Where art thou going in such a hurry?" Ekka demanded.

"I am on a pilgrimage," Ki-Gor replied, "and my time is short."

"What kind of a pilgrimage, and where to?"

"That does not concern you, my precious young whelp," Ki-Gor said, and then looked around him swiftly. The trail had at last broken out of the jungle on to open veldt. He pointed to a hill a half mile ahead.

"When we get to the top of that hill," Ki-Gor said, "our paths separate. Off to the left, you will see a river about three miles away. It will be safe, open country and you will be able to strike across it until you come to that river. A very short distance up the bank, you will come to a village. Find the head man and tell him that Ki-Gor sent you. He will treat you kindly for my sake, and he will protect you from Makaka and the Gwembi."

"Wait a minute!" Ekka puffed as he scrambled along beside Ki-Gor's long legs. "What is all this nonsense about our paths separating? Art thou not coming to the river with me?"

"No. I shall be veering southward," Ki-Gor answered.

"Then, I too will be veering southward," Ekka declared.

"Do as you please," Ki-Gor shrugged. "But you will not be coming with me."

To Ki-Gor's consternation, this last statement brought forth a howl of dismay from Ekka.

"BUT OF course I am coming with thee!" the boy screamed. "And why shouldn't I?"

"Softly, softly," Ki-Gor admonished. "Let us get this matter straight. You cannot go with me. There are many reasons why you cannot go with me, but one reason is enough—I am in a great hurry and you cannot keep pace with me."

"I will keep pace with thee, Ki-Gor!" Ekka cried. "I will keep up! I will run my legs off!"

"No, no!" Ki-Gor exclaimed impatiently. "You don't understand!"

"Look at me!" Ekka gasped, running furiously beside Ki-Gor. "Look at me—I am easily keeping pace with thee!"

"Yes, and hard put to it," Ki-Gor said, ironically, "when I am merely strolling along at a third my usual pace. Come now—we are almost at the top of the hill. You can cut over to the left, there, and go straight to the river—"

"No, no, no!" Ekka stopped dead, and burst into a paroxysm of sobbing. "Unfeeling brute! Thick skinned ape! Of what use to save me from the torture of the Gwembi, and then leave me alone on the veldt for the lions to eat!"

Ki-Gor stopped and glared exasperatedly at the boy. What spawn of the devil had he rescued who turned on him and plagued him for his pains? And how was one to treat such a wilful, maddening child?

"Look here, you," Ki-Gor said firmly. "There are no lions about. Between here and my friends over on the river, you will probably run into not so much as a dik-dik. You have four hours of daylight left to complete your journey, and you need only two, if you will but stir those spindly legs of yours a little. Now, let us have no more nonsense. You go on your way, and I will go mine. I can afford to waste no more time on cry-babies. Farewell."

With that the jungle man turned on his heel and strode up the hill. Ekka stared after him unbelievingly and then burst out into a flood of insults.

"Pig!" Ekka screamed. "Ugly wart hog! Go ahead! Desert a helpless child in the middle of a wilderness! I hope the Gwembi come after me and take me again! Then thou wilt be sorry!"

That last despairing suggestion startled Ki-Gor, although he did not slacken his pace. He had overlooked the possibility of the Gwembi wrathfully following on behind. And yet the possibility remained. He turned it over in his mind as he ascended swiftly to the top of the hill. The more he thought about it, the more he realized that he had made Ekka's life his affair, and that he could not go off and leave the boy if he was still in some danger.

Ki-Gor sighed as he reached the top of the hill. There were two courses open. Either he escorted Ekka to the friendly river tribe, or he allowed the boy to come with him for another day. If he went with Ekka to the village on the river, it would mean that he would be going at least eight miles out of his way. On the other hand, if he took Ekka with him on his direct route eastward, there would be other friendly tribes he could leave him with.

Of the two alternatives, the latter would probably lose him less time, although it carried the disadvantage of Ekka's noisy and tiresome company. Ki-Gor had already become thoroughly sick of the boy's unceasing, impertinent chatter. However, there was nothing for it. Ki-Gor halted and looked back down the hill.

Ekka was standing where Ki-Gor had left him, and a shrill stream of vituperation continued to come from the boy's mouth. Ki-Gor waved a beckoning arm, impatiently.

There was a moment of silence. Then with a triumphant shout, Ekka broke into an awkward, knock-kneed trot up the slope. Almost at the same instant, Ki-Gor looked over the boy's head and was glad he had not deserted him.

For his startled eyes beheld a party of naked blacks pouring out of the jungle three hundred yards along the trail behind the boy.

Ki-Gor calmly trust his spear point down into the ground, unslung his bow and fitted an arrow. The party of blacks broke out into shrill cries as they caught sight of him on the hill top. Ekka threw a startled glance over his shoulder, and immediately redoubled his pace.

"The Gwembi!" he shrieked, as he neared Ki-Gor. "I told thee they would come after me!"

"Have no fear," Ki-Gor answered. "I won't let them touch you."

"But they are so many!" Ekka cried, gasping for breath. "And all in full war kit!"

"Sit down beside me," Ki-Gor commanded, "and don't worry. The Gwembi are no warriors."

HE WATCHED the oncoming blacks with a contemptuous smile on his bronzed face. There were twenty-five or thirty of them leaping along the trail, shouting and brandishing their spears. They began to slow down a little at the foot of the hill. Evidently their warlike spirits were a little chilled by the grim, uncompromising figure of the jungle man. Their progress became slower and slower until they reached a point about fifty yards down the slope from Ki-Gor. Then they came to a full stop, and huddled together uneasily. A large globular figure hovering safely in the rear, Ki-Gor recognized as "King" Makaka.

There followed a few moments of confused muttering. Then a querulous voice floated up to Ki-Gor.

"We have no quarrel with thee, Ki-Gor. Do but give up the boy—he belongs to us—and go thy way in peace."

Ki-Gor made no answer.

After a long silence the voice came again, even more querulous.

"The boy, Ki-Gor—he is appointed to die. Turn him over to us, and we will not harm thee."

Ki-Gor let out a gusty laugh, and the Gwembi jumped nervously.

"You chicken-hearts!" Ki-Gor cried. "You could not hurt Ki-Gor! Go back to your village quickly before you get hurt! Ki-Gor is quick to anger and terrible in war, a mighty killer—cross him not!"

A resentful murmur went up from the Gwembi, and once more Makaka's voice croaked forth.

"Be warned, Ki-Gor! We are many against thee!"

"Silence, O Fat Caterpillar!" Ki-Gor spat out. "Do not try my patience too far! I intend to waste no more time here. Go now and do not try to follow me farther, or I will bring fearful disaster on your heads. I will count three and when I have finished, if you have not started home, one of you is a dead man already! I will begin the counting now.—One! Two—"

He lifted the great bow.

But that was enough for the Gwembi. With shrieks of terror, they broke and ran down the hill, led by their peerless warrior, Makaka. Ki-Gor watched them rush out of arrow-shot, a grim smile on his face. Then he turned to Ekka, who was looking at him with an awe-stricken face.

"Come," he said, "we must be on our way. We will not be troubled by Makaka again."

Ekka shook his head wisely. "I hope thou art not wrong," he said.

CHAPTER V

TWO DAYS LATER, KI-GOR sat on a rock and stared morosely at the rising sun. Beside him Ekka was juggling three pebbles and carrying on a rapid-fire though entirely one-sided conversation. Finally Ki-Gor could stand it no more.

"Silence!" he roared. "Will that tongue of yours never cease clacking in your empty head—not for one moment?"

He glared at the boy, and anybody but Ekka would have been warned by such an expression. But not Ekka. He laughed gaily.

"Ohee, Ki-Gor!" he cried delightedly. "Thou art such a lovable jungle-ish lout of a fellow! What wouldst thou do without Ekka to lighten the brutish darkness of thy days with gay quips and witty jokes?"

Ki-Gor groaned inwardly. Ekka's idea of a witty joke was to run off the trail and hide. Four times he had done that already, and on two of the occasions the city-bred boy had blundered on to feeding lions. Ki-Gor did not dare count up the precious hours the boy had cost him while he went to his rescue. Each time the boy took the rescue completely for granted.

In fact, Ekka seemed to take Ki-Gor completely for granted. He was irresponsible and irrepressible. He talked incessantly, his mind being as agile as his body was uncoordinated and clumsy. Ki-Gor was beginning to loathe the child, and yet for the life of him he could not get rid of him. Ekka clung to him like a leech.

Ki-Gor had tried to abandon him twice, but each time the boy set up such a howl that there was nothing to be done but wait for him to catch up.

But now Ki-Gor was getting desperate. He saw no reason why he should be saddled with Ekka any longer—especially when the boy was such a drag on him, at a time when every day counted. There were but sixteen days left to fulfill the commands of the Priestess of the Moon.

The worst of it was that Ki-Gor still had no idea of how to go about finding the star at mid-day or the cold ray of the sun. He had built up one forlorn hope within himself, and that was to find his old friend Tembu George.

Tembu George had been born George Spelvin in Cincinnati, U.S.A. He was a giant Negro who had been a Pullman porter and ship's cook, among other things. One day he had jumped ship at Mombasa, walked inland and had been enthusiastically adopted by a Masai tribe. Ki-Gor had met George soon after Helene had dropped into his life, as a result of the crack-up of the plane she had been solo-flying across Africa. And the huge American Negro had proved to be a staunch friend and genial companion of Ki-Gor's and his lovely red-haired wife.

After the failure of Tsempala to help him, Ki-Gor had drifted eastward without conscious thought that in that direction lay the country of the Masai and Tembu George. But gradually the realization dawned on him that he was drawing nearer the home of his friend, and that the colored man might be able to help him. For George, in spite of an indolent, good-natured exterior, had a sharp alert mind. Moreover, he had traveled over a good deal of the earth's surface. Decidedly, Ki-Gor thought, he should get to George as fast as he could.

However, he was still a good three day's journey from George's stamping grounds—three days of hard, fast traveling alone. But with Ekka on his hands, there was no telling how long it would take.

Somehow or other, he had to get rid of Ekka.

Gloomily, Ki-Gor swept the eastern horizon with his eyes. To the southeast, great mountain peaks raised silvery heads against the sky. The northeast was less rugged, although it was wooded, rolling country. Suddenly, Ki-Gor got an idea.

He remembered that his friends the Banda people lived toward the northeast, and not too far away—perhaps fifteen miles. He would take the pestiferous Ekka to the Banda and make them keep the boy prisoner for two or three days. Long enough, at any rate, to allow Ki-Gor to get a good safe distance away, too far for the boy to be able to catch up with him.

This trip would be off Ki-Gor's route, but in the long run it would pay to make the thirty-mile extra trip. Ekka would be off his hands for good, and he could travel swiftly to the country of the Masai.

"COME, O Chatterbox," he commanded, rising to his feet, "we must be on our way."

"Restless lion of a man," Ekka complained. "Must every day be a headlong rush to somewhere? Can we not take our time one day?"

"One more day we must hurry," Ki-Gor said amiably. "Tomorrow will be easier for you."

Already Ki-Gor felt better, just at the prospect of finally getting rid of the exasperating boy. Good-naturedly he parried the boy's suspicious questions concerning the change of direction to the northeast. And good-naturedly, he prodded the boy into maintaining a brisk gait. By paying attention to Ekka more than he had ever done, thus flattering the child's enormous ego, he managed to keep him going at a remarkably fast pace. For four consecutive hours, Ekka trotted by Ki-Gor's side. Only once did he express any great desire to stop. That was when he caught sight of a small spitting cobra beside the trail. Ekka wanted to stop and tease the cobra for a while. But Ki-Gor swiftly killed the snake, and Ekka, after one bitter exclamation of regret, picked up the pace again.

By early afternoon, they reached the village of the Banda.

Not long ago, Ki-Gor had rescued the daughter of the Chief from a gang of Arab slave-dealers. This daughter, a crippled girl named Luma, was among the first of the Banda to catch sight of Ki-Gor and his young charge. She uttered a glad cry of welcome and immediately gave orders to prepare a feast in honor of Ki-Gor's visit. The jungle man was loath to spend any more time than he had to in the Banda village, but he realized that it would be discourteous of him to decline the feast. So he resigned himself to staying on until after sundown.

The one consolation was that once he had left the Banda village, he would have left Ekka behind. He sought the earliest opportunity to get Luma aside and ask her to have Ekka gently but firmly confined for a day or two—long enough so that Ki-Gor could be far away by the time the boy was released. This, Luma readily agreed to do, and Ki-Gor sighed with relief. Already he felt as if a tremendous burden had been lifted off his back.

The Banda village presented a scene of bustling activity as preparations for the feast went on. But, about an hour before sundown, the preparations were suddenly interrupted when a terrified villager came tumbling down the trail from the east.

"Invaders!" the villager cried. "A war party! Huge men—Gallas or Somalis! What will we do!"

There was a rush for weapons. Ki-Gor seized his spear and bow and ran out the trail to the eastward, accompanied by a half dozen Banda youths. They had not gone far when from a ridge top they described the strangers. It was a formidable party of sixty or seventy immensely tall men dressed in tight white robes. But they were not Gallas, nor were they Somalis.

They were Masai. And at their head was Tembu George.

The big American Negro's eyes widened in astonishment as he beheld Ki-Gor bounding down the trail toward him.

"Ki-Gor!" he shouted, in his deep musical voice. "My gravy, wheah did you come f'om?"

"I was on my way to your country," the jungle man explained.

"Well, I was on muh way to find you!" said George.

"To find me?" said Ki-Gor with a sharp glance.

"Yeah, I heard you was in bad trouble."

"You heard I was in trouble?" Ki-Gor said, puzzled.

"I sho' did." George threw a glance behind him, and lowered his voice, even though the conversation was in English. "Th'ough the Brotherhood of the Dog!"

"Ah," Ki-Gor murmured, remembering Tsempala's drums.

"But," George went on, "I heard you was a long ways away—to the west. I didn't rightly get jest whut yo' trouble was, but jest's quick's I could, I gathered up these yere Morani and came 'long fast."

"You're a true friend," Ki-Gor said sadly, "but I'm afraid your Morani warriors will be of no use in this situation. However, I did want to see you and tell you what has happened. It might be that you would have some ideas. Come, let's go back to the Banda village and I will tell you everything."

A curious, seemingly irrelevant thought crossed Ki-Gor's mind. And that was if he had not come out of his way to leave Ekka at the Banda village he would have missed George altogether. So, for once, Ekka had in a sense brought him luck. He dismissed the thought from his mind and started in to tell George everything that had happened beginning with the ill-fated safari with Prince Datu.

"MAN, THA'S awful!" George said, when Ki-Gor had finished. "I don't know any place wheah the stahs shine in the middle of the day, any more'n I know a place wheah the sun's rays is cold—mid-day or any othuh time. Looky yere, Ki-Gor, don't you think the best thing would be jest to go on ovuh to Dera Daga with my Masai and clean up on them Lunanda?"

"No, George," Ki-Gor shook his head, wearily. He explained what King Mboko had said regarding any attempt to rescue Helene.

"Lordy!" George ran a huge hand over his head. "Whut we-all goin' to do, Ki-Gor?"

"I hoped you would have an idea," Ki-Gor said.

"Well, I ain't. Not right now, anyways," George said, unhappily. "But it looks like I bettuh git one—quick."

By this time, they had reached the gates of the Banda village. Reluctantly, George dismissed his faithful Masai warriors and sent them back to their homes. Then, deep in thought, he accompanied Ki-Gor to the house of the old Chief, where he was soon invited to attend the feast in Ki-Gor's honor.

Throughout the feast, George remained deep in thought, saying only a few words now and then, when good manners demanded. However, young Ekka was very much in evidence, full of brash conversation, and playing mischievous practical jokes at the expense of the hospitable Banda.

"I see what you mean about that kid, Ki-Gor," George was once moved to say. "He is really a pesky brat, an' I'm sho' glad you're gettin' rid of him tonight."

By pre-arrangement, Luma, the Chief's daughter, lured Ekka away when the feast was nearly over. She came back presently with an enigmatic smile on her face.

"Ekka does not know it yet," she whispered to Ki-Gor, "but he is a prisoner. We will keep him confined for two days. After that, I think he will be glad to stay with us. As a matter of fact, he is not a bad boy, really. He is very bright for his age. I think I will adopt him."

Ki-Gor smiled dubiously. "Very well," he said, "but I am glad he is to be your responsibility and not mine."

Shortly after that, Ki-Gor noticed George's eyes on him.

"Have you an idea, George?" he asked, half smilingly.

"Not much of a one," the big Negro admitted, "but mebbe it's enough to go on."

A wave of hope went over Ki-Gor and he stood up and began to make his farewells to the Chief of the Banda and his daughter.

CHAPTER VI

AS THE CAMPFIRES OF the Banda village began to disappear behind them in the darkness, George told Ki-Gor what was on his mind.

"Now, I don't really know nothin' 'bout these yere cold rays of the sun," he said. "But the only thing I c'n figger is—if you want the sun to be cold, you jest bettuh go somewheres wheah the climate is cold. If ever'thing else is plumb cold, seem to me that ol' sun got to be cold, too."

"It's reasonable," Ki-Gor said. "I had thought a little bit along those lines, myself."

"It's the only thing I c'n think of," George went on. "Now—I reckon the coldest place on earth is the No'th Pole. But we ain't got time to go up theah. *But*—jest southeast of heah, two days journey—they is some plenty high mountains. The snow nevuh leaves the top of them. Mebbe it's cold enough up on top o' them to cool off the sun."

"It's worth trying," Ki-Gor agreed. "Now, what about the stars at mid-day?"

"Tha' s one that's got me buffaloed, Ki-Gor," George admitted. "But let's see if we cain't find that cold sun, first. Aftuh that, we c'n staht figgerin' about them stahs."

"The Priestess of the Moon," Ki-Gor recalled, frowning, "stated the problems the other way around. The stars first, then the sun."

"I don't reckon it make much difference," George said. "Long's you find 'em both, sometime."

The giant pair were going at a swift pace through the pitch dark African night. Fortunately, a small but swift river ran in a southeasterly direction from the Banda village—exactly the direction George had indicated that the tall mountains lay. And guided by this stream, the two friends traveled all night long.

By sun-up they had put a safe distance between themselves and the pestiferous Ekka. They stopped to eat a little breakfast.

"Ovuh theah is yo' mountains," George stated, pointing at a mass of tumbled snow-capped peaks to the southeast. "Now, they's two ways of gittin' to 'em. We c'n bear off heah to the south for a while and then circle eastwards—that way is good goin' all the way. Or, we c'd cut straight across this yere desert ahead of us. That would be shorter, but it would be almighty hot!"

Ki-Gor gazed out across the great arid depression that lay like a huge dry moat between him and the mountains. It was a true desert. The tumbling stream beside him cascaded down from the veldt into it, and after a few miles thinned out and disappeared.

"If it is shorter," Ki-Gor said, "let us go across the desert, no matter how hot it is. George, it is just fifteen days before the next full moon."

George made no answer, but stood up and looked gloomily back up the little river in the direction from which they had come. Something back there appeared to catch his eye, for he kept on staring, and a little frown gathered on his forehead. Ki-Gor followed his gaze. Some distance up the river, a dark object was bobbing in the current.

"Are you looking at that log?" Ki-Gor queried.

"Yeah," George answered slowly. "But it ain't jest a log. Look like somepin' is hangin' on to it. Some kind of animal or—no! By gravy, it's a human!"

A dreadful premonition crept into Ki-Gor's mind. It was a human, all right—a small human. And as the log came nearer and nearer, borne along on the breast of the swift current, it became only too apparent who that small human was. Ki-Gor blew through his teeth angrily and waded out into the river. As the log careened past him, he reached out and snatched off the limp figure clinging to the rear end.

With a happy sigh Ekka collapsed into Ki-Gor's arms.

With a stunned look, George watched Ki-Gor wade ashore and lay the child on the bank.

"Man," George breathed. "Tha's really a problem-chile you got there an' no mistake!"

Ki-Gor glared down at the unconscious boy as if he'd like to kill him. Presently Ekka's eyes fluttered open.

"Try to desert Ekka, would you?" he whispered weakly. "Leave him behind with a pack of jungle yokels, would you? Well, I showed you! I'm half drowned, and every bone in my body has been smashed by the rocks—but I showed you you can't desert Ekka!"

Ki-Gor let his hands fall helplessly to his sides.

"Mm-*mm!*" George murmured. "Whut kin you do with somebody like that!"

IT WAS an hour before Ekka was fully revived from his hair-raising journey on the log. He was a mass of bruises, but he had broken no bones. And his triumph at out-witting Ki-Gor and the Banda acted like a tonic on him. He declared himself ready to go anywhere, although he swayed on his feet when he said it.

Ki-Gor was at his wit's end. He could not afford to slow down his rate of travel to accommodate the boy. At the same time, he could not bring himself to abandon him on the great veldt. Finally, he reached out and seized Ekka by the nape of he neck.

"Look you, little fiend!" he snarled. "I ought to leave you here for the lions to eat! For some reason I cannot. So we will take you with us. We are going straight across that desert down there, and George and I will take turns carrying you on our shoulders. But you behave yourself from now on, or by the gods I will give you such a thrashing that you will wish you had never left the Banda people. Do you understand?"

"Hooray!" Ekka cried, completely unabashed. "The big black elephant"—pointing at George—"shall carry me first!"

Ekka was not much of a burden to men of such extraordinary strength and endurance as Ki-Gor and George. However, even without Ekka to carry, the journey across the desert would have been arduous enough. And Ki-Gor drew a sigh of relief when, toward the end of the afternoon, the ground began to slope upward consistently and the shaly gravel underfoot began to give way to short grass.

The late afternoon sun still beat unmercifully on their backs, however, and Ki-Gor longed for a shady spot to rest for a few minutes. But the country they were entering now offered little promise of relief from that blistering sun. It was a wide belt of treeless foothills where shade of any kind was at a premium. Ki-Gor resigned himself to endure the next two hours as best he could. The sweat poured down his brown body in rivers as he trudged uphill, and even Ekka lay limp and silent on his back.

"Man! It sho' is warm, hereabouts!" George exclaimed. "Heah, lemme carry that brat for a while now, Ki-Gor."

"No, he's all right," Ki-Gor said, looking at George with a wry smile. "It's very warm, but tomorrow we will probably wish for some of this heat."

His eyes swept the bare foothills and lifted toward the giant snow-capped peaks beyond. Then they flicked back to a point in the foothills again. Something had caught his attention. It was a round black spot.

"George," the jungle man said sharply. "Over there a little to the right—what is that?"

"Whut is whut?" George said, staring. "Oh, you mean that black patch—hey! Wait a minute! Look like it might be the mouth of a cave! That whut you mean?"

"Yes!" Ki-Gor cried. "That's what I thought! A shady place to rest!"

"Man, that would sho' be a treat!" George rumbled delightedly. "Don' let's waste no time gittin' ovuh theah!"

Without any question it was a cave mouth and a very curious one. It was a fairly wide opening, perhaps six feet in diameter. But it looked as if it had once been much taller and wider.

"Say, you know somepin'?" George said, as they stood in front of the opening. "This yere ain't no natural cave, I don't think. It look to me like someone dug a hole in the side of this yere hill—and dug it a good time ago!"

George was manifestly right, Ki-Gor thought as he scrutinized the spot. It certainly looked like a man-made opening in the base of the hill, which Nature had encroached upon during the course of years.

"Yep! That's whut it is, all right!" George exclaimed. "See, they's another one ovuh thataway—only that one's most filled in! Say, you know somepin', Ki-Gor? I think we found ourselves an ol' deserted mine!"

Ekka slipped off Ki-Gor's back, then, and trotted to the cave mouth, where he stood for a moment peering inside.

"Hai!" the boy shouted delightedly. "This looks like fun! I bet I could hide in here, Ki-Gor, and you would never find me—never in the world!"

Ki-Gor gave a warning shout and lunged toward the boy. But he was too late. With a gleeful shriek, Ekka dodged into the black hole and disappeared.

"COME BACK!" Ki-Gor shouted wrathfully, running after the boy. But a cascade of impudent laughter floating back was Ekka's answer. Ki-Gor ran about ten steps and stopped. The transition from the brilliant sunlight into the darkness of the shaft had temporarily blinded him. George came stumbling along the passageway behind him, cursing.

"Man, if you evuh git yo' hands on that kid," George rumbled, "I hope you break his neck!"

And Ki-Gor, standing in that black cave, felt he would like to do just that. For as his eyes became adjusted to the darkness, he was able to see that the passageway divided just in front of him—divided into three separate shafts.

Which shaft had Ekka taken?

Just then, a faint cry floated through the caverns, as if from a tremendous distance.

"Ki-Gor! Ki-Gor! Come and get me! I've lost my way! I don't know where I am!"

That was merely the introduction to a night of trouble. Ki-Gor recognized immediately the fact that there existed a maze of caverns in the heart of that hill. And that to go very far along one of those shafts without leaving a trail of some kind to follow back, was to invite getting lost himself. With Ekka's cries growing fainter and fainter in their ears, Ki-Gor and George went out to the mouth of the cave, to discuss ways and means.

In the end it was decided that Ki-Gor would utilize the hours of daylight left to climb to the wooded slopes above them and bring back some rosinous sticks for torches, and, if possible, some vines. George would stay behind at the cave mouth in case Ekka located the cave mouth without help.

Night had fallen by the time Ki-Gor returned, and Ekka had not found his way out. But the jungle man had torch-sticks, and also yards and yards of slender vines in great thick coils. With these instruments he and George set to work exploring the shafts. With flickering torches lighting the way, they proceeded through the caverns, uncoiling the vines as they went, so that they could always retrace their steps.

Hour after hour, they searched without success. Now, they heard Ekka no more. Whether the child had gone to sleep, or whether something had happened to him, Ki-Gor did not dare speculate.

At daybreak, the two friends, haggard and red-eyed, were still searching. By this time they had run out of torches and vines both. Ki-Gor toiled up the mountain side again for a fresh supply, getting back to the cave about an hour before noon.

"Well, the kid's still alive," George grunted. "He's squawkin' his head off, somewhere's in theah."

With Ekka's shrill voice echoing through the shafts, Ki-Gor searched with renewed hope. And, sure enough, within an hour, he and George turned a corner and came upon the child.

He was squatting on his heels in the middle of good-sized rock-hewn chamber. He blinked contemptuously at the torches.

"Well," said Ekka, "it took you two great boobies long enough to find me!"

It was all Ki-Gor could do to keep from cuffing the child's impudent face.

"I could have gotten out by myself," Ekka went on, "but it's still night time outside, and I thought I was safer down here."

"You have lost track of time, little chattering monkey," Ki-Gor said, with considerable restraint. "It is not night time, but the middle of the day. And how could you have gotten out by yourself?"

"See that hole halfway up the wall?" Ekka demanded triumphantly. "It goes outside. And it is, too, night time. You can see the stars shining."

The skin on Ki-Gor's back began to prickle. What was the boy saying?

Less than an hour before, Ki-Gor had observed the sun nearly overhead. Without a word, he handed his torch to George and stepped over to the shaft that Ekka had indicated.

The opening was about four feet above the cave floor. Ki-Gor bent down and peered into it. For a moment he could see nothing. Then, like a revelation, he could see the opening at the other end. The shaft led steeply upwards at a forty-five degree angle. At the other end, there seemed to be a small deep blue disk.

Ki-Gor's heart pounded in his ears as he realized that the deep blue disk was a patch of sky.

Then he saw three stars winking.

CHAPTER VII

A FEW MINUTES LATER, he and George and Ekka burst out of the main cave mouth. They winced and blinked from the brassy glare about them.

The sun was exactly overhead.

Ki-Gor felt a little dizzy. "George," he said. "Was it true? Did I see some stars back there in the cave? Or was I dreaming?"

"Oh, no, you saw 'em, all right," George replied emphatically. "An', come to think of it, I ought to of known 'bout that. Sho', pop! I remember when I was a li'l bitty kid I heard someone say that of you went way down to th' bottom of a deep well, you c'd look up and see the stahs shinin' in the middle of th' day. That theah shaft back in theah is kind of like a well—deep enough so it shut off the sunlight an' let you see the stahs."

"Yes," Ki-Gor said, deep in thought. "The Priestess of Dera Daga sent me to find the stars at mid-day. I did not know they existed. Now, I find they do. So, George, that means that somewhere—somewhere the sun's rays are cold at high noon."

"Tha's right," George said heartily, "an' I think we goin' to find that place up yonduh on the mountain. Whut do you say we git goin'?"

"Yes," Ki-Gor said. His eyes fell on Ekka. The boy had a stick and was prodding a large, crab-like creature in front of the cave mouth. Ki-Gor strode over and swept the boy up in his arms.

"Come, O Child," he said, gently, "leave that venomous beast alone. It is a black scorpion, and if it should sting you with its upraised tail, it would hurt you badly, and you might die."

"Wah!" Ekka exclaimed impatiently. "What a big, overgrown booby thou art, Ki-Gor! Forever frightened at thine own shadow!"

Ki-Gor made no answer. His mind was too full of the unexplainable fact that this infuriating child had been the unconscious instrument of fate. Without his devilish prank, Ki-Gor would never have discovered the stars that shine at mid-day.

Ekka wriggled his way around on to Ki-Gor's back, and a moment later the jungle man with his friend George at his side started climbing toward the snow-covered peaks up ahead.

They had gone several hundred yards when Ki-Gor swung around for a last look at the cave mouth. He gave a startled grunt. For a moment he thought he saw a lone black man standing there looking up toward them. It was only for a fleeting moment, though. Ki-Gor blinked and then the black man had disappeared.

"George," Ki-Gor said, "didn't you send all your Masai Morani home?"

"I sho' did," George replied promptly. "Why?"

"Because I thought I saw one of them just now—down below by the caves."

"Tha's funny," George said. "It couldn't have been any of my boys, I'd be pretty sure."

"Well, I only caught a quick flash of him," Ki-Gor admitted. "But he was carrying a long spear. It looked like a Masai spear."

A CRUEL wind whistled down the wild, rocky gorge, blowing great clouds of fine, stinging snow. The three wayfarers bent their heads away from the cutting particles. Behind them, a huge red sun was swiftly dropping below the western horizon.

"My gravy, Ki-Gor!" George shouted. "I b'lieve we're on the right track. It's almighty cold, already, an' we still got a long ways to climb!"

The giant Negro's teeth were chattering in spite of the fact that he, like his two companions, was covered with sheep skins from top to toe. It was fortunate, Ki-Gor reflected, that they had found the tribe of sheepherders, high up on the mountain side, and had purchased the skins to keep them warm on their expedition up the great mountain.

"Yes, *suh!*" George shouted. "Ef it's cold right yere, whut's it go' be like when we git to the top o' that big baby up yonduh!"

George waved a great hand toward the huge peak that towered above them in frigid majesty. The last slanting rays of the dying sun were casting an unspeakably beautiful rosy glow on the spire-like summit.

Ki-Gor gazed silently at the beautiful spectacle. It would be cold up there—colder than anything he had ever experienced. But he was prepared to endure it. He was prepared to endure anything which would save Helene from the Crocodile Pool.

And there were just twelve days left to fulfill the commands of the Priestess of Dera Daga.

"Come on," Ki-Gor said. "Let's go as far as we can before it gets too dark to see our way."

"Right with you," George responded. "I think mebbe we c'n make the top by noon tomorrow."

There came a piteous wail from Ekka as he saw the two rise up. The cold and the altitude were too much for the scrawny little Bantu child. Ki-Gor picked him up with a sigh, and labored up the gorge after George.

Later, Ki-Gor wondered how they ever survived that night. The cold was unbelievable. They had climbed far above the timber line, and there was nothing to build a fire with. So the three huddled together in a sheltered spot and somehow lasted out the long hours of darkness.

As soon as it became light enough to distinguish objects, even vaguely, the climb was resumed. More than anything, Ki-Gor wanted to reach the summit of that mountain by high noon. There, he was confident, the sun's rays would be cold, and the second command of the Priestess would be fulfilled. After that, it would remain only to dash back the long distance to Dera Daga in time to arrive before the next full moon.

It was brutally cold going up that west slope of the great mountain. For most of the morning the trio were in the shade of the peak, alternately trudging through deep snow and traversing rough, bare rock. It was George who pointed out an easier route to the top. To their right the mountain fell away to the south with a more gradual slope.

Ki-Gor quickly decided that George was right, and that the long way around might prove in the end to be the shortest route to the summit. Immediately, the party turned to their right and crossed the steep west face toward the south. Relieved from the gruelling test of climbing, the trio made good time. Even Ekka stopped whimpering and danced along ahead of his two guardians. In a short time they had nearly left the shadow of the peak. Before them lay a dazzling sunlit snowfield. Ekka dashed ahead out into the sunlight. There he stopped and raised his arms.

"Hai!" he shouted joyously. "The good sun! For the first time in two days I am warm!"

A thrill of horror went through Ki-Gor. Did the child say the sun was warm?

A moment later he stepped out into the sunlight. George stepped up beside him. The two old friends looked at each other mutely, tragically.

The sun had about two hours to go before it would reach the zenith. But its rays slanted down on the shoulders of the travelers and suffused them with an all-pervading warmth.

KI-GOR STOOD in stunned silence as the heat poured down on him. Already his sheepskin clothes were almost too warm. George broke the silence.

"I'm sorry, Ki-Gor," he said in a low voice. "I gave you a real bad steer. Why, I sweah, the sun up heah is 'most hotter'n it was down on that desert."

Ki-Gor stood motionless, without answering.

"Whut we goin' to do?" George asked humbly. "I ain't got anothuh i-dea."

When the jungle man raised his head, a ferocious scowl contorted his brow.

"I have tried," he said in a flat, dangerous voice, "and I have failed. If, up here, the sun is hot—then there is nowhere on earth where it is cold. There is no time left to search for these cold rays of the sun. We have barely time as it is to get back to Dera Daga before the full moon. Come, let's start right now. Somewhere on the way, we will try to work out some plan to rescue Helene."

"All right, Ki-Gor," George said slowly. "I'm with you. But f'om whut you already told me about them Lunanda, I reckon we'll have a job on our hands."

"We'll do it somehow," Ki-Gor said grimly. Then he called to Ekka in Swahili. "Come, Little One. We climb no longer, but instead we go down the mountain as fast as we can go."

"If we stay right on this ridge," George offered, "and go south for a while—then curve around west, I think we'll make bettuh time. Don't look to me like the snow is so deep, that way."

"Good," said Ki-Gor. "Now, let's go."

Ekka was delighted with this manner of travel. He found it much more enjoyable to go running and sliding down a sunny slope than to toil upward in deep shady snow. It was swift, easy going, and much more exciting than toilsome climbing.

Within half an hour, the trio had come to the bottom of the main peak. A great snow-field now led off to the westward at a much gentler declivity. It was like a great white road, a mile wide, that swept downward toward the first scrub trees that indicated the timber line. Without hesitation, Ki-Gor led his companions down this route with long swinging strides.

It was George who first noticed that there was solid ice under the thin coating of snow.

"Hey, Ki-Gor!" he shouted. "Wait a minute!"

The jungle man halted and looked around impatiently.

"This yere field of snow," George said. "It's layin' on top of a lot of ice. This yere is really a kind of river of ice. They's a word for it in English—now, whut is it? Oh, yeah, I remember, now. It's called a *glacier.*"

"A glacier?" Ki-Gor repeated. "Well, what does it matter?"

"Well, seem to me," George went on, "that these yere glaciers is kind of dangerous to go walkin' round on. Mebbe we bettuh kind of take it easy along yere."

Before Ki-Gor could reply, there came a delighted cry from Ekka, who had wandered away some distance.

"Come quickly!" the child shouted. "It is so beautiful! It is like a cave, but so beautiful!"

A moment later, George and Ki-Gor peered over Ekka's shoulder at a great crevasse. It was a slanting crack about six feet wide that sliced downward through the blue ice at an angle.

"It is so beautiful!" Ekka said again and crept nearer to the edge.

"Be careful, O Child," Ki-Gor growled, and reached out a hand toward the fascinated boy.

Then, suddenly, without any warning, Ekka's feet flew out from under him. Ki-Gor grabbed at him frantically—and missed.

There was a despairing shriek, and Ekka plunged down into the crevasse.

The two men stood transfixed with horror as the agonized scream rang in their ears for a long moment, faded a little, and then—abruptly stopped.

A HIDEOUS silence hung over the glacier as Ki-Gor stretched out his full length, drew himself carefully forward, and peered over the lip of the crevasse. Because the crack was not vertical and slanted off at an angle, he was able to see along it for about twenty feet. Beyond that was a blue-black vagueness. How far down the crevasse went, there was no way of telling.

Ki-Gor twisted his head around and looked up at George.

"I am sick at heart," he said. "His life was my affair. I should not have let him go so close to the edge."

"Now, come on, Ki-Gor," George said, "that ain't right! You warned him and you tried to grab him. You cain't take—"

"Now he is dead," Ki-Gor said woodenly, "and it is my fault."

George hesitated, groping for the most comforting word he could think of, when suddenly there came a faint sound which made both of them stiffen.

"Whut—whut was that?" George whispered. Both men strained their ears.

Then the sound came again—a faint, distant wail.

"Ki-Gor! Ki-Gor! Come and get me!"

"Oh, my lawd!" George exploded. "He ain't dead! Hey!—whut you fixin' to do, Ki-Gor?"

But the jungle man made no answer. He had whipped out his great hunting knife and was busily chipping a great niche in the ice of the crevasse. "Man! you're crazy!" George shouted. "You cain't possibly go down theah!"

"He is still alive!" Ki-Gor said through clenched teeth. "And I must get him!"

George fell silent then, knowing that no power on earth could dissuade Ki-Gor from the task he had set for himself. But the next half hour graved some new lines on the big Negro's broad face. There was nothing for him to do but stand by helplessly while his friend set out to do the impossible.

Swiftly and surely, Ki-Gor chipped handholds in the ice as far down as he could reach with his long arms. Then, he got up, turned around, slipped one leg down the crevasse until the foot reached the lowest of the niches he had cut. Slowly, then, he lowered the other leg and finally his whole body.

Clenching the knife between his teeth, he dug both hands into niches and carefully released his feet. In a moment, he was stretched full length against the cold, sleek ice. His two hands alone held him steady and kept him from sliding down the precipitous ice-wall after Ekka.

Now came the test.

With George's anguished eyes on him, he lifted his right hand, took the knife from his mouth with it, and began to chip a new handhold lower down. While he did this, he was supporting his entire weight on the fingers of his left hand.

Presently, the new handhold was finished. The knife was returned to his mouth, and his right hand got a grip on the new niche. Gently, he shifted his weight to the right hand, and released the left hand.

With infinite care, he let his body slide downward until his right arm was quite straight. And then, with his left hand, he cut a new handhold.

In this manner, alternating handholds, did Ki-Gor slowly cut a ladder down the bleak face of the crevasse wall. George watched him in silence until he disappeared in the shadows of the great crack in the ice.

For a while after that—after he lost sight of Ki-Gor—George Spelvin lost track of time. He lay in a sort of horrified stupor, his head at the edge of the crevasse, his eyes glued to the shadows below.

Actually, measured by minutes and hours, Ki-Gor was not gone long. But it seemed like an eternity to the big American Negro, before his searching eyes made out a vague shape down in the crevasse. His heart began to beat a wild, joyous rhythm as the shape grew clearer.

Ki-Gor came up his ladder much faster than he went down, even though Ekka's limp form was draped over one shoulder.

"He is all right, I think!" Ki-Gor shouted cheerily. "Just badly frightened. The crack gets narrow gradually, and he must have been able to slow himself down before he hit bottom."

Ekka was crying softly as Ki-Gor bore him upward. He stopped crying when they came to a spot ten feet below the top of the crevasse, and looked upward with a tear-stained smile. George watched the pair, fascinated as the pale sunlight filtered through the ice-roof above them.

"Ah! Ki-Gor!" Ekka said, squinting his eyes. "I never thought Ekka would see the sun again."

Involuntarily, Ki-Gor twisted his head around to look up at the ice wall that hung over his head. And then suddenly he began to tremble so violently that he nearly lost his grip on the fresh niches.

He was looking straight up at the ice overhang. A blinding glare of diffused light made him close his eyes.

"George!" he whispered. "The sun! Is it overhead?"

"Why—why, yes!" George answered with a quick upward glance.

"Ah!" said Ki-Gor, and rested a moment against the ice. "I can see it, George! I am looking at the sun at high noon! And its—*its rays are cold!*"

CHAPTER VIII

LATE THE NEXT MORNING, Ki-Gor and his companions halted, gaunt and footsore, beside the old deserted mine where the stars had shone at mid-day. The trio had not stopped to eat or sleep since they had left the crevasse in the glacier. But now George insisted that they rest in the shade of the caves for a few hours. Ki-Gor gave in eventually, knowing that they were in no shape to traverse the desert during the heat of the day. Ekka was far too exhausted to get himself lost in the caverns again, so Ki-Gor told himself that they would not have to worry about that.

After a few hours of slumber, Ki-Gor went outside the cave and searched the ground for tracks. He did not have to look far. There were two sets, one fresher than the others, but both left by the same man. Moreover, Ki-Gor found several small punctures in the turf here and there beside the foot marks. A Masai spear has a two-foot long slender metal spindle embedded in the butt end. These punctures could have been made by a spindle like that.

Ki-Gor could make nothing of this unseen lurking stranger, but he did not waste much time looking for him. There was no time to waste. Instead, he went into the cave and awakened George and Ekka. There was nothing to eat, but Ki-Gor knew they would find food on the other side of the strip of desert if they set out right away.

The jungle man's plan was to make a bee-line for the big west-flowing river which he had come up with Tsempala's two Kroo boys. If possible he hoped to strike the river above the great falls, and locate the friendly river-tribe that lived there. They would give him a boat and perhaps some paddlers. Once the falls were past, they could make swift time downstream to the point where the man called Lebo, the Dog Brother, had given Ki-Gor his boat. From there, they would cut across the veldt due south, retracing Ki-Gor's steps back to Dera Daga.

It was by far the quickest route, and its only drawback lay in that it went close to the Gwembi village where Ki-Gor had rescued Ekka. It was conceivable that the fat chieftain who called himself King Makaka might make an effort to recapture Ekka. But Ki-Gor had scant respect for such frail, rickety forest-blacks as the Gwembi.

However, as these thoughts went through his mind, Ki-Gor realized that the first consideration was to get started across the desert before them. Ekka was about to set up a clamor at resuming the journey thus, without food to assuage the gnawing hunger in his stomach. But he somehow caught the urgency of the occasion and followed his two guardians quietly down the bare hillside to the gravel of the desert.

They reached the veldt on the other side just after sundown, and Ki-Gor stalked some sleepy ground-hens, bearing them back in triumph to serve as the first meal the trio had eaten in more than twenty-four hours. After the meal Ki-Gor allowed his companions to stretch and loll back luxuriously for just one hour. Then, although it was pitch dark, he announced that they would resume the dash toward Dera Daga.

All during that night march, George marveled at how Ki-Gor could find his way with no landmarks to guide him—nothing but the brilliant tropical stars overhead. Yet when day broke, Ki-Gor seemed to know exactly where he was.

There was only the briefest stop made for a hasty breakfast of fruit and nuts. Then Ki-Gor led his friends onward, promising them that they could sleep during the heat of the day, when the blazing sun made travel more arduous.

They soon struck a well-worn trail which Ki-Gor remembered following in the opposite direction. It led ultimately to the Gwembi village, through it, and to the river. As he led his companions along it now, he inspected the wind-blown dust of the trail for tracks. For miles there were none, or what spoors there were, were so old as to be nearly obliterated.

BUT ABOUT three hours before noon, a fresh track appeared in the dust, a splay-toed Bantu spoor. And every now and then, a slight puncture appeared beside the foot-marks, a puncture that might have been made by the spindle of a Masai spear.

This single spoor carried along the trail for some two miles, and then suddenly turned off into the short new grass of the veldt. Without stopping, Ki-Gor threw a shrewd glance around, and noticed a small clump of trees and bushes not far away on the crest of a small rise of the ground.

"George," he murmured, "we will go on for a little distance, and then I drop off to one side. You keep on going until you are out of sight of that grove. Then stop and wait for me. I will not be long."

Five minutes later, Ki-Gor was crawling silently on his belly toward the clump of trees. The grass was too short to afford any great cover, yet the jungle man's movements were so skilled that only an alert, expectant pair of eyes could have distinguished his tawny form.

He reached the grove unchallenged and wormed his way noiselessly into the protecting undergrowth. Then he began a silent but thorough investigation of the grove.

He had not far to go to find what he was seeking.

A tall black was sound asleep under an ironwood tree. A Masai spear lay beside him, but the man was not a Masai. He was dressed like a Lunanda.

Ki-Gor studied the slumbering face, and tried to recall who this Lunanda was. Then he remembered. It was Aku, the hunter who had shown his malice toward Ki-Gor by speaking up during the trial on the top of the pyramid at Dera Daga. Ki-Gor looked at the Masai spear again. It looked familiar.

It was his own.

For several minutes, Ki-Gor regarded the sleeping Lunanda hunter. At last, he had found the explanation to several matters. Who had stolen his spear—the identity of the strange Bantu who had trailed him from Dera Daga all the way to the old deserted mines.

For a brief moment, the jungle man considered waking up the hunter, and at the point of his spear, demanding his business. On second thought, he decided against it. It would take precious time. Also, if Aku slept on while Ki-Gor continued his way, he would never know that his prey had slipped past him. Ki-Gor was not afraid of the man, but he did not want to waste any precious time on his account. Quiet as a ghost, he slipped out of the grove and rejoined his waiting companions.

"Don't talk yet," he murmured in answer to their inquiring looks. "We must keep going—faster than ever."

After they had gone several miles, Ki-Gor was faced with a decision to make as regards their route. Their trail took them, he knew, ultimately to the river near the village of the friendly river-blacks. But it did not go in a straight line. Instead it curved around in a wide sweep through the Gwembi village. It would be miles shorter to cut across country to the river.

However, there was a reason for the trail making such a wide detour.

The country between them and the river was an impassable jungle swamp. By himself, Ki-Gor could easily have negotiated it, merely by taking to the trees. But George and the city-bred Ekka could not travel the tree route.

Therefore, they would have to stick to the path, even though it was longer, and even though it led right through the village of the hostile Gwembi and their vengeful chieftain, "King" Makaka. Ki-Gor did not anticipate any real trouble from the Gwembi, no matter how hostile they were. Furthermore, if the trio were able to maintain the pace they had been going, they would pass through the Gwembi just before dawn the next morning.

THIS, HOWEVER, was a problem. Ki-Gor now wanted to push on without stopping for a mid-day nap. Having overtaken and passed the mysterious Lunanda hunter, he wanted to keep his advantage. But, Ekka was already querulous from fatigue, and even huge George was getting dull-eyed. Ki-Gor took the child up on his back, and persuaded his giant friend to keep going as long as he could.

So they pounded along the trail through the broiling heat of the day into the comparative coolness of late afternoon. But when the sun went down, George suddenly wilted.

"I sho' am sorry, Ki-Gor," he said in a muffled voice, "but I don' guess I c'n go anothuh step without a little shut-eye."

That was that, and Ki-Gor hunted out a safe place for his exhausted companions to sleep. Even his own iron stamina was weakening somewhat, but he planned to stay awake and watch the trail. If Aku, the hunter, came by, Ki-Gor wanted to know it.

An early moon, now more than half full, lighted the trail perfectly, and Ki-Gor found a spot where he could command the path without being seen. He sat down with his back resting against a rock, and settled down to waiting.

But fatigue and the monotony of watching a deserted trail had its effect. Before the moon had climbed to its highest point in the sky, Ki-Gor's head drooped forward until it lay on his knees, and he went sound asleep.

It was pitch black when he woke up. The moon had gone, and by that fact he realized that he had slept many hours. He rose up, inwardly raging at himself, and woke his companions. Silently, the three groped their way back on to the trail and resumed their journey.

Ki-Gor was out of patience with himself. Not only had he lost precious hours in getting back to Dera Daga, but he had delayed long enough so that he and his friends would have to go through or by the Gwembi village in broad daylight. Furthermore, he now did not know whether Aku, the hunter, was still behind him, or had passed by during Ki-Gor's lapse into slumber.

On an impulse, he dropped to his knees and sniffed the dew-dampened dust of the trail. There was an unmistakable scent of Bantu. It was a single Bantu, at that.

There was no way of knowing, of course, whether that Bantu had been Aku. But, considering that most Bantu will not travel by night, Ki-Gor judged that the spoor had been left by a man fired with determination and driven by a purpose. That description might fit Aku. Ki-Gor decided that it would he safest to assume that Aku was now somewhere ahead of them along the trail.

It was almost time for the sun to rise, but the wayfarers on the trail were still in comparative darkness. The reason for this was that the trail had long since left the veldt to plunge into thick jungle. It was not many miles now to the Gwembi village.

As time went on, Ki-Gor strode along, growing more and more tense. Any moment now, he might expect the bushes on either side of the trail to erupt a shooting black brandishing a great broad-bladed spear.

THE TRAIL now began to veer to the right, and Ki-Gor knew that shortly they would come upon the squalid huts of the Gwembi. Suddenly Ki-Gor realized that there was a complete absence of the ordinary sounds one expects to hear from human settlements. In fact, an abnormal stillness was hanging over the jungle.

In a flash, Ki-Gor guessed what was about to happen. Aku would not be lying in ambush alone. He would have prepared the Gwembi.

"George," he murmured, "I think we are going to have a little trouble. Keep Ekka between us, and protect the rear—"

Before he could finish, the forest around them sprang into life. A hideous concerted yell went up and Gwembi leaped out of the bushes from all sides.

Ki-Gor's taut nerves relaxed. Action was always better than waiting. He uttered a glad shout, slipped his hand down to the butt of his eight-foot spear. Then he slashed it horizontally across the path in front of him. Three Gwembi tribesmen went crashing to the earth under the impact of the ironwood rod.

"Give 'em hell, Ki-Gor!" George shouted gaily behind him. "This'll be easy! These boys ain't the champs!"

It was not precisely easy, but as George observed, the Gwembi were not champion warriors. Moreover, they had sacrificed the value of their numbers by attacking in the close quarters of the trail. Ki-Gor moved forward slashing them down with his tough spear-haft, as if they were so many canes of bamboo. Behind him, big George was coolly battering down more Gwembi, while in between, little Ekka screamed with delight and triumph.

Once, his voice was raised in terror as one of the Gwembi wriggled through and seized one leg. But Ki-Gor spun around and felled the black with a swift battering blow.

In a few moments, the Gwembi began to falter. When their first rush did not succeed they began to lose taste for the whole affair. Ki-Gor seized the opportunity.

"Come on, George!" he shouted, and started to trot forward into the village itself.

There came an enraged cry from in front of him, and another party of Gwembi poured out from behind the huts. Leading them was a tall figure carrying a Masai spear—Aku the hunter.

At once, Ki-Gor realized that this would not be so easy. Unlike the Gwembi, Aku was a resolute man. Furthermore, he was armed with a splendid weapon, a spear that was four feet longer than the ironwood spear in Ki-Gor's hands.

The Lunanda warrior was shouting commands to the Gwembi, ordering them to encircle their prey while he engaged Ki-Gor in front. And Ki-Gor knew then that he had to dispose of Aku quickly, before the Gwembi behind him on the trail could take heart and rally. If he got Aku, the Gwembi would collapse.

Trusting George to protect himself and Ekka for the moment, Ki-Gor suddenly sprinted forward. Aku fell back a pace, the great spear leveled. Ki-Gor feinted with his own spear, but Aku was not to be fooled. The huge Masai blade licked out at Ki-Gor's bare stomach.

Ki-Gor swiftly twisted away. But the thrust barely missed. Like a flash Ki-Gor cut downward with his spear-haft. The Masai spear was battered downward momentarily. But before Ki-Gor could spring forward, the great blade swung up again.

For a moment, the jungle man was off balance. A triumphant snarl contorted Aku's black face and he lunged forward, spear leveled.

Ki-Gor's own spear was point down in the ground. There was no time to lift it. But he still gripped the butt end. With a grunt, he heaved upward with it. The stout haft engaged the hissing Masai blade and deflected it six inches from its course. Four inches would have been enough.

Now Ki-Gor leaped. This time it was Aku who was off balance. Ki-Gor's left fist hooked around like a sickle, caught the Lunanda in front of the right ear with a crunch. Aku toppled forward with a groan, and Ki-Gor seized the Masai spear from his nerveless fingers.

He was not a moment too soon. A half dozen Gwembi flung themselves on top of him. But he shook them off with one motion and then sent his two-foot blade sizzling through an unhappy warrior in front of him.

That was enough for the Gwembi. With shrieks of terror, they dodged back to the shelter of their huts. Ki-Gor glared down at Aku.

The hunter had drawn himself up to his hands and knees. For a second, Ki-Gor was tempted to snuff out his life with one twisting spear-thrust. Then he changed his mind. There had been enough killing. Ki-Gor hesitated a moment. Then he prodded the groggy hunter contemptuously.

"Get up, O Murderous One!" he growled. "You are returning to Dera Daga with us!"

CHAPTER IX

LIKE A GREAT GHOSTLY lantern the full moon hung in the sky. Its cold beams shone palely on the dark, mysterious ruins of Dera Daga. They reflected whitely from the decaying sides of the Pyramid and revealed the silent crowd of Lunanda massed around its base.

But those moonbeams could not penetrate the black, oily waters of the Crocodile Pool that yawned evilly before Helene, wife of Ki-Gor. She stood calm on the awful brink, a length of thin chain about one wrist, while a dozen black shadows crouched behind her.

Up on the top of the Pyramid, the harsh voice of the Priestess broke the brooding silence.

"O Moon-God! Listen to thy people! We are gathered here to await the arrival of one who was sent away to prove his innocence of a crime. Full twenty-eight days hath he been gone. It is declared that if he doth not appear in that time, then shall he be judged guilty of murder, and his hostage thrown into the Pool!"

The Priestess stopped and bowed her head amidst an awful silence.

Then, raising her face to the moon like one drugged, she intoned stiffly:

"Hostage of Ki-Gor, prepare to meet thy fate."

A thrill of horror shot through Helene. Could this happen to her, to be mangled by loathsome crocodiles, while Ki-Gor wandered helplessly in some far-off region—trying to fulfil the ridiculous demands of that dope-crazed old woman?

But before she had time even to cry out, two husky warriors grasped her and started down a rope ladder into the Crocodile Pool. They carried Helene to a little rocky promontory, all the while casting nervous glances at the hideous reptiles which lay sleepily on the farther bank of the Pool.

Fear lent speed to their hands as they fastened Helene's chains to a staple fastened into one of the rocks on the promontory. Then, as one of the sleepy crocodiles stirred lazily, they scampered for the safety of the rope ladder.

The wife of Ki-Gor was left alone.

Helene began to breathe faster. Yet it was a purely physical, purely automatic reaction within herself. Her mind was singularly clear, and what was more, her mind was unafraid. Something of the fatality of Dera Daga had communicated itself to the beautiful wife of Ki-Gor. She stared impersonally at the evil waters of the Pool.

What was to be, would be.

As in a dream, she saw the eyes of a crocodile blink open, fasten in brute wonderment on her. Heavily, the beast lumbered to its feet and slid like a great log into the black waters of the Pool.

Helene closed her eyes.

Suddenly, the silence of the night was broken by a mighty shout:

"Ki-Gor comes, O Priestess!"

At the sound of that beloved voice, Helene's calm left her. She had to fight to keep from laughing hysterically. Twenty-eight days Ki-Gor had been gone. And while she had never doubted that he would return in time to save her—

"Here, Ki-Gor!" she screamed. "In the Pool! Help me, Ki-Gor!"

The scaly snout of the crocodile appeared at the edge of the Pool. On short legs it pulled itself upon dry land and commenced to slither toward her.

"Ki-Gor!" Helene screamed again.

There was a terrific roar, scarcely human, emanating from the foot of the Pyramid. Then Helene's straining eyes saw the great figure of her mate bounding to the edge of the Crocodile Pool, and throwing himself down the sheer, slippery walls.

The crocodile's snapping jaws were almost within arm's reach now. But Ki-Gor's racing form came hurtling. He flung himself on the crocodile's back and his hunting knife rose and dipped with great, lethal strokes. The hideous saurian writhed furiously, its tail threshing dangerously near Helene. Ki-Gor's knife sought out the crocodile's tiny brain. The brute threshed once, convulsively, then subsided in a limp heap.

Ki-Gor hurried to Helene's side.

"I'm caught, Ki-Gor," Helene sobbed. Over her shoulder she saw the other crocodiles, aroused now, and starting to swim toward them. "Oh, Ki-Gor, what shall we do?"

Without a word, Ki-Gor bent to the chain holding Helene. His bronzed face was stern as his great hands took hold of the chain close to the staple. Helene was watching his face; she saw it tense as Ki-Gor's mighty muscles contracted. There was a grating sound and suddenly Helene was free, the length of chain dangling from her wrist. Ki-Gor lifted her, chain and all, and carried her in his arms to the wall of the Pool.

"O Priestess, I have returned within the twenty-eight days allotted… although barely in time, it is true. Let down thy rope, that I may inform thee of my discoveries."

There was a stir upon the brink of the Pool. Suddenly, a rope slithered down the wall, and Ki-Gor grasped hold of it. Helene put her arms around his neck and Ki-Gor mounted hand over hand.

Gently, Ki-Gor carried her to where George Spelvin and a small Negro youth stood. Then, handing her over to George, he turned and started climbing the stairs to the top of the Pyramid.

The moment of Ki-Gor's inquisition had arrived!

KI-GOR ADVANCED steadily toward the Priestess, and came to a stop ten paces from her. He folded his arms across his chest, then addressed her:

"I have returned, O Priestess, having fulfilled your commands. I bring with me two friends who will corroborate my words."

"Thy friends are useless, O Ki-Gor," the Priestess croaked. "Describe what thou sawest, and we will judge from thy words whether thou truly fulfilled the Missions. First, didst thou see the stars shining at mid-day?"

"I did."

A murmur went up from the crowd.

In measured words, Ki-Gor described precisely the place and the conditions under which he saw the noon-day stars. When he finished there was a long pause. Then the Priestess spoke.

"Well and truly hast thou spoken, Ki-Gor! There is no doubt of the truth of thy words. Tell us now of the second Mission."

Carefully, Ki-Gor detailed the scene on the glacier.

Again the pause. And again the Priestess spoke.

"Clear enough it is, Ki-Gor, that thou witnessed the sun at high noon when its rays fell cold on thee. No one living of the Lunanda hath seen solid water as thou hast described it. Yet there is such a thing, as the ancient songs of our people do testify."

The Priestess paused again with bent head.

Now, Ki-Gor awaited the Third Condition, which had not been named. He wondered what it would be.

The Priestess spread her arms wide.

"NOW, KI-GOR," she chanted, "forasmuch as thou hast well and truly performed the tasks set before thee in order to prove thy innocence, it remains for thee to satisfy the Third Condition. Thou shalt answer a question regarding thyself. Thou hast killed a fellow-man—whether by accident, negligence, or design—thou killed him. Now, thou askest that thy life be spared. Tell us, O Ki-Gor—hast thou ever shown mercy to an enemy and spared his life? Answer, Ki-Gor, and answer truly!"

Ki-Gor stared at the old Priestess. How strange was Fate! He marveled at the inexplicable chance which had furnished this denouement.

He said measuredly, "Do not take my word for it, O Priestess. The man whose life I spared is here. Let him step forward and admit it. Aku! Aku, the hunter!"

An astonished murmur broke over the Lunanda, as a figure broke through the crowd and came slowly up the stairs to the top of the Pyramid.

"It is true, O Priestess!" Aku the hunter said in a flat voice. "I followed Ki-Gor, believing him guilty of murdering Datu. I planned to kill him in revenge. But he defeated me in battle, and even as he held my life in forfeit, he spared me—"

"Enough!" the Priestess cried. "Thou hast satisfied the Third Condition, Ki-Gor! I now pronounce thee not guilty and not accountable in any way for the death of Prince Datu!"

INSIDE KING Mboko's royal guesthouse, Ki-Gor, Helene, and George sat facing Ekka. The youth stood before them, eyes fixed on Ki-Gor.

"How couldst thou think I'd ever desert thee, Ki-Gor?" Ekka said finally.

"I would consider it no desertion," Ki-Gor said patiently. "But this is something which you must choose for yourself. You may come with me if you wish. Without you, I might never have discovered the cold sun and the mid-day stars. For that I am deeply grateful and I will grant any wish of yours."

"Suppose then," Ekka said, "that I wish to stay with thee?"

"Then stay with me you may," Ki-Gor said promptly. "But King Mboko and Queen Goli have lost their only son, and the Lunanda have lost a future king. Mboko is taken with you and has asked me to give you to him. He will adopt you and bring you up as his own child and as heir to the throne of Dera Daga. That is more than I could ever offer you, and it would be wrong of me to stand in your way if you wished to accept King Mboko's offer."

Ekka flung himself into Ki-Gor's arms.

"Ah, thou great booby!" he cried affectionately. "How thou must love Ekka! Yet, how can I turn down an opportunity to be a king?"

"You cannot," Ki-Gor said simply.

"You are right," Ekka said, getting to his feet. "If Fate has thrust a future kingdom upon me, I fear I must accept. Although"—Ekka shook his head dubiously—"how thou wilt ever get along without me to help thee, I don't know."

George Spelvin smothered a smile and said in English, "Man, he sho' is goin' to make a wonderful king!"

STORY XI

WHITE SAVAGE

CHAPTER I

FOR TWO NIGHTS AND a day, Helene had rested secure and unworried in the great baobab tree. Ki-Gor had left her two big gourds full of water and plenty of biltong to eat. In addition there was the juicy, tangy fruit of the baobab to be had for variety. Ki-Gor had used the greatest care in selecting a safe spot to leave Helene while he made a swift trip on the back of Marmo, the elephant, to the country of Tembu George.

The small river which tumbled through the rugged, almost mountainous country flattened out at this point for a short distance into a considerable swamp, emerging after less than a mile into a swift rock-banked water-course. The baobab tree grew on an island in the middle of the swamp commanding a view not only of the swamp but of the mountains to the north and west, and the veldt to the east and south. Ki-Gor had been confident that Helene would be perfectly safe in the great tree, as long as she did not descend from it until he returned from his visit to Tembu George.

And for two nights and a day, Helene had taken her ease in the tree and felt not the slightest prickle of fear.

But here at noon of the second day, Ki-Gor's wife realized suddenly that she was uneasy about something. The ominous quiet of the jungle, broken only by the slow drip-drip of moisture from the broad leaves of the baobab tree, was fast getting on her nerves. She roused herself and climbed up from the cool shade below to the upper branches of the huge tree where she could look out toward the horizon. Not that she expected to see Ki-Gor astride Marmo coming across the veldt yet. He had said only that he would return sometime during the second day, without specifying any particular time.

It was just that Helene felt more comfortable, in spite of the grueling heat, up there out of the brooding shadows of the swamp. She reflected on the impulse that had brought her and Ki-Gor up into this rugged north-eastern country which was so far from their home. The mysterious jungle telegraph had brought news of war—widespread and terrible. White men and black, the news had reported, were fighting other white men and black men on a grand scale. The jungles of Uganda, the mountains of Kenya, the deserts of Jobaland, and the wastes of Abyssinia and the Great Rift were resounding with gunfire and the screams of dying men. The civilization which Helene had abandoned to come and live with Ki-Gor as his wife in the steaming Congo jungle had followed her with all its implacable hatred and terror.

Not even in their cozy island home had she and Ki-Gor remained untouched by war. Accordingly, they had journeyed northward through the restless forests to see for themselves what was happening to their Africa.

Suddenly, Helene's thoughts were interrupted. Away to the north where the river entered the swamp, a swarm of wild parrots rose from the trees screaming raucously. Helene stiffened. What had caused

that? Then, a moment later, a shrill chattering went up and climbed to a steep crescendo as a tribe of monkeys joined the parrots in sounding the alarm to the denizens of the swamp. In a few moments, the noontime hush was gone, replaced by a great clamor as the jungle people announced to each other that there were strangers in the swamp.

HELENE STRAINED her eyes toward the north where the alarm had first sounded. She could see nothing, but her heart began to beat faster. It was not likely that Ki-Gor was coming from that direction. He had gone straight east, and besides he usually went unnoticed by birds and animals as he sat motionless on the back of the great elephant. Helene turned her head and gazed eastward.

Far away on the dry grass of the veldt, she made out a gray object. As she watched it, it grew larger. That, she decided, was Marmo. But what was causing the commotion in the swamp?

Helene slipped down the great tree to a fork about thirty feet above the ground. From there she commanded a view of the sluggish main current of the river. In a few moments she heard human voices raised in angry shouts. It sounded as if a half dozen men were bickering at the top of their lungs. Gradually, the voices grew nearer.

Helene could not make out any words, or even what language was being used. Minutes passed, and still no one appeared within her vision. She considered climbing up the tree again to see how close Ki-Gor was getting, but curiosity impelled her to wait. She wanted to see the owners of those strange yammering voices.

After a long interval, the strangers came into view. And a noisy crew it was. There were about a dozen tall black askaris in tattered uniforms struggling through waist-deep water beside the main current of the river, their extended arms holding military-type rifles away from the water. A stocky, unhappy-looking white man headed the column. Behind were four native porters carrying a crude litter on which a gray-mustached white man was lying with closed eyes. On the river beside this odd procession floated a dugout canoe carrying two black paddlers and a third white man.

This man was making most of the noise. He was broad shouldered and evil of face. He wore a battered sun-helmet, and the ragged remnants of a white uniform. And he was directing a ceaseless stream of vituperation at the less fortunate members of the party who were struggling on foot through the swamp. The askaris were shouting back in exasperation. They looked like Somalis, and Helene thought she recognized several Somali syllables. That gave her no clue to the nationality of the white men. But whatever their nationality, she did not like their looks.

With a shock, Helene suddenly thought of Ki-Gor. How long had she been down there in the fork of the baobab? Longer than she realized, probably. It would be just as well, she thought, if Ki-Gor kept out of sight of this heavily armed safari. She decided to go up the tree and see how close he was getting. She shifted her weight to start climbing, her left hand groping for her little throwing-spear.

But it was a hasty stab she made with that left hand. Her knuckles grazed the slender shaft which was resting point downward in the crotch of the tree. Helene jerked her head around with a thrill of dismay to see the little spear wabble out of the crutch. She clutched at it despairingly. The spear hesitated for a second, tantalizingly out of reach, then plunged down.

With horrified eyes, Helene watched it go, apparently straight for the dugout canoe. It finally hit the water with a little splash right beside the bellowing white man.

A sudden shocked hush went over the safari. Helene promptly ducked around the tree out of all possible sight from below and began climbing swiftly. In a moment, enraged cries floated up after her.

Helene knew that the party below could not possibly see her, but she was thoroughly vexed with herself for her carelessness. It had revealed to the safari that someone else was in the swamp. What they would do about it she did not know. She was not especially worried about that. Under Ki-Gor's tutelage, she had learned to make her way through treetops very handily, so that even if one of the blacks was sent up the tree after her, she felt sure she could easily get away from him.

The clamor underneath the tree grew fainter as she slipped deftly upwards into the upper branches. Perhaps, she reflected, the strangers would not attach any importance to the falling spear. They might think a lone Pygmy had thrown it, and go on their way.

BY NOW, Helene was high enough to see out over the veldt. What she saw made her gasp. The gray blob she had seen earlier had been Marmo all right, and Ki-Gor was astride his broad neck. But the elephant had come on very fast and was at that moment at the very edge of the swamp. The only trouble was that Ki-Gor had directed

Marmo considerably to the south of the baobab tree. If he kept on and came into the swamp at that point, he might conceivably run straight into the strange safari!

Helene thought swiftly. That must not happen. To be sure, it was not likely to happen if the strangers continued to be as noisy as they had been. Ki-Gor would hear them and be warned. Helene cocked her head and listened. There was not a sound from below.

That was bad, Helene reflected. Quickly, she decided to go down the tree and reconnoiter. If the safari was gathered silently on the island below, looking for the owner of that dropped spear, Ki-Gor might well blunder into them.

As Helene descended, still no voices reached her ears. Presently, she found a hole in the screening leaves through which she could look straight down. The safari was not there.

Cautiously, Helene went down farther until she was back in the big fork. There was not a sign of the party. Evidently, they had not bothered too long about the spear, but had proceeded downstream. Helene searched the scene with keen eyes for a long moment. Then, slowly and carefully she crept down the thick vines on the trunk to the ground.

She paused at the edge of the water and listened intently. There was a faint rippling sound and she jerked her head. Upstream, a pair of snowy egrets rose from the still waters and flapped majestically away. Helene stepped into the water. She must slip through the swamp and try to intercept Ki-Gor before he could by any chance run into the safari.

The river there was only about five feet deep, but Helene preferred swimming it to the slow business of wading neck-deep through it. When the water reached her waist, she launched herself forward into a gentle breast-stroke.

She had not gone ten feet, when her heart leaped into her mouth. A dugout canoe shot out from a thicket across the stream straight toward her. The two black boys paddled furiously, and the evil-hunking white man in the stern yelled in triumph. Helene flung herself around, churning the brown water furiously. She threw herself on the island just as the dugout touched it. Picking herself up, she scrambled toward the base of the baobab tree. The ground jarred under heavy feet pounding behind her, and the man's rasping voice bellowed. With a sob, she leaped into the vines. And just as she did, a rough hand closed over one ankle.

She kicked out frantically and lunged upward. But relentlessly another hand gripped her other ankle. Although she clung to the vines for dear life, the man hauled her downward mercilessly. Helene gave a despairing scream.

"Ki-Gor!"

She suddenly let go of the vines and twisted around, flailing her small fists at the man's swarthy face.

"Ki-Gor!" she screamed. *"Ki-Gor!"*

The man bellowed wrathfully, pinned her arms to her sides, and picked her up. Then he carried her struggling and screaming to the dugout. A few moments later, the canoe pushed out into the shallow current. Helene sat trembling in the bottom, her wrists firmly bound behind her back and a dirty handkerchief tied around her mouth.

"Porco Dio!" the white man exclaimed, licking his lips. *"Ecco—la bedda fighia!"*

Helene's eyes widened with astonishment. The man spoke Italian—and with a strong Sicilian accent. In the days before Helene had forsaken the brilliant world of society to live in the jungle as Ki-Gor's wife, she had spent a great deal of time in Italy. The peasants around her villa near Palermo had said *"Bedda fighia"* for *"Bella figlia,"* meaning "beautiful girl."

The man leered at her with an evil chuckle. Suddenly, he broke off and jerked his head. There was a thunderous crashing off to one side. Helene's heart leaped as she made out the gigantic form of Marmo plunging toward them through the swamp. The white man in the canoe gave a nervous shout and drew a heavy military automatic.

"Avandi!" he shouted, and the two canoe boys dug paddles into the water. As the canoe shot downstream, Helene stared back agonizedly. She chewed futilely at the gag over her mouth, and wrestled in vain with the rope on her wrists. If only she could scream now!

MARMO BURST out on the river about twenty yards above the speeding dugout. Ki-Gor crouched up on the elephant's great shoulders, throwing-spear poised in his right hand. A gurgling scream came from Helene and she rolled on her side in the narrow canoe-bottom. The Sicilian snorted wrathfully and struck her a stinging blow on one knee.

Ki-Gor saw it.

"A-a-arrgh!" The war-cry of the White Lord of the jungle went crashing through the swamp. With agonized eyes, Helene saw him heel Marmo behind one great ear, saw the huge beast swing around and plunge after the dugout. Sheets of water were tossed to either side as the elephant dropped into a shuffling trot that was deceptively fast.

Again and again Ki-Gor roared, his bare bronzed arm holding the throwing-spear aloft. A gleam of fear lurked in the black eyes of the man in the canoe. He raised the automatic and aimed it at Ki-Gor's massive torso. Helene threw herself against his knee just as the gun roared.

Marmo trumpeted with pain, and Helene knew the bullet had hit him. Again she flung herself at the white man's legs, just as his gun spatted for the second time. His furious curses were drowned out by the elephant's high-pitched squeal. Helene felt a terrific blow on her shoulder and fell forward face down in the boat. Before she could struggle up, the automatic roared twice more.

Marmo was making the swamp hideous with his trumpeting. His great ears were flapping, and his horny trunk was flailing the air.

The action had been so swift that Helene saw the dugout was at the lower end of the swamp already. In a few moments, the river would emerge on to the veldt. Marmo had not been able to overtake them.

In fact, Marmo had slowed down appreciably. Helene could see Ki-Gor urging him on desperately. Then the Sicilian fired two last shots, and the elephant swerved aside with a despairing shriek and plunged out of view into the screening undergrowth.

Cold fear clutched at Helene's heart. What would Ki-Gor do now? He had been afraid to throw his spear for fear, probably, of hitting her. Now, Marmo had suddenly failed him—how could he hope to overtake the speeding canoe?

Marmo still trumpeted and crashed and splashed, although Helene only caught fleeting glimpses of his great hulk. The white man in the dugout snarled at the screen of bushes and reloaded his gun. By now, the canoe was almost out of the swamp. Helene, staring ahead, saw the main safari drawn up on the right bank of the by now swifter flowing current. Then something to her left caught her eye.

It was a human figure running at tremendous speed along the left bank. Already it was abreast of the canoe, and rapidly gaining on it. Helene held her breath. Would her abductor see that speeding figure? It was Ki-Gor.

Apparently the Sicilian did not see the jungle man—at least not until Ki-Gor was fifty or sixty yards downstream of the canoe. Then an astonished Sicilian curse ripped out. Ki-Gor was hurtling down the bank toward the water. A second later he plunged in. At the same moment, the army automatic went off with a deafening roar by Helene's left ear. She squeezed her eyes shut as the gun spoke again and again. The canoe was bearing down toward Ki-Gor's bobbing head and curving arms. Tiny cascades of silver marked how close the bullets came to the rolling bronzed body in the water.

But as the gun roared again, Ki-Gor disappeared. Just one or two swirling eddies and an ever-widening circular ripple marked where he had been. A snarl of triumph jumped from the Sicilian's mouth and Helene sat paralyzed. Had Ki-Gor been hit by a bullet—or had he just dived?

Seconds went by—and every second an eternity for the beautiful girl in the dugout. She knew that Ki-Gor could stay under water for more than two minutes at a time and yet—. Evidently, the Sicilian was a little uneasy. He barked some commands at the paddlers, and they began to veer the dugout toward the right bank where the askaris were gaping expectantly.

SUDDENLY, THE foremost paddler screamed. A brown arm snaked out of the water over the side of the dugout. As the Sicilian bellowed with rage and fright, the canoe tipped sharply to one side, sprang back to an even keel again, and then tipped again. This time the gunwale went under and the canoe kept on rolling until it was upside down.

Helene had just time to take a deep breath before she rolled into the water. It was a hair-raising moment for her, gagged and bound as she was, hand and foot. But as she sank toward the bottom of the river, completely helpless, she had a curious faith that Ki-Gor would not let her drown. He must have seen that she was tied up before he set out on his long underwater swim. Therefore, after he had tipped the canoe over, he would be bound to come to her aid.

But the long seconds went by and Helene kept on sinking, rolling like a drowned rat. Her lungs began to ache, and sudden terror swept over her. She twisted and arched her body and kicked her bound legs frantically. Then a hand closed over one knee, and for an awful moment she held herself rigid. Something tugged at the rope around her shins, and again at the rope on her wrists. With a rush of unspeakable relief, she spread-eagled her arms and legs and shot up to the surface.

As she gulped down fresh air into her tortured lungs and shook the water out of her ears, she could hear the frightened bellowing of the Sicilian, and more faintly, the angry shouts of the men along the bank. Ki-Gor's head emerged glistening beside her. He took the knife from between his teeth and spoke in a low voice.

"Dive," he said, "and swim downstream. Stay underwater as long as you can, and when you come up for air, dive again as quick as possible. I'll be beside you."

With a quick glance to get her bearings, Helene took a deep breath and dived like a porpoise. Not even Ki-Gor was a better swimmer than she was. Back in the world of society, she had been a noted sportswoman, and had excelled particularly in swimming and high diving. At times like this, and indeed on many another occasion since she had joined forces with Ki-Gor, this skill had been very useful. Side by side, now, she and Ki-Gor stroked downstream under the surface of the river.

When they finally came up for air, Helene was surprised at the distance they had gone. Evidently, the current was much swifter than she had realized. They were so far downstream that the askaris did not see them. However, they both prudently submerged again and helped by the ever-increasing velocity of the current went even farther. A third stretch under water carried them around a bend out of sight of the safari, and the jungle couple pulled themselves out of the racing waters on to the rocky bank.

CHAPTER II

"WELL!" GASPED HELENE, AT length. "*That* was a close call!"

"Yes," Ki-Gor growled, blue eyes glinting. "Tell me—how did that man capture you? And why? And who was he?"

"Well, he laid in wait for me," Helene said. "I don't know why he captured me—unless he just took a fancy to me. He was an Italian."

"An Italian!" Ki-Gor said with a frown. "Then what is he doing down here? Tembu George told me the Italians had been driven deep into the north."

He went on to tell Helene the war news of East Africa as received by their old friend whom Ki-Gor had just visited.

"We've got to find Marmo," he concluded. "The old beast has been shot at too often. When that man's bullets pricked his hide, he simply stampeded. The worst of it is"—he added with a rueful expression—"that I had some presents from Tembu George to you tied on Marmo's back."

"Presents!" Helene cried. "What kind of presents?"

"Different kinds," Ki-Gor shrugged. "You'll see them as soon as we find Marmo. Oh, I have one of them with me!"

He reached down into his tight leopard skin trunks and pulled out a small cloth bag. Helene opened the draw-string of the bag and shook out some brightly colored stones into her palm.

"Rubies!" she gasped. "And emeralds! Oh! aren't they beautiful! And perfectly huge stones! Oh, George shouldn't have done it!"

"I'm glad you like them," Ki-Gor said casually. "They're very pretty. But I don't see what use they are."

"Strictly speaking," Helene admitted, "they aren't useful. But I'll get a lot of pleasure out of them, just the same. Here, you'd better keep them until we get back home."

Ki-Gor replaced the little bag in his trunks and stood up. "Come along," he commanded. "Our first job is to find our friend, Marmo. After that, we'll think about what to do with the Italian and his safari."

They climbed up from the river over tumbled semi-eroded boulders to the crest of the high bank. They were at the edge of a considerable forest which stretched away to their right downstream along the river. To their left, the trees gave way to open veldt. The swamp and presumably the elephant were upstream to their left, but if they went in that direction they would come in plain sight of the Sicilian and his safari—there being very little cover. So Ki-Gor headed straight into the forest, planning so make a wide circle away from the river.

It was difficult going through the semi-jungle, and Helene gave a cry of relief when they shortly came out on a narrow foot-trail.

"We'll follow this," said Ki-Gor, "and see if it opens on to the veldt a safe enough distance from the river."

He stood aside and waited for Helene to precede him. She stepped along the trail briskly, following it around a gradual curve. Halfway around the curve, she suddenly halted.

A small black child about eight years old was standing in the middle of the path, looking very startled.

"Well—hullo, little one," Helene said, in Buganda. "Where didst thou come from? And where is thy mother?"

For a second the pickaninny stood without a word. But its eyes rolled, and its little face twisted with dread. Then it suddenly turned and ran shrieking with terror down the path. She stood perplexed and waited for Ki-Gor to hurry up beside her.

"Probably never saw a white person before," Ki-Gor explained.

"I don't know," said Helene slowly. "I've had pickaninnies run from me before—but not like this one. Why, he acted as if I were a ghost—or some dreadful apparition of some kind."

The child was still shrieking down the trail somewhere out of sight.

"We'll wait a moment," Ki-Gor said. "His mother will probably come running after him."

But several minutes went by and no mother appeared. And the pickaninny kept on wailing.

"This is ridiculous!" Helene exclaimed. "Do you suppose the little thing wandered away from home and got lost?"

"It may have," Ki-Gor admitted. He raised his voice. "O Mother!" he chanted in Buganda. "Come and fetch thy man-child who is lost!"

THE PICKANINNY stopped wailing and there was dead silence. Ki-Gor again addressed the absent mother. But there was no answer. Then the child started screaming again.

"It's lost, all right," Ki-Gor said, and paused. "I suppose," he said with a sigh, "that we ought to take it to the nearest village, even if it delays us a little. The leopards wouldn't let a child that age survive very long."

"No, you're quite right," Helene agreed. She could not resist adding, "But you survived, Ki-Gor. And you were just about that age, weren't you, when you were left alone in the jungle?"

"Yes, just about," Ki-Gor said seriously. "But I think I was a little bigger. And when something scared me I didn't yell. I didn't make a sound. I just climbed the nearest tree and went up into the topmost branches and stayed there."

Helene smiled proudly. "I bet you were bigger," she said fondly, "and I bet you were tougher, too."

"Probably," said Ki-Gor. "You have to be to stay alive very long in the jungle. Well, let's pick up the child. You talk to him. He should be less frightened of a woman."

They found the pickaninny about fifty feet beyond to one side of the path. He was trying pathetically to hide underneath a banana bush. When Helene spoke to him, he broke out again into furious screams and scrambled blindly away. Ki-Gor took a hand in pleading with the child, now, but that only made matters worse. The child was apparently insane with terror. He crawled up the trunk of a dead tree which had broken off about ten feet above the ground and clung there gibbering and writhing in spite at anything Ki-Gor could say.

Finally, the jungle man threw up his hands in defeat. "It's no use," he said to Helene, "we'll just have to leave him."

He took Helene's arm and propelled her back on to the path. When she would have spoken, he put a finger over his lips. They went on down the trail a short distance.

"Now," Ki-Gor whispered. "I don't understand this. That child shouldn't be as frightened as all that of us. You wait here—I'm going back and watch him for a little while. We can't leave him alone, that's certain. I'm going to keep an eye on him."

Soundlessly, Ki-Gor drifted back up the trail, stepped off into the undergrowth, and quietly circled around to a spot close to the broken tree. The child was moaning softly now, lifting a tear-stained face now and then and looking around fearfully. Ki-Gor was not too encouraged over the chances of ever coaxing the child down. It was a very peculiar thing, this awful terror of white people. Many was the pickaninny who had run from Ki-Gor, but none of them had been as terrified as this one. And furthermore, they had run from him merely because he was a stranger, not especially because of his white skin. Children under ten years old, Ki-Gor had found, rarely paid much attention to the differences in people's color.

Suddenly Ki-Gor abandoned his thoughts and began testing the air with his sensitive nostrils. A scent, sharp and sour, had drifted downwind to him. Ki-Gor stiffened. It was a cat of some kind, probably a leopard. A twig snapped nearby, and Ki-Gor slowly turned his head in that direction. His eyes patiently searched the bush and in a moment picked out the menacing form. It was a leopard.

The unsuspecting child was now about over his spell of crying. He gave a few spent sobs, then gulped and moved about on the tall stump preparatory to coming down. But his protracted howling had attracted the leopard, and the great cat eased forward for the kill. Ki-Gor's hand crept down to the knife at his waist. He would have to strike before the leopard sprang. A child so small would be killed by one blow of those massive fore-paws.

The leopard was upwind of Ki-Gor and completely oblivious of his presence—oblivious of everything except its prey. Nearer and nearer to the broken tree the leopard crawled, the black tip of its tail twitching restlessly. Six feet away from Ki-Gor, it crouched, cruel claws digging into the earth.

Ki-Gor's knife was out now, and his muscles ready. The leopard's hind-quarters raised slightly and swayed. Ki-Gor sprang.

He had timed it perfectly. The leopard itself had been on the split-second verge of leaping. Ki-Gor's spring caught it completely unawares. There was a confused scream from the beast and it scrambled sidewise in confusion. But quick as it was, Ki-Gor was quicker.

He was on the creature's writhing back, his left hand pinning the flat evil head to the ground, his right hand descending with tremendous force driving the knife-blade deep between the leopard's shoulder blades. There was a gurgling screech, and the leopard's hind claws ripped great gashes in the ground. Ki-Gor drove the blade home, and the brute suddenly went limp under him.

THE JUNGLE man parted the bushes and looked up at the pickaninny. The child was silent for a change, and gazed at him stiff with horror. Ki-Gor reached down and dragged the leopard into full view.

"He would have eaten thee up, O little one," Ki-Gor said calmly. "But I killed him, because I am thy friend."

The child apparently was unable to utter a word.

"Now wilt thou let me take thee home to thy mother?" Ki-Gor said, sheathing his bloody knife and walking coolly to the base of the broken tree. Helpless tears rolled down the child's ravaged face, but he made no sound. Fatalistically, he climbed down the stump a few feet and put his arms out to Ki-Gor.

The jungle man stepped out onto the path with the pickaninny huddled in his arms and called to Helene. Then he bent his head down.

"Which direction lies thy home, O little one?" he asked.

The child looked up at him wonderingly for a moment, then pointed a finger up the trail in the direction from which Ki-Gor and Helene had originally come.

"That way," whispered the child. "But are you truly going to take me home?"

"Yes, we will take you home," Ki-Gor answered patiently.

"Will you not eat me, then?"

"Of course not," said Ki-Gor with a smile. "Why shouldst thou ever think we would eat thee?"

"My mother told me," the child said, gaining courage, "always to run from the White Ones. They will drive a stick through me and roast me over the fire."

"That is nonsense, little one," Ki-Gor said. "Thy mother has never seen us before. How can she know whether we would eat thee?"

"Aye, but she *has* seen you," the child insisted. "She has seen you when you came in the night and took away my sister."

"Hush, little one," said Ki-Gor, "we did not take away thy sister."

"What a terrible story to tell a child!" Helene said in English.

LESS THAN a mile along the trail, they came upon the village. It was a scattered group of miserable huts clustered under the trees not far from the river. Such a village was indicative of one of those feeble, undernourished, debased tribes of forest blacks which were so common in the Congo lowlands, but were rather unusual in the Uganda heights.

The stupefying heat of early afternoon held the village now in its heavy grip. No person or thing stirred among the shapeless huts. A small mangy dog lay asleep in the shade of the nearest dwelling, and somewhere a woman was crooning sadly and tunelessly.

Ki-Gor set the pickaninny down on the ground. The child stood trembling for a moment, and clung to Ki-Gor's hand.

"Fare thee well, little one," Ki-Gor said. "Go straight to thy mother and don't go wandering off alone again."

The little dog woke up with a start and began barking furiously. The crooning stopped and a young woman appeared at the doorway of the nearest hut. Her eyes rolled as she saw the child standing between Helene and Ki-Gor. Then she screamed at the top of her lungs.

"The White Ones!" the woman shrieked. *"The White Ones!* They have my child!"

And still shrieking, she leaped forward. With lightning speed she scooped up the child. Then her right hand shot out and clawed viciously at Helene. Caught completely by surprise, Helene just did manage to dodge out of the woman's reach. Ki-Gor sprang forward quickly between Helene and the woman, but wisely did not touch her.

For by now, her shrieks were answered all over the village, and women poured out of the huts like black ants. In less than a minute, Helene and Ki-Gor were ringed around by scores of spindle-legged black women, their faces distorted with savage rage and all screeching venomously.

"The accursed White Ones!"

"In broad daylight!"

"Kill them!"

"Give us back our children, Accursed Ones!"

"Give me back my husband!"

"Give me back my sister."

Ki-Gor had not the faintest idea of what the women were raving about, but he did know that this riot scene would quickly grow dangerous if something were not immediately done about it. He stepped forward a pace and threw his arms up over his head.

"Silence!" he roared.

A startled, grudging hush followed the command. Ki-Gor fixed a stern eye on the mother of the child.

"There is some mistake here," he said emphatically. "It seems you have suffered from the deeds of some white men. We do not know who they are, nor have we any connection with them. This is the first time we have ever come to your village—or even to this region. Far from harming any of you, we have saved this child from leopards and brought him safely home. I tell you this not to gain your thanks, but just to show you that we are not your enemies. Stand back now, and let us depart in peace!"

He swept the ring of black faces with a wary glance. The women murmured in indecision, and Ki-Gor felt that he might have made his point. He was not afraid of them, but at the same time he did not want to hurt them. Weak, depraved creatures that they were, they had evidently suffered from the depredations of some villainous white men and Ki-Gor felt sorry for them and was ready to stretch his patience to the limit. Who those white men could be, Ki-Gor did not know. Unless, the thought suddenly occurred to him, it was that strange Italian who had tried to abduct Helene up the river. Helene had observed two other white men in the safari.

Suddenly an old crone pushed herself forward through the crowd of women. Her skinny hands clawed the air vindictively, and her voice was raised in a shrill cackle.

"O women of the Balelu!" she stormed. "Are you going to believe the lying words of this monster? Look at him! The very color of his skin—abnormal, hideous white—marks him as our deadly enemy! You have caught him in brood daylight—are you going to allow the Accursed Ones to get so bold as to come into our village in broad daylight and try to carry off a little child?"

CHAPTER III

KI-GOR TENSED HIMSELF FOR the reaction of the rest of the women to the crone's words. However, it was slow to come. Only a few of them mumbled agreement with the old hag. Ki-Gor seized upon their indecision.

"As I said, O women of the Balelu," he declared, "I do not know who these white-skinned persons are that you call the Accursed Ones. But do not make the mistake of thinking we belong to them because our skin is white." Ki-Gor paused and smiled slightly. "You cannot tell the inside of a coconut from its husk."

Again the women murmured, and one or two of them giggled. Ki-Gor felt that he had made his point. But the old woman started yammering again, and in the midst of it there came a yell from the jungle. Ki-Gor looked back quickly, and saw a dozen or so men of the tribe running down the trail into the village.

Instantly the uproar began all over again. Ki-Gor strode out to meet the newcomers, hands upraised in a gesture of peace. But the men of the Balelu seemed to be thrown into the same desperate rage at the sight of the two whites as their women had been before them.

"Death to the Accursed Ones!" yelled the foremost of the men, and flung his spear straight at Ki-Gor. The jungle man skipped lightly to one side and plucked the flying weapon out of the air.

"Stand back!" Ki-Gor shouted wrathfully. "We are not the Accursed Ones! We are peaceable strangers!"

To emphasize his point, Ki-Gor brought up one knee and broke the spear across it. The men hesitated a moment in awe, but the old woman kept on shrieking, and incited by her voice the men started yelling again. Two more spears came flying at Ki-Gor. He caught the first and dodged the second. With hysterical cries, three Balelu men rushed straight at Ki-Gor.

Not for a moment did the jungle man doubt his ability to cope successfully with the situation. Rather was he exasperated at the misdirected animosity of these poor puny blacks. He had no desire to kill or injure any of them—he simply wanted to leave the village without further trouble.

But the skinny blacks had gone completely berserk, and Ki-Gor knew he had to act swiftly. As the three who were charging him came within a spear's length, he battered down all three assegais with the haft of the one he had caught. Then, quick as a cobra, he lunged forward, seized the nearest man around the waist. He lifted the frail body up in the air and flung him straight at the rest of the Balelu men behind him.

The hapless black crashed into the little knot of advancing men, and knocked half of them down. The rest halted uncertainly.

"Fools!" Ki-Gor roared. "Leave us alone! We do not wish to hurt you! I could kill the lot of you in the twinkling of an eye! But you see! I do not deign even to use weapons on you!"

The man he had thrown through the air was picking himself up groggily as were the others whom he had knocked down.

"Learn your lesson, O Men of the Balelu!" Ki-Gor cried. "Leave us alone, and I will not harm you! Attack us, and I will go through you like a whirlwind!"

The men of the Balelu lowered their spears and looked at each other dazedly.

"We are going away now," Ki-Gor declared, quick to follow his advantage. "Let no one make a hostile move, or I will wreak a terrible vengeance!"

A glance behind him showed Ki-Gor that the women of the tribe were now falling back and opening a way between them through the village. The Balelu men, shuffling uncertainly, were still blocking off the trail by which he and Helene had come. Ki-Gor took the easier route. He murmured to Helene and she walked briskly through the lane of women. Ki-Gor bent a last stern glance at the men, then turned his back on them and followed Helene through the village.

In a few seconds they were on a broad path that led to the river. When they reached the river bank, three hundred or so yards away, Ki-Gor looked back. The Balelu were gathered in a silent knot back in the village staring after them.

"WELL!" SAID Helene with a sigh of relief. "That was a nasty little situation! I'm glad we got out of it without any more trouble. I felt sorry for those poor creatures."

"So did I," said Ki-Gor studying the trail.

"Who do you suppose the Accursed Ones are?" Helene said.

"I don't know," Ki-Gor said. "There are always bad white men to prey on weak ignorant tribes like the Balelu."

"Wait a minute!" Helene exclaimed. "It's probably that Sicilian and his crew. He was as evil-looking a white man as I expect to meet! He and the others would be capable of any kind of villainy, I should think!"

"Yes," Ki-Gor replied with a frown, "except that the way those Balelu acted—I have a feeling that the Accursed Ones have been in this region for some time. That Sicilian's safari up the river looked like complete strangers. His askaris were Somalis. I think they were on their way in here for the first time. Besides, they had guns, and the Balelu acted like people who had never heard of guns."

"Why, yes," Helene said slowly, "they did, at that. Then, who are the Accursed Ones?"

"I don't know," said Ki-Gor. "But we are going to keep our eyes open for strange white men until we leave this country far behind."

The choice of routes open to Ki-Gor now was a poor one. The trail they were on bent leftwards and followed the river downstream. There was no trail to the right going upstream, which was the direction Ki-Gor would have preferred to take. Furthermore, the river bank was rocky and difficult to traverse.

"The only thing to do," Ki-Gor told Helene, "is to follow the trail downstream for a while so that we leave the Balelu village behind. After that we'll decide what to do next."

The region presented peculiarly broken country. A succession of hills not tall enough to be dignified by the title of mountains rose from the treeless veldt. And in among the hills were thickly wooded kloofs that reminded Ki-Gor of similar country far to the south in the Transvaal. The river beside the jungle couple showed as many varied aspects as the country it traveled through. Farther upstream it wound sluggishly through a swamp that was typical on a small scale of the lower reaches of the Congo. But here by the Balelu village, it coursed rapidly between rugged rocky banks as it dropped off the plateau toward lower ground to the south.

Travel along its boulder-strewn banks would have been slow and tedious had there not been the trail which Ki-Gor and Helene now pursued downstream. It was narrow, this trail, hardly wide enough for two people to walk abreast in as it twisted between high ledges and impassable thickets. But it was well-worn, and Ki-Gor suspected that it was probably centuries old, like many another travel-trail in Africa. For the half hour or so that the jungle couple followed it, the trail never lost sight of the river. Ki-Gor stopped several times and studied the stream and the opposite bank.

The other side of the river was just as thickly wooded and on rather higher ground which sloped upward to a long ridge.

"I wonder whether we should try and get over to the other side," Ki-Gor reflected during one of the halts. "The Italian and his safari are on that side, and I would like to get a good look at them. We could keep on upstream then to the swamp and see if we can't find our faint-hearted friend, Marmo."

"How would you get across?" Helene asked. "Are you thinking of swimming?"

"The current is quite swift," Ki-Gor remarked, staring at the swirling eddies.

"It is," Helene agreed, "but if we wanted to chance it, I think we could make it across."

"It would be too dangerous," Ki-Gor said. "I think we'll go along a little further. If we can find some tall trees with vines we might be able to swing across."

"I can swim anything you can, you know," Helene reminded her husband.

"I know you can," Ki-Gor smiled. "But since you left the other world to come and live with me, I've led you into too much danger. Not that I meant to—but things worked out that way."

"Don't ever worry about that," Helene said loyally. "When I think of the idle, useless life I used to lead, I feel a little ashamed. It was such a boring life, too. Why, I used to have to manufacture thrills for myself. Like that solo plane flight from Dakar across Africa. And if I hadn't cracked up in the middle of the jungle, and you hadn't come along and saved me—well, I suppose I'd still be manufacturing thrills, instead of trying to avoid them. Right now, Mr. Ki-Gor, it's thrill enough just being your wife."

Ki-Gor grinned down at her and took her hand and swung it happily—his characteristic expression of purest happiness.

"Come along then," he commanded. "We'll stay on this side a little longer, and see if there isn't some easier way of crossing this river besides swimming it."

TEN MINUTES later, Ki-Gor halted abruptly and stared. Helene followed his gaze, and blinked in astonishment.

"Why the river—" she exclaimed, "it's—it's disappearing!"

The river did exactly that. A rocky shoulder of the river jutted out at right angles from it and formed a broad barrier right across the path of the river. But the river, instead of being deflected by this barrier, went straight ahead into a cavernous hole in the high shoulder. It was an unusual phenomenon, but by no means an impossible one. Centuries past, perhaps, an earthquake had set a large landslide in motion, and then during the course of more centuries, the river had bored a subterranean passage for itself through the soft sandstone.

What was even more remarkable, however, was the fact that the well-worn trail along the river followed the river straight into the wide cave mouth. A lesser trail branched off to the left away from the river and up over the barrier-hill. But to Ki-Gor's keen eyes the path that kept on into the cave was the main one.

Ki-Gor's curiosity was aroused. What sort of an underground water-course was this? How far did it go, and above all why should a trail go right along into the natural tunnel? Did it mean that the underground channel was of brief duration? Or was it an indication that there was a considerable cave beyond which might be inhabited?

Ki-Gor strolled forward to the cave mouth. On an impulse, he dropped to one knee and scrutinized the floor of the trail. There was not much to learn from the solid rock. He bent over and sniffed. His sensitive nostrils caught a faint whiff of Bantu—a Bantu odor which was somehow *not* a Bantu odor. It was an extraordinary and puzzling fact, this last. Again and again, Ki-Gor sniffed the trail. It was a human scent, left by bare feet. It was not the odor of a white man, at least none that Ki-Gor had ever yet smelled. Yet it was not quite right to have been left by a Bantu-speaking Negro. Possibly, Ki-Gor reflected, the spoor might have been left by some of the mixed tribes to the north, Masai, or Gallas, or Somalis. But what would any of them be doing in this Uganda fastness?

Added to the difficulty of identifying the strange spoor was the fact that it was an extremely cold trail. In the course of time, three people, at least, had been by there. But how many more there might have been, Ki-Gor was unable to tell.

Somewhere in the distance there was a sustained and muffled roaring as if there were a falls or a rapids in the subterranean river. The wind whistled down the kloof and around the mouth of the cave.

Ki-Gor took a few steps inside and peered inwards for several minutes trying to get his eyes accustomed to the darkness. However, he could not see much except that the river took a sharp bend to the right shortly after it entered the hill.

A voice spoke at Ki-Gor's ear, and he jumped a little, not realizing that Helene had followed him.

"I don't think I like this place," Helene was saying. "It sort of gives me the creeps."

It gave Ki-Gor the creeps a little, too, but he did not like to admit it.

"Why should it give you the creeps?" he asked quickly. "It's a very good cave. See—the roof goes high up out of my reach. It's dry, and it's well venti—venti—"

"You mean ventilated?" said Helene.

"Ventilated, yes," said Ki-Gor. "See how the wind blows through here? This would be a good cave to live in. You could put some big thorn bomas at each end to keep the wild animals out."

"Maybe some of them are already in here," Helene suggested.

"Maybe," Ki-Gor conceded. "But there are humans in here, too. Or they passed through, along thc trail. Let's go in a little way and see how big this cave is."

"Oh, let's not, Ki-Gor!" Helene said. "It's too spooky. And besides, what will we gain by it?"

"Nothing, I suppose," Ki-Gor replied. "I'm just curious, that's all."

HE TILTED his head back and gazed at the high ceiling of the cave. Once upon a time the river bed had been much higher. Swirling, pounding freshets had poured in there, making a great cauldron that had sculptured the soft rock in graceful curves. Ki-Gor murmured admiringly and looked downstream at the point where the river bent to the right and the cave bent with it.

"It's nice," Ki-Gor commented, and his voice rang hollowly over the soft swishing of the water. Suddenly a crackling evil chuckle floated toward them from the river. Helene jumped.

"What—what was that?" she gasped.

Ki-Gor pointed to the river. Helene peered through the dim light at the swirling water.

"No—over there," Ki-Gor said, indicating a semi-circle as wide as a punchbowl hollowed out of the rock bank. The chuckle sounded again, and Helene felt pretty sheepish. It was nothing but three little whirlpools gurgling in the hollowed-out place.

"You see?" said Ki-Gor. "Things that frighten you in the dark are so often nothing at all. Just little eddies in a river."

He moved ahead farther into the cave, and Helene was too humiliated to protest.

Several times, as he pursued his leisurely course, Ki-Gor bent and sniffed the trail again. But the faint spoor was the same as that outside the cave mouth, and told him no more than it had out there. Apprehensive in spite of herself, Helene stayed dose behind him. They were rounding the bend in the cave and there was less and less light to see by. There was, however, just enough illumination to make out the succession of high vaulted chambers which the river had hewn out of the rock. By now, too, the water course itself was lower, having cut a channel that was, in spots, as much as fifteen feet lower than the floor level of the chambers.

Ki-Gor was going very slowly and cautiously now, stopping frequently while he peered ahead, trying to pierce the dense darkness with his remarkable eyes. On many an occasion in the past, Ki-Gor had demonstrated to Helene his extraordinary faculty of seeing in the dark. His night vision was practically as good as a cat's. No person, human or brute, can see where there is complete absence of light. Certain nocturnal animals are able to expend the pupils of their eyes so that they utilize every tiny beam of light. These cats, or bats, or owls, are thus said to be able "to see in the dark."

Ki-Gor had developed this power to an amazing degree and he proceeded to make use of it now. Being careful not to look backwards toward the daylight that was reflected from the mouth of the cave around the bend, he moved slowly forward, examining the gloom of the cave. The size of the place amazed him. Across the river on the right bank, he could see the glistening ceiling curve downward to the floor, leaving only a narrow shelf on that bank. But on the left side of the river—the side he and Helene were on—the side wall was lost far away in the shadows. The smooth floor stretched away out of sight, broken here and there by smooth humps and loose boulders. Now and then the ceiling dipped only to slant upwards again, giving an extraordinary vaulted effect. Except for the swishing, gurgling song of the river, and the distant, muffled sound of falling water, the great cave was ominously silent. Not so much so a bat twittered in that somber nether-world.

AS KI-GOR advanced farther and farther, the noise of the falls grew perceptibly louder. The jungle man guessed that the river must drop over a precipice soon after it left the cave at the other end. The falls could not be within the cave, or else the noise would be deafening.

By now, too, the faint illumination reflected from the entrance of the cave had almost completely gone. Nothing but a vast blackness stretched before Ki-Gor's questing eyes. He stopped abruptly, and Helene walked blindly into him.

"Oh!" she gasped. "I didn't see you, Ki-Gor! I can't see anything! Oh Ki-Gor! Let's go back! I don't like this!"

Ki-Gor was just about to agree, when he saw a light.

What sort of a light it was, or where it came from, Ki-Gor had no idea. It just seemed to materialize from nowhere. One minute there was nothing, the next minute there was this curious indefinite glow, faintly greenish in color. Ki-Gor stared so long and hard that the indistinct patch of light began to waver before his eyes. He took several strides forward. It seemed to him that the light grew a little brighter. Although it was so dim and so diffused that it was hard to tell how far away it was.

Ki-Gor went ahead a dozen paces, and then another dozen, then stopped in amazement. He was practically standing over the patch of light. He beat over and saw the source of the light—a small man-made lantern.

A moment's examination showed that the lantern consisted simply of a candle set in a cylinder made of horn set under a conical top made of heavy hard wood. The candle-wick was tiny, giving a tiny flame, and the horn case was so thick as to be only slightly translucent. The result was a dim diffused glow which would be useless anywhere but in the stygian darkness of that cave.

Ki-Gor straightened up wondering. The lantern was concrete evidence that the cave was inhabited by human beings. But what kind of human beings, Ki-Gor reflected, would construct such a curiously inefficient lantern as this one sitting in the middle of the trail?

It suddenly occurred to the jungle man that it was not prudent, to say the least, to linger very long beside the lantern. Whoever owned it might he nearby, and whoever owned it *might* be friendly—or might not! Ki-Gor moved warily away from the lantern.

All of a sudden an ear-splitting scream rang through the cave. It was a split-second before Ki-Gor realized that it was Helene.

"*Ki-Gor!*" she screamed again, in a voice frantic with horror and revulsion. "Help me! Ooogh!"

He sprang toward her. At the same moment, something slithered around his right leg, just below the knee. Quick as a cobra it coiled around his calf in lightning spirals. A heavy weight hit his shin with sickening force. Ki-Gor staggered off balance and shook the leg violently. But the coils tightened and something dragged heavily on the leg. Another heavy weight now crashed into his chest. Gasping for breath, Ki-Gor flung himself to the ground.

But as he went down, something seemed to explode with a yellow flash inside his head, and then he knew no more.

CHAPTER IV

KI-GOR HEARD SOMEONE GROANING in the distance. The groaning came nearer. Gradually the realization dawned on Ki-Gor that it was he himself who was groaning. His head ached fearfully. He tried to reach a hand up to touch it. Then he discovered that he was lying on the ground and that his arms were pinned to his sides from shoulder to wrist by yards and yards of rope coiled tightly about his torso. Evidently he had been knocked unconscious by some kind of missile, and then promptly had been trussed up in this efficient manner.

Although he had not opened his eyes, he was aware that a light of some kind was shining on his face. A desultory murmur of soft voices sounded close by. Probably his mysterious captors were sitting around him waiting for him to return to consciousness. Ki-Gor decided to keep his eyes closed a little longer and listen to those soft voices. Already he had caught a few words here and there. The language of his captors was a Bantu dialect very similar to Buganda.

Suddenly, Ki-Gor thought of Helene, and his heart sank. What had happened to her? The last thing he remembered before he was knocked out was her appalling scream. Had she been hit on the head, too? The soft voices murmured on around Ki-Gor, while his thoughts raced through his aching head.

Then another voice broke in, and a thrill of joy shot through Ki-Gor. The voice was Helene's.

She was speaking slowly and laboredly in Swahili. Why, Ki-Gor did not at first understand, because Helene had become quite fluent in Swahili.

"You are bad men," she was saying, "to attack my husband and tie him up. He is a great lord, a *bwana mkubwa.* Many warriors serve him, and they will come and kill you all."

A chorus of soft snickers greeted Helene's pronouncement. Then one of the soft voices replied in Swahili.

"Where are those warriors now, if he is a *bwana mkubwa?* How come it that a *bwana mkubwa* goes traveling abroad to a strange country attended only by a woman?"

There was a silence. Helene evidently could think of no adequate answer to the question. Her questioner finally snickered and began talking to his fellows in the Buganda dialect. Then Ki-Gor understood that Helene had pretended ignorance of Buganda, and spoke halting Swahili, so that the strangers would talk freely amongst themselves, and possibly reveal their intentions.

"A clumsy deceiver, this woman," said one of the voices, "but handsome in a peculiar way."

"How handsome?" another voice said scornfully. "She is the right color, but that is about all. Nothing but skin and bone—ugly deep-set eyes—and very peculiar hair. Is that real hair?"

"It's fastened to her head," the first voice said. "I pulled it to make sure—hers and the man's, too. I admit it's funny hair—long, and perfectly straight, and such an odd color."

"The man is certainly an ugly brute," a new voice commented. "Did you ever see such a nose in your life? It makes you think of an eagle."

"And the size of him, too! I hope you used plenty of rope."

"An elephant could not get free of the rope we put on him. Have a look at him—he's stopped groaning."

"He's about to wake up, I think. He must have a skull like a rhino to survive that crack on the head."

"Maybe he didn't."

"He's all right"—Ki-Gor sensed the light being held over his face—"There's no bleeding at the mouth or ears."

It was time, Ki-Gor decided, to open his eyes. He uttered one last groan and fluttered his eyelids.

"Ah!" said one of the voices. "He's awake!"

Ki-Gor opened his eyes a tiny crack and found himself looking straight into the lantern. He turned his head aside, still keeping his eyes half-shut. Three faces were bent over him, staring down. They were typical Negro faces, with full pouting lips, flaring nostrils, short kinky hair growing in little tufts on long narrow skulls. But there was something out of place.

For a moment, Ki-Gor thought his eyes were playing tricks on him. Then he thought it might be the dim lantern. He closed his eyes and opened them again suddenly. The faces were still there and there was still something very wrong about those faces. The back of Ki-Gor's neck prickled.

Those Negroes had white skins!

THE SHOCK of this discovery did not prevent Ki-Gor's mind from working like lightning. In a flash it came to him why the poor miserable Balelu had flung themselves so desperately at him and Helene. He and Helene had white skins, and undoubtedly these white-skinned Negroes had been terrorizing the Balelu, abducting their children and otherwise earning the name of "Accursed Ones."

While his thoughts were racing along these lines, Ki-Gor calmly studied the faces that were leering down at him. In truth, they were strangely repulsive. Not only were their skins ashen-white, but so were the woolly tufts on their heads. And the pupils of their eyes were completely colorless, while the whites of their eyes were a hideous pink. Never in his life had Ki-Gor seen such creatures.

Vicious and repellent were those faces that stared down at him, but Ki-Gor had to admit that they were proud and resolute. And considering that these extraordinary cave-dwellers had him completely in their power, he knew that he would have to summon up all his craftiness if he was to get himself and his lovely wife out of this ugly situation.

"Peace to you, O White Ones," he said calmly. "This is surely a rough greeting to extend to ones of your own color who come to pay you a friendly visit."

The White Ones exchanged startled glances. Ki-Gor was fluent in Buganda, and besides he had imitated their inflection and intonation perfectly.

"Who are you that speaks with a smooth tongue?" one of them asked bluntly.

"I am Ki-Gor," the jungle man said cheerfully, "and you?"

"I am Naga," said the man, "Chief of the Tenzori. You say you come on a friendly visit? Your woman tells a different story. She said you are a great bwana with many warriors serving you."

"That is true," Ki-Gor said evenly.

"You are on a friendly visit," Naga pursued, "yet you creep silently into our cave, and when we capture you, you tell us lies about a host of warriors."

"Listen, O Naga," Ki-Gor said good-humoredly. "I left my warriors at some distance from your cave. That was the first indication of my friendliness. I did not creep into your cave, as you assert. I came in boldly and called out several times. Is it my fault that none of you heard me? Finally, I stood over the lantern fearlessly and showed myself to any who might see. None of my actions have been unfriendly."

The three White Ones looked at each other again.

"He might have called out," one of them admitted. "We were at the Waterfall and thus did not hear him."

But the one called Naga did not look convinced. He turned to Ki-Gor again, his face stern.

"Where do you come from?" he demanded.

"From a far land," Ki-Gor replied promptly. "But news of the white-skinned Tenzori reached us even there. As you scc, my woman and I also have white skins. We determined to come and see you and exchange friendly words."

"You have white skins," Naga said coldly, "but your features are not as ours. Do you live in a cave?"

"Listen, O Naga," Ki-Gor said. "Gladly will I answer all your questions. But first be good enough to loosen these ropes. They are squeezing the breath out of me. If you are afraid of me"—Ki-Gor smiled ironically—"you may bind my wrists and ankles. But, at least, give me a chance to breathe."

There was a long pause, while Naga bent a calculating look at Ki-Gor. Finally he nodded.

"Lift him to a sitting position," he commanded, and several hands hoisted the helpless jungle man upright. Ki-Gor saw now that there were many of the dim lanterns, and he counted at least a dozen chalk-white Tenzori moving silently among them. Twenty feet away sat Helene. She was unbound except for a coil of rope around her ankles. Ki-Gor noticed that the end of the coil was tied around a good-sized stone. It came to him now how the Tenzori had captured him and Helene so easily. Their ropes were crude lassoes, except that instead of loops on the end they had stone weights. The ropes were swung in a wide arc. When they touched their victims, the stone weights caused them to coil around the legs, arms, or even torsos which might be touched.

"NOW," SAID Naga, and Ki-Gor saw that the Tenzori chief had a formidable looking weapon in his hand. It was a long, slender, curved knife, and it looked extremely sharp.

"This will not hurt you," Naga said, and rested the edge of the knife on Ki-Gor's leg just above the knee. Then Naga drew the blade lightly and swiftly across the leg. Ki-Gor scarcely felt it. And yet a broad dark line suddenly appeared on his thigh as the blood welled out of a cut four inches long.

A wolfish grin spread over Naga's ghastly face. "Did you hear," he said softly, "about our Tenzori knives."

"No," Ki-Gor admitted, "but I see they are very good knives."

"Very good," said Naga. He got up and came around and stood behind Ki-Gor. The jungle man felt something cold just barely touching his throat.

"The rope," Naga said, "is being taken off as you requested. You will remain very still until I give you the word."

Ki-Gor did not move so much as a muscle, while the ropes were unwound. Then he felt his wrists seized and placed together behind his back. Automatically, Ki-Gor clenched his fists and swelled the cords of his wrists. A voice complained behind him.

"Come," said Naga, "relax."

The blade pressed ever so slightly at Ki-Gor's throat and he relaxed his wrists. But when the wrists were finally tied up, he was interested in feeling how loose the bonds were. Evidently, the Tenzori were extremely weak-muscled.

"Get up," Naga commanded, "we will go to a more comfortable place to continue our conversation."

A strange procession wound along the path by the river now. A single silent Tenzori led the way with a dim lantern, stepping leisurely and sure-footedly. Behind him came Helene, stumbling blindly in spite of the lantern in front of her. Three more of the strange white Negroes separated her from Ki-Gor, with Naga close behind him. The rest of the Tenzori followed the chief.

Ki-Gor wondered why Helene stumbled so much. The trail was smooth and the lanterns, though dim, shed enough light for him to see his way perfectly. Then he realized that Helene had not developed his capacity for "seeing in the dark." But the Tenzori certainly had. They moved as surely as if they were walking in broad daylight. It gave Ki-Gor an idea. He began to stumble deliberately.

"What is the matter?" said Naga with a soft chuckle.

"Your lanterns are so dim," Ki-Gor complained. "I can't see my way. How is it that you move so easily?"

"There is plenty of light for us," Naga boasted. "In fact, we could go just as easily without the lanterns. We Tenzori have remarkable eyes. Or we seem to have, compared to those people who come to our cave from the outside. The Balelu, for instance."

"The Balelu?" said Ki-Gor innocently. "Do they come in here?"

"Oh yes," Naga said. "But they do not come like honored guests as you do. They come as hostages."

Ki-Gor wondered how hostages were treated, if honored guests walked with bound wrists.

He was soon to find out.

After a little more than five minutes of walking, the procession left the river-trail and turned off to the left between two enormous boulders. These great monoliths, so huge that their tops were lost in the obscurity of the great cave, appeared to be a sort of gateway to an inner cave—a cave within a cave.

This was an immense chamber dotted with the lanterns of the Tenzori. A score or more ghostly white forms came running toward the newcomers, and stood around exclaiming as Naga informed them about what had happened. Naga's words were innocent enough—"We have guests, O Tenzori, and as you see, they have white skins like us"—but Ki-Gor caught a hidden undercurrent that did not make him feel any easier in his mind.

The jungle man was mildly surprised, however, when the Tenzori chief ordered his wrists unbound, and bade him be seated on a large flat rock covered with skins. He was even more surprised when Helene was permitted to sit beside him. Then Naga, himself, sat down facing them about ten feet away, flanked on each side by three Tenzori tribesmen with bared knives.

"We will eat presently," said Naga, "but now we will talk. You will tell me about your country."

HE TURNED to a waiting tribesman and issued orders. Helene took the opportunity to speak to Ki-Gor for the first time since they were captured.

"What's going to happen to us?" she murmured hurriedly in English. "I've never been so scared in my life!"

"Don't worry," Ki-Gor muttered. "We'll get out of this somehow. I have never seen white Bantu before—"

"I have heard of them," Helene broke in. "They are called Albinos. That's the English word for them."

"Albinos?" said Ki-Gor puzzled.

"Yes, they are freaks of nature. They're found among men and animals, and even plants. You've probably seen animals that are normally dark colored that are pure white instead."

"Yes," said Ki-Gor slowly, "I saw a white springbok, once—and a wild dog, too, that was white with pink eyes."

"Albinos," said Helene. "These men have pink eyes, you notice? They're supposed not to be able to stand very strong light."

"That's why their lanterns are so dim," Ki-Gor agreed. "So, if we can just get out of this cave, we don't have to worry about them."

"Except at night," Helene pointed out.

"Oh, yes," said Ki-Gor. "That's when they go out, of course. No wonder the Balelu were surprised to see white-skinned people out in the sunlight."

At this point, the Tenzori chief turned his face toward them expectantly, and Ki-Gor broke off. There was a moment's silence, which was accentuated rather than broken by the sustained muffled roar of the distant waterfall. The noise of those falls had grown progressively louder the deeper the cave had been penetrated until by now Ki-Gor was sure that they could not be far away.

"Now," said Naga, "tell me about your country."

"Willingly," Ki-Gor answered promptly. "What would you like to know?"

"Everything."

"Very well, then," said Ki-Gor. "Would you like to know how far away from here it is?"

"Yes."

"It is farther than a man may travel on foot during two moons," Ki-Gor stated roundly.

Naga made no comment, but disbelief was written all over his ghostly face.

"You are wondering," Ki-Gor went on, "how we could have heard of the Tenzori at such a distance. You are also wondering, no doubt, *what* we heard about the Tenzori."

"Yes—I am," Naga said after a pause. "What did you hear?"

"We heard," said Ki-Gor, "that you go out at night to the village of the Balelu and carry off their children as hostages. Is that true?"

"Yes, that is true," said the albino chief. "But how could you have heard that?"

Naga had forgotten that he himself had told Ki-Gor that not long before.

"We heard it," said Ki-Gor. "But we heard no reason for it. Why do you keep Balelu children as hostages?"

"We get almost all our food from the Balelu," Naga replied. "Sometimes they object to our taking it. At those times it is well to have hostages."

"Ah!" cried Ki-Gor. "Then it is true that you sometimes sacrifice your hostages to a powerful god?"

This was nothing but a very wild guess, but evidently it hit close to the mark. Naga looked quite startled. Then he smiled.

"This very evening," he said, "you will see a sacrifice to the God of the Waterfall."

"It is good," said Ki-Gor evenly. "It is true, of course, isn't it, that the Tenzori are not able to stand strong light in their eyes?"

"Yes," Naga admitted, "but we make up for it. We can see in the dark."

Ki-Gor smiled inwardly. What had started out to be a questioning of him by Naga, had now been completely reversed. He was asking the questions. He pressed home his advantage and bit by bit added to his store of information concerning this strange tribe of cave dwellers. Naga, far from objecting to the questions, answered them willingly and seemed to grow more and more affable as time passed.

IT WAS not a pleasant picture, this life of the Tenzori which gradually unfolded itself to Ki-Gor. The albinos depended for their very existence on ruthless extortion of the Balelu and other related forest tribes in the vicinity. Those miserable blacks under the best circumstances barely raised or hunted enough food for their own needs. Yet almost every night they were visited by wraithlike figures who flitted through their dark villages collecting provender for the fifty-odd albinos in the cave, and the fifty-odd hostages who were forced to live with them. Frequently, the Balelu lost their heads and made desperate and futile attempts to resist the never-ceasing encroachments of the Tenzori.

Promptly, then, the albinos sacrificed one of their hostages, and news of the sacrifice was speedily carried to the long-suffering blacks. There was never any wholesale slaughter of hostages. For one thing, the captured blacks served in a dual capacity as slaves as well as hostages. Naga proudly took Ki-Gor and Helene on a tour of inspection back to the bank of the river. There, they saw one group of forlorn blacks laboriously fashioning horn lanterns. Another group was dipping candles. Ki-Gor noted with interest that the fuel used in the cave was some sort of peat, that smoldered and smoked but did not flare up in bright flames to hurt the weak eyes of the albino masters.

Farther downstream, a group of Balelu squatted around another peat fire. They were the cooks for the cave. Naga bade his guests to sit and eat. It was a very poor meal of leathery unleavened dough-cakes baked on hot stones, and tasteless under-cooked fish. These fish, Ki-Gor learned, were the only food which the Tenzori did not rob from the unfortunate Balelu. They were taken from still backwaters of the river—large, carp-like fish that were snow-white and totally blind.

By now, the noise of the waterfall was so loud that conversation could only be maintained by shouting. Evidently, the other end of the cave was not far away. At Ki-Gor's request, Naga escorted them in that direction.

As the first gray signs of reflected daylight began to lighten the blackness of the cave, a wave of inexpressible relief went over Ki-Gor. He had not realized how oppressive the darkness had been. Soon it became light enough to see that both banks of the river were converging, and that the current was growing swifter. And as the light increased, the sound of the falls grew increasingly louder. Ki-Gor was a little surprised that the albino chief kept on going toward the daylight without fear for his eyes. Then it occurred to him that the day was growing old, and that it must be getting on toward sunset.

A few moments later, Ki-Gor saw that that indeed was the case. The river, and the cave with it, took a sharp bend, and less than a hundred feet beyond was the other opening of the cave, a great half-moon lying on its flat side. Apparently, the soft blue twilight beyond was not too strong for Naga's eyes, for he led the way to the very edge of the cave mouth.

Here, the river poured over a precipice fifty feet high and leaped down to a wide deep pool below. A big flat ledge projected out into the daylight beyond the wide arch of the cave mouth. Naga walked out on the rock and stood blinking downwards. He beckoned to Helene and Ki-Gor to join him. Ki-Gor cast a wary glance behind him and then went out and stood beside the albino chief. He filled his lungs with the fresh air and looked longingly at the forested slopes on either side of the great pool below.

Suddenly, Ki-Gor realized that the river furnished the only exit from that end of the cave. No trail led downward beside the falls, nor was one possible there. The river evidently issued forth from a sheer cliff. On both sides of the vaulting waters there was nothing but smooth rock that dropped away almost perpendicularly. This was not an encouraging feature to Ki-Gor. He did not know whether he and Helene would have any difficulty leaving the Tenzori. But if trouble should develop, Ki-Gor would like to have had a choice of two exits from the great cave. As it was, they must go out the way they came in. It was not likely that anyone would survive a trip over those falls.

His eye followed the powerful stream as it curved over the lip of the precipice and thundered down into the pool below, boiling and foaming. Due perhaps to the peculiar acoustic properties of the cave, the very noise of the cascade had a menacing metallic sound. Ki-Gor turned away frowning.

A CLAMMY hand touched his shoulder, and Ki-Gor saw that Naga was cupping a hand around his mouth.

"Come back," the albino shouted over the roar of the falls. "You will see a sacrifice to the God of the Waterfall!"

As Ki-Gor stepped off the ledge back into the cave mouth, he saw a crowd of ghastly-white Tenzori blinking in the soft daylight. He took Helene's hand and marched toward them. They fell away on either side to make room. A sudden booming sound made Ki-Gor whirl around.

Naga was squatting under the rocky arch. Beside him was an enormous drum. The albino chief threw his head back and uttered a thin unearthly wail. The crowd around Ki-Gor and Helene answered with a savage chanted note. Then Naga smote the drum with a thick short stick. Again he wailed, and again the crowd answered. In a few short moments, a measured rhythm was established between the drum and the voices—a rhythm which gradually begun to quicken.

Uneasy alarm began to creep over Ki-Gor as the din mounted high over the roar of the falls. The chalky faces of the albinos twisted into horrible ecstasy and one by one they begun to draw their long curved knives from their belts. Slowly and gently, Ki-Gor pushed through them to the side of the trail, one arm around Helene. Then he turned and planted his back against the rock wall of the cave and watched the proceedings with a grim eye.

The great drum was throbbing faster and faster interspersed with the shrill yelps of the albinos. They were swaying ecstatically now, and here and there arms shot up in the air brandishing knives.

The cave mouth was a deep blue color as the daylight rapidly faded, and only a pale sickly light illuminated the frenzied scene on the river bank. Automatically Ki-Gor selected the nearest three albinos to jump on in case the insensate mob should turn on him and Helene. With one of those knives in each hand, he calculated that he could slash a gory pathway back into the cave. It would be a fearful and desperate task to get himself and Helene through that serried mass of hideous gray-white bodies—.

Suddenly, the drum doubled its tempo, the yells of the Tenzori mounted to a wild shriek. Ki-Gor stepped in front of Helene, muscles and nerves tingling. A second later, he drew a deep breath and relaxed. The albinos nearest him had turned their backs to him and were staring upstream. They were jumping up and down, now, and a forest of white arms writhed upwards. A black form was being passed from hand to hand over the heads of the shrieking albinos.

It was a Balelu stripling. In the dim gray twilight, Ki-Gor could barely make out the youth's face, stiff with horror, and the agonized rolling of his eyes. The miserable creature had lost all hope. With limbs limp, he passed from hand to hand without a struggle of any kind.

Ki-Gor felt a pang of pity for the poor wretch. Yet he knew there was nothing he could do for him. Any attempt to interfere with the sacrifice would not only not succeed, but would probably result in the destruction of himself and Helene.

As it was, Ki-Gor had not the slightest idea of Naga's intentions toward them. They had been left apparently unguarded during this appalling sacrificial ceremony, although scores of tossing white heads still filled the pathway between them and the inner cave. However, as long as the young Balelu was being manhandled up to the ledge over the waterfall, the frenzied albinos seemed to be paying no attention to Ki-Gor and Helene.

The jungle man began to inch his way back along the trail, keeping Helene between himself and the sidewall of the cave. His hands itched to snatch one of those cruel knives from a waving white hand, but cold reasoning advised against attracting attention. Progress was slow, and they had by no means penetrated to the rear of the mob, when a final climactic yell announced the actual moment of the sacrifice.

Ki-Gor looked back over the milling heads. The Balelu boy stood with sagging knees silhouetted against the arched cave mouth. The drum was throbbing unbearably. As Ki-Gor watched with a horrid fascination, another silhouette appeared—a paler one. One hand was upraised and Ki-Gor guessed, although he could not see it, that the hand held a slender curved knife. Closer and closer to the Balelu youth crept the second silhouette. Of a sudden the Balelu youth came to life. His arms writhed unhappily over his head. He turned, took two strides, and flung himself off the ledge into the waterfall.

INSTANTLY BEDLAM broke loose in the cave. The Tenzori shrieked like maniacs, spun around like tops, embraced each other in a frenzy. And as if by a signal, they all began to surge back from the cave mouth. Ki-Gor flattened himself against the rock wall at the side of the trail, and extended a protecting arm across Helene's body beside him.

But frenzied though the Tenzori were, they swarmed past the jungle couple without paying them the slightest attention. It was as if Ki-Gor and Helene had not been there. And sometime during the passage of the howling mob toward the heart of the cave, the drum stopped beating.

It did not take long for the fifty-odd albinos to throng past. Ki-Gor stared after the last of them as they disappeared upstream, and the noise of their triumphant shrieks died away. A sardonic voice sounded close beside him, and Ki-Gor jerked his head around. It was Naga.

"You brought us good luck," the albino chief said.

"How is that?" Ki-Gor said coldly.

"The victim," said Naga with great satisfaction, "jumped off the rock of his own accord. Most of them have to be cut badly with knives, and even then, we have to throw them off ourselves. The God of the Waterfall much prefers to have his victims jump off by themselves.

We should have good luck tonight with those troublesome Balelu. They have been growing restive recently."

"Do you go out soon?" Ki-Gor inquired.

"In a little while," Naga replied. "Just as soon as it is completely dark outside."

"I think we will go with you at the same time," Ki-Gor announced casually.

Naga seemed surprised. "But you have only just come," he protested. "Do you make a journey of two moons distance to visit the Tenzori—and then only stay a few hours?"

Ki-Gor paused. That was a shrewd thrust of Naga's, and it required a smart answer. Unfortunately, Ki-Gor could not tell Naga the truth, which was that he disliked and feared these albinos and wanted to get away from them at the earliest possible moment.

"We have stayed but a short time," he admitted finally, "but we must go soon. We have other business."

"I am sorry," Naga said, and sounded quite hurt. "Our hospitality has not been good, perhaps."

"Oh, no," Ki-Gor replied politely. "You have been very courteous."

"Perhaps it was our food, then?" Naga pursued. "You did not like our food? I admit it is not always good—"

"Of its kind it was good," Ki-Gor replied. He thought he saw a possible opening here. "But, as it happens, we are meat eaters. We have come a long distance on traveler's rations. My wife and I crave meat."

"Ah," said Naga. "We Tenzori like meat too. But those miserable Balelu are such poor hunters that they very seldom have any decent meat for us. But, look you, Ki-Gor! Perhaps they will have some tonight. Stay here tonight—get some sleep—and perhaps in the morning we shall return with better food!"

Ki-Gor shook his head, but before he could speak, Naga was talking again.

"Or better still in the morning you can go hunting yourself and bring us back a fine buck!"

Ki-Gor thought that over. There was a certain advantage in waiting for the return of day to leave the cave. Because if he and Helene left the cave during daylight, the weak-eyed albinos could not possibly pursue. Not that Naga's present attitude suggested that they might pursue—but Ki-Gor was not inclined to trust the Tenzori chief in spite of his ingratiating attitude. But Naga's words were fair enough, and it might be good policy to seem to fall in with his suggestions. There was another possibility, too. If Ki-Gor agreed to spend the night in the cave, there might be an opportunity to slip out after the Tenzori had all left to go marauding. There was a chance, of course, that Naga would leave some guards to prevent Ki-Gor and Helene from doing just that thing. But Ki-Gor was confident that he could handle the guards if there were not too many of them. And if there were too many, then he would wait until the morning to decide what to do.

"Very well, Naga," Ki-Gor finally said. "We will accept your last suggestion. We need sleep, for we have been traveling hard for many days."

Ki-Gor said that deliberately to put Naga off guard—although there was more than a grain of truth in it. Helene had rested, but Ki-Gor had spent the last two days almost continuously on Marmo's back. Ki-Gor was not lying when he said he needed sleep.

LESS THAN an hour later, he and Helene watched the Tenzori file out of the huge inner chamber, watched the row of bobbing ghostly lanterns disappear between the enormous boulders which formed the natural gateway. For a long time, the jungle man sat cross-legged on the flat rock piled high with skins that had been assigned to him and Helene as a pallet for the night. The combination of the inky black cave and the muffled lulling roar of the waterfall acted to make him extremely drowsy. But with a tremendous effort of will, he kept his tired body upright in a sitting position, and waited until he was reasonably sure that Naga had led his ghostly tribesmen out of the cave into the night air.

Finally he got up stiffly and touched Helene on the shoulder. "Come," he said, "let's see if we can find our way out of here."

Slowly and quietly, the jungle couple groped their way in the direction of the boulder gateway. This was not so difficult as it might have been if Ki-Gor had not orientated himself quite accurately before the last of the procession of lanterns had disappeared from view. It was slow going, however, especially as Ki-Gor allowed for the possibility of a trap being laid for him. He carefully felt out every foot of the way before going forward.

Just about the time that Ki-Gor figured they should have traversed the great chamber, he became aware of a faint illumination coming from somewhere. With a little shock, he realized that he could see a vague silhouette—one side of one of the boulder-gates. There was a light beyond those gates.

Silent as a cat, Ki-Gor stood up and stepped around the huge boulder. There were several Tenzori lanterns placed across the trail which led back to the upstream mouth of the cave. Beside them squatted at least six of the albinos with drawn knives.

One of them stood up and came toward Ki-Gor.

"You are not sleeping well, Bwana Ki-Gor?" the man said pleasantly. "Is there something we can do for you?"

Ki-Gor felt suddenly very tired. He might have known that Naga would have left guards to prevent him from leaving.

"Yes," he said stiffly, "I am thirsty and I came to get a drink of water."

"The water is not good to drink," the man said, "it tastes bitter. But we have some hot tea brewed, will you have some of that?"

"Very well," said Ki-Gor. He reflected that he would stay out there a few minutes drinking the tea. It would give him an opportunity to look over the situation. If there were no more than six guards, he might risk combat with them—knives or no knives. Helene was back in the darkness out of sight.

The man brought a gourd-cup full of a warm aromatic liquid. It smelled agreeable and Ki-Gor tasted it cautiously. The flavor was not especially pleasant, being rather acrid. That was not unreasonable, considering that it was probably made from the river water which the man had said was bitter. However, Ki-Gor was really thirsty and he quickly drained the cup. He handed it back to the albino and was about to ask him for a second cup, when he began to feel curiously dizzy. He could not focus his eyes properly on the albino in front of him. The dimly lighted scene commenced to waver and swoop. His legs, of a sudden, felt too weak to support his weight. His head was uncontrollably heavy and fell forward on his chest. Enormous weights pressed his eyelids down.

"The tea!" Ki-Gor murmured wrathfully. "It's drugged—"

KI-GOR WOKE up with the feeling that somebody had been tugging at his shoulder for a long time. With a great effort he opened his eyes and looked up into the leering face of Naga.

"You have had a long sleep," the albino chief chuckled. "It is nearly dawn outside."

"Why did you have me drugged?" Ki-Gor demanded thickly.

"I did not," Naga replied. "You asked for the tea. I did not think to warn you that the tea which we all drink is a mild drug. Living in a cave as we do, we do not go to sleep and awake with the sun. So we all need something to help us sleep."

This Naga! He was always ready with fair words! Ki-Gor wished his own brain could clear itself of the clouds.

"Where is Helene?" he demanded.

"She is still asleep," Naga informed him, and then quickly added, "Are you going hunting? Isn't dawn the best time to hunt?"

"Yes, it is," Ki-Gor said, his mind still foggy.

"If you want, I will show you your woman," Naga said. "But as long as she is still asleep, why disturb her? By the time you come back—if you start now—she will be awake."

Everything the albino chief said seemed so logical and so persuasive, and yet Ki-Gor felt that somehow something was wrong. But his brain was still in too much of a stupor for him to figure out just what was wrong about the situation.

Almost before he realized it, Ki-Gor found himself walking upstream along the well-worn trail. Naga and several albinos with lanterns were trotting along with him. The Tenzori chief was explaining that the only weapons they could provide were the long knives, Ki-Gor's Balelu spear having been lost in the river the day before.

Presently, the blackness ahead lightened to a dingy gray, and the albinos slowed down and stopped.

"In a little while," said Naga, "you will come to the bend in the cave. From there you can see the mouth of the cave. Follow the river trail, turn and go through the Balelu village and thus on out to the veldt where you will find buck in any quantity. You need not worry about the Balelu. They will still be asleep—the lazy dogs!"

A few minutes later, Ki-Gor watched the faint lanterns go bobbing back into the recesses of the cave. His brain was just now beginning to clear, and he was pondering why Naga and his men seemed to be in such a hurry to leave him and go back to the other end of the cave. He turned and walked slowly around the bend. A gust of fresh air blew gratefully in his face, and Ki-Gor quickened his steps.

By now, he was convinced that Naga had put something over on him. Just what it was, he did not know. But he was sure he had made a grave mistake in leaving Helene to the tender mercies of the suave albino chief. The more he thought about it, the more he was convinced that Naga in persuading him to go hunting was merely getting him out of the way for the time being. For what reason, Ki-Gor could not guess.

The jungle man decided to go as far as the mouth of the cave, gulp in some fresh air, gratify his eyes with some daylight, and think over the problem. He was still a hundred feet from the cave mouth, when his nostrils caught a strong odor of wood-ashes and charcoal. He strode forward puzzling over that. He did not recall any campfires near the cave mouth. Fifty paces farther on, he stopped and stared at the floor of the trail.

The remains of a large fire were strewn all over the wide path. A quantity of charred sticks and half-burned faggots were scattered in a broad irregular ring around a large pile of silvery ashes. One tiny wisp of smoke showed how recently that fire had burned itself out. It had not been there the day before when Ki-Gor and Helene had entered the cave.

Who had built that fire? And what was its significance?

Ki-Gor stepped warily around it. It suddenly occurred to him that the Tenzori did not build the fire. Their weak eyes would never have been able to stand the light of the flickering flames.

Then who did? The Balelu?

Like a flash it came to Ki-Gor. Of course, the Balelu had built the fire! They had somehow found out the weakness of the albinos. Bright light! At last the helpless Balelu had discovered a defense against their oppressors. They had come and set a roaring fire going at the cave mouth. That fire had blocked the Tenzori into their cave as effectually as if it had been a huge rock. And there was nothing to prevent the Balelu from doing that every night, until the malignant albinos were starved into a desperate and hopeless sortie.

No wonder Naga had wanted Ki-Gor to go hunting!

THEN ANOTHER thought struck Ki-Gor. He walked past the dead embers toward the arched cave mouth. His nostrils tickled with a faint smell of Bantu borne downwind to him. He nodded his head with a sardonic smile. Could it be that there were already some Balelu lying in wait outside the cave?

The only way to find out without exposing himself to a possible ambush was to take to the river, which Ki-Gor did. The current even there was too strong to swim against, so the jungle man pulled himself slowly and carefully upstream by the rocky bank.

Even before he reached the actual mouth of the cave by this means, he saw the Balelu. There were more then twenty of them, grimly lying in wait. Ki-Gor knew then that Naga had not intended that he should ever return.

Carefully, the jungle man retreated downstream the same way he had come up. At a safe distance within the cave, he pulled himself out of the river and set off down the trail. But he had taken only a few steps when he thought of something. It would not be unlikely that the albinos would have set watchers along the trail, just in case he should escape the vengeful Balelu. He went back to the remains of the fire, and collected a quantity of charred sticks. Systematically, he smeared his face and body with charcoal. His idea was to give the Tenzori as little of him to see as possible.

Finally, satisfied that he had reduced his visibility considerably, he set off once again for the other end of the cave. Halfway around the bend, he slowed down and dropped to all fours. Then, pressing close to the rock wall, so as to present as little silhouette as possible to anyone who might be watching for him, he crept forward.

His progress was necessarily very slow this way, and Ki-Gor wanted to get back to Helene as fast as possible, but he forced himself to go on in that manner until he should be deep into the cave. That circumstance saved his life in a way that he did not anticipate.

He had gone almost all the way around the bend in the cave—there was scarcely enough reflected light at his back for him to see his way—when it happened. His left hand sliding over the smooth rock floor of the trail suddenly grasped empty air. If Ki-Gor had not instantly stopped, he would have tumbled straight into a yawning pit that stretched the width of the trail.

Still on his hands and knees, he concentrated his eyes on the semi-darkness in front of him. There was most certainly a pit there—where none had been before. It was as long as the trail was wide, about ten feet, and it was perhaps six feet across. Ki-Gor lowered his head and peered down into the depths.

At that, it was not so deep that Ki-Gor with his remarkable eyes could not see the things writhing at the bottom. The pit was crawling with snakes—chalk-white snakes, like the Tenzori themselves.

Ki-Gor tucked in his breath thoughtfully. Evidently the albinos could slide or tilt a rock to one side and expose this fearful trap. The unwary stranger would step right into that writhing, venomous mass.

He would be dead within a half hour.

NOW, KI-GOR knew that Naga had expected him to die. The wily albino had sent him unsuspectingly out into the Balelu ambush, and just in case he escaped them, had laid this surer death in the path back into the cave. What other traps, Ki-Gor wondered, might lie ahead of him? And why exactly, Ki-Gor wondered, did Naga want him to die?

The likeliest reason—and Ki-Gor's scalp prickled at the thought—was to have him out of the way so that he could not interfere with whatever plans the albino chieftain had in store for Helene. Ki-Gor rose swiftly to his feet. He must get to Helene without a moment's delay.

He peered for a second into the awful blackness ahead of him. Beside him, the river chuckled evilly. Far away, the waterfall roared forebodingly. Suddenly, Ki-Gor's heart turned over.

Far away, over the sound of the waterfall, there was a resonant thump. A pause, and then came another thump. The drum! The Tenzori were sacrificing another victim to the God of the Waterfall!

With a snarl, Ki-Gor stepped back a pace and leaped across the pit of white snakes. Unhesitatingly, he plunged into the fearful blackness and sped along the trail. In a few moments, he had left all light behind, and was following the trail only by a sort of sixth sense. There was no time now for caution. If there were more traps ahead, or if Naga had left some skulking watchers along the path, there was no help for it. Ki-Gor simply had to get back to Helene, and get there fast.

The drum beats were sounding a little faster now, and louder, as Ki-Gor flung himself through the darkness. And presently, a faint wail came to his ears. There was no question about it—the Tenzori were sacrificing again.

But this time who was their victim?

ALTHOUGH IT seemed like hours to Ki-Gor, it was in reality only a few minutes before he sighted a row of dim lights ahead. The drum was throbbing maddeningly now, and the high-pitched yells of the Tenzori sounded clear above the sound of the falls. As Ki-Gor pounded down on the row of lanterns across the trail, a pair of albinos leaped up with yelps of alarm.

But before they could swing their weighted ropes, Ki-Gor was upon them, the long Tenzori knife glistening in his right hand. Once to the left he slashed, and once to the right, and then kept straight ahead hardly breaking his stride. More lanterns loomed up in front of him, but there were no Tenzori there. Only the miserable Balelu hostages huddled together along the river bank while the drum banged and the albinos shrieked their bloodlust.

Ki-Gor swept onward past them, past the huge boulders which formed the gateway to the inner chamber, toward the gray daylight which was beginning to be reflected on the cave wall ahead. The drum was booming furiously now, and just as Ki-Gor rounded the last curve, a hideous concerted yell broke out.

A second later, Ki-Gor came in sight of the leaping, howling mob of albinos. Above and beyond the forest of upraised, gesticulating arms, a slender sacrificial victim stood on the ledge above the waterfall. One look at that figure silhouetted against the gray dawn, and Ki-Gor knew the worst.

It was Helene.

CHAPTER V

CROUCHING BACK IN THE darkness behind the boulder gateway, Helene had heard the conversation between Ki-Gor and the Tenzori guards. She heard Ki-Gor ask for the drink, and heard the albino's answer. Then when the albino had brought the tea, she waited tensely. Finally she heard Ki-Gor groan.

"The tea! It's drugged—"

For a long, awful moment Helene debated with herself whether to creep back to the pile of skins or to go out and show herself. In the end, she flung herself out of the gateway.

"You beasts!" she cried, as she saw Ki-Gor lying full length on the cave-floor. The albinos looked up at her with horrible smiles. She leaped forward and would have kneeled by Ki-Gor's prostrate form. But the albinos rose up to meet her and closed their gray hands over her bare arms. With a scream of loathing, she flung them off. For a brief time, she fought like a tigress and gave a good account of herself against the slight-muscled albinos. But eventually their numbers prevailed. Her arms and legs were firmly bound together, and four of the guards carried her back into the inner cave and laid her still screaming and struggling on the pallet of skins.

Not long afterwards, she heard the sound of many voices. A score of bobbing lanterns came toward her, and presently Naga was standing beside her, leering down at her. He paused only for a moment and did not speak to her. Then he rejoined the group of his tribesmen, and they all squatted down within earshot of Helene and began to discuss the events of the evening.

Helene understood most of their conversation, although they did not know that, and what she heard plunged her into the deepest despair. Evidently, the Tenzori had not been able to leave the cave at all, that night. The only exit from the cave had been blocked by a huge bonfire, evidently set by the Balelu. It was the most effectual barrier that could have been erected, because the weak-eyed albinos could not come close enough to the blaze to put it out.

Apparently, this was the first time that this had ever happened, and it represented a serious problem for the Tenzori. They could not go out by day, and if the Balelu continued to keep a fire going at the cave mouth every night, it would not be long before the Tenzori would be starved out.

Naga had apparently shouted to the Balelu to hold a conference, which they had agreed to. And in that conference, the Tenzori chief had persuaded the Balelu to discontinue the business of setting fires at the mouth of the cave. In return for that, he had agreed to hand over to the Balelu one of his tribe as a hostage. This hostage, Naga promised, would be the biggest white man in the cave. With mounting horror Helene heard the albinos plan to trick Ki-Gor into walking alone out of the cave mouth. He would all unsuspectingly deliver himself straight into the arms of the waiting Balelu.

THE NEXT eight hours provided Helene with probably the most dreadful ordeal of her life. She was forced to lie bound and helpless and listen to the repulsive albinos plot sure death not only for Ki-Gor but for herself. Superstitious Bantu that the Tenzori were, in spite of their ghastly color, they decided to sacrifice Helene to the God of the Waterfall at dawn. The god, in their opinion, was angry at them and thus permitted the Balelu to contrive the ingenious idea of building the fire at the cave mouth. The god therefore should be placated with the finest victim obtainable, and Helene was chosen.

Only two things sustained Helene through that dreadful night, and allowed her to preserve her sanity. One was her own above-normal courage. The other was an almost mystical belief in Ki-Gor's strength and cunning. During her short but adventurous life with Ki-Gor in the jungle, they had both found themselves in many a desperate situation. And every time, when all hope seemed lost, Ki-Gor had somehow found an escape, or somehow turned certain disaster into brilliant victory.

This situation, Helene had to admit to herself, looked perhaps worse than any she had been faced with before. But she obstinately clung to the hope that somehow Ki-Gor would not be taken by the Balelu, but would come back in time to save her from being pushed off the ledge into the waterfall. Although, if Ki-Gor did come back to her, she hardly knew how he could get her out of the cave alive with odds against him of more than fifty to one.

The rope around her wrists was cruelly tight. The Tenzori had gained a healthy respect for her strength, and they had bound the wrists so ruthlessly that her hands soon began to get numb. In an effort to get some circulation into her hands, she began to work them back and forth. At first, she could hardly move the wrists even a fraction of an inch. But after a while, it seemed to her that she had gained a tiny bit of play in the rope. It was enough anyhow to encourage her to keep on.

Under circumstances like that, it is hard to judge the passage of time, but after what Helene supposed might be an hour's time, she had actually loosened the bonds enough to permit some circulation into her hands. But at what a cost to the skin of her wrists! The constant chafing of the tender skin against the rope had burned and cut so badly that Helene could feel the sticky blood oozing down on to her hands.

But even though every move soon became torture, Helene kept on working her wrists. If she had loosened the ropes a little bit, perhaps she could loosen them even more. The Tenzori were apparently satisfied to leave her alone, and as long as they did that, she intended to devote herself to the task of somehow getting her wrists free.

The night dragged on, and Helene patiently and painfully worked on those bonds. After a while, it seemed as if she would have to stop from sheer agony. But manfully she kept on. Sometimes the pain made her feel faint, and she was tempted to lie back exhausted and close her eyes in the escape of sleep. But each time she drove herself to new efforts.

But flesh and blood can stand only so much. There came a moment when Helene knew she had to stop. Her wrists felt as if someone had been at work on them with a hack-saw. She sat up straight and eased the sticky rope down off her wrists on to her hands as far as they would go. It was an automatic gesture to free her wrists of anything touching them.

To her stunned amazement, the loosened loops slid right down to the knuckles of both hands. Once more she tensed the tortured muscles of her wrists. One after another, she managed to push the loops over the knuckles. How long the final operation took, she could not have judged, but at last she sat panting and joyful, hardly able to believe that her hands were free.

Unhappily, her joy was short-lived. There was a movement among the Tenzori, and several of the ghostly lanterns came bobbing toward her. Panic-stricken, Helene lay down quickly with her hands behind her back. Hastily she pulled the loose rope close to her body, and then rolled over on her back on top of them. Her poor wrists hurt excruciatingly under the weight of her body, but she bit her lip and lay silent as the Tenzori came to her and held their lanterns over her.

It seemed an age to Helene while the albinos stared at her. The pain was shooting up both arms from the wires, and it was all she could do to keep from crying out. Somehow she managed to last out until the Tenzori finally lowered their lanterns and went away. They had not noticed that she had slipped the bonds on her wrists!

SHE LAY still for a long time in spite of the hideous pain it cost her, just in case the albinos might return suddenly. After what seemed like a safe interval, she struggled to an upright position. It should be easy enough with her hands free to undo the ropes winding around her ankles.

But now the blow fell. She made the crushing discovery that her hands had stiffened and puffed up so from the lacerations of the wrists, that she could scarcely move her fingers. No matter how high her courage or strong her will power, she had not the strength or the control over her fingers to free her ankles. It was heartbreaking.

Dully, she laid her head on her doubled-up knees and waited. She had done her best and it was not enough. If she was to be saved, Ki-Gor was the one who would have to do it.

Yet through the remainder of that dreadful night Helene still hoped. Even when the Tenzori came back and clucked with astonishment at the sight of her wrists. When they cut the rope at her ankles, and led her out to the sacrificial ledge—even then, Helene still believed that Ki-Gor would come back. And exhausted with pain and lack of sleep that she was, her mind was nevertheless clear and unafraid when

Naga's great drum began to throb.

Ignoring the drum and the savage crescendo of the Tenzori voices, she stepped coolly to the rim of the lodge and gazed down at the waterfall, and the wide blue pool fifty feet below. Idly she tried to estimate the depth of that pool. Naga's stick was beating faster and faster on the skin drumhead, and the Tenzori were whipping themselves into a frenzy, but Helene felt curiously detached. It was as if she were watching someone else—some other white woman who happened to be called Helene—who was the intended victim of the savage albinos. She noted without excitement that the ceremonies were nearing their climax, and her only thought was that Ki-Gor would have to come soon.

Her back was turned to the cave and the maniacal mob of albinos when a challenging, shattering roar sounded above the din.

"A-a-a-arrrgh!"

Helene turned with a smile and saw Ki-Gor slashing his way through the milling mass of ugly gray-white bodies toward her.

Ki-Gor had come!

CHAPTER VI

THE SIGHT OF HELENE—*HIS* Helene—standing on the sacrificial rock instantly threw Ki-Gor into a blind berserk rage. Sounding his terrible war-cry, he leaped high into the air and came down feet first on the heads of the rearmost Tenzori. Four of them were crushed before the fury of his charge, and his right hand clutching the slender knife descended twice like lightning. Two more repulsive gray bodies fell with red blood spouting.

Ki-Gor chopped downward again swiftly, and then realized that his frail weapon had broken off at the hilt. Unhesitatingly, he flung the hilt away, and hauled down two more albinos with his bare hands. Then a mighty leap and he was again trampling gray heads beneath his smashing feet.

The drum had stopped and the savage chanting of the Tenzori had changed to cries of terror as the berserk jungle man ploughed a fearful furrow through their serried masses. The unexpectedness and the fury of Ki-Gor's attack had thrown them into momentary confusion. Furthermore, they were jammed together so closely along the narrow trail, that they were unable to defend themselves.

Ki-Gor had swiftly seized another knife to replace the broken one.

But the new weapon soon snapped off from the force of Ki-Gor's murderous slashing. Again and again, he wrenched knives from upraised hands about him and hewed a passage through the human wall, leaving a bloody trail behind him.

He had cut his way almost half the distance through the shrieking mass of albinos, before Naga came to life. The albino chief ran out on the sacrificial ledge shouting commands. In a few moments he was able to restore some of the Tenzori from their initial panic. And while the Tenzori were slight of muscle, they were undeniably resourceful and resolute.

A number of those whom Ki-Gor had left behind him in his whirlwind attack suddenly closed in on his rear. Ki-Gor felt a searing pain on his back as one of the razor-edged knives licked across it. He whirled and swept three of the attackers to the earth. But he suddenly realized the precariousness of his situation. Even his mighty prowess could not prevail against a clever foe if he had to fight in four directions at once. He realized that he had to get to one side of the trail or the other, immediately. He must either get the cave wall at his back, or else stand on the very brink of the river where the swarming albinos could not get behind him.

A position on the river bank would give him greater freedom of movement than one with his back to the cave wall. Accordingly, he battered a path to his right, and a moment later was fighting triumphantly with his back to the river.

By now his original fury had given way to cold implacable hate. He had a Tenzori knife in either hand now, and he was using them deftly and carefully so as not to break the slender blades. His long arms gave him the advantage of reach, and enabled him to keep the Tenzori away from him while he edged down the river bank toward the sacrificial ledge.

For a time these tactics prevailed, and Ki-Gor gained several feet toward his precious goal. But the Tenzori soon divined what he was up to, and at a shouted command from Naga, three of them flung themselves simultaneously at Ki-Gor. Swift as a snake, Ki-Gor's two knives licked out and caught two of the albinos in the throat. They fell gurgling and choking against his knees. But the third one stabbed at Ki-Gor's left side.

The jungle man jerked his elbow back and all but deflected the wicked blade. At the same time, the surviving albino grabbed his left arm with both hands and swung himself off the ground. Seeing Ki-

Gor's plight, several other Tenzori sprang forward.

Ki-Gor could not spare his right hand for an instant to dispose of the albino hanging on to his left arm. He fought the newcomers off and shook his left arm desperately. But the albino clung like a leech. Ki-Gor's situation was not good. The two Tenzori lying against his legs and gushing blood in their death throes hampered his movements badly.

HE TOOK a swift step to one side, and again shook his left arm. This time he got rid of the tenacious albino—but at what a cost! Released from the weight of the albino, Ki-Gor lost his balance for a second. He crossed his right foot to save himself, but suddenly there was no footing. The rock there was covered with fresh blood, slippery as grease.

For two awful seconds, Ki-Gor skated drunkenly on one leg, clawing the air wildly, trying to regain his balance. He got his left foot to the ground too late. Now both feet shot out from under him grotesquely. He felt himself going inevitably over backwards—straight into the river.

He heard Helene's scream and a yell from the Tenzori. Then his head hit the water. His feet came over in a somersault, and he felt himself sink deep into the river. With a prodigious effort, he jackknifed himself and kicked himself frantically toward the surface. He was scarcely a hundred feet upstream of the falls—it would be a miracle if he reached the bank before he was swept over. Even as his powerful legs kicked, Ki-Gor doubted whether he would make it. The swift current was rolling him over and over like a log, dragging him inexorably downstream. A fearful thought flashed through his mind as he fought the water. What if he did not make the bank? What would happen to Helene?

Just then his head shot up out of the water and he saw with grim clarity that the worst was going to happen. He was ten feet from the bank, but he might as well be a hundred. The powerful current was bearing him resistlessly straight to his doom. He caught a glimpse of the wildly excited Tenzori thronging the bank. Then he was looking straight up into Helene's horror-stricken eyes. She was screaming something at him, but he could not hear her above the roar of the falls.

Three more heartbeats and he found himself poised on the oily brink staring straight down at the pool fifty feet below. He seemed to hang there for a fearful eternity, defying gravitation. It was as if he had no connection with that prodigious weight of water which pounded the pool below into boiling froth. In a few scant seconds, those tons of water would be cascading down on his helpless body, beating it to a pulp—

Now, at last he felt himself going over. Nothing could save him now, he thought. But his last thought was for Helene. What would happen to her?

As the current swept him over, it also seemed to throw him forward. Half his body came out of the water. Mechanically, almost unconsciously, he gave one last convulsive kick. For a brief astonished moment, he realized that he was clear of the water, and dropping through empty air. Automatically, he contracted the muscles of his twisting body. He arched his back, threw his legs back and up, flung his hands forward and down. A split-second later, he hit the water head first with stunning force.

The world began to go black before Ki-Gor's eyes. He was barely conscious of bring engulfed by white bubbling water. Then he found himself on the surface gulping air, while great drops of water showered down furiously on to his head. Again the world seemed to disappear, and he felt himself bring sucked down under the raging foaming water. The next thing he knew was that he was trying to breathe but could not. Some relentless hand seemed to have him by the throat choking the life out of him. Half-conscious though he was, Ki-Gor could not help but see the grim irony of surviving the fifty foot drop only to die anyway through drowning.

He was gasping, and coughing and choking, but something or someone far away told him not to give up the fight. His legs kicked and his arms flailed, but they felt so heavy—so heavy—

THE NEXT thing that Ki-Gor was conscious of was acute pain in his scalp. He felt as if someone were trying to pull all his hair out by the roots. He was doubled up and gasping, but at any rate he was not dead yet. He suddenly vomited a quantity of water, and then he was gulping great mouthfuls of air. Consciousness now began to flood back. He realized that he was floating on his back on the surface of the water. He realized too that someone was actually pulling his hair. Someone, in fact, was towing him through the water by his hair.

Who was it? Who had entered the pool and dragged him out from under the falls? His eyes could see that he was well away from the bottom of the cascade. His mysterious rescuer was making heavy work of towing him. He could hear gasping sobs behind his head.

Ki-Gor tried to kick his legs, but evidently he was too weak to accomplish more than the feeblest of motions. Suddenly, the gasps behind him stopped. There was a tremendous sigh, and then the sound of heavy breathing. Then a pair of arms twined themselves around his shoulders, and he felt himself dragged into shallow water, the gravel scraping his back.

By now, Ki-Gor felt strong enough to try and lift himself to a sitting position. More and more, he wanted to see his rescuer. He could not imagine who it could be. As he put his hands down on the gravel at his sides and feebly lifted himself up, he heard a joyous cry. A shower of water descended on him. He looked up and saw a head bending over his. It was Helene.

"Thank Heaven!" she exclaimed. "Your eyes are open! Oh, darling, are you all right?"

Ki-Gor nodded. For a moment he could not speak. His life had just been saved by a miracle, and it was his own Helene who had performed that miracle.

"Can you move your arms and legs all right?" Helene asked anxiously.

Ki-Gor nodded again and smiled. Carefully, he flexed each knee in turn, and then with a tremendous effort he strained upward on his hands and managed to sit upright.

"Oh, be careful, darling!" Helene cried.

"Don't worry!" Ki-Gor finally spoke. "See? I'm all right."

"Oh! Thank goodness!" Helene said, with a long happy sigh. "Darling, I'll never know how you came out of that without breaking any bones! Your diving form is not very stylish. Although, at that, you did protect your head, and you arched your back enough so that your body was deflected up to the surface. And I guess nobody else but Ki-Gor could have thrown himself clear of the waterfall, the way you did."

Ki-Gor eased himself back until he was resting on his elbows; he was still very weak.

"Wait a minute," he said, "I want to ask you some questions. How could you get down to the pool so quickly?"

"Me?" Helene laughed. "I did the craziest swan dive of my career. I only had room for about six running steps—"

"You—you dived?" Ki-Gor gasped. "Off that ledge?"

"I certainly did," Helene said. "You didn't know it, but I used to be quite an amateur diver. That was back in the days when I was a social butterfly, long before I met you. We had a big pool on my father's estate on Long Island, and I used to practice by the hour off the high board."

KI-GOR GAZED up to the top of the waterfall. There were several tiny white figures up there standing on the ledge, hands over their eyes. The returning daylight was already too strong for the weak-eyed albinos to stand.

"You dived—off there!" Ki-Gor repeated in awed tones.

"Yes, as I say," Helene went on matter-of-factly, "there wasn't much room for a running start, but I gave the takeoff everything I had, and I just did manage to clear the bottom of the falls. Then I saw that you were being sucked under, so I just went in and got you."

"Just—went—in—and got me," Ki-Gor said slowly. "Oh, Helene! There isn't much I can say. But you were wonderful—to risk your life to save me."

"Oh, darling!" Helene said, and her eyes grew moist. "Life wouldn't be worth living without you to share it with. And I'm so glad I could—just once—be of some use. You're continually getting me out of some trouble or other—I'm such a helpless boob!"

"Helpless—what?" Ki-Gor said curiously.

"Helpless boob. Boob—that's an old-fashioned slang word which describes people like me—"

"Look!" Ki-Gor interrupted. He was staring at Helene's wrists. "What happened?" he demanded.

"That's a perfect illustration of what I mean," Helene said, and went on to tell him about slipping her bonds the night before. "But you see?" she concluded. "I only got so far and then failed. Just a boob, that's all—"

"But they must hurt terribly!" Ki-Gor broke in.

"They're not so bad, now," Helene said. "The water cooled them off a little, and took down some of the swelling. At least, I can move my fingers now. Enough to hang on to that mane of yours," she added with a grin.

Ki-Gor felt his scalp with a rueful smile. "I thought you were going to pull it right off," he said.

"Well, anyway," Helene said happily, "it was one way of getting out of that cave. I was beginning to think we weren't going to escape from those horrible albinos, at all."

"But we did," Ki-Gor said, "thanks to you. And we're safe from them now. They can't come out of the cave until nightfall. And by that time, if we haven't found Marmo, we'll be in some good safe place with a big fire going. Now, the first thing to do is to find some herbs to soothe your wrists."

The jungle man got up slowly and stood unsteadily on his feet.

"Oh!" cried Helene, staring at him. "You've got some terrible cuts, darling!"

"They're not serious," Ki-Gor said, disdainfully. "It's a good thing those Tenzori are such puny men. These wounds aren't as bad as your wrists—come, we'll attend to them."

With that the couple waded ashore, Ki-Gor still feeling very shaky. It took him several minutes to negotiate the steep grassy bank above the pool, and he stood panting for a moment at the top and glanced around him.

"We finally got on the other side of the river, Helene," he said humorously. "We can go up over the hill, there"—he indicated the spur which came down from the ridge to the west, the spur through which the river flowed forming the great cave—"over that hill and then upstream on this side until we get back to the swamp. I hope we'll find Marmo somewhere in the swamp."

"We'll have to look out and not bump into my Italian friend," Helene remarked. "He was on this side of the river, don't forget."

"I haven't forgotten," Ki-Gor said grimly, recalling another score he wanted to settle. Then his mood suddenly changed as his right hand accidentally grazed the waistline of his leopard-skin trunks.

"Look!" he said delightedly, pulling forth the little bag. "Even after going over the falls, I've still got your pretty stones!"

"Oh, how wonderful!" Helene cried. "Let's see them!"

Ki-Gor shook out some of the emeralds and rubies into his great palm, and Helene gazed at them appreciatively. Suddenly, there was a crackling, rustling sound to one side of them. They both whirled in time to see some bushes parting. A burly white man in soiled white clothes stepped out of the bushes and pointed an automatic at them.

"Bedda figghia!" the stranger exclaimed, showing tobacco-stained teeth in an evil smile.

CHAPTER VII

"MY LORD, IT'S THE Sicilian!" Helena exclaimed. Then something snapped within her. She had been through too much trouble recently to be bothered with this brute again. She fumed on the man and poured a stream of vituperation at him in fluent Italian.

The man's eyes widened in amazement. Then he began roaring with laughter, but all the time kept the gun leveled.

"The pretty girl is glad to see me, is she?" he shouted in his thick Sicilian dialect. "Well, strike me dead! And her big wild husband, too? And what are you both looking at?"

The man strode toward them. Ki-Gor poured the gems back into the little bag, and would have replaced it in his trunks. But before he could do it, the man had reached his side. He jammed the blunt nose of the automatic into Ki-Gor's ribs and wrenched the bag away.

"I saw them!" the man shouted triumphantly. "Jewels, hey? Precious stones! And they came from that cave up there, I'll bet, didn't they? You two come along with me—I want to talk to you."

Ki-Gor, of course, had not understood a word the man had spoken, but his intentions were plainly indicated by his gestures with the gun and with the bag of gems. Even if Ki-Gor had been in possession of his full strength, there would have been little he could do as long as the man kept him covered with the automatic. As it was, he could only comply with the man's demands and await an opportunity to catch him off guard.

Ki-Gor looked curiously at Helene who was continuing her shrill denunciation of the stranger in his own language. Somehow the jungle man could not take the situation, bad as it was, too seriously. After the recent terrible ordeal among the macabre denizens of the cave, a single white man did not seem to present such a problem. There was something almost comically villainous about this man, too. His ragged, soiled clothes, his scraggly black beard, and his loud boisterous voice—all indicated a man of low origin, recently elevated to power.

But comically villainous or not, the man proceeded to act rapidly. He shouted something to Helene and made a beckoning gesture with the gun. Ki-Gor looked at Helene.

"He says for us to come with him," she interpreted.

Ki-Gor hesitated. The man watched narrowly. Then he suddenly raised the gun and fired it into the air. Instantly there was a crashing in the bushes, and shortly three tall askaris came panting out. The bearded man gave a brief order, and the askaris advanced on Ki-Gor rifles leveled.

"Tell him we will go with him," Ki-Gor said to Helene.

They were prodded several hundred yards to a strange untidy camp. There were eight additional askaris there, and a stocky, grizzled unhappy-looking little white man. A third white man was lying on a litter with his eyes closed. This man had finely chiseled features and a luxuriant gray mustache, and Ki-Gor guessed from the high flush on his cheeks that he had fever.

The bearded man—his name, Helene found out, was Maledetto—commanded the jungle couple to sit down. Then he shook the gems out of the little bag into his hand and gazed at them greedily. He asked Helene some questions, which, of course, Ki-Gor could not understand. Helene, evidently, was in violent disagreement with him and shook her head vehemently. Finally she turned to Ki-Gor.

"This idiot," she fumed, "is convinced that we found the stones in the cave. He has an idea that the cave is probably full of loose rubies and emeralds. I tried to tell him it wasn't so, that they came from somewhere toward the east, but the fool won't believe me."

Maledetto suddenly interrupted Helene in his crude dialect, and got up and stood menacingly over Ki-Gor. Helene turned pale. Again Maledetto spoke to her. Reluctantly, she turned back to Ki-Gor.

"Oh, the stupid brute!" she cried. "He says he is going to have you whipped until you confess that you got the gems in the cave!"

Ki-Gor got slowly to his feet, in spite of shouted commands from the Sicilian. Maledetto backed away, knuckles white on his gun hand. But Ki-Gor looked around at the askaris behind him and spoke to them in Somali.

"Who is this grandson of a baboon? Is he truly your master?"

THE ASKARIS were startled at being spoken to in their own tongue. Then they looked embarrassed. Finally one of them answered.

"Aye, he commands us while our Capitano lies sick of the fever."

"A sad day it is," Ki-Gor commented, "when proud Somalis must obey such a stupid pig."

Before the askaris could answer, Maledetto sprang forward snarling. He halted himself abruptly and shouted some commands. Three askaris promptly made for Ki-Gor with wolfish grins.

"Stupid pig maybe," said one of them, "but whoever commands must be obeyed. We are to tie thee up and beat thee, O Strange White One."

With Maledetto's gun on him, Ki-Gor could do nothing. The askaris tied his arms over his head to a stout low-hanging branch. When Helene saw what was happening, she let out a shriek and threw herself incontinently at the Sicilian, and pounded her fists on his breast. He swept her aside contemptuously, and barked another command. One of the askaris began to take off his uniform belt. Just then a new voice, a strange weak voice, was heard calling quietly.

"Tenente Maledetto!"

Ki-Gor twisted his head and saw Maledetto staring across the campsite. Following his eyes, Ki-Gor saw that the man on the litter was sitting up The flush was gone from his face, and he looked pale and exhausted. But his eyes glittered and he rasped some commands at the askaris. The Somalis looked at each other disappointedly. Again the man on the litter spoke, and this time the small grizzled man walked shouting into the midst of the tall blacks. Reluctantly, the askaris untied Ki-Gor's wrists. Helene was already on her feet walking toward the man on the litter.

"Grazie!" she cried, and continued in Italian, "Thank goodness there is an Italian gentleman present to curb this Sicilian ruffian!"

The man struggled to his feet and delivered a courtly bow.

"Buon' giorno, signora!" he said. "All Sicilians are not ruffians. Allow me to present myself, your faithful servant. I am Count Roberto di Ghiscardi, an old Sicilian name if there ever was one. I have the honor to be a captain in the army of His Excellency the Duke of Aosta. This Fascist dog, Maledetto, attached himself to us during the confusion attendant on our withdrawal from Reshiat."

The Count paused momentarily and looked at Helene with a mischievous smile.

"To the British, perhaps," he continued, "our withdrawal might have looked like a rout. But I think we might have made a better showing there if we had had a few more real soldiers, and fewer political soldiers like this brave Maledetto here. How he ever attained the rank of lieutenant is a mystery to me. However, he had that rank, and when I fell sick, he assumed the command of this little force. Now, that will stop. I shall resume command, myself."

"You are most gracious, Count Roberto," Helene said. "May we speak in English? My husband does not understand—"

"Most certainly," the count said in purest Oxonian. "My English is not so pure as the signora's Italian, but it will suffice."

"The count is far too modest," Helene smiled. "Very well, then. This is Ki-Gor—and I am his wife."

"Ki-Gor!" Count Roberto exclaimed. "I believe I have heard of him—back in the blessed days of peace. I am honored to meet you, sir. Are you not at some distance from your usual haunts?"

"Africa is my home," Ki-Gor replied pleasantly. "And you—?"

"Count Roberto is a captain in the Italian Army, Ki-Gor," Helene explained. "His detachment has been split off from the main forces."

"Oh," said Ki-Gor curiously. "Then you have come a long way from Abyssinia."

"We have," the count acknowledged. "My intention was to lead my little force somehow to Axis-controlled territory. That is something I should like to discuss with you—but first, I must attend to some details here. You are of British origin, I believe, and it is a melancholy fact that your country and mine are at war. I am unfortunately obliged to inform you that you and your beautiful wife are prisoners of war. However, I will accept your parole without question. You understand the matter of parole, do you not, Signor Ki-Gor?"

"Yes," said Ki-Gor thoughtfully, "and we will give you our parole, freely—"

"Excellent!" said Count Roberto. "And for your shameful treatment while I was asleep, a thousand apologies. Maledetto shall be disciplined. He will be stripped of his rank, and will be placed under arrest. With your permission"—the count bowed—"I will attend to that, this moment!"

THE COUNT'S eyes blazed and his mustache bristled righteously, and he proceeded to pour out a torrent of blistering Sicilian at Maledetto. The little gray-haired man—apparently he was Sergeant Gianni—marched briskly to the black-bearded lieutenant and took his gun from him, while the askaris looked on stolidly, with occasional sidelong glances at each other.

Maledetto protested volubly, but the count shouted him down. Then at another command, Sergeant Gianni trotted over and took the bag of gems from Maledetto, and brought it to the count.

"Again my apologies for this greedy Fascist dog," said Count

Roberto, handing the bag over to Helene. "He is the son of a blacksmith—no recommendation to a gentleman. Mussolini is also the son of a blacksmith, you know."

Helene thanked him profusely and started to explain about Maledetto's conviction that the stones had come from the cave. But Count Roberto waved the explanation aside.

"It is not his business or mine," he said, "where the contents of this bag came from—they belong to you, Signora. The matter is closed. And now, Signor Ki-Gor, I should like to discuss some geography with you. First I must confess that even before I fell sick, we were hopelessly lost. Now, of course, I have not the faintest idea where we are. You cannot honorably give me directions as to how to reach territory or men friendly to my side. That would be giving aid and comfort to the enemy. But could you at least give me some idea of where we are at this moment? So that I can make my dispositions accordingly?"

Ki-Gor smiled a moment before he spoke. Then he said, "Nothing I could tell you would aid you much, and it certainly wouldn't comfort you. I have just visited the Ngombi-Masai, who live not far from here. They are well informed about the movements of the armies, and from what I learned from them, you are cut off on the north, east, and south from your friends. Twenty-five hundred miles to the west is Dakar but you would never get there."

"How do you mean?" the count asked, frowning.

Ki-Gor explained some of the insuperable difficulties in the face of such a march. The little force, Ki-Gor said, would soon run out of ammunition, would undoubtedly be ambushed and slaughtered by any one of a score of blood-thirsty tribes before it ever got half way across the Congo.

"Why don't you surrender to the nearest British forces?" Ki-Gor said in conclusion.

"Not," said the count with dignity, "until I have exhausted all other possible alternatives."

"Very well," Ki-Gor shrugged, and looked around the brush-enclosed camp site. "Then there is something you should do right away. You are in the midst of some unfriendly tribes right here. This camp would be a bad place to be caught by any of them. I advise you to move to some better place. You should have open country all around you, so that no one can come within spear range of you unseen."

"Sensible, sensible," Count Roberto said, nodding. "We will move immediately. Are they very dangerous, these tribesmen you speak of?"

"No, not very," Ki-Gor said. "Ordinarily, they would make no trouble, at all. But they have been mistreated by men with white skins, and now they are desperate. I don't think they are in sufficient numbers to be a real danger, but it would be best to be on your guard."

The count looked curiously at Ki-Gor. "You say they have been mistreated by white men?" he said.

"That is a long story," Ki-Gor said hastily, "and one that you'd find hard to believe. First, let us move this camp."

CHAPTER VIII

ACCORDINGLY, THE LITTLE GROUP soon got under way with its second-in-command under technical arrest, and its prisoners of war free on parole. The nearest open country was the spur across the river, and the little column halted at the base of the steep ascent while Ki-Gor spoke a word of caution to the Italian captain.

"There is one bad thing about climbing up there—we will be seen by the Balelu. But then, if they haven't discovered you yet, they will sooner or later. Their village is only a half a mile away, or three-quarters at the most, and as I said, they are hunting men with white skins."

"I see," the count reflected. "Well, one thing is certain—these Somalis of mine are great soldiers, but they come from the desert and are not so effective in the close confines of the jungle. We will proceed up the hill and risk being seen. Then if we are attacked we can give a better account of ourselves."

The climb was made slowly. Evidently, the native porters and paddlers had deserted the day before, and rather than use Somalis as litter-bearers, Count Roberto left the litter behind and walked. The count had recovered somewhat from his fever, but was still quite weak, therefore necessitating many halts on the way up the grassy slope. The last stop was made within two hundred yards of the crest of the ridge. Ki-Gor, who had been searching all points of the compass with his eyes, volunteered to go on ahead to the top by himself and scout the country.

But, even as he was speaking, a chorus of shrill cries sounded in the distance. Ki-Gor spun around and pointed. There, at the foot of the hill, at almost the very spot where the little party had issued forth from the tangled forest, were a score or more of naked blacks. They were Balelu, obviously, and they came bounding up the slope. Ki-Gor smiled grimly. It was just as well that Count Roberto had accepted his advice and withdrawn from the jungle. Sooner or later, these Balelu would have come upon them, and while Ki-Gor held them in contempt as fighters, he conceded they would have had a certain advantage if they had caught the Somalis in the shadowy tangle of the forest.

"Now that this party has seen us," Ki-Gor said to the count, "it is of no value to try and keep hidden any more. Go on up to the top of the hill. I will lag behind and speak to them."

"Speak to them?" Count Roberto cried in astonishment. "What? Alone and unarmed? They will kill you, won't they?"

"I don't think so," Ki-Gor said. "I will give them something to think about."

Count Roberto shook his head wonderingly. "These English!" he murmured.

Helene looked at her husband anxiously, but when he quietly told her to go along with the count and the others, she went without question. She did not want to particularly, and she was a little afraid that Ki-Gor was taking too much of a chance in facing the advancing Balelu unarmed. But she realized that Ki-Gor knew what he was about, and she trusted him to handle himself shrewdly.

Ki-Gor strolled downhill toward the twenty-odd shouting Balelu, alone and unarmed. At first, the blacks scented a victim and leaped ardently up the slope toward him. But when they were about a hundred yards from him, Ki-Gor stopped and stood with hands nonchalantly on hips and feet spread, and gazed over their heads. The advancing group of Balelu slowed down and stopped shouting. By the time they had covered another fifty yards, they were traveling at a walk, and were edging close to one another.

Ki-Gor grinned to himself. Having gained a psychological advantage, he proceeded to an old trick of distracting attention—one which he had used successfully before in similar situations. He lifted his right hand off his hip and pointed dramatically over the heads of the oncoming Balelu. They all promptly halted and whirled around to look in the direction of Ki-Gor's pointing finger. Before they could turn around again, Ki-Gor had filled his lungs.

"Beware!" he roared. "Beware, the invisible ju-ju! It is right over

your heads this instant—ready to pounce down and snuff out your lives! You cannot see the ju-ju—it is invisible. But it is there. Know ye, O miserable Balelu, that Ki-Gor is displeased! Twice now have you attacked him without cause! Ki-Gor is Ki-Gor—he is no gray-faced Mid-Mountain Dweller—he is no pink-eyed Tenzori! Look you—Ki-Gor can gaze into the sun, the way no Tenzori can do, as you well know!"

DELIBERATELY, KI-GOR turned and looked over his left shoulder up at the sun. The Balelu stared in fascination, and up near the top of the ridge, Helene and Count Roberto and his party halted and watched silently. Ki-Gor snapped his head front.

"Begone, Miserable Balelu!" he thundered. "Do not again mistake Ki-Gor for a sickly Tenzori! Twice Ki-Gor will forgive you! A third attack will bring swift and furious punishment! Go! Go—before he loses patience and unleashes the fearful, invisible ju-ju on your unlucky heads!"

For a brief moment, the puny blacks hesitated in awe. Then one of them gave a frightened yelp and bolted down the slope away from Ki-Gor. Instantly, the rest followed suit, and the little band that had a few minutes before been leaping the hill in such warlike fashion, now streamed away in terrified rout.

As Ki-Gor rejoined his party, he saw that Helene was holding a rifle, one obviously borrowed from one of the Somalis. She was holding it muzzle sloping downward, as if she had just lowered it from a shooting position.

"I thought you'd get away with it all right," she laughed, in answer to Ki-Gor's inquiring look, "but I thought it would be just as well to cover you—just in case."

Ki-Gor smiled in wonderment. "I never thought of that," he said simply.

It was not far now to the top of the ridge. Ki-Gor took the lead, and even before he reached the actual crest, he received a disagreeable surprise. The base of the hill was swarming with blacks.

The entire length of the trail along the river was crowded with Balelu, spears gleaming in the morning sunlight. And at the entrance to the cave, they were overflowing up on to the lower slopes of the hill itself. Ki-Gor frowned. There were so many of them, they could not all be Balelu. There were literally hundreds of black warriors down there. Evidently, the Balelu had gathered kindred tribes from miles around in a desperate effort to conquer the oppressive Tenzori once and for all.

Ki-Gor's sympathies were entirely with the Balelu, but this concentration of force had come at an awkward time for him and Helene, and for Count Roberto's little force. Particularly, as he could see that some of the allies of the Balelu were far more competent looking warriors than the feeble Balelu. He threw a quick glance to the right and observed that the small party which he had just routed with his threatening words were hurrying around the base of the hill above the waterfall. Apparently, they intended to join the main body of blacks.

Ki-Gor threw himself to the ground and shouted to Count Roberto.

"Lie down—quickly!" he cried. He hoped that they would not be seen until that first group of Balelu joined the rest with a story of mighty ju-ju.

But a chorus of yells from below which swelled and spread told him he had been seen.

"Too late!" he called out to the Italian captain. "They saw me. I'm afraid some of them will have to be shot. Keep your men under cover of the grass if you can. I will threaten those foolish Bantu once more with a ju-ju. If they still come on, I will raise my arm and let it fall. That will be a signal for you to fire a volley."

Count Roberto issued rapid orders, and the Somalis crawled through the grass grinning and ranged themselves in rows on either side of Ki-Gor. Then the jungle man stood up once more, and his thunderous voice sounded from the top of the hiltl.

"The ju-ju!" he roared. "Beware the invisible ju-ju! Come no farther or it will strike you dead!"

The advancing horde slowed down and grew quiet for a moment. Again Ki-Gor roared his warning.

"You will see no spear, no arrow! But there will be the sound of a great bough snapping off a tree, and an invisible bee will buzz into your midst carrying death and destruction! Be warned and come no farther!"

The vanguard of the swarming blacks hesitated. They were strapping men in brown skin kilts, and they were obviously made of sterner stuff than their cousins, the Balelo. Several of them leaped forward with shrill cries, and instantly the whole line surged up the hill.

Ki-Gor raised his right arm, and let it drop. Count Roberto spoke and eleven rifles cracked.

THE SOMALIS were aiming downhill, and in consequence, some of them overshot. But six bullets found their marks in the serried mass of blacks, and the effect was instantaneous and devastating. One of the six victims was hit in the head and died without a sound. But the other five leaped high in the air shrieking and notching their throats or shoulders or wherever they were hit. The rest of the advancing blacks halted in consternation, and a concerted moan of terror went up on all sides.

"The ju-ju has struck!" Ki-Gor cried bitterly at them. "You were warned and did not heed the warning! Back now—before the ju-ju strikes again! Back! For your lives!"

The blacks screamed with terror and fought each other to get away. The horde which was a moment before swarming up the hill now melted away, leaving six victims on the slope. The panic spread behind the fleeing vanguard, and shortly the entire group of Balelu and their allies were in desperate, fear-driven flight.

Count Roberto and Helene came and stood beside Ki-Gor and watched the rout.

"Remarkable!" the count said wonderingly. "I wish we could have driven the Abyssinians as easily as that, six years ago. Well, Signor Ki-Gor, I am most indebted to you. You are, if I may say so, a most valuable prisoner of war!"

Ki-Gor looked down thoughtfully at the aristocratic little Italian. "Are you going to try to go to Dakar?" he asked casually.

Count Roberto shrugged. "It seems ridiculous," he replied, "but what else can I honorably do? My men still have some twenty rounds apiece, they still obey me, I am able to stand on my feet—. Considering those things and in the absence of any orders from my superiors, I must carry on, as you British say."

"Mm," Ki-Gor murmured. Then he said softly, "You will never make it to Dakar, Count Roberto—it is impossible. You would be throwing your life away needlessly. And also the lives of the people in your force."

"Ah, do not worry about that!" the count smiled. "It would be inhuman of me to make you and your wife go with us. I have been thinking about that, and I have decided that the only thing to do is to release you. After all, you were not captured in a combat between British and Italian forces. You were merely abducted at the point of a gun by that rascally politician, Maledetto. Signor Ki-Gor, it gives me great pleasure to announce to you that you were never legally a prisoner of war, and that henceforth you and your charming wife are free to go your own way."

"And our parole?" Helene broke in.

"You are free," Count Roberto said, "therefore, there is no longer a question of parole. Now, in this new event, Signor Ki-Gor, what are your plans?"

Ki-Gor turned and looked shrewdly northward, up the river. He pointed along the west bank, the opposite bank from the one which he and Helene had come along the day before.

"My wife and I," he said, pointing, "by ourselves, would go along that bank until we came to the swamp. Then we would cross the swamp and go east to the land of the Ngombi-Masai. It is healthier country there—open veldt, with plenty of game, and with room to see your way and to see who is near you. I will guide you, if you want."

"Ah!" the count murmured, and thought for a moment. Then he said, with decision, "You are right. We will maintain ourselves on the veldt as long as we can. And I accept your offer to guide me, most gratefully, Signor Ki-Gor."

"It will be tricky," Ki-Gor warned. "The quickest and shortest way from this dangerous spot is straight down the hill where the blacks were, and along the trail they are still fleeing. It will mean going right through the Balelu village. But the Balelu have just had a bad scare. If we go now, immediately, before they have a chance to recover from that scare, I think we will get through the trail and the village without any attempt by them to attack."

Count Roberto's answer was immediate. "I place myself in your hands, Signor Ki-Gor. Here, take this pistol of Maledetto's and lead the way."

Ki-Gor nodded, accepted the automatic and handed it to Helene. "She knows better how to use these than I do," he explained. "I will pick up one of those assegais down the hill. The guns of your men should all be loaded, although I hope they will not need to use them."

The count sang out a command, the bolts of the rifles snicked, and Ki-Gor started down the hill.

The river trail was still crowded with frightened blacks, and, in fact, there were still some left at the base of the hill, who were unable as yet to get on to the trail. When they saw Ki-Gor and his party advancing downhill toward them, they redoubled their efforts to get away. Some of them did not wait to follow on to the trail, but merely dived in a panic into the tangled jungle at the base of the hill.

This did not displease Ki-Gor, who foresaw that the Balelu and their friends would not summon the courage to attack for a long time. He maintained an even unhurried pace, and allowed the last of the panicky blacks to get well out of the way before he arrived at the foot of the hill. Once there, he led his party straight down to the river trail, and presently stood in front of the cave mouth waiting for them to assemble there.

The askaris looked curiously into the cavernous opening as they went past, and Ki-Gor stepped toward Count Roberto with the intention of warning him about them. But before he could say anything, Maledetto was yelling at the top of his lungs. The Fascist had ducked into the cave mouth and looked around. He had stooped and picked something up from the rock floor of the trail.

He came lunging out, shooting and holding the object out in his hand. It was a ruby.

How Ki-Gor could have dropped the gem, he did not know. But drop it he evidently had, and to Maledetto it was positive proof of what he had been contending all along—that the cave was full of precious stones.

"The man is a fool!" Ki-Gor shouted at Count Roberto. "There is no time to go in there! Every moment now is precious—we have to keep on going while the Balelu are still afraid of us!"

Count Roberto pushed his way through the askaris to the shouting Maledetto and snatched the ruby out of his hand. Then he barked commands and rejoined Ki-Gor. The askaris fell in behind and followed up the trail, but they were obviously reluctant to leave the cave, and Maledetto, bringing up the rear, was still protesting loudly.

"RICHES!" HELENE heard him scream. "Countless riches! Give us ten minutes in there, Capitano, ten paltry minutes! We can all pick up a fortune in ten minutes! Look—that enormous ruby! It was lying on the ground in the middle of the trail! I beg of you, Capitano—just ten minutes!"

Count Roberto marched grimly forward behind Ki-Gor and did not deign to answer the Fascist. But now some of the askaris began to join in with Maledetto's pleading, and before the party had gone twenty paces from the cave mouth, the murmurs grew too loud to be ignored any longer. The count wheeled around and shouted. But human greed was more compelling than discipline.

Maledetto suddenly turned and sprinted back toward the cave. And as one man the Somalis rushed after him. Count Roberto shouted impotently at them, raised his automatic and fired once into the air over their heads. But the askaris, led by Maledetto, only ran the faster. The count spat out a furious Sicilian oath and aimed his automatic straight at his rebellious men. Ki-Gor reached over and caught his arm.

"Don't waste your bullets," the jungle man advised grimly. "They will not last long in there."

"What do you mean?" the count said, with a startled look.

"There are people living in that cave. They are clever, cruel people, and right now they are in a bad mood."

"Well, then," the count said, starting forward, "I must get them out."

"It's too late," Ki-Gor said, as the last askari disappeared into the shadows of the cave mouth. "You can do nothing for them now. Save yourself and your faithful one, here."

Ki-Gor pointed at little Sergeant Gianni, standing imperturbably awaiting orders with his gun at his shoulder. Count Roberto hesitated a moment, then finally lowered his gun and nodded. Just then there came a sound of a distant, anguished scream.

Muffled and indistinct as it was, it was a harrowing, bloodcurdling sound—the wail of a soul in torment. There were shouts then, and a fusillade of shots. But the first scream continued and seemed to grow louder.

"Dear Heaven!" Count Roberto muttered. "What has happened?"

It sounded now as though a full-fledged battle were going on inside the cave. But on top of the noise of hoarse shouting and gunfire, that appalling scream hung on the air and grew louder and closer. Then, after what seemed like an interminable interval, Maledetto burst out of the cave mouth.

The man had gone completely off his head. Wordless shrieks poured from his mouth and his arms thrashed about wildly, beating and plucking at his body and at his legs.

"Ki-Gor!" Helene cried. "What are those white things on him? They aren't pieces of rope—"

"They're snakes," Ki-Gor replied laconically, as Maledetto spun around like a top and then flung himself into the river.

Count Roberto stood transfixed with horror. Ki-Gor touched his arm.

"Come," the jungle man urged. "You can't save any of them, and there isn't a minute to lose if we are to get through the Balelu village safely."

The count turned away slowly.

"Poor ignorant brute!" he muttered. "But he brought it on himself. Too bad it couldn't have been his master—his leader, Benito—and the rest of that vile crew who have so dishonored the name of Italians everywhere!"

Then Count Roberto di Ghiscardi followed Ki-Gor and Helene up the river trail with the faithful Sergeant Gianni at his heels.

The jungle man took care not to set too fast a pace, even though he knew that every minute was precious. But he had caught a glimpse of Count Roberto's face, and he could tell that the aging aristocrat was feeling the effect of his recent fever. He was hardly in condition to stand up long under prolonged activity and excitement. And yet the desertion and loss of the eleven askaris might complicate the business of getting away from the Balelu. Now, instead of a party of sixteen, there were just three men and a woman. When the Balelu saw the sadly reduced party, they might still be too terrified to attack—or they might not.

WHEN HE arrived at the point where the trail turned away from the river to go through the Balelu village, Ki-Gor hesitated. The wisest course would be not to traverse the village at all, but to leave the trail and follow the river bank. But one look at the tumbled boulders and tangled bush that lined the river, and he knew Count Roberto would never make it. So they would have to go through the village after all, and risk a possible attack.

Ki-Gor spent a few seconds rapidly explaining the risks to the count. That gentleman nodded quietly.

"We are soldiers, Gianni and I," he said. "Signor Ki-Gor, lead on!"

Ki-Gor looked up the trail grimly. A scant three hundred yards was the village, a few of its miserable huts visible from where he stood. He could see no humans, the incident at the cave mouth having given the fleeing blacks a chance to draw ahead and clear the trail.

"Keep your guns ready," Ki-Gor said, and strode forward.

The Balelu village was completely deserted by the time the four whites reached it. But a suspicious quiet hung over the thick jungle that surrounded the clearing, and Ki-Gor sensed the presence of the hundreds of blacks lying hidden in the underbrush. Without a word the four walked through the village—Ki-Gor in the lead, then Helene, then the count, and finally little Gianni. Ki-Gor's steps were unhurried and his actions unworried. But with every casual glance to one side of him or the other, his alert eyes were not missing a single detail, and his marvelous ears were tensed for the slightest sound.

He began to hear sounds, too, before he reached the other side of the village. First, a sibilant whisper, then another less cautious, and more joining in even more boldly, until the entire forest around them broke into audible murmurs. And what the hidden Balelu were saying was:

"They are so few! Only four!"

At the other side of the village, Ki-Gor stepped aside to allow Helene to lead the way, and then fell in himself behind Sergeant Gianni. Ki-Gor knew Bantu, and he knew that even with the fear of mighty ju-ju over them they could not resist the attraction of overwhelming odds in their favor. He suspected that the Balelu might begin a wary pursuit; and he was not wrong.

They had left the village about two miles behind them when the jungle began to thin out, and Ki-Gor breathed a little easier. They could not be far from open veldt now, and so far there had been no sign of Balelu in their rear. If there was to be an attack, Ki-Gor preferred it to come after he had got his party out on the veldt. Not that four people with three guns would have an awfully good chance against hundreds of blacks, but at least they stood a better chance in the open than they would hemmed in by jungle.

But just at that moment, as if matters were not bad enough, Count Roberto gave a groan and stopped.

"What a fearful bore!" the aristocrat said dryly, and sat down heavily in the middle of the trail. "But I'm afraid I've got to rest again. My legs feel absolutely like pieces of soft rubber. As a matter of fact, you know, I think you had all better go ahead without me. I'm afraid I'm simply endangering your lives—"

"No, Count Roberto," Ki-Gor interrupted gently, "we're not going on without you. Rest easy for a while, and then we'll go on for a short distance and we can rest again. We'll soon be out of the jungle and that—"

Ki-Gor suddenly jerked his head around and stared back up the trail.

"Here they are," he said grimly. "Up Count Roberto and over to this tree. Sit down with your back to it and hold your fire until I tell you. Tell Gianni to kneel the other side of Helene."

THE BLACKS were pouring down the trail without a sound, and that was a bad sign. Whether they still believed Ki-Gor could perform ju-ju against them or not, they were coming on cold-bloodedly, desperately. Ki-Gor's heart sank. It was a bad position to be caught in. There were enough scattered trees around to afford plenty of cover to the attackers and yet not enough to confine them to the trail. Even now the Balelu and their allies were spreading out on both sides of the trail.

Ki-Gor lifted his assegai high in the air and shook it.

"A-a-a-arrrgh!"

His war cry thundered out on the air. A menacing, nasal yell answered it and the blacks broke into a run.

"Be ready, Count Roberto!" Ki-Gor cried. The nearest blacks were no more than thirty yards away.

"Fire!"

The rifle and the two automatics spoke and three blacks went kicking. But instead of recoiling, the horde of blacks came straight on. Ki-Gor saw that Sergeant Gianni was ready to fire again.

"Fire as fast as you can!" Ki-Gor cried. "We're in for it!"

The second volley did not seem to deter the Balelu, but when the guns kept spitting, the foremost of the charging blacks swerved aside. The whites were shooting deliberately, making every bullet count. For a moment, Ki-Gor thought the blacks were stopped.

But a fresh contingent poured up from behind with savage yells and leaped forward at the little party. Three of them went down, but the rest came on without hesitation. Ki-Gor stepped out from the tree, gripping his assegai hard.

He was not fooling himself into thinking that, single handed, he could hold off hundreds of blacks for very long. It was simply a case now of selling his life as dearly as possible.

Just before the blacks reached him, he heard an extraordinary sound above the Balelu cries. It was extraordinary because he did not expect to hear an elephant trumpeting in the midst of a battle.

The elephant trumpeted again, and a thrill of hope shot through Ki-Gor. He swung the assegai by the tip-end and swept three frenzied blacks to the ground.

"A-a-a-arrrgh!" Ki-Gor cried. "Marmo! Marmo! Here!"

As if in answer the trumpeting sounded again, high and shrill and growing nearer. Ki-Gor launched himself into a group of Balelu and literally smashed five of them down with the battering assegai. The sound of shots from Helene and the Italians was echoed by other shots somewhere. Ki-Gor spun around like a demon at some Balelu who were coming around behind him. At the same time he heard a mighty crashing.

Suddenly, the Balelu were crying out in dismay, and some of them began to run away. The woods began to ring with the sound of shots and a new deep-throated shout went up. Bewildered with joy, Ki-Gor saw Marmo rushing toward him—and on the elephant's back was Tembu George!

BEFORE KI-GOR quite grasped what had happened, the fight was over and the Balelu were in full flight. Tembu George was down on the ground gripping Ki-Gor's shoulders in his huge black hands, and all through the woods streamed a horde of immensely tall black warriors. The Masai!

"Man, I sho' called it close!" Tembu George rumbled. "But s' long as I made it in time, I ain't got no kick!"

"But George!" Helene exclaimed, coming up. "What on earth made you come, and how did you ever find us?"

"Marmo!" said the huge American Negro in explanation. "He show up last night. An' you know how you feel if a man's horse come along and the man ain't on it? You jest git on out and find out whut happen to yo' frien'."

"Only instead of a horse, this time it was an elephant," said Helene.

"Yassum," George chuckled. "Here, Ki-Gor only jest lef' us a little while befo' sittin' on top of Marmo. So when Marmo come back 'ithout no Ki-Gor, why we-all jest put on our runnin' shoes and come a-runnin'. We might have missed you too, because Marmo took us 'long ovuh yonduh to a swamp. But we hear some shots goin' off ovuh here, so we made tracks."

"Well—" Ki-Gor sighed. "Thanks to you, good friend, that you did. You saved our lives."

"Aw, shucks, Ki-Gor," George said. "We jest help get the fight ovuh quicker, thassall. Ain't nobody evuh go' get Ki-Gor down—I don't care how many they is of 'em."

Just then, a young white man appeared behind George. There were several tall askaris with him, in British uniforms.

"I brought someone with me," George said, "an' I'd like to interduce him. This here, Ki-Gor and Mrs. Ki-Gor, is Lieutenant Costello of the King's African Rifles. He was staying ovuh the night with us, him and his men, and he wanted to come along."

Ki-Gor shook hands with the pleasant, hawk-faced young man with the trim black mustache.

"Pleasure to meet you, Ki-Gor," said the lieutenant. "Heard a great deal about you, of course."

Suddenly, Costello stiffened and stared past Ki-Gor's right arm. "I say!" he exclaimed. "What have we got here? Italians?"

"Permit me to present myself, Lieutenant," said Count Roberto di Ghiscardi. "Capitano di Ghiacardi of the Army of His Excellency, the Duke of Aosta. We're supposed to be at war, of course, you and I. Forgive me for not immediately opening fire at you. Unfortunately, I have expended all my ammunition fighting off a common enemy."

"Most assuredly, I shall forgive you, Captain," Costello said gravely. "It's a fearful disadvantage during war time—being out of ammunition."

"It is, you know," said the count. "Now, here's what I propose. You are an officer and a British gentleman—"

"Irish," Costello corrected.

"Even better," said the count, without missing a beat. "You are an officer and a gentleman—surely you will grant me a truce long enough to remove myself and my force to a defensible position."

"Couldn't be a fairer request," said Costello, without a smile. "But wouldn't it save a lot of trouble if you just surrendered to me? You'd have lots of company—probably meet a lot of your old mess-mates and friends."

"An attractive prospect, I admit," said the count. "But as long as my commanding officer holds out, how can I honorably surrender when I am—"

"I beg your pardon, Captain," Costello interrupted, "but your commanding officer has surrendered."

"No, no," said the count indulgently, "I mean the Duke of Aosta."

"Well, then, so do I," said Costello triumphantly.

THERE WAS a little pause, then Count Roberto said slowly, "The Duke of Aosta has surrendered?"

"He has, Captain."

"On your word as an officer and a gentleman?"

"On my word as an officer and an Irish gentleman."

"Ah," sighed the count, "then I am quite sure further resistance would be futile. Lieutenant, I surrender myself and my force into your hands."

"Captain, I am most honored. Pray, where is your force?"

"Right here," said Count Roberto with a weak gesture toward little Gianni, "Sergeant! Attention! Reverse Arms!"

"I'll accept your parole, all-inclusive, Captain," said Costello. "You can tell your force he can keep his arms. Jolly good soldiers, you Italians, when you're properly led."

"And when we have a good cause," Captain Roberto murmured. "Er—forgive me, but I'm afraid I have a touch of fever. Do you mind if I sit down?"

With that the count's knees buckled. The devoted Gianni leaped forward and eased him to the ground. Ki-Gor knelt down and put a hand on his forehead while young Costello leaned over, murmuring anxiously. A look of concern came over Ki-Gor's face and he moved his hand down to the count's chest. After a long moment, he stood up.

"He was a brave man," Ki-Gor said.

"Ah, the poor man!" Costello murmured. "He was on the wrong side of this mess and he knew it."

The young lieutenant stood up straight and saluted, and Sergeant Gianni burst out into unashamed tears.

COUNT ROBERTO DI GHISCARDI was buried at sundown with full military honors. After the ceremony the party moved out on to the veldt where George's tall Masai warriors had prepared a camp. George had already bathed and dressed Ki-Gor's innumerable minor wounds, and the jungle man was glad enough to sit quietly by the huge fire and eat his first meal in many hours. Big George proposed a punitive expedition against the Balelu the next day, but Ki-Gor vigorously opposed the idea, and went on to explain how the Balelu were the victims of the albino Tenzori.

"Hm," George murmured, as Ki-Gor concluded his narrative of the events in the cave. "Man, them Tenzori is bad clear through! Funny thing—they have to have white skins, ain't it?"

"Well," Lieutenant Costello smiled, "I'm still young for my age, but I've already discovered that there are white men—and white men."

"You is plumb right, Lieutenant," George said. "How about it, Ki-Gor?"

But Ki-Gor was fast asleep.

Made in the USA
Columbia, SC
27 June 2019